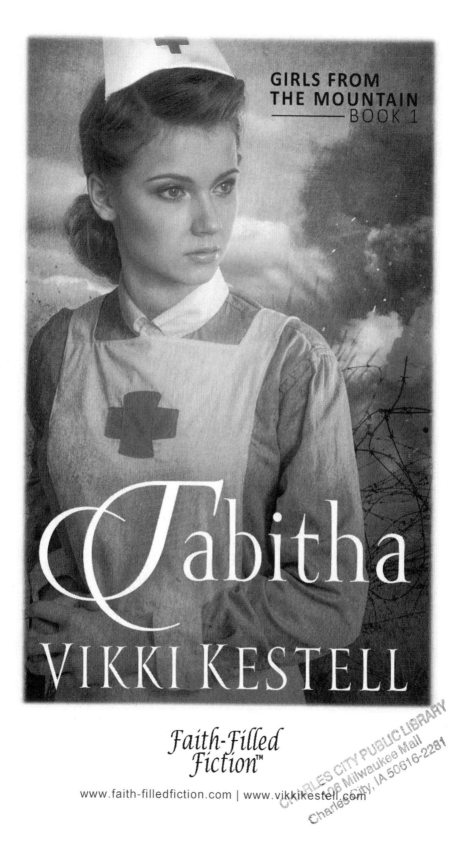

GIRLS FROM
THE MOUNTAIN
BOOK 1

Tabitha

VIKKI KESTELL

*Faith-Filled
Fiction*™

www.faith-filledfiction.com | www.vikkikestell.com

Tabitha

Girls from the Mountain, Book 1
©2015 Vikki Kestell
All Rights Reserved
Also Available in Kindle Format

Other Books by Vikki Kestell

A Prairie Heritage

 Book 1: *A Rose Blooms Twice*, **a free eBook, most online retailers**
 Book 2: *Wild Heart on the Prairie*
 Book 3: *Joy on This Mountain*
 Book 4: *The Captive Within*
 Book 5: *Stolen*
 Book 6: *Lost Are Found*
 Book 7: *All God's Promises*

Nanostealth

 Book 1: *Stealthy Steps*
 Book 2: *Stealth Power*, **fall 2016**
 Book 3: *Stealth Beyond Borders*

 The Christian and the Vampire: A Short Story,
 a free eBook, most online retailers

Tabitha

Copyright ©2015 Vikki Kestell
All Rights Reserved.
ISBN-10: 0-9862615-3-X
ISBN-13: 978-0-9862615-3-4

"A timeless story of redemption and hope, *Tabitha* will pull at your heartstrings and delight you with its rich characterization and impeccable details. *Tabitha* is a book you will not soon forget."

~~**Chautona Havig,** Author of Christian Fiction without Apology or Pretense—Lived, Not Preached

From the author of the groundbreaking series, **A Prairie Heritage**, comes the compelling story of fiery-haired, fiery-tempered Tabitha Hale. Rescued from a life of depravity, Tabitha gives her heart to God and her life to nursing.

As this tenacious, redeemed woman perseveres toward her vocation, her temper and stubborn independence threaten to derail her aspirations. Will Tabitha pass the trial by fire that is necessary for God to truly use her?

When the Great War erupts in Europe, Tabitha hears God asking her to nurse the war wounded. However, because America has not joined in the fight, Tabitha has few options.

Will the elite British Nursing Service make a place for her? Will they accept the services of an American volunteer?

And what is Tabitha to do with her feelings for Mason Carpenter, the man who simply refuses to give up on her? Is it even possible for God to ordain a shared future for two such different people, both with fervent callings upon their hearts?

Will Tabitha and Mason overcome the obstacles that stand between them?

Revisit Palmer House—a most extraordinary refuge for young women rescued from prostitution. Renew your acquaintance with Rose Thoresen, Joy Michaels, and the others who live at Palmer House. Glimpse the years between *Stolen* and *Lost Are Found*.

Tabitha, **Girls from the Mountain**, Book 1

WHY THE SERIES TITLE, "GIRLS FROM THE MOUNTAIN"?

A short excerpt from *The Captive Within.*

Denver, 1909.

Joy was thoughtful. "You said something just now..." You called them *girls from the mountain.* I rather like that."

"Certainly less degrading than 'former prostitutes.'" Grant smiled his endearing half-smile.

"Perhaps that is how we should refer to them from now on. Of course, when the Lord gives us women from Denver, the phrase will no longer apply."

"Denver is surrounded by mountains. I don't see a problem with it. It could be our own little code for the young ladies of Palmer House."

Joy nodded. "I like that."

Girls from the Mountain is a follow-on series to **A Prairie Heritage**. Each book can be read as a "standalone" volume, but having already read **A Prairie Heritage** may increase your enjoyment. *A Rose Blooms Twice*, Book 1 in A Prairie Heritage, is free on Kindle and most eReading platforms.

DEDICATION

For the selfless nurses
of the Great War and beyond.

ACKNOWLEDGEMENTS

Many thanks to my esteemed teammates,
Cheryl Adkins and **Greg McCann**,
who give selflessly of themselves
to make each new book the most effective
instrument of God's grace possible.
I love you.

Cover photography by **Damon Jasso**.
Cover model by **Beth-Grace**.
Cover by **DogEared Design**.

TO MY READERS

This book is a work of fiction,
what I term Faith-Filled Fiction™.
While the characters and events are fiction,
they are situated within the historical record.
To God be the glory.

SCRIPTURE QUOTATIONS

The King James Version (KJV)
Public Domain,
and
New Living Translation (NLT).
Scripture quotations marked NLT
are taken from the Holy Bible,
New Living Translation, copyright 1996, 2004.
Used by permission of Tyndale House Publishers, Inc.,
Wheaton, Illinois 60189.
All rights reserved.

℘ROLOGUE

But where sin abounded,
grace did much more abound.
(Romans 5:20b, KJV)

JULY 1911

Rose Thoresen sighed and folded her hands upon her desk in the great room of Palmer House. Her account books, filled with sums and figures waiting to be worked, lay neglected before her. It was late morning but already Rose's bones were weary of sitting.

I never used to tire so easily, Lord.

Shaking her head, she reflected on her sixty-three years and how quickly they had seemed to pass ... how odd it was to gaze into a mirror and view a stranger: a woman aging gracefully, but not the figure of youth she expected, the young woman who still resided in her heart.

Rose rubbed her arm where, not many months before, a bullet had torn skin and broken bone. The bone was healing, but her arm often ached. Its ache reminded her that the man who had shot her had meant to kill her—*and had failed.*

"I thank you again, Lord, for your many mercies," she whispered.

Rose leaned back against her chair and closed her eyes. She listened. The house was quiet.

Too quiet.

Too still.

Too empty.

Most of the young women of Palmer House were away for the day, gone to their places of employment. Even Rose's daughter Joy had departed the house this morning, surprising them all. Joy had left the house in the watchful company of her employees, Sara, Corrine, and Billy, to catch the trolley into downtown Denver.

Tabitha had accompanied them.

Tabitha has been Joy's caring shadow during these dark weeks, Rose acknowledged.

Unable to return to nursing school in Boulder until the onset of the fall term, Tabitha had stayed close to Joy. She had seen to it that Joy ate enough and had helped Joy navigate the treacherous and painful road of mourning and loss. Not that anyone could walk that road for another. Nevertheless, Tabitha's steadfast presence had eased many of Joy's burdens.

Yes, with chin lifted and mouth set in resolute lines, Joy had marched out the front door to resume management of the fine furnishings store she owned—the store she *and Grant* had established and poured their hearts into together.

Grant! Gone to Jesus now these many weeks.

And baby Edmund. Still missing.

Mr. O'Dell. Absent from Denver, working himself into the ground to find and retrieve Edmund.

So many losses.

Rose turned her head and heeded the creaks and groans of the stately old mansion they called Palmer House.

Marit and Breona, Palmer House's cook and housekeeper, were about the day's business, but they moved with soft footsteps and spoke in subdued voices—as though the noise and bustle of daily activities might violate the holy hush that persisted in the house.

Even Mr. Wheatley puttered noiselessly about in Palmer House's expansive yard, his dear old face creased with the weight of grief they all carried in one measure or another.

Rose massaged her throbbing arm, and her heart ached in tempo with the knitting of her bones. The absence of baby Edmund's coos and gurgles made the empty echoes of the old house all the more difficult to bear ... even though more time had passed without him in their lives than the scant three months he had been with them.

Lord, I am always grateful when Mei-Xing returns from work in the evening with our little Shan-Rose, Rose prayed.

Mei-Xing's daughter, coming up on a year old now, was a blessing they all cherished—even though her very presence underscored Edmund's conspicuous absence.

Father God, Rose entreated, *I ask you to fill our hearts and this house with happiness again, because we cannot bear this sorrow. I pray for Mr. O'Dell who is searching so diligently, so earnestly, for our little man. I pray you would fill him with strength and courage. In all these things I trust you, Father God, for in you, the lost are found.*

Rose huffed and glanced down at her accounts. Just as she took up her pen, the front door of the house opened and she heard the patter of footsteps. Seconds later she glimpsed Tabitha's flaming hair as she crossed the entryway.

Rose stood and went to meet her. "Tabitha! Are you home so soon?"

The young woman, perhaps age thirty and the eldest of their "girls from the mountain," turned and entered the great room at Rose's question. The two women placed their cheeks together in warm greeting.

"What I know about fine furnishings would not fill a teacup," Tabitha laughed, more than a little chagrined, "and, truly, Joy does not need me at the store. Sara, Corinne, and Billy are more than enough staff for their customers' needs."

She stared at the floor. "I am so glad Joy has returned to work. It is an important step for her. But I am afraid I find myself at rather loose ends right now."

"Ah." Rose studied Tabitha, admiring the woman's brilliant green eyes edged with dark auburn lashes, admiring the thick, fiery locks Tabitha pinned upon her head in such a practical manner. "How many weeks remain before you return to school?"

"I have counted three times," Tabitha confessed, "but it is still nine weeks. I fear I shall go out of my mind if I do not busy myself with some productive work in the interim."

"Perhaps you could volunteer at the hospital?" Rose suggested. "With the training you received during your first term at nursing school and the practical experience you gained nursing all of us during last winter's influenza, surely they could find use for your capable hands?"

"Yes, I did think of that. I even spoke to Dr. Murphy and he is willing to write a letter of recommendation."

Tabitha broke off and frowned, and Rose wondered where her thoughts had turned.

"What is it, dear?" she inquired.

"I find it odd that, just as I make up my mind to go down to the hospital, I balk at doing so. It is as though ... as though I am supposed to be doing something else, yet what that 'something else' might be eludes me."

Rose pursed her lips and breathed a silent prayer. "Tabitha, I have something I have been praying over, but, well, perhaps we could speak of it over a cup of tea?"

Tabitha's brows lifted. "I should be glad to hear your proposal." She hurried off to make a tray for them.

Rose's eyes followed Tabitha. *I doubt my suggestion will make you glad in any respect, dear girl, but if my idea is from God and is for his glory, he will speak to your heart and do the convincing.*

Rose finished the sums she had neglected and tidied up her desk while she waited for Tabitha to return. Perhaps ten minutes later, Tabitha entered the great room with a tray set for two.

They sat in worn but comfortable upholstered chairs, facing each other across a low table. Rose poured the tea and handed Tabitha her cup.

Tabitha looked to Rose. "Can you tell me of your idea now?"

Rose blew on her own steaming cup. "Yes, but perhaps we should pray first?"

Again Tabitha's brows levered upwards, but she did not answer. Instead she nodded her agreement. The two women placed their cups on the table between them and joined hands.

"Father, thank you for the fellowship Tabitha and I share in Jesus Christ. We ask that you guide our conversation. And we ask that you move our hearts to follow yours, wherever you may lead us. Amen."

"Amen," Tabitha echoed. She picked up her cup. "Now I am *very* curious!"

"Yes, well..." Rose paused and then dove in. "I have been praying about some of the young women at Palmer House writing small books, personal accounts that would contain their ... testimonies. The accounts would not be for public consumption, but for the benefit of newcomers to Palmer House, now and in the future."

She glanced at Tabitha to see how she was receiving her words.

Tabitha's forehead puckered in puzzlement. "Testimonies? I am not familiar with that word."

"Hmm. What I mean to say, Tabitha, is that your testimony—the account of what God has done in you and for you—could aid other women, women whose past lives are similar to yours but who, perhaps, have not experienced similar redemptive outcomes. Not as yet anyway."

She wet her lips with a sip of tea. "I am asking you to consider writing the story of your journey to the Savior."

"The story of my j-journey?" Tabitha stuttered over the last word.

"Something of a memoir, dear. So that others, other women such as yourself, can come to know Jesus and his saving power in the same way you have experienced it."

"You want me to write about ... before?"

Their eyes met.

Rose's steady gray eyes did not blink as the two women searched each other's heart. Rose wanted to be honest with Tabitha.

"I believe the Lord would have you write about the choices you made and their consequences, Tabitha. Yes, you would write about the sin that ensnared you but—and this is much more important—you would also write about the grace Jesus extended to you. How he sought you, found you, and redeemed you from your choices and sin."

Rose sipped her tea and added, "We do not wish to glorify sin or dwell on the past. However, we, as followers of Christ, should anchor our testimonies in what we were before he saved us so that our great God receives the glory that is due him, and so that others can receive hope— hope for their own lives. The Apostle Paul said it this way, *Christ Jesus came into the world to save sinners; of whom I am chief.*"

Tabitha swallowed and the anxiety that radiated from her was palpable. Her cup and saucer clattered together as she set them on the table. "I-I am not sure I could do that, Miss Rose. I do not wish people to know..."

She said "people," but in her mind's eye she fixed on one individual in particular: *Mason Carpenter*, a man whose esteem she did not wish crushed by a detailed account of her past with all its ugliness. Although Tabitha had discouraged Carpenter in the most unmistakable manner, the man continued to call upon Palmer House—ostensibly to provide support for the house's ministry, but also to pay informal court to her.

He has been a tremendous blessing to us, Tabitha admitted. His financial gifts and other services had kept Palmer House solvent through the recent turbulent events—the attack on Rose and abduction of baby Edmund in April and, not long after, Grant's death.

When Carpenter had first expressed an interest in her, Tabitha had not spared his feelings. No, she had been blunt. Severe. She had, with dispassion, recounted the origins and purpose of Palmer House— including her own reasons for living in the house. In fact, she had done her best to revolt him, to shock him into retreating!

But Carpenter had not been the slightest bit dissuaded—not from supporting the house's ministry and certainly not from asking after her frequently. He had taken care not to push in or make himself unwelcome to her, but he had lately begun attending services at Calvary Temple, the same church the family at Palmer House attended: Calvary Temple, the unconventional Denver congregation that met for services in a former warehouse.

No, Carpenter's unhurried, steady attentions showed no signs of abatement, and Tabitha had no wish to wound or shame him.

Rose responded, "Your story would be available only to the women the Lord asks us to love back into wholeness—not to the general public. No copy would ever leave this house."

Tabitha nodded, but her expression reflected worry.

"I understand how difficult telling your story might be, which is why I thought, perhaps, we could do it together," Rose added.

Tabitha wrapped her arms about herself and shivered. "Do it together?"

VIKKI KESTELL

"Yes. If you felt you could speak openly to me, then I would take notes and write the first draft of the manuscript." She paused and then shrugged, "Who knows? Perhaps the recounting of your journey would be cathartic and would bring God's grace toward you into sharper focus."

Tabitha glanced away, clearly conflicted. Rose allowed her to think in peace as she sipped her own tea. They remained in silence for a long while.

As she waited, Rose prayed within herself. *If this is of you, Lord, then you will show us the way. I fear nothing in this world anymore, with one exception: I fear not following closely after you. If it is Tabitha's decision not to share her testimony at this time, then you will open another young woman's heart to do so. I trust in you, my Lord.*

Tabitha was lost in her own thoughts for so long that Rose began to gather up the tea things, including Tabitha's cup of very cold tea.

At last Tabitha whispered, "Do you think... do you think my testimony might help another girl not to make the mistakes I made?"

Tabitha turned toward Rose and tears glistened in her eyes. "I can scarcely bear to consider what my own willful nature—and my unbridled temper—cost me."

"My darling girl, I am much less concerned over the choices and mistakes you made years ago than I am with how our Lord Jesus saved you *out of all of them*. It is human nature that we rarely care about our great God of grace until we, personally, see that we have a need for him, no? Jesus came to seek and save those who are lost—and I care a great deal about the lost who might see themselves in your story. I believe your testimony will cause the hearts of many women like yourself to turn to him."

Rose hesitated. "It will not be easy, Tabitha, remembering and talking of the life you lived before Jesus rescued you."

Tabitha stared at her hands. "I would only need to tell you? You would write it out?"

"We would do it all together, dear. Every part." Rose hesitated. "We have nine weeks. I do not know but that it may be the work of more than nine weeks, but we can be well begun in that time."

Tabitha swallowed again and nodded. "I ... suppose I am willing to at least try."

Rose took her hands. "Then let us give this to our Lord and trust him for the outcome. Nine weeks will give us a good start—and let us start today, now, while our determination is fresh."

They cleared away the tea things and Rose selected paper and pen.

"Where should I begin?" Tabitha asked.

12

"Perhaps we should start at the place where you made your first wrong choice?"

Tabitha hmmed. "Yes. I know exactly when that was."

"Very well. Take a moment to compose your thoughts and then begin."

Tabitha shifted and looked around the room as though she wanted to flee the memories in her head. "I ... well, I should say that my name is Tabitha Kathrine Hale."

"I did not know your middle name." Rose smiled. "It is beautiful and suits you."

"Thank you, Miss Rose." Tabitha rested her chin upon her folded hands.

"I probably should begin, then, when I was fourteen ..."

PART 1:
A BAD BEGINNING

The eye that mocks a father
and despises a mother's instructions
will be plucked out by ravens of the valley
and eaten by vultures.
(Proverbs 30:17, NLT)

$\mathcal{C}$HAPTER 1

ARIZONA TERRITORY, 1895

I sighed and wondered again what was keeping Cray from his dinner. Sweat and dirt ran down the back of my neck and I swiped at it. I was angry, of course.

I was almost always angry lately. Bile and discontent had taken up residence in my belly. They lived and thrived there, seething and churning, until they climbed up my throat and erupted in heated words.

"Here I been a-cookin' an' bakin' over this hot fire and he ain't got th' decency t' come eat?" I grumbled. I was incensed at Cray's thoughtlessness. "He can't leave off a-workin' when day is done?"

Down in my gut the anger swirled. I wanted to say more, much more, but I wanted to say it to Cray's face. I held one hand over my eyes and squinted west into the scorching light, scanning the path that wended down the hillside not far away. I saw no sign of Cray and his mule.

The late afternoon dragged on toward sunset, and the sun still burned, hanging like a bloated, shimmering orb in a blindingly blue sky. The day's heat was beyond anything I had endured in my short fourteen years. Even the scorching skies of west Texas, under which I had spent my childhood, had been nowhere near as merciless as the searing desert of southern Arizona.

During the day the air inside of our small tent grew so hot that it sucked the moisture from my lungs: If I inhaled, fiery billows seared my chest. So I spent the long hours outside, hunkered down in the tent's scanty profile, the single refuge to be found for miles.

Every hour of the day I had to shift the box upon which I sat so as to remain within the tent's shadow; every hour of the day the sun's blazing furnace intensified.

When blessed night arrived, the stifling heat retreated but slightly; by daybreak the temperature was already clawing its way up to blister and torture the land—and us—once more.

And we had been camped in this awful place for two weeks.

I lifted my dry eyes to the path that led up the craggy hillside.

Still no sign of Cray.

Four months back, Cray had begged me to leave my folks. He pleaded with me to leave them, leave their pretty little patch of land alongside a seasonal Texas creek, and venture west with him to seek fortune and glory in the Arizona gold fields.

"There's gold to be had in Arizona Territory, Tabitha, just by pickin' it out of the sides of hills," he bragged with shining eyes, "and the price of gold is goin' up like fireworks on the Fourth o' July. Why, once I get my share, we'll be set for life. I'll never have t' work again."

The first time Cray came to call on me, my folks had studied him with misgivings. They did not come out and say as much, but I knew they did not care for Cray.

Then I overheard Daddy tell Mama, "Thet boy ain't got the sense God give him." A moment later he added, "And he's wild. A dreamer. Too much like *her*."

It was true. I had an unruly streak as wide as the day was long, and I was drawn to Cray, pulled to him by the thrilling, adventurous future he painted for me. Life on my folk's little spread was spare and it was good—but it was the same, *always the same*, day in and day out, year after year.

I rebelled against a life of monotony, of that dreary sameness—a future that held nothing different, only more of what I already knew and, with youthful contempt, despised.

My wild streak was companion to an even wilder temper, and I often allowed my temper to rule me. I was an only child—spoiled, headstrong, and willful. My folks loved me, but they scarcely knew how to curb the unrestrained young woman I was growing into.

To listen to my mother, my hot, rebellious disposition was a great weakness. I know now how right she was, but at that time? When I heard what Daddy said—about Cray being too much like me?—it rankled my temper, and I set my jaw and my obstinate will against my folks' wisdom.

And Cray? I think he was bedazzled by my red hair. He raved over what he called "the unflawed beauty of my milky complexion" and "the glowing flames of my long tresses." My young, inexperienced ego swelled, and I preened under such high praise.

Cray certainly had a way with words! And as the days went by, he pressed me harder to leave with him.

The life Cray promises will be better than this dismal old farm, I had assured myself when Conscience raised its unwelcome head. Oh, I knew that running off with Cray was not right. It went against everything Mama had taught me about decency, and I told Cray as much. I challenged him to prove my folks wrong.

In response Cray had pledged me a ring, a church wedding, and a house. Oh, he promised so many things! But always, "As soon as I make my fortune."

Finally, I gave in.

One cool morning, Cray and I headed for the Arizona gold fields. I rode behind Cray on his pony until we reached the southwest edge of the New Mexico Territory and entered Arizona Territory. There Cray traded his pony for a pack mule named Sassy. He poured most all of his cash into the tools and supplies he would need to work his mine. Last of all, he bought a claim, a claim he was told would yield more than enough gold to set us up for life.

What we had found when we arrived at the claim was uninhabitable desert, vast wastelands, and an empty, gutted pit in the side of a mountain. The claim may have boasted of gold at one time, but its treasure was long gone when Cray paid good, cash money for it.

Disheartened and with little cash left, we bought what supplies we could in a disreputable boomtown called Fullman. Then we walked on into the desert where rumors promised better prospecting. Sassy carried our tools and tent, a couple of weeks' of food—if we were careful—and two large casks of water.

When we arrived at *this* spot, two weeks back, weary in foot and heart, I spied a patch of green at the base of the hillside over yonder. I called Cray's attention to it because the green was so out of keeping with the bleak shades of brown surrounding us.

We searched for and found the spring that fed the green patch. It was not much more than a slow seep, really. The tepid liquid dribbling up from the ground was likely the only water source for miles around. Cray studied the rocky hillside above the water and decided the looks of it suited him.

"That there rock face has gold in it, or m' name ain't Cray T. Bishoff," he had muttered.

We dug a basin in the earth to catch the water from the seep, and each day I strained what pooled in the hole through a scrap of canvas. It was not much, that little bit of water, but it was enough to keep us and Sassy alive day to day.

Cray erected our tent on a low mound nearby, one of the thousands of mounds just like it dotting the desert around us. Then fourteen long, scorching days dragged by.

As the sun drooped closer to the horizon, I stood and put my hand to my eyes to shade them. In every direction I turned, the view was the same. Undulating dunes and gullies. Sparse cacti and brush. The same landscape in every direction except for the hillside Cray had climbed with Sassy this morning.

The low hill just west of our tent, the one Cray had staked our futures on, was the lone geographical variation within sight. Not another marker stood in the wild, barren land to hint at where we were. Not another vestige of human life stirred.

I again stared into the distance. Not for the first time did the notion of being left alone and adrift in this bleak wasteland cause my breath to hitch in terror.

"Where is he?" I whispered.

Cray never missed an evening meal, little though it was.

Cray had been enthusiastic when we had arrived at this place. "I'll find gold here. I know I will—that hill has the look of it," he boasted. "And when I've made my fortune, we'll go back to Texas. I'll buy me some land and some cattle."

He had stared with fierce determination at its rocky face. "Yep. I'll get the gold first. Land and cattle next."

"And then we'll get married?" I had demanded. My words were sharp. The shine had worn off our relationship in the few months we had been together. We quarreled more than once during our fruitless travels, and I often gave Cray the rough side of my tongue.

"Oh, sure, sweetheart. Sure. We'll get married." But he had frowned and seemed distracted as he said it.

Cray had left off reciting the promises by which he had lured me into coming with him. The very absence of such assurances frightened me.

"Like you promised," I insisted, my temper—and apprehension—ratcheting up another notch.

He had rounded on me then. "Y'know, Tabitha Hale, no man can abide a nagging woman. You'd best consider that."

His cold, detached tone and the way he had clenched his jaw shocked me. I recoiled as surely as if he had slapped me.

Later, after my distress calmed, I finally admitted to myself that I had made a mistake—a horrible mistake. Cray was not the man I had thought him to be, any more than I was the sweet, biddable woman he had thought he was getting.

Cray had begun his prospecting that first morning with optimistic energy; he returned that evening wordless. The next day he clamped his lips together and, with Sassy in tow, hiked up the hill again. That night he came back to camp, dour and uncommunicative.

I did not question him. I already knew what he had found. Nothing. No sign of the precious ore he yearned for. Yet he kept at it, day after burning day. Each morning, with the mule following on a lead, he went in search of his treasure. Each evening he returned, sullen and less talkative —until fourteen sunrises and sunsets had passed and our supplies were spent.

Tabitha glanced up into Rose's face. "My folks were right, you know. And it is clear to me now, sixteen years later, how this one, willful choice—my decision to run off with Cray—set in motion the direction of my life, the downward course that would end in my ruin."

Rose, dismay growing in her heart, tucked her chin to her breast and gripped her pen tighter.

Tabitha picked up where she had left off.

The following morning, Cray seemed easier, lighter of heart. He packed his gear on the tired mule with purpose and added extra water for the animal. He ate the small breakfast I prepared for him with dogged determination and took his packed lunch from my hand. For a change he said goodbye to me instead of grunting his thanks and stalking wordlessly toward the hill.

Now, hours later, the sun at last slid down the golden horizon. Long, deep fingers of shadow—the heralds of approaching night—lengthened around the tent and across the desert floor. I used the sticks I had gathered during the day to build up the fire. Cray would need light to find his way to me in the dark.

I hugged myself and tried to recall the exact words he had muttered when he tugged on the mule's lead and turned to leave. What was it he had said?

"Goodbye, Tabitha. You wish me well, now."

I licked my chapped lips. I was restless. Edgy. The hours dragged on and Cray did not appear. I lay down on the blanket inside the tent but could not sleep.

The next morning, before the sun commenced its ponderous journey across the sky, I hiked up the hill to Cray's dig. It took me two hours to reach the rock face where the holes and tailings from his pick and shovel were evident.

No sign of the mule. No tools or pack. No Cray.

I dragged myself back to our campsite. Exhausted and near to panic, I drank my fill of the water that had accumulated in the seep. Then I collapsed in the tent's shade.

I have to know for certain, I told myself. *I have to know*.

I took a deep breath and ducked inside the tent. There I rummaged through our scant possessions. As my alarmed imaginings had suggested, most of Cray's clothes were gone. He had left only the few ragged things he wanted me to wash and mend.

To keep me from suspecting.

I shuddered. Cray was not coming back. *He had left me.* Left me by myself in the desert!

Rose and Tabitha were silent, held taut and wordless by a shared horror. But Rose could not stop shivering—the last sentence of Tabitha's account burgeoned with dread. Awful, terrifying dread.

Many minutes later, Tabitha resumed her whispered narrative.

I spent the remainder of the day crouched beside the tent either sobbing in terror or raging at Cray for his duplicity. Darkness again crept across the desert. I stared at the fire and rocked back and forth, keening into the empty sky.

Alone! I am alone!

Sometime in the night I shook myself and faced the facts: *If I do not fend for myself, I am going to die*.

Fullman, where we had bought our last supplies, lay a full day's walk due east of our campsite. Surely Cray had to have gone there? It was the only point of "civilization" either of us knew of.

I swallowed hard at my memory of Fullman. The town consisted of a few rows of clapboard houses and businesses surrounded by a great tent city, a swelling, noxious collection of ragged canvas shelters. The most prosperous-looking of the buildings had a store on one side of it and a bar on the other.

The prospectors camped around Fullman were lean and dry, desiccated from their fevered pursuit of gold. They outnumbered the women of the town ten times over—yet as Cray and I had purchased our meager provisions, it was not the hunger for gold I had glimpsed in those men's eyes. No, they had stared with avarice at my red hair; they had raked my body with ravening eyes.

I trembled at the remembrance and babbled within myself, *Cray had to have gone to Fullman, and I must go there and find him. Surely he will take me back! He must!*

For a second night I did not sleep. I passed the long minutes and hours in anxious watchfulness. Every noise and every rustle reminded me that, while the desert appeared empty to the human eye, many creatures stalked, crept, and slithered upon its face.

In the early morning, as the desert floor lightened, I packed only what I absolutely needed to survive the walk to Fullman. I left the tent and the few pots and utensils. I strained all of the water that had pooled in the seep overnight and poured it into the coffee pot and a lone glass bottle—the only containers left to me since Cray had strapped both casks and our canteen over Sassy's back and taken them with him.

Three handfuls of oats remained of our foodstuffs. I cooked the last of them, ate part of the congealed mess, and scraped what remained into a kerchief that I knotted and tucked into a pocket. I rolled the rest of my clothes into a bundle and pinned my only hat securely in place. Over my hat and around my shoulders I draped my shawl as a tent against the blistering sun.

I fingered the bottom of my skirt. I had stitched four half dollars into its hem as insurance before I left my folks' farm. Maybe, somehow, the coins would help me leave Fullman and get to a place where I could send a wire to my folks asking for help.

That morning I envisioned the thin little creek meandering by my parent's land, and it had never seemed so sweet, so desirable. The sameness of each day on their farm—tending the animals and garden, doing the cooking, laundry, and cleaning—had never held such appeal. True, it was a boring life, but it was *a life*—not the certain death awaiting me upon this wasteland.

I have shamed my father and mother. Will they take me back? I wondered. *Will they allow me to come home?*

Certain that the coins were secure in the hem of my dress—but not at all certain or secure in my own heart—I set my face toward the rising sun.

I walked all day, walked until dark was falling on the land. I had eaten the oats tied up in the kerchief and drained the last of the water hours ago.

I would have missed the town and wandered on, out into the desert, if not for the scents that reached out to me. The odors of smoking fires and smoldering grease drew me a little south. Kept me from losing my way.

My feet ached. My throat and tongue were dry as dust. I was exhausted. But I had made it; I had arrived in Fullman.

Fewer tents than I remembered stood between me and the rows of buildings at the center of Fullman.

I waited until the night was fully dark. I trod by ragged shelters as quietly as I could manage. I avoided campfires where men sat and talked and drank with each other. I threaded my way through the canvas outskirts of Fullman until I reached the clapboard buildings.

I stumbled up onto the planked walk in front of the store. The sign on the door read "Closed." I glanced around in the dark, unsure of what to do next. Raucous singing, piano music, and smoky light issued from the saloon only feet away.

I crept around the side of the store and sank to the dusty earth. *I'll just sleep here. No one will see me in the dark,* I told myself. *I'll find Cray in the morning.*

I was not at all certain I wanted to find Cray, but I was frightened nearly out of my mind *not* to find him. A woman alone in a place like this? And I was only fourteen, after all. Scarcely a woman.

I turned sideways and leaned my head against the rough planks.

And slept.

CHAPTER 2

I felt the appraising stares on me before I came fully awake. Or perhaps it was the gamey stench of unwashed bodies that woke me. I jerked and pushed myself up to sitting. My muscles cried out as I did so; sometime in the night I had slumped over sideways and slept bent over for hours. Wiping a grimy hand across my face I pried my eyes open.

At least ten men, backlit by glaring midmorning sun, circled around me. My breath caught. They might have been vultures circling their next meal, as intent as they were.

"She ain't dead," one muttered.

"I sawed 'er first. I claim 'er," another growled.

He nudged one of the men aside; two others pushed him back.

"We'll see 'bout that!" one of them snarled.

My shawl had slipped to the ground as I slept. I fumbled for it and wrapped it about my shoulders; my hands clutched it to my bodice. With my back to the rough wood behind me, I shimmied to my feet.

I mustered courage I did not know I possessed. "I ain't belong t' any of you-all," I spat. My voice rasped with need for water—and with fear. "I-I'm a married woman. You-all jest move aside an' let me pass."

Lie though it was, I would stick to the "married woman" tale— because a single woman alone in this God-forsaken land? An unmarried woman had no protection at all.

The men were as depraved as I remembered them. They did not budge. Their eyes swept over my body; a few of them sniggered. Their intent was clear.

As though responding to an unheard signal, hands scrabbled for me, grasped and clawed at my clothes, and I had nowhere to run. I was backed against the building. A shriek filled my mouth and spilled into the open air. I screamed and kept screaming.

"Step aside, boys. You have no business here."

The sinews in my neck cracked as I craned my head to see who had spoken. A few of the men, while grumbling and complaining, started to back away, but others, their hands still grabbing at me, did not. Through their numbers I caught sight of a tall, slender woman.

"Help me, lady! Please! Help me!"

"You, Bill Plant! And Wendell Meyer! Take your filthy hands off this poor girl. Get away now, or I will fetch Big Jim to clear you all out."

The woman folded her arms and waited. Muttering dark threats, the mob started to break. I clasped my shawl tighter about myself as if it could shield me from further violation. I fixed my eyes on the woman who tipped her head on its side and considered me.

"You are Tabitha Hale, are you not?" The woman swayed as she approached me. It seemed a well-practiced movement, that swaying of skirts and hips, both feminine and alluring. "Cray told me to expect you."

"Cray? Is-is he here?"

I was so eager that I leaned toward the woman and caught the powdery scent of her cologne. I examined her face. She was not young but she was not old, either. Delicate lines etched her beautiful skin like the crazing of fine old porcelain. Her hair, a dark brown shimmering with strands of silver, was swept up and pinned upon her head. Delicate curls dangled by her ears and trailed along her neck.

In every way, she was polished. Well-spoken. Sophisticated. Genteel. Everything I was not.

"No, I am afraid he left yesterday," the woman murmured, her voice soft and sympathetic, "but he asked me to . . . look after you. We agreed that I would."

"Oh." I was stunned. Cray had well and truly left me! But he had, at least, made some sort of provision for me, had not left me to fend for myself?

For the moment I forgot how Cray had abandoned me to the desert— where I might very well have died.

"My name is Opal." The woman smiled and looked me over. "You look done in, Tabitha. May I suggest a hot bath, a good meal, and a long sleep in that order? How does that sound?"

"Thet . . . sounds right good." I had to concede that I was almost as filthy as the men who had attacked me.

An' I prob'ly smell as bad, too, I admitted.

"Well, shall we take care of you? We cannot leave you out here another moment. Those jackals cannot be trusted to behave, you know."

I nodded. I was still dazed, but I was grateful. "Thank ya fer savin' me."

Opal's smile stretched her mouth and made even more of the tiny lines appear in her face, but they were pleasant enough lines. Only her eyes did not truly smile. "I own this store. Let us go up the back way to my apartment where you shall have privacy."

Opal led the way up a back staircase to the second floor. It was still early; the bar next door was dark and silent. The entrance at the top of the stairs opened to a hallway. Opal turned right and stopped at the door on the end.

"This is my private apartment. Please rest yourself here while I make arrangements for your bath and a hot meal. Drink as much of the water by my bed as you wish. You must be parched, you poor dear."

I gaped when Opal opened the door. The room was not large, but it was artfully arranged. The bed was spread with a gay silk coverlet, the windows with thick drapes. A dressing table and a floral-patterned screen graced one corner of the room. A pitcher and washbasin painted with roses sat on a small table near an overstuffed arm chair.

"Sit here, Tabitha," Opal suggested.

I collapsed into the chair Opal indicated.

She poured a tall glass of water from the pitcher and handed it to me. "Drink as much as you like, but start with small sips, yes?"

I nodded and sank deeper into the chair. It was all I could do to not drain the glass of its tepid water. I sipped at the glass, placed it on the table, and leaned against the chair's back to pace myself.

"I need to give instructions for your bath. I will return in a few minutes." Opal glided from the room, closing the door behind her.

I must have dozed off in the chair. When I awoke, a hip bath sat on the carpet in front of the bed and two young women were filling the bath from steaming tea kettles. I sat up and watched them empty the water into the tub.

"Hello," I offered when they finished.

One of them, a young woman with glowing auburn hair, smiled. "Hello. I'm Amber. This here's Saffron." Saffron's skin and eyes were a deep glossy black. Her eyes glittered and her white, even teeth gleamed against her ebony skin as she smiled and examined me, but she said nothing.

I nodded. "I'm Tabitha. Thanks fer fetchin' m' bath."

"Sure thing," Amber replied.

They came with filled kettles several times more before Amber murmured, "That should be enough." She slanted brown eyes toward me as though she wanted to say something, but Saffron touched her arm. Amber shrugged, and they left.

As soon as the door closed, I stripped off my dirty clothes, sank under the hot water, and allowed the liquid heat to heal my aching feet and muscles. I sighed and sank lower.

Later, my hair washed, combed, and drying, clad in a robe Opal had loaned me while someone washed my clothes, I tore into the meal one of the girls placed before me. I wolfed down the biscuit first and then attacked the chicken and mashed potatoes.

I was still gnawing on a drumstick when Opal returned bearing another tray.

"I am glad you have a good appetite, my dear," she murmured. She set the tray down on the bed and poured from a flowered teapot into a delicate china cup. "Perhaps a cup of tea to finish your dinner? I've added extra sweetening to it to strengthen you."

"I'm obliged to' ya," I replied.

Opal took my plate away and handed me the cup and saucer. I balanced them on my knee, thinking how pretty their pattern was.

"Thank ya ever s' much for all this," I said, staring at the steaming tea. "Don' know how I can ever repay ya."

"Do not concern yourself, my dear. As I said, Cray and I have an arrangement. He took care of everything."

I sipped on the tea. It was strong and hot and sweet and warmed my stomach, even after the bath and the meal. "Did he? But still, he left town 'thout me?" I frowned, wondering how I would find him or, at the least, reach a bigger town, one with a telegraph.

"Yes. We can talk about such things tomorrow when you are recovered from your ordeal. I shall just brush your hair while you drink your tea."

Opal moved behind me and fingered my hair. "You have such beautiful hair, my dear. Such fire!"

"Thank ya. Cray . . . Cray always said he loved m' hair."

I sipped on the strong brew again. I did not recognize the flavor. It seemed . . . a bit off, but its sweetness was welcome. I sipped again.

"Yes, I can certainly understand why." Opal gathered my thick mane and drew a brush through it. She brushed with a soothing rhythm and soon my hair dried under her ministrations.

I found myself yawning. "Goodness—I'm s' sorry. 'Fraid I'm a-gettin' right sleepy again."

"You have endured a terrible experience, my dear, so your fatigue is to be expected, no? Finish your tea and I will get you into bed."

Opal poured a little scented oil into her hands, rubbed them together, and then ran her fingers repeatedly through my hair. The scent of the oil filled the room.

"What's thet?" I asked as I made myself finish the tea. My hand felt weak and the teacup rattled as I placed the saucer on the little table next to my chair.

"Just some perfumed oil. To relax you a bit more."

"Relax?" My tongue seemed stiff.

"Are you finished, dear? Ready for bed?"

I did not answer. I could not seem to string two words together.

Opal helped me to the bed but it was all I could do to sit on its edge. She slid the robe from my shoulders and helped me to lie down.

I lay blinking slowly under the sheet.

What is happening?

She had not been gone more than a minute when the door opened and closed again. I heard Opal speaking from just inside the room.

"You may have your way with her, Mr. Ward, but remember this: I expect you to break her in gently. She should be compliant enough and I will not tolerate any marks on her. Do you understand?"

"Sure, Opal, sure."

"Very well, then," Opal opened the door and slipped from the room. A shadowy figure neared the bed and leaned over me.

"Who . . ." My mouth would not form the words I wanted to say.

Three times that night men came into the room. I knew what they were doing, but I had no voice to object, no strength to fight them.

I could only endure.

Rose's pen upon her notebook quivered. Her entire body trembled with an outrage she did not know how to express in a godly manner. At the same time, she ached with a sorrow that threatened to undo her.

Tabitha stared at something unseen and tears streamed down her cheeks and dripped from her chin. She was lost in her own thoughts, her own pain, and did not notice Rose's struggle. Tabitha's hands clenched and unclenched until Rose saw how red the woman's fingers were becoming and placed her own hands upon Tabitha's to still them.

"That is enough for today, dearest," Rose murmured.

O Lord, O Lord! Did I not hear you? Was this a horrible mistake?

Tabitha's eyes blinked rapidly and she returned to consciousness of the place and time. She glanced at Rose, weariness upon her brow. "I have not thought of all that for a while," she whispered. "I-I have refused to think on those days for many years."

Rose swallowed. "I understand why." She moistened her lips. "I had no real sense of what I was asking of you, Tabitha. Perhaps I was wrong to ask such a thing. Perhaps—"

"No!" Tabitha's temper, often lurking just under the surface, flared, and her one-word response was sharply spoken.

She regretted her outburst immediately. "Oh! Oh, I-I am so sorry."

Rose moved to sit next to Tabitha. She wrapped her arms about the younger woman and Tabitha leaned into Rose's comforting embrace.

"Tabitha, you said 'no' to my suggestion that we stop. Can you tell me why?"

Tabitha shuddered but nodded. "It is hard, dredging up the sordid details after all these years. But I am beginning to see how it could help. I want . . . I want to try."

"Are you certain?"

Tabitha sat up and inhaled deeply. "Now that I have begun, I do not want to stop until I recount the very moment Jesus came to rescue me. I must tell it all so that my story ends in hope."

"As you wish, dear girl," Rose responded. She took up her pen and, shaking her head, silently reread the last lines. "This . . . woman. This *Opal*."

"Yes. Opal." Tabitha spoke the name with soft dismay. "You know me, Miss Rose. As you might imagine, even at fourteen I was a handful."

Tabitha twisted a napkin in her hands. "Opal may have bent me, but she did not break me. Not entirely. And not right away. However, it was not for lack of effort on her part."

CHAPTER 3

ate the following day when whatever drug Opal had given me had worn off, she came back to her room. "It is time for us to talk, Tabitha. Get out of bed and get dressed."

She sat in the same chair I had sat in the night before and addressed me as I, groaning, sat up in the bed.

Well, I cursed her. I cursed Opal with words I'd often heard Cray use, words foreign to my tongue but suited the burning rage I felt toward Opal.

Then I saw the man watching from behind her chair twitch his shoulders. He was a hulking mountain of a beast with a protruding jaw and dull, piggy eyes. His hair, cut in a ragged line around his collar, was the same dull brown as his eyes.

He flexed his hands, clenching his fists by his side, and the muscles on his arms bulged like thick tree limbs. He was a monster. A freak of nature.

"You will curb your tongue, Tabitha," Opal said softly.

It was not a request. The menace in those few words made me wonder how I had so utterly misjudged her the day before.

I saw my clothes, washed, dried, and folded, on the end of the bed. Remembering the coins I'd stitched into the hem, I covered myself with the sheet and grabbed at the skirt.

The four half dollars were gone.

"Where are m' coins? M' money?" I demanded.

"We will not speak until you have dressed," Opal answered.

With one eye on the menacing figure standing behind her, I scooted behind the dressing screen and pulled on my clothes. It was not easy—my body ached from the rough treatment of the previous night. I flinched when I bent over to put on my shoes. All the while, I seethed, but my anger was a thin veneer atop the horror of the night before.

Then I stood before Opal, defiant and smoldering, but holding my tongue in check—for the moment.

She watched me and was amused. Her amusement only made me angrier.

"I want m' money," I said through gritted teeth. "Ya ain't got no right to it. I want t' leave Fullman. Now."

She chuckled under her breath. "Yes, I am sure you do. However, as I mentioned yesterday, I have an agreement with Cray."

"Ya lied to me," I hissed.

"Not at all, I assure you," she smirked. "Cray, in return for all the supplies he requested, traded what he had to offer. It was an equitable exchange. It was advantageous for both of us."

Her gaze studied me in a detached, practiced manner. "You are thin and have not come into full womanhood yet. We need to fatten you up a bit."

"I want m' money," I insisted.

Opal sighed. "I want to speak the truth to you, Tabitha, so there will be no hard feelings between us. When Cray arrived a few days back he offered you to me in return for a grub stake so he could continue his search for gold."

"O-offered me? I-I don' understand."

Opal smiled. "It is not the first time a man has traded a woman for supplies, my dear. What is important now is that you understand *how things are* and cooperate."

I still could not fathom Opal's words. "Are ya sayin' he *sold* me?"

The events of the night before swept over me and so did panic.

"But he ... he cain't *sell* me! He don't *own* me!" I was sputtering, unsure of how to proceed.

"Ah, my dear. So many things in this life are not as they seem. Whether he had the 'right' to sell you is inconsequential. You are here. I have already invested in you. And now you will work for me."

"I—" The horror was just beginning to dawn on me. "Work fer ya?"

"Why, yes. In addition to the store below us, I also own the saloon next door. News of your arrival has already made quite a stir. The men are looking forward ... to getting to know you better."

As though I would blithely accept and accommodate her instructions, she waved her hand and continued. "Working hours are six in the evening until one in the morning. You may sleep until ten each morning if you like. I prefer my girls well rested and in good spirits.

"However, you must be present at the table for the morning meal at 10:30. After we eat together, I will assign chores. If you complete your chores in a satisfactory manner, you may use the time remaining for your own pursuits—but you may not, *ever*, leave this building without permission. Then, promptly at three in the afternoon, you will wash, fix your hair, and tend to your clothes."

She examined her hands. "Yes, about the clothes. Amber is making over a dress for you right now. I want it understood that you will receive this dress in good condition and you will keep it in good condition. Every afternoon at 4:30 we will meet again for dinner. If you are not properly turned out, you will leave the table and repair whatever part of your toilet is lacking."

She looked hard at me. "I do not save back food for girls who are late or unprepared, and we do not eat again until the following morning, so have a care. Take your clothing and appearance seriously."

"I ain't doin' any of thet," I spat at her. "I'm a-leavin' this god-fersaken place. T'day."

Opal smiled her amused smile. "Let me introduce you to Big Jim, Tabitha."

She crooked her finger at the monster near her elbow. With more speed than I could believe, he lumbered toward me. I bolted for the door but he cut me off and spun me around. His hands grasped my neck, and he lifted me from the floor.

No matter how hard I hit him or raked him with my fingernails, Big Jim did not loosen his hold around my neck. He held me straight out in front of himself, his arms fully extended so I could scarcely reach his face.

Oh, I bloodied his cheeks and his eyes in those first seconds, indeed I did—but it seemed to make no impression upon him. He simply stared at me with those little piggy eyes and squeezed. He squeezed hard enough that soon I could not breathe, could not swallow. I felt the enormous strength in his thick fingers and I knew he could snap my neck with little effort—but he was not trying to kill me outright.

He squeezed until I floundered and twitched, my feet dangling above the floor, until I had no air left. Until I hung limp and yielding in his hands. Until the room dimmed and sparks of light were all I could see. Until I was certain I would die.

I think Opal murmured something. I cannot really remember. Big Jim dropped me to the floor and I lay there, helpless and motionless except for the bit of air seeping back into my lungs.

Opal bent over me. "That had to have been unpleasant, Tabitha, and I am certain you would not like to repeat this experience. So have a care: I do not tolerate insubordination or a poor attitude in any of my girls. Do you understand?"

Big Jim loomed behind Opal. He twined his hands together behind her shoulder where I could see them. A silent threat.

"Do you understand, Tabitha?" Opal asked again.

I gritted my teeth and nodded.

"This place is played out," Opal announced at breakfast two months later. "I invested my working capital here because I believed it would grow, that the miners would put down roots. Sadly, I was mistaken.

"We will be moving to Silver City next week. I do not plan to stay there long; I've set my sights on returning to Kansas City, my home town, as our permanent destination. When we have earned enough in our next town, we shall start east."

I barely listened. An insistent vow played in my head: *I will kill Cray Bishoff if ever I find him.* It was, in fact, all I thought of, all that kept me moving through each day ... and each night.

"Pass the butter, Red."

I ignored "Amber," as she was called. I knew it was not her real name. All of Opal's girls were renamed for colors or colored stones. Opal tried calling me "Ruby" to fit into her naming scheme, but the men all asked for "Red," so she relinquished Ruby and called me Red.

I despised the moniker and I despised *her* for shackling me with it. I particularly hated hearing the men talk about me and ask for me using that despised name.

"Hey, Red. Pass the butter?"

When I still did not respond to Amber's request, her elbow nudged me in the ribs.

My hand snaked out of its own volition. The resounding crack of my palm on Amber's face echoed through the kitchen. I do not know why I did it. I knew I would be punished, but I could not restrain the ever-simmering rage in my breast.

"Red!" Opal was on me in a trice. She may have been an older woman, but she was still strong, and she was ruthless. Opal grabbed me by my hair and yanked me backward. My chair toppled to the floor with me in it. Opal sat on my chest and held me down.

"Get Big Jim in here," she hissed.

Amber ran to do Opal's bidding. The other women, three of them, eyed each other uneasily. I had been nothing but a vexation to Opal since the day she had told me how Cray had "sold" me to her—and this would not be the first punishment Opal ordered Big Jim to dish out.

Big Jim shambled into the room with Amber peering from behind his bulk. "Yesh, Missh Opal?"

"Take Red upstairs and discipline her, Big Jim. This time, I do not care how marked up she is—just not her face."

I swore and struggled violently under Opal's knees. I wanted to run, but Big Jim grabbed my arm and yanked me to my feet. He lifted me so that my toes were unable to touch the floor. I managed to rake the nails of my free hand across his face one time before he shook me so hard that my teeth rattled.

Opal smoothed her skirt. "I want this girl *compliant*, Big Jim. If she will not bend to my bidding, I will get rid of her."

She hissed in my direction. "You are more trouble than you are worth, Red, but let me tell you something. You think life with me is bad? *Here* you receive enough to eat and are treated well enough as long as you are productive and obedient, but know this: I could sell you today to any of six men in Fullman and not lose a minute of sleep over it."

She sat, shook out her napkin, and placed it across her lap with that air of sophistication she had perfected.

"Take her out of here, Big Jim."

The man swung me over his shoulder like so many pounds of potatoes in a sack and hauled me, shrieking and cursing, up the stairs.

I screamed with rage until I screamed in pain.

For a time, I gave Opal nothing to complain about.

Her threat to sell me to one of the disgusting men of Fullman's tent city had frightened me more than she knew.

We moved to Silver City and, after four months there, Opal hired two men and their mule-pulled wagons to cart all of us and our things to Santa Fe. When we had gone far enough east to have skirted the nearby mountain range, we turned north and followed, roughly, the muddy river our drivers called the Rio Grande. The trip took three weeks and was hard on all of us, body, mind, and temper.

Most of the journey it was easier to walk than to ride in the wagons. Our bones were stiff and bruised from the wagon's continual jolting.

As I walked, I stared out onto the desert with its distant craggy mountains, red-rock bluffs, dangerous crevasses, and endless vistas. I was again terrified of being abandoned, left alone in the wasteland—and for good reason: The men Opal hired were as disreputable and untrustworthy as one might imagine.

Opal, to her credit, was no fool. She used both a carrot and a stick to keep the drivers in line—the carrot being one of us girls each night, the stick being Big Jim. Oh, the drivers were right to be as afraid of Big Jim as we girls were: At a word from Opal, he would have killed the drivers and never batted an eye.

In that respect, we girls were grateful for Big Jim's protection. Without him we feared the two drivers would have killed Opal—and taken us. I harbored no illusions that we would have survived long in their "care."

After the long, difficult trek, we arrived in Santa Fe. It was a strange town, bustling with three diverse populations, Indian, Spanish/Mexican, and white American.

Opal regarded the straggling adobe buildings and narrow, dirty streets with distaste. We all wrinkled our noses over the odors of meats cooking with unfamiliar spices. Opal hurried us into a boarding house where we bathed after so many days travel and washed our clothes.

We were exhausted, but Opal was up and about early in the morning. She arranged for the owner of the boarding house to pack enough food to feed us for the day. Then she hurried us again, this time to the train depot. We boarded the train, and she had Big Jim guard us while she dealt with the two drivers. Sullen-faced, they took her money, climbed aboard their wagons, and drove away.

After the jarring passage from Silver City to Santa Fe by wagon or foot, the train was a delight. Oh, the railcars were still filthy and hot, but riding by train was far easier than walking or riding in a wagon. And faster. We arrived in Kansas City in three days' time. This leg of our journey ended in the bustle and stench of Kansas City's stock yards.

To Opal, however, Kansas City represented opportunity. Once we were away from the trains and cattle, we found ourselves in a much more gentrified town. Opal again installed us in a boarding house and left Big Jim in the hall outside of our rooms.

I thought of climbing out a window and running away, but we were on the second floor and the ground sloped steeply away from the house. It would have been a dangerous drop. I was too scared of what the fall to the ground might do to me—and the other girls watched me closely anyway. They would not allow me to do anything that would put *them* in jeopardy without alerting Big Jim.

Apparently Opal was a good business woman: She had saved much of the money she made from the women and alcohol she served in Fullman and Silver City. Within a week of arriving in Kansas City, she located and purchased a house. We girls worked hard under her direction to ready the house and, within a second week, we were set up for business again.

Opal laid great store by manners, elegance, and sophistication. She invested money in the house's furnishings and the girls' clothing.

She drilled us relentlessly in conversation and diction. She strove extra hard to eliminate my crude, illiterate, west Texas dialect, slapping or pinching me if I lapsed into countrified speech.

She also trained us in "charm," but what I am referring to is the art of wit and guile—all aimed at flattering our customers and encouraging them to spend more money.

At every turn, Opal sought to raise the standards of her house and so attract a wealthier clientele—men to whom money presented no impediment.

Opal graced her parlor with the best looking and best "turned out" of her girls, those who could converse in an intelligent, clever manner. She was always on the lookout for new girls who, with a little training, would be an asset to her house.

At the same time, Opal could not abide a girl who, after many lessons, continued to use incorrect grammar and whose speech or accent remained coarse. Opal could not ask top dollar for *those* women, so any woman who could not—or would not—be improved, she sold off to cheaper, less discriminating brothels.

We heard whispers about the "working conditions" in those places, rumors about the squalid cribs and the customers who were allowed to mistreat the girls.

I was not obtuse: I watched Opal sell off girls who did not comply with her standards, and I did not want to be one of them. I also had no desire for Big Jim to repeat the last beating he'd given me back in Arizona.

So I learned what Opal demanded of me and I performed as she required. In fact, because of my flaming hair, I became one of Opal's "first" girls, the ones who were in demand, the girls men reserved ahead of time and paid a premium to do so.

How did I survive? How did I bear the horror of that first year? Bereft of hope, I shut my feelings away. I denied the cries of my heart until I was numb. It was not long before I learned how liquor, too, had the power to temporarily deaden my pain.

You see, every drink a man bought for me (watered down, of course) was money in Opal's pocket. You can imagine then, how she encouraged her girls to drink. Besides, Opal knew that a drink-addicted prostitute was easier to control. Like the other girls, I gave in to alcohol. I was able to face each evening by looking forward to the drinks with which eager men plied me.

I stayed out of trouble for a while, but the self-preserving restraint I exercised over my unruly temper started to shred, to unravel. One morning I awoke and realized that my birthday had passed. I was now fifteen years old—and had been for an entire month.

The fact that I'd forgotten my own birthday, that no one else had remembered it, that no one cared that my birthday had passed unnoticed—or ever would care—struck deep into my heart. I peered ahead into my future and all I could see was another fifteen years, perhaps twenty, of the same corrupting life.

Soon after we arrived in Kansas City, a new girl, a lovely, delicate brunette with milky white skin, joined the house. Her real name was Pauline, but Opal, in keeping with her theme, bestowed the illustrative name of Pearl upon her.

Pearl was, perhaps, nearer the age of thirty than twenty. She had been raised as a gentlewoman, a spinster who had never been required to work. Apparently, Pearl had fallen upon hard times and had no family to help her. Opal had glimpsed Pearl's manners and beauty and had swooped in to "rescue" her.

From her first day in Opal's house, I knew Pearl would not survive long. She'd been beaten into compliance like the rest of us, but she had no inner reserves upon which to draw. The crushing blow of being forced into prostitution had broken her spirit, and she succumbed to the snare of alcohol almost immediately.

I do not know how she managed it, but within three months of joining Opal's house, Pearl was drunk nearly all the time. She no longer cared for her clothes as Opal demanded. Her face was chronically swollen, her eyes bleary from drink, her pearly white skin a sallow, sickly yellow.

The rest of us edged away from her, knowing one morning she would be missing, sold away. The morning I awoke and realized that I had missed my own birthday, Pearl was gone.

That was the morning I stopped drinking. That was the morning, deep in my breast, my temper's tamped-down embers again glowed hot. It was not long before my smoldering anger showed itself.

As I related earlier, I despised the name Opal had foisted upon me and the many "gentlemen" who asked specifically for "Red." Out of my anger, I invented many small ways to rebel against those men. My favorite game was to (carefully, of course) denigrate those who denigrated me.

During the clever banter of the parlor or bedroom, I delivered subtle jabs to the men who used me. I enjoyed watching my barbs strike their mark, all while maintaining an innocent or come-hither expression.

Some customers were not quick or astute enough to see through my sweet, guileless façade; others smarted under my verbal gibes. If they reddened or grew cross, I soothed them with smiling platitudes—but it was a dangerous game I played, baiting these men.

And then, of course, I made a mistake: I leveled my stinging wit at the wrong man.

He was small in stature and carried a chip on his shoulder because of it. He was a mean, vindictive little man, but he was intelligent.

He grasped my veiled insult to his size. The scene he caused in Opal's parlor—and my subsequent punishment—are still etched on my mind, but I do not care to rehash the details.

Suffice it to say that it was a very bad night for me.

❧ ✳ ☙

CHAPTER 4

Early the next morning, while the other girls still slept, Opal woke me. She bid me to rise and pointed at what I was to wear—my old dress, the one I had been wearing when I came to her.

"Come down to the parlor when you are presentable," was all she said.

When I stepped into the parlor, Big Jim stood ready at Opal's elbow.

A large, vulgar-looking woman, all the more slovenly in appearance for her soiled skirt and shirtwaist, looked me up and down. "Aye. She'll do." She latched on to my arm with a hand like a manacle.

I clawed at the hand—until Big Jim flexed his fingers.

"What are you doing?" I stared at Opal. I was bruised and in a great deal of pain from the beating I'd received the night before. But I was still defiant.

"Meet Ethyl Moyer," Opal muttered through thinned lips. "I have loaned you to her for a time—time enough, I hope, for you to learn *gratitude*. You are one of my best moneymakers, Red, but your attitude creates more difficulties than benefits for me. Your attitude must, therefore, be corrected. When you have learned to be *grateful*, and when you beg me to take you back, I will *consider* doing so."

Big Jim walked with us to Ethyl's wagon and waited until I was seated next to Ethyl. The woman did not release my arm until she'd clamped a chain about my wrist. I screamed and pulled at the chain until Ethyl backhanded me across the mouth. Still I screamed and struggled. She used her fist then. When I stopped struggling, she released the brake and picked up the reins while I cradled my bleeding mouth.

An hour later we arrived at a building every bit as slovenly as Ethyl herself, and I began to understand what Opal meant by "learning to be grateful."

I had been with Ethyl two months when I began to feel unwell. I was tired all the time, even in the morning, and parts of my body were tender and sore. A customer complained to Ethyl about me. He told her that I whined that certain things hurt me. Ethyl stripped me down, examined my body. She said I was pregnant.

Tabitha looked away. "You and I have spoken of this, Miss Rose. Ethyl brought in a woman to-to 'take care' of the baby. Is it all right if I do not speak of it again?"

Rose nodded. "It is not necessary. I will pray about how to write this part. Surely some of the girls who read your account will . . . relate?"

"Yes, that is likely. I-I, well, after the abortion, I became sick—so sick! For a long while I ran a fever and tossed in pain upon a cot in a back room. The sweat poured from my body for days. I think Ethyl figured I would die, and she stopped feeding and caring for me. But I did not die."

"No," Rose whispered. "God preserved you."

Tabitha sighed and took a sip of water. "Yes, he preserved me. But, as you know, because of the infection I contracted, I will never have children."

She rolled her shoulders to ease the tension in them and continued.

During the long weeks while fever festered in my belly, anger and hatred festered in my heart. After my body healed, Ethyl put me back to work, but I was not the same girl. I would never be again. Within a week I was causing trouble—insulting customers, provoking other girls, defying Ethyl. Anywhere and in any manner I might vent my anger, I did.

I did not care if Ethyl starved me. I no longer worried about the beatings—I simply went elsewhere in my mind.

I just did not care anymore.

"Yer not worth m' time, Red," Ethyl snarled at me. "You hev cost me more money'n you'll ever make up t'me."

She dragged me back to Opal and shoved me through the front door into Big Jim's arms. It was a triumph on my part. A small victory that reinforced my resolve.

"I'm shut of 'er, Opal," Ethyl declared. "A worse bargain I ain't ever made."

No sooner had I been reinstalled in Opal's house than I rebelled against her rules. It was as though the old Tabitha had been asleep—and had revived. I stared at the world with wide-open eyes, and everything I saw, *I hated.*

Every outburst and disobedience earned a punishment: Opal starved me. Big Jim beat me. Opal allowed customers free reign with me. Nothing mattered and nothing changed. I may have feigned defeat more than once after a punishment, but only until the bruises faded.

As soon as the pain eased, my resentment flared back to life, and I invented a myriad of ways to express my fury. The customers complained to Opal that I was not "accommodating" enough.

Indeed, I hated the men who expected me to smile and please them. Customers who were drawn to my bright hair were as quickly driven off by my caustic tongue. My behavior and reputation caused nothing but problems for Opal and, no matter the punishments, I celebrated the few little victories I managed.

Opal's other girls steered clear of me—they had all learned the hard way. However, I hated them just as much as I hated Opal. In fact, I hated everyone.

But most of all, I hated Cray Bishoff.

Someday I will find you, I vowed to him in raging thoughts. *Someday I will find you and make you pay.* I fantasized on meeting him again, of surprising him. And I planned in detail how I would kill him. The time I spent thinking and plotting filled my waking hours and haunted my sleep. It was all I lived for.

Of course, Opal wearied of my surly moods and the problems I caused. At one point, she managed to sell me to an unwitting customer, a man who had admired me from afar but who knew nothing of my, er, disposition. He was a man Opal felt "would suit" my temperament.

Yes, he was strong and determined, but I did not care. I made his life a misery. Two weeks later he dumped me back in Opal's arms and demanded his money back.

"Glad to be rid of you, you red-haired hellion," he breathed in my ear as he turned me over to Big Jim.

Opal stared at me, her hands fisting and unfisting at her sides. "Lock her in the attic, Big Jim," her words grated through clenched teeth. "No water. No food. She will stay there until she capitulates. Or until she dies. I do not care which."

Big Jim hauled me up the three flights of stairs until we reached the attic. He pushed me inside and I heard the rattle of the lock on the door as he fastened it. I took a deep breath, confident that I had scored another victory, and looked around.

The attic was empty except for the trunks we had used on our trip from Silver City. Dust motes floated in the air, in cracks of light coming from a vent at the front of the house.

When the sun set, the attic settled into darkness. I hauled a trunk to the vent, stood upon it, and tried to peer between the slats. All I could see were rooftops across the street, but even they were shrouded in darkness.

I heard muffled voices from the floor below and lay flat on the dirty floorboards, my ear to them. I could not make out any words, only a little laughter and movement. Then doors closed and sounds faded.

They have gone downstairs, I thought, *to begin the night's work.* Soon they would be bringing customers to their rooms. I did not want to hear any of that activity.

Unexpectedly, the door to the attic opened and Big Jim lumbered over the threshold. He placed a chamber pot on the floor.

Nothing else. No blankets. No water. Nothing.

I was left in the attic, without food or drink, for four days before Opal appeared at the door. I was as near death as a person deprived of water can be. I lay curled upon the bare floor, my muscles contracted in spasms from lack of water. I had not given Opal the pleasure of hearing me beg and scream for something to drink—but then again, by the time I was ready to scream, my throat had been too dry to utter more than croaking sounds.

Opal nudged me with the toe of her finely polished shoe. I moved my mouth and tried to blink, but the lids scraped painfully across my dry eyes. I gave up and kept them closed.

Opal squatted near me. "This must be your choice, Tabitha," she whispered.

I was, in some withered part of my mind, surprised to hear my name, my real name, but I could not respond.

"This must be your choice," Opal repeated. "You must choose now if you wish to live or die. If you choose to die, very well. You will not suffer much longer. Another day. Perhaps two, at the most."

I turned her words over in my head. It was hard to think, to string the thoughts together and make them stay put. *Another day. Perhaps two.* I was past the frantic pain of thirsting. It would not be too hard to … let go.

"However, if you choose to live, you must decide *now* that things will be different." Opal's voice cut through my confused thoughts. "If you choose to live, you must change your mind and do all that is expected of you. No more rebellions. No more problems. Do you understand?"

As best as my distressed mind could, I weighed the two options. Slipping farther away would be easier. The worst was over.

Except for the sudden niggle, a frisson of fear that quivered its way through my chest.

"If you choose to live, Tabitha, you must capitulate to me. *Now.* Choose, Tabitha. If you agree to surrender to me, open your eyes."

She waited for my answer.

That fear, *the fear of death*, trembled in my breast. The door to eternity loomed before me, and what lurked beyond it terrified me. I could not let go. I wanted to! Oh, I wanted to! I wanted to slip into oblivion, to float far away from all pain and sorrow.

But the fear in my heart was not convinced that painless bliss awaited me if I let go. I was scared of what lay on the other side. I was not ready to die, and I knew it.

Opal urged me to surrender to her and live. She urged me to choose. Choose? Did I have any choices left? No, choice for me was dead.

And so I was beaten. I had fought long and hard, but I was defeated.

As real, as vivid as the unmistakable rending of a length of fabric, I heard—*I felt*—my will and my heart tear apart. My broken will fluttered downward, into the abyss. What remained of my heart lay bleeding and mortally wounded in my breast.

I opened my eyes and surrendered.

Tabitha dropped into a silent preoccupation with her own thoughts. Rose turned from her scribbled notes to watch her.

"What are you thinking now, Tabitha?" she asked gently.

Surprised from her reverie, the red-haired woman smiled. "Actually, I was thinking of how, at what could be deemed the second-lowest point in my life, God reached out to me."

Intrigued, Rose leaned forward. "Tell me what you mean."

"I could not have known it then, but the fear I felt, the fear that kept me from choosing death, kept me alive for the next thirteen years. And even though I thought that I had come to the end of myself, I still had not reached out to God, had not called out to him."

"And?"

"And I think he placed that fear in me so that I would choose to live. He kept me going, kept me alive, all those years that followed after, so that when just the right time came, my heart would be ready."

"*In the fullness of time, God sent his Son,*" Rose whispered.

"Yes. In the fullness of time." Tabitha's mouth quirked in wry humor, "I thought I was at the bottom, but I had not yet reached the end of myself, the place where I would, finally, cry out to God, and ask for his help. I had not yet met Cal Judd."

Rose shuddered at the mention of Cal Judd. She could absorb no more of Tabitha's revelations today, so she glanced at the clock on the fireplace mantelpiece. "Goodness. We have been here for hours. Shall we break off for the day, Tabitha?"

Tabitha nodded her agreement. "Tomorrow, then?"

"Yes," Rose replied. "As soon as the girls leave for their work and the house quiets."

❧ ✳ ❦

CHAPTER 5

Rose and Tabitha seated themselves in the same places they had occupied the day prior. Breona, her black eyes dancing with intrigue, placed a tea tray between Rose and Tabitha.

"Thank you, my dear Breona!" Rose exclaimed. "How very thoughtful."

"Ye was both bein' as parched as th' ground in July yesterday." Breona wiped her hands on her apron. "Will ye be talkin' fer hours agin t'day?"

Rose glanced at Tabitha. "Perhaps. We shall see how it goes."

"Shall ye be needin' onything from me?"

"No, dear one, but thank you for asking."

Having received no word or hint to assuage her curiosity, Breona shrugged and left the great room, closing the door behind her.

"Did you sleep well last night, Tabitha?" Rose inquired. Her own sleep had been restless and her dreams uneasy, disturbed by the details Tabitha had shared with her.

"Yes. I am surprised at how well I slept, actually," Tabitha responded. "To be truthful, the sharing of my past with you is causing me to appreciate God's grace toward me so much more than I had."

She glanced up at Rose from under downcast lashes. "I think I had not realized that I still felt a great deal of shame about my past. And yet, as I spoke of the things I had done, the woman I used to be, the shame seemed to ... slip away. Does that make any sense?"

"It makes sense to me, Tabitha," Rose replied. "I believe that God's children cannot testify to his gracious forgiveness in our lives without first acknowledging that for which he has forgiven us."

Rose tapped her pen on the notebook already filled with so many lines and mused, "I wonder if those individuals who have lived 'good' lives do not sometimes struggle to see their need for God's grace and forgiveness."

"Well, *I* certainly do not struggle to see that need," Tabitha sniffed.

She and Rose laughed a little.

"Shall we begin again?" Rose asked. "Perhaps at this point you might move your story ahead, closer to when Jesus met you."

"That is a good proposal, Miss Rose. I do not wish to dwell overmuch on those evil years." Tabitha's brows drew together. "I will take up my tale not long before I was moved to Denver."

KANSAS CITY, 1907

I stared from my second-floor room to the busy street below. I was not really taking in the sights; rather, I was allowing my thoughts to wander ... allowing them to fret and grow anxious about the future.

Eleven years had worn their way through my life. For eleven years I had performed, complied, and obeyed as Opal required. I was now twenty-six years old, a well-practiced prostitute, utterly dead in my heart. Yet somehow, I had managed to maintain a "lively" enough pretense on the outside to suit Opal's purposes these many years.

But now Opal was ill. Her skin, once beautiful in its porcelain clarity, hung from fragile bones in paper-thin folds. She looked every year of her life—and more.

She is dying, I made myself acknowledge. *I have seen the signs before; I recognize them.*

Indeed, over the last decade, I had watched two of Opal's girls march toward death in similar fashion. Opal was dying of consumption.

The harbingers of death by the dread disease were clear enough: A cough that would not abate, that sent the older woman into spasms where she could not catch her breath; coughing spells that more and more frequently ended in blood-soaked handkerchiefs; a persistent fever. And Opal had lost a great deal of weight. Far too much weight.

She would not be coming back from this sickness.

What will become of us girls when she dies?

In a deep corner of my heart I clutched at and gripped a tiny, brittle hope, a hope that when Opal passed, I might be free again and make my way home to my parents.

My folks. Are they still living? Neither of them would be old yet, but life on a farm was arduous, and disease and injury were ever-present in the world, threatening even the hardiest of bodies.

Like Opal's.

Opal's ever-present shadow, Big Jim, was also older by eleven years. He was just as massive, just as strong as when I had first laid eyes upon him, but he was not as light on his feet as he had been in his younger days.

Big Jim was, like the rest of us, preoccupied with Opal's condition. I could see from the concern glinting in his simple-minded eyes that he, too, knew Opal would not rally. As I watched him, I probed for the right opportunity to flee. I would have to be quick and have a good plan.

I left off staring out the window and came to the table when called.

In the years following my surrender to her, Opal had built on to her house. Twelve girls now sat down to the morning meal. Usually Opal presided at the table, but she had sent word that she would be taking her breakfast in her room.

For the third morning in a row.

Instead, Big Jim and two other hired men like him kept watch over the table. Their sole job was to keep us girls in line.

While I ate, I covertly studied the three men. I was not sure if Big Jim had thought ahead, had thought about what would become of Opal's "business" when she died.

His eyes shifted uncomfortably from watching us girls to watching Marco, a younger, smarter version of himself. Marco, in my estimation, was an ambitious type, the kind of man who would make a move to take over Opal's business the moment she was no longer able to give orders.

But Opal was not at quite that point yet; no, she was not about to allow a *coup* to topple her rule. Not over her own house!

Tensions in the house were rising, however. I would have to time my escape to dovetail with the power struggle I could feel looming near—when Opal's attention was elsewhere.

But all my scheming did not foresee Opal's preemptive move.

Only two days later, she called all of us—working girls and hired muscle—into the parlor. She looked somewhat better, stronger than she had for a while. Certainly she had taken pains with her toilet and dress, even though her clothes sagged upon her exceedingly thin frame.

As I studied her, I wondered what it was that I sensed about her. I was mildly disconcerted when the word "relieved" came to mind.

Relieved?

"Ladies," she nodded at the dozen women who worked for her, "and gentlemen." Her last word held a degree of sarcasm, and she fixed on Marcos, in particular, as she addressed us. She drew herself up in her chair.

"I have an announcement to make." She again surveyed us, considering each of us for a moment. Then she sighed, and a bit of vitality seemed to seep from her.

"But first, Big Jim, would you kindly show our guests in?"

Big Jim ushered three men into the room, two of them impressive in their stature and girth. The third smiled at Opal and swapped a wad of chaw from one side of his mouth to the other.

"Miz Opal. Right good t' see ya lookin' s'fine t'day," he grinned.

Opal, a tight smile frozen upon her face, nodded like a queen to an inferior subject. "Mr. Jacobs. Thank you for your prompt arrival."

She inclined her head and Jacobs took a seat. His men stood behind him, hands clasped in front of their bodies, expressions inscrutable.

"Ladies," Opal began again, "and gentlemen," (this time there was no mistaking that she had fixed her gaze upon Marcos) "I wish to announce that Mr. Jacobs has made me an agreeable offer for my business. I have accepted his offer. As of this afternoon, Mr. Jacobs is the new owner of this house."

The tension in the parlor could not have been thicker. We girls, discomfited, stared from Opal to Jacobs and back while Jacobs leered at us, looking us up and down like so much meat on the hoof.

Marcos clamped his lips together in anger and evaluated Jacob's muscle. They, in turn, dropped their hands to their sides and held them in readiness, hinting at the guns that had to be hiding beneath their suitcoats.

"Marcos." Opal's voice broke through the crackling hostility. "Mr. Jacobs will not be retaining your services as he steps into his management of this house." She lifted an envelope with a weak, trembling hand. "Your pay. Please take it and excuse yourself with *my thanks*." Her address to Marcos, again, was laced with sarcasm.

Big Jim took the envelope from Opal's hand and held it out to Marcos. The man looked from the envelope toward Jacobs and his men and back. Finally, snatching his pay from Big Jim, he stormed from the room and out the front entrance.

"As I mentioned during our negotiations, Mr. Jacobs, you would do well to watch out for that one," Opal drawled.

She struggled to her feet and Big Jim assisted her. "And now, ladies," Opal wheezed, "I bid you farewell. Big Jim and I are departing for a warmer, drier climate, one better suited to my health."

With no further word, Opal, leaning heavily upon Big Jim's arm, walked from the house to a waiting carriage and drove away.

Tabitha's laugh broke Rose's rapt attention. "Well, *of course* Opal had planned ahead! We should have known she would. At least, *I* should have known. Apparently, Big Jim had already packed her clothing and personal belongings and removed them from the house."

Tabitha leaned back in her chair and closed her eyes. "As soon as the door closed behind Opal, we became acquainted with our new 'master': Jock Jacobs."

"Well, ladies! I'm right proud t' be yer new boss man," Jacobs grinned. He looked around for a spittoon. When he spied one, he spat toward it—missing it completely—and grinned again. "Y'all kin jes' call me Jock."

I do not need to say much about this period. Jock Jacobs was a pompous, vulgar man who lived to make money and spend it on debauchery. He had won a large cash pot in a poker game and, out of his winnings, he paid Opal a small fortune for her house and clientele.

However, his business practices drove off Opal's more discriminating customers in short order. In only six months the house had eroded to the level of a common bordello, a brawling, riotous whorehouse.

As keenly as I had hated Opal, I had also, on some level, respected her business acumen. But Jock? I not only despised Jock Jacobs; I loathed him for the crude, lowlife creature he was.

The house immediately began losing money—what with Jock drinking heavily every night and the loss of the "standards" upon which Opal had built her flourishing business. I watched Jock fritter away Opal's "good reputation" with growing concern.

Within a year, Jock had racked up serious outstanding bills with the house's creditors. The other girls in the house did not perceive how precarious the situation was, but I had an inkling.

One evening in the fall of that year, Jock closed the house for a private party. He lectured us on how important this party was and how he wished us to be on our best behavior, catering to his guests' every desire.

As it turned out, Jock had invited his guests to examine "his girls" and make offers for them. Of course, he did not say as much in front of us, but I caught on to his ploy. While the other women were doing their best to flatter the men and display themselves to their best advantage, I did the opposite.

My old tricks—my serpent's tongue and acid wit—were just as sharp and biting as they had been eleven years ago. In less than an hour, I had insulted and ridiculed Jock's every guest.

Of course, I paid a price for my rebellion.

When morning dawned and I awoke to lick the wounds of my beating, I was the only woman left in the house—and Jock was packing furiously to flee his creditors.

"Pack all yer things, Red," he hissed. "Put all yer whorin' clothes in thet trunk." He pointed to a small case.

When I hesitated, Jock grabbed me by the arm. "I would do ya in right now, Red," he snarled, "fer th' damage ya done me las' night, but I need th' cash you'll bring too much. I'll take ya with me t' Denver and sell ya off there. Nobody knows ya there."

He leaned into my aching, battered face, his boozy breath hot on my cheek. "An' if'n ya pull them same tricks in Denver? I'll wring yer neck fer certain, an' I ain't foolin' none."

Tabitha swallowed. "Jock had me put on a faded cotton dress and told me to hide my red hair under a bonnet. He loaded our things into a wagon and made me sit beside him on the wagon's bench. Then he locked a chain about my ankle—the kind used in jails—and I was too weak to fight him. He had bolted the other end of the chain under the seat of his wagon.

"We traveled a circuitous route to Denver. Jock was agitated and fearful that his creditors were chasing after him, so we took little-used back roads. He often pulled off the track into dense trees or brush. We would spend the day in hiding until Jock felt assured that no one was following close behind us.

"To the casual eye, he and I probably appeared to be a poor married couple hauling all of our worldly goods from one place to another. No one could see the shackle upon my ankle."

She shook her head. "These sordid details are not necessary, and I could have skipped them. I only bring them out because of what happened on the fourth afternoon of our journey."

We were far out into the country when we came upon a gathering of mostly colored folk. They were huddled up close to a tall black man dressed in a shiny black suit. He was a fine looking gentleman. He stood upon a packing crate, but he would have towered over the crowd without standing upon anything!

As it was, with the added height of the crate and the resplendent figure he cut, he reminded me of a war hero's statue rising up from the center of a city square.

The man was speaking and gesturing. We could not hear him yet—but the crowd was attentive. More people were coming. They drew near and then pressed in closer as he spoke.

I so wanted to stop to listen to what the man was saying. I even asked Jock if we could pull aside for a few minutes to hear the man. Jock, however, cursed under his breath and kept the horses moving.

The dusty trace our wagon followed ran directly behind the man in the black suit. No one in the crowd paid us any mind as we trundled by, but I began to hear the man's words.

"The Bible say God *so loved* that he give his one an' only Son. God so loved! YAY-ess! I say it again, God *so loved*!"

He broke for a second to wipe his face with a handkerchief. "Well, sir, *what* did God love? The Bible say he loved the world. *The world*, folks! YAY-ess! The whole, wide world! *The world*—it mean' peoples. *The world*—it mean' *all* peoples. All peoples mean' *ever'* kind o' people!" he thundered.

The crowd was riveted—and I was, too. The preacher's voice was deep and melodic, rhythmic and enthralling. After each sentence he paused, just a bit. Each pause made me want to beg him, *Please do not stop!* And he did not.

He shouted,

"God give his Son fo' the rich, and God give his Son fo' the poor.

"God give his Son fo' the high, and God give his Son fo' the low.

"God give his Son fo' the black man, and God give his Son fo' the white.

"God give his Son fo' *all* men—we's all equal in his sight!

"Yea, an' I say!

"God give his Son fo' the drunks. God give his Son fo' the thieves.

"God give his Son fo' you, and God give his Son fo' me."

Jock swore and urged the horses to go faster. We were almost beyond the scene now.

Every part of my being, though, was captivated by that giant of a man preaching to the crush of eager people. As our wagon passed him by, my head and hips swiveled to keep him in view. I twisted as far as the chain around my ankle would allow me to. I could not take my eyes off him as his voice boomed over the heads of the throng facing him.

And then the preacher slowly turned. That black man in the black suit rotated away from the crowd and toward us. And as he was still turning he pointed. He kept turning until he was facing away from the crowd and his finger was pointing at *me*. And that man shouted,

"God give his Son fo' the prostitute, God give his Son fo' the whore!

"God give his Son fo' the vilest of women—don' you run from God no more!" And he pointed at me. *At me.*

The sudden change and intensity in Tabitha's tale had stunned Rose. Her mouth hung agape, her pen stilled.

"Miss Rose, his finger did not merely wag in my direction. No, he lifted his finger toward heaven and when he brought it down, it was extended directly at me."

Tabitha pointed at Rose and repeated, "God give his Son fo' the *vilest* of women—don' you run from God no more!

"I did not know what he meant, Miss Rose. I heard the words and they resounded within me. No, resounded is not the right word. When he pointed his finger straight toward me, his words landed like a thunderclap upon my soul! I knew what he said was important, that he had spoken something momentous, but I could make neither head nor tails of his words: *God give his Son fo' the vilest woman—don' you run from God no more.*"

Tabitha shook herself. "Even after we were out of earshot, Jock was still turning the air blue with curses. While he railed against the roadside preacher, I shut him out, closed myself up inside, and repeated the preacher's words,

"God gave his Son for the rich, and God gave his Son for the poor. God gave his Son for the high, and God gave his Son for the low. God gave his Son for the drunks. God gave his Son for the thieves. God gave his Son for you. God gave his Son for me.

"I pondered those words within myself until I had them memorized, but I kept wondering, *If what the preacher says is true, if God gave his Son for me, what does that mean?* You see, Miss Rose, I had no religious training. I had never been to church. I did not know the Bible. I could not fathom what the preacher man had shouted. I could not understand it.

"But a tiny flicker of, I suppose it was curiosity, ignited in my heart. And I asked, *Who are you, God? Who are you, the God of whom the preacher spoke? Are you real? Where can you be found?*

"I did not expect an answer, really, so it was with some surprise that I thought I heard—or rather I felt—a single word land in my belly. It landed in what felt like the deepest part of me."

Tabitha lapsed into a quiet contemplation and gave no indication that she intended to finish her narrative.

When Rose could bear the silence no more, she touched Tabitha's hand. "Tabitha? Which word?"

Tabitha started and looked slightly confused. "I beg your pardon, Miss Rose?"

Rose leaned farther across the little table and the stone-cold tea things. "You said that you felt a single word land in your belly. Which word, Tabitha?"

"Oh! Yes." Tabitha swept a wisp of hair behind her ear and her eyes lit. "The word I heard down deep inside of me was *wait.*"

❧ ✹ ❧

CHAPTER 6

When Mei-Xing brought Shan-Rose home that evening, the toddler was whimpering and running a slight fever. Tabitha immediately became engrossed in helping Mei-Xing care for the little girl.

"Perhaps we should put off our sessions. I would like to give my time to Shan-Rose while she is ill," Tabitha suggested.

"Yes, I concur," Rose answered. "We are making splendid progress on your testimony. I have many notes to review and write up, but my other responsibilities must be feeling a bit neglected. This interlude will allow me to catch up with my household duties and, perhaps, begin to write out some of my notes."

In the face of Tabitha's assurances, Mei-Xing returned to her work as Mrs. Palmer's assistant the following morning.

And as it happened, Rose and Tabitha did not resume Tabitha's recitation of her story for nearly two weeks.

That afternoon their Pinkerton friend, O'Dell, returned from his travels to report on his search for Joy and Grant's infant son, Edmund. He spent an hour closeted in the parlor with Joy and Rose, sharing what little news he had.

Balancing his ever-present bowler hat on his knee, he faced the two women, bereft mother and grandmother. To Rose's eyes, O'Dell appeared weary and discouraged. Joy was composed as O'Dell gave his report.

"I am sorry that I do not have much new information to convey to you, Joy," he began. Our assumptions—such as they were—led us to believe that Dean Morgan left Denver by motorcar, taking Edmund with him. We also believed that Morgan had a companion, the wet nurse Fang Hua Chen hired to care for her grandson.

"Since our initial findings, two of Fang-Hua's co-conspirators have provided us with the identity of the wet nurse; however, we were unable to uncover any family connections other than her deceased husband and infant in the Seattle area."

"She had lost a baby?" Joy blinked as she tried to envision the woman who, most likely, was caring for Edmund.

O'Dell nodded. "A few weeks prior to Edmund's abduction."

"Then … she would be more likely to be … kind to my baby boy?"

O'Dell and Rose both understood where Joy's questions were heading. Rose looked at O'Dell and nodded.

O'Dell, speaking carefully, answered Joy's question. "Joy, my understanding is that the woman was suffering from her losses and took the job Fang Hua offered her so she could care for another baby. Yes, I believe she is being kind to Edmund. I cannot believe otherwise."

He ran a finger around the inside of his collar as if it felt too tight. "We received a report of one sighting that seems to confirm those assumptions. Morgan required gasoline for his motorcar. Since facilities where he might purchase gasoline are not numerous, Pinkerton focused its attention on a two-hundred-mile radius around Denver—in all possible directions—and all facilities within that radius where Morgan could have refueled.

"The difficulty in that approach is that the sale of gasoline is a new kind of business not confined to specific locations. Gasoline is sold at coal yards, factories, or out of an enterprising businessman's back door. Where to buy gasoline is frequently communicated by word of mouth—which works for us, by the way.

"Once Morgan was out of his familiar surroundings, he would have to look for signs advertising the sale of gasoline or ask locals where he might purchase it. An attendant at a general store in Pueblo, Colorado, recalls a man with a woman and infant asking for directions to purchase gasoline for their motorcar."

O'Dell turned his hat around on his knee. "The southeast direction of Pueblo from Denver gave us a general direction to go on. We refocused our radius."

Joy leaned forward, eager to hear more.

There was no more.

O'Dell looked down. "We have been unable to find any further witnesses who remember Morgan buying or asking about gasoline. I am sorry, Joy."

"But what does that mean?" Joy clutched her mother's hand and tried to remain calm.

Unable to remain seated, O'Dell stood to pace—but the parlor gave him no space to do so. He rounded his chair and held on to its back. "It does not mean that we give up, Joy."

"Give up? Who said anything about giving up?" Joy was strangling Rose's hand in her effort to stay composed.

O'Dell stared at the floor. "You asked what it means that we have found no further witnesses to Morgan's route."

His voice softened, "It means we have no leads to follow at present. From Pueblo, Morgan could have gone in any direction. It is unlikely that he turned north, of course, but he could have gone in any other direction."

The small room lapsed into silence for a time.

Finally Joy murmured. "I see."

"I would like us to pray," Rose's suggestion was too strongly worded to be ignored.

O'Dell again took his seat and the three of them bowed their heads together.

"Lord, we can do nothing apart from you," Rose prayed. "This task, this mission to find Edmund, is beyond our abilities—but O Lord, nothing is too difficult for *you*. We confess that we trust you, Lord, and we commit Edmund into your care."

After three days, everyone in the house knew that Shan-Rose had recovered from her illness when her energy returned and she refused to stay still. The next day the child, as was her custom, accompanied Mei-Xing to Mrs. Palmer's house, where the housekeeper generally watched her.

However, that same morning, Joy came down with a severe cold. Tabitha confined her to her bed in the cottage out back of Palmer House.

"You likely caught this cold from Shan-Rose, Joy, but you must understand that you are more susceptible to illness at this time, while you are still grieving," Tabitha admonished her friend. "Sarah, Corrine, and Billy have the shop in hand, so do not worry. Only rest."

"It is hard to rest," Joy murmured, "when my mind refuses to let me."

Tabitha placed her hand on Joy's forehead and made light, soothing circles on it with her fingers. "I can only imagine that is so. Still, you *are* running a fever, Joy. You must rest—and you must not expose the remainder of the house to your illness, particularly Marit."

Palmer House's beloved cook was very pregnant with her second child.

"Oh! You are right, of course."

Joy sighed and turned on her side. Tabitha pulled the covers up around Joy's shoulders. She sat beside Joy, stroking her back until Joy's even breathing and relaxed muscles told Tabitha that her friend had slipped into slumber.

"She is sleeping now," Tabitha whispered as Rose peeked through the doorway. They tiptoed from Joy's little cottage together.

A week later when Joy returned to work, Rose and Tabitha again convened in the great room.

Rose perused her notes. "I have managed, stealing little bits of time here and there and staying up a little late at night, to write a draft from my notes up to when Opal moved her 'business' to Silver City. But please, continue with your story."

Tabitha nodded. "Yes. Time is moving toward the new school term more quickly than I imagined it could. I do want you to have all you need to write my complete testimony."

Rose turned to the last used page in her notebook. "Let me see. You left off at such an important place—on the road to Denver with this Jock Jacobs person. Just after you heard the roadside preacher."

Tabitha smiled. "With the word 'wait' warming my insides, the rest of the long journey to Denver was a little easier. When we arrived in the city, Jock installed us in a cheap boarding house. Then he went on the prowl for a "buyer" for me. He left me chained to the bed with strict instructions to the landlord that 'his wife was ill and was not to be disturbed.' He made sure that I did not call out for help by forcing laudanum on me before he went out."

Tabitha sniffed. "I do not know how many days I spent in an utter haze, but I do not believe they were many. One morning Jock did not force the drugged drink on me. Instead, he had me bathe, dress, and fix my hair."

She glanced at Rose. "We got into his wagon. When we arrived at our destination, I looked up and read the sign: *Silver Spurs Bawdy Hall*."

CHAPTER 7

DENVER, 1909

She's 'bout as mean as a snake, but with regular, ah, *persuasion*, she's a good little money-maker. Ain'tcha, Red?" Jock rolled his chaw around in his mouth and spit into the general direction of an ornate brass spittoon.

As usual, he missed his mark and failed to notice—*or care*—that the disgusting wet blob had landed shy of its mark and had splattered, instead, upon the expensive carpet nearby.

From under my lowered gaze I watched the large man sitting at a desk in front of us: He, too, noticed Jock's miss. His jaw flexed and his expression stilled.

Jock gripped my arm tighter and growled. "I said, 'ain'tcha, Red?' You answer me, now. I don't want Mr. Judd here t' think you're unmanageable."

But I refused to answer and fixed my eyes instead upon the stain overspreading the carpet's floral pattern; I studied a cream-colored tea rose as it turned a nasty shade of rusty red-brown.

When I did not answer, Jock pinched my arm. I flinched yet remained stubbornly mute. Jock, concerned that his sale was going south, dug his fingers into my arm until his nails broke skin.

I cursed Jock inside, but I would not give him the pleasure of answering. I was determined to sabotage Jock's "sale." I do not know what I thought I would do if I did ruin his sale—given Jock's threats.

The man behind the desk smiled and tapped a finger on the desk's blotter. "Tell you what I am going to do, Mr. …."

"Jacobs. *Jock Jacobs* at 'cher service, Mr. Judd." Jock preened and added, "Like I said b'fore."

Judd's eyes narrowed. "I *beg* your pardon, Mr. Jacobs."

In the same way that Jock had not noticed Judd's reaction when Jock's stream of tobacco juice missed the spittoon, he now failed to discern the way Judd's eyes narrowed and glittered with disdain.

"No 'fense taken, Mr. Judd," Jock replied.

A brighter man than Jock might have perceived the decided chill in the other man's manner, but Jock was not bright. Nor was he observant.

I, however, was nothing if not observant. I lifted my eyes to Judd's and allowed him to see the anger smoldering there.

My bruises were fading, but the beating had done nothing to shake me from the old anger. It had utterly taken hold of me.

Amused, Judd smiled at me in return. Cal Judd's complexion was ruddy; his eyes a striking pale blue. Something flickered in those pale blue eyes. Something dangerous. I swallowed and allowed my eyes to drop.

"Tell you what I am going to do, Mr. Jacobs," Judd said again. "I'll take—*Red*, did you call her? I'll take Red off your hands. I am certain I can provide suitable…*persuasion* if it is required."

"Well, well. I'm right glad t' hear it, Mr. Judd. M' asking price is two hunnert dollars." Jock's hands twitched. He was already counting the bills, counting how he would spend them.

"I'll give you one hundred."

Jock frowned. "Well, now, m' price is two hunnert. She's worth ever' dollar, and tha's a fact."

Judd flicked open a small knife and proceeded to trim the nails on his left hand. "Two hundred dollars, Mr. Jacobs? Why, Red here runs a little long in the tooth, don't you think? What is she? Twenty-eight? Twenty-nine? Not exactly in the first blush of womanhood. Certainly too old for you to be asking prime rate."

Jock flushed. "But she's 'sperienced. Good little whore, she is! An' the men love thet red hair. Ask fer her by name."

Judd slowly stood up. From his seat behind the desk he'd given the impression of mild, gentlemanly decorum, but now he towered over Jock. His chiseled features hardened and he leaned forward—just enough for Jock to, finally, take notice.

"Ninety dollars."

Jock's mouth opened in dismay, the wad of chaw peeking out from between his cheek and lower jaw. "But-but-but you just offered a hunnert!"

"Yes, and every moment that goes by, the price will drop."

"But—"

My snort of derisive laughter interrupted Jock. Despite the iron grip he had on my arm, I sneered at him.

Jock reacted as I had known he would. "Why you no-good, lazy—" He swung his fisted hand to punch my face—and found his fist caught in a larger, stronger one.

"Can't have you damaging the merchandise, Mr. Jacobs, not—" Judd's eye flashed. "Not if you expect a deal."

While Jock considered the bull of a man who held his hand captive, he moved the wad in his mouth around and packed it under his bottom lip, "Hunnert dollars."

"Eighty-five. I did warn you, Mr. Jacobs."

Jock opened his mouth to protest again—and promptly closed it. He sputtered and then growled, "Done." He released my arm and gave me a little shove in Judd's direction. "Good riddance, Red. Ya bin nuthin' but trouble t' me."

"Welcome to the *Silver Spurs*, Red."

I looked again into Judd's cool blue eyes and shuddered. The amusement I'd seen there scarcely hid the cruelty beneath.

Tabitha had been staring into space as she recited her tale. She came to herself and looked toward Rose.

"You are already familiar enough with Cal Judd and the kind of monster he was. I will not say too much about my short interlude at the *Silver Spurs*. I will only say this: Where Opal and Jock had struggled in frustration to bend me to their will, Cal Judd looked forward to the task with relish. I was not at the *Silver Spurs* long before I realized that Cal had only taken me off Jock's hands for the pleasure of breaking me."

Tabitha shook a little and averted her eyes. "The thing is, hate and anger are what had kept me going during those years with Opal and, later, with Jock. I hated nearly everyone with an intensity that burned my soul. I was always angry, always ready to blow up at any provocation—even when I was forced to keep it tamped down.

"Well, Cal *wanted* to see my hate, so he toyed with me. He provoked and prodded my anger and hate purely for the enjoyment of crushing me under his thumb.

"For the first time in all those years, hate was not enough to strengthen me. For the first time, I was terrified and near to despair. The voice I had heard deep inside me had said, *Wait*, but I had been at the *Silver Spurs* only three months when I came to the end of my rope. I could not wait any longer. I knew Cal planned to kill me for sport, and I knew that no one would care when he did."

Tabitha sighed. "I remember, quite vividly, the morning I determined to deny Cal Judd that last bit of myself. I decided to end my own life. I would not have been the first whore—or the last—to choose that way out. Especially when death seemed like the only option. Some women I knew drowned themselves in alcohol to make life bearable, but many, like me, just wanted the pain to stop for good.

"The cribs—the cramped rooms where we were confined and where we conducted our business—were on the second floor, but the *Silver Spurs* also had an attic and a trap door to the roof. The roof was the highest point in the house. I made up my mind that morning to climb onto the roof and jump to my death."

Rose's breath caught in her chest. "You have never spoken of this, Tabitha."

"No, but I should have. Even as filled with hate and anger as I had been, I had not known real despair until I came under Cal Judd's control. My decision that morning was the true lowest point of my life. I came to the end of myself, and it was necessary that I did.

"I cried out against all the injustices of my life, and I wept as I had not wept in years. Not for the first time, I wondered what I might have become if I had not followed Cray Bishoff into Arizona. Would I have had a husband? A home of my own? Children?"

Tabitha bowed her head. "All those 'might have beens,' the possibilities that *never would be*? They stripped away whatever rebellion I had left. From the depths of my brokenness, *I called out*. I did not know to whom I was calling, but I called anyway. I begged the God of the tall, black preacher to help me."

She was quiet for so long that Rose leaned toward her and touched her hand. "What happened, Tabitha? What happened that night?"

Tabitha roused. "That night I felt… heavy, weighted, without strength, as though climbing the few steps to the attic and through the trap door was too much effort. Instead, after my last customer left, I fell into a deep sleep.

"The next morning, for a second time, I planned to end my life that night—and found myself, *again*, weeping and calling out. I thought I was just… finally breaking to pieces, like Judd wanted."

"And then?" Rose asked softly.

Tabitha chewed her lip before she whispered, "And then I heard that voice. In my head, I think. It might have been in my heart. I do not know. It was just *there*, not out loud, but I heard it anyway. So clear. So very clear."

"That voice?" Rose stared hard at Tabitha.

"Yes, like before! It was the same simple, soft voice I heard on the road to Denver. All it said was, *Wait. I am coming for you. Wait for me.*"

Tabitha tipped her head over a little. "It was the same word that had dropped into my belly when we passed by the preacher in the black suit."

She shook her head. "It was the same word, *Wait*. But the voice added, *I am coming for you. Wait for me!*"

Rose shivered. "*I am coming for you?* What did you think it meant?"

Tabitha shrugged and rubbed at the tension in her shoulders. A wisp of flame-tinged hair came loose from the knot at the back of her head and curled down her neck. "The voice said to *wait*, so I waited. I did not know what I was waiting *for*, but I kept waiting and looking, all that day, all that afternoon."

Tabitha laughed, a bit embarrassed at the memory. "I thought I might have become unhinged, you know? But when I looked inside and recalled that voice, it was too true. Too pure to ignore.

"I waited into the evening. The night started as most did, but I was distracted. I kept looking and expecting, as though something were about to happen. When a customer left my room, I would pace. I found myself quite excited, as though something momentous was close at hand.

"I was between customers and pacing when I heard a commotion, the shouts of two men running through the upper hallway of the *Silver Spurs*, throwing open the doors to the cribs. I knew Cal Judd was in a room not far from mine. He was with a young girl they called Monique.

"I did not know what was happening, but Judd never allowed disturbances to escalate. I expected him to burst from Monique's room any moment, shouting for his men. All his men wore guns, and I was afraid that there would be shooting. I opened my door a crack anyway and peeked through—and saw Marshal Pounder at the far end of the hall. Someone shouted his name, *Pounder!* and he ran from the farthest end of the hall toward me. I did not know him then, but I saw the badge on his chest. He stopped at Monique's room and went inside.

"Two of Judd's men thundered up the stairs and into the hall just then. Pounder stuck his shotgun out the door to Monique's room and yelled, *You men throw your guns out on the floor!* Judd's men dropped to the floor and did as Pounder told them, and Pounder stepped back into the hallway.

"Then this man wearing a bowler hat—I did not know Mr. O'Dell then—backed out of Monique's room, dragging Monique by her wrist. He stopped in the doorway and I heard him snarl, *Open this door, Judd, and you'll catch a bullet*. He and Monique started down the hallway toward Marshal Pounder and the stairs. As he passed my door—"

Tabitha broke off. She stared over Rose's shoulder.

"What, Tabitha? What did you do?"

"Not me," Tabitha breathed in wide-eyed wonder. "The voice! It said, *Now! Go! Go with them!* I threw open my door as the man in the bowler hat passed. He turned and pointed a small gun at me. I held out my hands and I begged him, *Please! Please take me with you!* He was angry—just worried, I think—but I begged him again, and he beckoned me to follow behind, so I did."

Tears were trickling down Tabitha's face now, but she smiled as though she'd said something humorous.

"What is it?" Rose demanded. She was present with Tabitha in her story, standing in the doorway, watching O'Dell and Pounder rescue fifteen-year-old "Monique" whose real name was Monika Vogel.

Rose was distressed that Tabitha had broken off her story. "Please tell me what happened next," she breathed.

"It is just that I was barefoot and, um, not fit to be seen in public, Miss Rose. Remembering the situation just now, it struck me as amusing. You see, all I had on was a dressing gown, and not a proper, concealing wrapper either."

"You…everyone could see through your gown?" Rose blushed.

"Oh, yes. Indeed they could. I suppose it is irreverent to speak of it, but I cannot help but consider the, er, *sight* I must have been and laugh a little about it."

Rose arched one brow. "I suppose it could be likened to how, when God finds us, we are clothed in the 'filthy rags' of our sin?"

"Yes! You have hit upon it, Miss Rose!"

Tabitha shook her head and then sobered. "Mr. O'Dell and Marshal Pounder took Monique and me down the stairs into the saloon and out the front door—right out from under Cal Judd's guards. We jumped into a waiting motorcar and raced away. Later, at the Pinkerton office, O'Dell gave me a man's coat with which to cover myself."

She smiled now. "A few days later, Marshal Pounder took me up the mountain to Corinth to meet you."

"I remember." Rose smiled back. "We have covered a lot of ground since then, haven't we, Tabitha? And God has done so much in that time."

"So much," Tabitha agreed.

"You were the touchiest of all our girls when we left Corinth for Denver and opened Palmer House," Rose reminisced. "Your heart was scarred and hardened. We never knew from one moment to the next how you would respond—if you would explode, or if you would bolt and leave us. But you did *not* leave, and I am so glad."

"I could not leave," Tabitha whispered. "I wanted to leave, oh! so many times! But I could not. I had to stay true to the voice that told me, *Wait! I am coming for you.*"

She sobbed once. "And then, finally, *I met him*—and when I did, I knew it had been *Jesus* who had spoken the word '*Wait*' out in the country when the preacher man pointed at me. It had been *Jesus* who told me, '*Wait! I am coming for you!*' And it had been *Jesus* who said, '*Now! Go with them!*'"

"Can you talk about meeting Jesus, Tabitha?"

Tabitha glanced up at Rose. "It was that morning, not long after we had moved into Palmer House. I know you remember. Things were not going well—no, it was worse than that. I think your vision for Palmer House was crumbling and near to falling apart. And I was the source of a lot of your problems."

Tabitha sighed. "Well, I was up to my old tricks, was I not? Every chance I got, I sowed strife and discord. I ridiculed and vexed the other girls, I rebelled against the house rules, and I found ugly ways to vent my anger. Yes, I was still so angry, still full of hate! You might have saved me from Cal Judd and a life of prostitution, but nothing had changed on the inside. I was still the same wounded and lost woman.

"But that morning at breakfast, you did two things, Miss Rose. First, you gave each of us girls an ultimatum: Make a decision to stay or to go. If we were to stay, we had to live up to the house rules. If we decided not to obey the rules, you said, then we were choosing to leave.

"Your ultimatum shook us, Miss Rose. As much as it would have grieved you to have any of us leave Palmer House, we knew that you were serious."

"And what was the other thing that morning, Tabitha?"

"Well, you asked us not to make our decision until after Bible study. And then you preached the most beautiful lesson. You told us about the captive within each of us. I can still remember your exact words: *We are, all of us, held captive by the thoughts and judgments we—and others—hold against us. But no one can keep you a captive if you choose instead to be free in Jesus.*

"Then you told us that Jesus was calling to us! *Come to me! Come to me all you who are weary . . . weary, worn, and heavy-burdened. Come to me, and I will give you rest for your souls.* And you asked us if we were ready to give our heavy burdens to Jesus.

"It was as though I were the only one in the room. Every part of my being was just as you had described: weary, worn, and heavy-burdened.

"Oh, I longed to be free! At that very moment, I surrendered myself to Jesus—and the weight of sin and bondage lifted!

"I am so humbled, so grateful! When, in my brokenness, I called out—even when I was filled with such darkness—Jesus heard me and answered. And he has forgiven me! Oh, he has forgiven me for so many things! He took those heavy burdens away and filled me with peace—the only peace I had ever known."

Rose clasped Tabitha's hands. "And I am so glad, Tabitha. So very, very glad."

The two women were quiet for the space of several minutes before Rose commented in a quiet voice, "Tabitha, you spoke of hate earlier, the hate you had for the man who left you alone in the desert and who, er, sold you to Opal."

"Cray. Cray Bishoff," Tabitha whispered.

"What became of the hate you had for him, Tabitha?"

Tabitha considered the question. "I am not sure."

Rose hesitated. "Have you ... have you consciously ... deliberately forgiven him?"

Tabitha frowned. "I do not know, Miss Rose. I try not to think about him or any part of my past."

"May I suggest, dear Tabitha, that you consider forgiving him? I suggest this not because he deserves your forgiveness or has asked for it, but because forgiving those who have wounded us sets us free. And I would have you perfectly, completely free, my daughter."

The red-haired woman nodded and bowed her head. "Lord, I forgive Cray Bishoff. I forgive him for leaving me alone and ... for selling me to Opal."

She shuddered then, and her shoulders shook. "I forgive him, Lord, as you have forgiven me in Christ. I let go of the hate I have held toward him. Father, please set me free in every part of my life so that I can glorify you with every part of my being."

"Amen," Rose murmured.

ᑕHAPTER 8

I n the time remaining before Tabitha left for school, Rose and Tabitha met together one or two days a week to go over the growing manuscript. Sometimes their sessions lasted only an hour, after which Rose would, carefully and prayerfully, write out what Tabitha had shared.

Other days they would meet for a longer session, talking over what Tabitha had recounted until Rose had a better grasp of the details—and a better sense of how the Lord would have her write what Tabitha had revealed.

It was important to them both that Tabitha's testimony reflect the grace that God extended to her, that it demonstrate the healing power of the Gospel.

Two weeks before Tabitha's scheduled departure for her next term in Boulder, Rose closeted herself in her bedroom to work exclusively on Tabitha's account. She delegated her other responsibilities to Breona or Tabitha.

Just before Tabitha was to leave, Rose offered Tabitha a portfolio. "I have completed the draft of your testimony, Tabitha. I am certain that it is not quite perfect yet, but it is close. Will you read it before you leave and give me permission to write out three copies and have them bound?"

Tabitha stared at the notebook but did not extend her hand to take it. "I do not think I need to read it, Miss Rose. I trust you. We have discussed all the details, and I pray the final product will be all we wish it to be."

Rose tapped the portfolio with an absentminded finger. "Would you allow me to show it to Joy? And perhaps Sarah? I am considering asking Sarah to be the next to write her testimony."

"Of course but ... perhaps after I leave?"

"As you wish, my dear," Rose replied. She hesitated, and Tabitha sensed her indecision.

"What is it?" Tabitha asked.

Rose smiled. "I was just wondering about something, but perhaps we'll speak of it later. You have already overstretched your emotions these many weeks by revisiting the events of your past."

Tabitha blinked. "I know God has forgiven me and he will sustain me. I would rather know what it is you are wondering."

Rose took Tabitha's hand and cradled it in both of hers. "As a mother, I could not help but wonder about your parents, if perhaps they would not want to know that you are alive and doing well." She gazed into Tabitha's face, seeking her response.

Tabitha looked down to hide her sorrow and regret from Rose. "I would not want my folks to know all this." She gestured toward the notebook and its precious but painful contents.

"You know that Mei-Xing felt the same way about her parents? Yes, the truth hurt them for a time, but... but in the end, what Jesus did for Mei-Xing made her past of no consequence to her mother and father. Mei-Xing's relationship with her parents was restored, and God received the glory."

When Tabitha did not answer, Rose asked, "Do your mother and father know Jesus the way you have come to know him?"

Tabitha's head jerked as though she had suddenly realized something significant. "I had not thought of that," she confessed. "I know my mother tried to show me right from wrong, but we never went to church or read the Bible. I cannot say that she was a Christian. I cannot say that she had a real, a *living* relationship with Jesus. I-I am certain my father did not."

She turned her face to Rose's. "It has been sixteen years since I left home. I do not even know if they are still alive."

"Would not you rather know if they are alive than continue on without knowing?" Rose studied the young woman, concern written on her brow. "If my daughter were missing, I would long for her every day of my life. I cannot but think that your mother still longs to know that you are alive and safe."

Rose paused and thought for a moment. "You were only fourteen when you left home. Your parents cannot be too old yet? Surely they are younger than I am?"

Tabitha nodded in agreement, so Rose added, "Perhaps, more importantly, if they are still living, you may have the opportunity to lead them to Christ and an eternity in heaven. However, the longer you wait to be reconciled to them, the greater the odds will be that they have passed on."

Tabitha's lips parted as she frowned and thought on what Rose said. "Do you... do you really think I should write to them?"

Rose nodded. "Yes, I do. However, you should pray before you start your letter. Let the Holy Spirit lead you as you write."

"I will," a sober Tabitha agreed.

By then, everyone in Palmer House knew that Rose and Tabitha had been working on Tabitha's testimony, although no one had heard the details.

Now that the account was close to completion and Tabitha's departure for school drew near, Breona and Marit had taken it upon themselves to declare a dinner celebration.

At Palmer House, Breona commanded the housekeeping and Marit the kitchen. Even on a good day, the house's newer girls lived in fear and awe of Breona and Marit and their strict—although generally cheerful—standards.

Marit (who owned to a matchmaker's heart and wanted everything to be "just right" for the celebration) had schemed to include several guests—certain *gentlemen* guests—in the festivities. However, with Marit's baby presumed to be two weeks overdue, the Palmer House cook's usually sunny disposition was nowhere to be found.

So while Breona and two of the girls of Palmer House undertook the actual work, a very pregnant and notably grumpy Marit directed the cooking and table arrangements from the confines of a kitchen chair.

Even Marit's husband Billy, home early from work in Joy's fine furnishings store, jumped to obey his wife's rapid-fire instructions and commands. At the same time, he kept little Will, their rambunctious three year old, out from underfoot.

"You, Olive!" Marit snapped, "Vatch how you cut those vegetables, ja? All the same size, if you please—as I've told you many times now!" and "Vaht are you doing vit that dough, Gracie? Not like that! Must I show you again—"

"Nay, Marit, I'll be showin' her," Breona cut in. "Ye air not t' be on yer feet." She wagged a wooden spoon and waved Marit back to the chair.

Marit sank onto the hard kitchen chair with a sigh and a grumble. She eased her swollen feet and ankles upon a stool and sighed again. "Ven vill this little one come? Oh, this baby needs to come *soon*."

"Aye, an' we air *all* a-prayin' in earnest for *that*," Breona muttered under her breath.

"Amen," breathed Gracie and Olive at the same time.

"I heard that!" Marit shot back.

Breona, her back to Marit, grinned, and Olive and Gracie bent over their work to hide their smiles.

Alone in the room she shared with another girl, Tabitha prepared paper and pen and then bowed her head. Her heart was troubled at the prospect of writing to her folks, but she knew it needed to be done.

O Lord, she prayed, *I will not deny that I am terrified of writing to my mother and father. What if they are already dead? Then I will know that my leaving drove them into an early grave! But Miss Rose is right— I cannot go on without knowing one way or the other, for perhaps they are still longing to know what has become of me.*

If they are *still alive after all these years, then I must ease their hearts, even if our renewed relationship requires that I tell them of my past. Please help me to know what to say. Please help me to share Jesus with them.* She paused and then added, *And please do not allow me to hurt them again, Lord.*

She remained, head bowed, until her spirit calmed and she felt the peace of the Holy Spirit urge her forward. She picked up the pen and scratched,

Dear Mama and Daddy,

I wanted to write and let you know how I am. I live, at present, in Denver, Colorado, with friends. However, I will be returning to nursing school in Boulder a week from today. I hope to complete my nursing studies a year from this spring.

More than anything, I wish to tell you how sincerely sorry I am for running away from home. My behavior has had many injurious consequences. I take responsibility for them all. I ask for your forgiveness, and I hope you will pardon me for the pain I have caused you.

Please write to me at the address below. I long to know you are both well.
Your daughter,
Tabitha Hale

Tabitha blew on the ink to dry her words and set about addressing an envelope with shaking hands. When the letter was sealed, she fixed a postage stamp to it and walked it downstairs to the outgoing mail. Then she returned to her room to dress for dinner.

Twenty-one Palmer House residents and three guests gathered that evening around the lengthy dinner table. The dining table was actually two well-used tables placed end-to-end to accommodate Palmer House's large family.

Although the table linens were patched and the place settings a mishmash of three patterns—and although the many chairs around the table were also mismatched, some barely serviceable—the twenty-four souls gathered to break bread together were happy and their conversation lively.

At a nod from Rose, Olive and Gracie (with help from Jenny and Flora, two of the older Palmer House girls) began to serve the dinner.

Marit raised her chin, about to issue some instruction to the girls, but Billy touched her arm.

"Let them be, dearest," he urged. "You must care for yourself and our baby right now. So rest. Enjoy your dinner and our guests. And let the girls alone. Breona will help if help is needed." Marit sat on Billy's left, and Billy had purposely placed little Will to his right, so that Marit would have nothing to do during the meal except relax.

As the young women served the meal, Mr. Wheatley, the house's grizzled caretaker—his hair standing straight up in white tufts over his head—told tall tales and teased the girls on either side of him. The girls, in turn, plied him with extra portions and hung on his every word.

Joy shared her day at her shop with her mother. Sarah and Corrine chimed in to add to Joy's narrative. Nancy, Alice, Flora, and Jane chattered about their workday—Nancy provided child care for a widower teacher and Alice, Flora, and Jane worked as seamstresses in Tory Washington's *Victoria's House of Fashion.*

Mei-Xing, home from her companion position with Mrs. Palmer, tended to her daughter, Shan-Rose, who was seated between Mei-Xing and her fiancé, Minister Yaochuan Min Liáng.

Breona found herself seated next to Isaac Carmichael, co-pastor with Minister Liáng of Denver's Calvary Temple. Breona alternately blushed and glared at Marit for arranging the seating so. Pastor Carmichael, on his part, was delighted with the seating arrangements and grinned his thanks in Marit's direction.

That left Tabitha seated between Pastor Carmichael and the final guest, Mason Carpenter. Tabitha, too, glared at Marit.

"Aw, please stop shooting those killing looks at Mrs. Evans, Tabs," Mason urged her. Tabitha knew that he was teasing her, and she pursed her lips, so as not to smile. The truth was, Mason Carpenter—as one of the house's greatest supporters—dined frequently at Palmer House. Not to mention that he called regularly to speak to Tabitha.

"Tell me about your day?"

"Oh!" Tabitha's exclamation slipped out before she had a chance to squash it.

"Something eventful, then?" he queried.

Tabitha, thinking on the letter she had just written, blushed.

Mason frowned. "I apologize, Miss Tabitha. I should not have pried. If you would rather, perhaps we could speak of your return to school? Have you made your plans?"

"Yes. I leave on the noon train next Thursday." Tabitha was relieved and mentally gave Carpenter points for his kind tact. She studied him out of the corner of her eye.

She assumed him to be in his late thirties, making him a little "old" to still be a bachelor—and an eligible one at that. Tabitha did not know how much money Mason Carpenter had to his name, but he lived the life of a gentleman at ease and was generous to many charities.

Tabitha noted that his thick hair was a little long. A brown lock curled down on his forehead. Every once in a while he swept it away with his left hand, the gesture totally unconscious. Then she realized he was speaking.

"I beg your pardon?"

He smiled. "It would be interesting to know where your thoughts wandered just now." He cleared his throat. "But I was merely inquiring as to whether you had arranged conveyance to the station for your journey."

"I, um, no, not as yet. I assumed that Billy—"

"Billy said he would be grateful if I could arrange your conveyance," Carpenter inserted smoothly. "He will be taking care of young Will while Mrs. Evans recovers from childbirth." He shot a glance across the table and quirked his brows. "God willing, she does not have to wait much longer."

"*Mr.* Carpenter!" Tabitha chastised him for alluding to Marit's condition, but she had cough to disguise and stifle a giggle.

"I beg your pardon, Miss Hale." Carpenter's face assumed penitent lines—all but his twinkling eyes. "So, may I offer my services to you next Thursday?"

"Why, I-I mean, um—"

"Excellent. I would be pleased to call on you at 10:30. I am certain that Banks will be able to load your trunks in a matter of minutes. I should have you to the station no later than 11 a.m. Plenty of time, I should think, to buy your ticket, enjoy a light lunch, and see you to your seat when the train boards."

Tabitha skewered him with an arch look. "I have not accepted your offer, Mr. Carpenter."

"My *kind* offer, Miss Hale," he returned. "You would not inconvenience Billy when I have so *kindly* offered, would you?"

"Oh, bother." Tabitha picked up her fork and stabbed a slice of potato.

"Why, I'll take that as the gracious acceptance I know it to be."

Tabitha heard the smirk in his voice, but when she rounded on him he was savoring a bite of roast beef.

"Wonderful. Positively wonderful," he muttered, all innocence.

Tabitha shook her head and glanced across the table. Rose, Joy, and Marit were slipping smug, discreet smiles in her direction.

"Blast them all!" she muttered.

"I beg your pardon, Miss Hale?" Carpenter smirked again.

Tabitha growled and shoved the slice of potato into her mouth.

It was while Olive and Gracie were serving apple pie for dessert that Tabitha noticed the stillness on Marit's face. Tabitha observed Marit for a moment then turned to agree with Carpenter's comment on the pie.

"My own cook could take lessons on this pie," he raved—and shoved another generous forkful into his mouth.

"It is my favorite," Tabitha agreed. "Marit uses such tart apples but they never spoil the pie. Rather, they—" She was struck again by Marit's open-eyed stillness.

Carpenter leaned toward her. "What is it?"

Tabitha grinned and whispered back, "I believe the next little Evans will arrive tonight!"

A moment later, Tabitha observed Marit bite her lip and grimace.

"Excuse me, please," she murmured to Carpenter. Tabitha rose from her seat, as did the other gentlemen in deference to her. She walked around the table and bent toward Marit.

"Shall I help you to your cottage, dear?" Tabitha whispered to her. Marit and Billy's cottage—once the caretaker's quarters—was not far from Joy's little bungalow at the back of Palmer House's property.

"Oh, *ja*, please," was Marit's relieved response. She gritted her teeth again, and Tabitha waited until she relaxed to help her out of her chair.

"What's going on?" Billy demanded. Conversation ceased, and all eyes turned toward Marit and Tabitha.

"Oh, just a baby coming," Tabitha announced merrily.

Dinner was over.

Many hands reached to help Marit to the little cottage behind Palmer House, and it was Tabitha who gave orders now. "Breona, please have someone make up Marit's bed with clean linens? Yes; you should oversee them—you know what is needed."

She turned. "Will you girls heat water in the large kettle and begin clearing up the dinner things? Thank you. Oh, and would someone be so kind as to telephone Doctor Murphy?"

The guests—mostly ignored in the flurry of activity—excused themselves and prepared to depart. Carpenter's attention, however, was focused on Tabitha. His expression attracted Rose to his side.

"She is quite a capable woman, our Tabitha," Rose murmured.

"I could not agree more," Mason Carpenter replied. Pride shone in his eyes.

Tabitha, weary but joyous, delivered the news to Billy in the early hours before dawn. "You have another son," she announced.

"Another son!" Billy was bursting at the news.

"Yes, and he's just as plump and pink as a ripe peach!"

"And Marit?"

"She did well. Doctor Murphy says you may go out to see her and the baby in another five minutes."

Tabitha dropped into her own bed that morning, fatigued but content. "This, Lord, is the joy I would give my life to," she murmured before sleep took her.

Tabitha finished packing her small trunk and strapped it closed. "Not 'trunks,' Mr. Carpenter," she muttered. "Only the one." The lone trunk contained all she owned in the world, but it was enough.

Breona entered. "Mr. Carpenter ist here for ye, Tabitha. Should I be havin' Banks coome fetch yer trunk?" Her black eyes danced.

"Aye, mooch obliged if ye would be doin' so," Tabitha replied, mimicking Breona, laying on the accent.

They laughed together and Breona squeezed Tabitha's hand, two friends who were once adversaries. Tabitha's bitterness and animosity had antagonized Breona—had alienated everyone at Palmer House—when they first met. But the hardships through which they had fought, side by side, had changed all of that. Had changed *them*.

Banks, with a tip of his hat, hauled Tabitha's trunk downstairs to the waiting motorcar. When Tabitha descended after it, Carpenter met her at the bottom of the stairs.

"Only the one trunk, Tabs?"

"Mr. Carpenter, it is not appropriate for you to call me by my Christian name, let alone a diminutive of it," Tabitha admonished him.

Although I rather like it, she added to herself.

She was surprised when Carpenter's expression turned serious. Her eyes widened when he leaned toward her and whispered, "I would that it *were* appropriate for me to speak to you so, Miss Hale. And I would that it were my place to shower you with so many things that you required five trunks to travel and not the one."

Tabitha's mouth dropped open and she fumbled to speak. "You-you do not know what you're saying."

"Oh, I do. I assure you, I do." He sighed and stepped back into his more formal role. "I realize, however, that nursing is your calling—your God-given calling—and I would never knowingly interfere with what God has called you to do. I am willing to wait for you to complete your training and find your way to your nursing vocation. Indeed," he added as he took her arm and tucked it into his, "I am willing to wait as long as is needed."

Tabitha licked her lips nervously and could think of nothing to say. Rose stepped from the great room at that moment and saved her from needing to say anything. She held out her arms and Tabitha welcomed the excuse to detangle herself from Mason Carpenter's gentle hold.

"My dear girl, we will pray you often," Rose murmured into Tabitha's hair. "And you must come home for every holiday and break between terms. Palmer House will always be your home."

Tabitha gripped Rose. "Thank you. Thank you for… so many things."

"No," Rose answered. "You have enriched us in every way. We thank God for *you*."

Tabitha thought the drive to Union Station with Carpenter might be awkward given their exchange at the bottom of the staircase. However, from the time Banks closed the motorcar door until they arrived at the station, Carpenter did nothing but enthuse over his newest hobby.

"I have been taking rides in an aeroplane, Miss Hale," he announced. "Flying! I am absolutely smitten with flying. Have you ever flown?"

"No!" Tabitha's response was emphatic. "If God wanted us to fly, he would have given us wings."

Carpenter merely grinned and swiped at the curl of hair that slipped down upon his forehead.

A bit miffed—and a little troubled at hearing about Carpenter's reckless activity—Tabitha rejoined, "Mr. Carpenter, do you not have a business to attend to? Or are you merely one of Denver's idle rich, never engaging in a productive use of your time?"

He stared at her, suddenly serious. "I can assure you, Miss Hale, that I am never idle." He held her look. "Idleness is a sinful waste. I never take up an activity that will not yield a benefit or fill a need."

"Even a transient fad, such as flying?" she pressed.

He shrugged. "Perhaps flying is a fad at present. However, I see it figuring heavily upon the future."

Then he grinned, all seriousness gone. "And you cannot imagine the thrill!"

"I really cannot see the attraction."

"Ah, but you have not experienced it. My pilot is a great fellow. Canadian. He has a two-seater biplane, a trainer. And the sensation? The sensation is freeing; the views are breathtaking."

He sighed in anticipation. "When you come home next, I will ask you to come flying with me. By then I should have my own pilot's license, perhaps my own aeroplane! I am learning a fair bit of mechanics, too, which is most necessary when learning to fly."

Tabitha stared across the seat at the enigma that was Mason Carpenter. "Well, you do beat all," she muttered.

PART 2:
HOPE IN THE MIDDLE

*These trials will show
that your faith is genuine.
It is being tested
as fire tests and purifies gold
—though your faith is far more
precious than mere gold.
(1 Peter 1:7, NLT)*

$\mathcal{C}$HAPTER 9

FALL 1911

The work and pressure of nursing school were difficult and Tabitha had a lot to readjust to. Her fellow students were far ahead of her, and she had a great deal of catching up to do—and do well—if she expected to complete the three-year program and graduate with her class in the spring of 1913.

Tabitha had been away from the school since the spring holiday of the past April. She had been home between terms when Rose had been shot and wounded. When baby Edmund had been abducted.

In the chaos that ensued, Tabitha had chosen not to return to school as scheduled. She had, instead, remained at Palmer House to nurse Rose back to health and to help provide stability to Palmer House as the police and the Pinkerton Agency sought to find and restore Edmund to his parents, Grant and Joy Michaels.

At the time, Dr. Wellan, dean of the medical school, had agreed with her choice; Emily Van der Pol, Grace Minton, and the other Christian women who supported Palmer House and provided Tabitha's nursing scholarship concurred.

Then Joy's beloved husband Grant, already suffering from congestive heart failure, had worsened. Tabitha gave herself to nursing Grant, too, and had to inform Dean Wellan that her short furlough would be longer than she had expected.

After Grant passed away weeks later, Joy became Tabitha's primary concern. Bereft of husband and child, Joy needed a different kind of care.

In light of Tabitha's extended absence, the dean had questioned whether Tabitha's commitment to the difficult nursing program was as strong as was necessary to complete it. When Tabitha wrote to explain all the extenuating circumstances that kept her from her studies, Dean Wellan had ruled that she could not return to school until the fall term, "When Miss Hale may be able to give herself wholly to her studies," his letter had read.

Hanging over Tabitha's head, as she struggled to regain her footing at school, was the knowledge that if she failed to come up to completion standards, Dr. Wellan would keep her back an entire year.

Tabitha had not once regretted her decision or its consequences. She had told Rose, "My family needs me. This is where I should be as long as they need me."

However, during the months at Palmer House, Tabitha had forgotten how inflexible the school's discipline was and how difficult she had found it the previous fall term.

The rules for nursing students and staff were strict, with heavy emphasis placed upon personal virtue and an impeccable reputation: Every aspect of a nursing student's life was considered a reflection upon the integrity of the school and hospital.

Tabitha found comfort in knowing that Dr. Murphy, Rose Thoresen, and Pastor Isaac Carmichael had provided glowing letters of recommendation for her enrollment and acceptance into the school—and she was grateful that no one at school had an inkling about her past life.

Still, Tabitha found it difficult to submit to the school's discipline after months away from it. Being older at age thirty than most of the students in her class, she was considered by some of the staff to be too set in her ways to adapt to the rigors of nursing. The fact that she was behind in her studies and practicums placed even more pressure upon her.

The staff, for their part, extended her no slack, and the younger students, sensing that Tabitha was different from them in many ways, seemed to shy away from her.

Consequently, Tabitha's fall term got off to a difficult and painful start: During the first two weeks, she received two tongue lashings from instructors in front of her class and a mark on her record for poor performance.

You must buckle down, Tabs, she scolded herself, even as she blinked back angry and mortified tears. *You have given yourself to The Lord and his work; he will not allow you to fail. Every chastisement crucifies your old, ugly temper and purifies your character. So set your mind to the tasks at hand—and do not forget: The Lord is your Helper!*

She returned to class the next morning with a dogged resolve in her eyes. It was far later in the day—a day that had gone much better than the previous one had—when she realized she had called herself "Tabs."

"Oh, bother," she groused. Try as she might to block it, she often heard Carpenter's voice in her head.

The students' mornings were filled with lectures. Their afternoons were taken up with nursing practicums—small student groups performing specific nursing duties under the severe guidance of an instructor or an experienced nurse. When not in class or practicums, the students were studying.

For Tabitha, the walk across campus from her dormitory to classes or the hospital was generally a blur. She used the time to memorize study notes—and rarely paid attention to her surroundings.

One afternoon as she raced toward the hospital's imposing structure, Tabitha experienced the eerie sense of being watched. She slowed her pace and stopped, turning in a complete circle, not understanding what had distracted her, had caught her attention.

The grassy and tree-lined campus was still. Only a few other students and a pair of caretakers were in view, and they were preoccupied with their own activities.

Tabitha took a deep breath—and was surprised to see that the trees were beginning to turn color.

Fall is nearly upon us, she realized with a start, *and I had not even noticed!* She wasted precious minutes breathing in the brisk autumn air. Then she shook herself, glanced around again, and hurried on her way.

Silly me, she laughed to herself. *Imagining things.*

On Sundays, nursing students received the morning off to attend church and were allowed to collect any mail that had accumulated for them during the week. Soon Tabitha was receiving weekly letters from Palmer House.

Rose sent all of the latest news and included little notes from Breona, Joy, and others in the house. Rose's letters were filled with updates on Billy and Marit's new baby, Charley.

"Charles, named for Billy's father," Rose wrote.

Then she received a letter from Mason Carpenter.

My dear Miss Hale,

In the bustle leading up to your departure, I neglected to ask permission to write to you. I had intended to ask you after the dinner the week before you left, but little Charley so artfully timed his entrance that I did not see you again that evening before I took my leave. Even on our drive to Union Station a week later, we were so engrossed in our conversation around flying, that the request slipped my mind.

"*Our* conversation?" Tabitha had a different recollection of the ride to the train station. She clearly recalled Carpenter, eyes shining with enthusiasm, spending the majority of the short drive to the station describing the sensation of—and his complete infatuation with—flying.

"If memory serves," she chuckled, "*you* did most of the talking!"

She laughed again and finished the letter, quite enjoying the monologue of his life in Denver. She was impressed with the level of detail included in his observations of people and places. Rather than merely focus on what he did and saw, Carpenter wrote as though he saw into the hearts of those he encountered—and prayed for them accordingly.

Tabitha read his letter twice. Both times she was struck with the compassionate heart his written observations revealed.

The letter closed with,

I beg you not to hold my lapse against me! I do hope you will write soon and permit me to write to you on a regular basis. Denver is quite dull without you.
Truly yours,
Mason Carpenter

Should I write back? Tabitha was torn. On the one hand, she longed to receive his attentions; on the other hand ...

She shrugged. *What would be the purpose? We are not meant for each other—he could not possibly wish to go beyond a friendship given what he knows of my background.*

"And what he does not know," she added. "Besides, even when I graduate, my work will keep me busy twelve hours a day, whereas he is independently wealthy and would wish *his wife* to go into society with him."

It was the first time she had spoken the word "wife" aloud in connection with Carpenter, and it stung. *I can never be a wife*, she admitted to herself. *Not to him or anyone. Not with my past.* She looked down at the letter in her hands and shook her head. *Particularly since I can never have children.*

With a shaking hand, Tabitha placed the letter in its envelope and buried it in the bottom of her trunk.

She did not write back.

Tabitha had been at school three weeks when she picked up a letter with a Texas postmark. She stared at her name and address printed in crude letters on the front of the envelope, and her fingers trembled.

She recognized the hand: *It is Mama's writing!* She returned to the dormitory and found a quiet corner to open the letter. The missive was short, scrawled on a piece of brown butcher paper, but Tabitha devoured the words painstakingly printed on it:

Deer Tabitha,

We culd hardly beleve it when we got yor letter. Yor pa and I give up a long time back thinking weed ever no what becum of you. Pa is poorly. His chest is bad and he coffs a lot, but I ain't seen him so happy in years as when he red your letter. Was like a tonic to him, and he lays it by his chair to reed agin and agin.

I keep up the place best I can. Your pa does wat he can, too. We get by.

We forgive you, dotter, and we are so prowd you are aworkin to be a nurse. Tis a comfort to us to no you are well.

Pleese rite agin. Wish we culd see yor face.

Muther

After reading the letter so many times that she had memorized it, Tabitha went for a long walk, almost missing the dinner curfew. *I had forgotten how plain they were,* she thought, *how uneducated.*

Color crept into her face and neck as she realized how much Opal's strict standards of deportment had changed her, had reshaped her manner of speaking and behavior.

If I had stayed home, if I had stayed with my folks, I would still be as rough and simple as they are.

That night she wept into her pillow. *Oh, Lord! Who will take care of my father and mother in their ill health and old age?*

She copied her mother's letter word for word into a note to Rose. *What should I do, Miss Rose? Should I leave school to go take care of them?*

Even as she wrote her concerns, Tabitha felt no release to leave Boulder. Rather, the pull toward nursing grew stronger with each passing day.

Rose's response confirmed what she already knew:

Dearest Tabitha,

I am so grateful that your parents have replied to your letter and that they have forgiven you. This is the first step, I pray, in restoring your relationship with them.

As regards your question, I counsel you to pray and do as the Holy Spirit directs you. Let his peace be your guide. I know you will continue to write to your parents, sharing bit by bit what Jesus has done for and in you.

However, unless the Lord directs you to leave school, you must trust him to care for your parents, too.

All my love,
Rose Thoresen

Six weeks into the term, after many late nights of study and many long hours on her feet, Tabitha at last hit her stride with the rest of her class. A full night's sleep was something she had not enjoyed in quite a while.

It would still take her more weeks of late nights to cover the ground she had missed, but she pressed into the work and received no further chastisements or marks on her record.

Lord, you are my strength, she often prayed. *I am learning to lean upon you.*

The last thing she prayed as she slipped into sleep was, *Lord, why do I feel like someone is always watching me?*

September and October passed, and November came upon Boulder with frosty mornings and chilly winds. At the midpoint of the term, the nursing students were assigned to cohorts under the supervision of school instructors and began to work regular shifts in the hospital.

Cohort instructors were to assign their students to eight-hour shifts, six days a week, for the remainder of their schooling. The nursing shifts were in addition to classes and ran in conjunction with the practicums. The grueling program of practicums and work would ensure that the students, when graduated, had adequate hands-on experience in general nursing and three nursing specialties: obstetrics, pediatrics, and surgery.

The demanding pace served to weed out those women whose commitment to nursing was anything less than absolute—and students who made mistakes or who rebelled at the strict discipline were assigned punishment duties in addition to their assigned shifts.

Tabitha and five of her classmates were assigned to a cohort under the supervision of a staff nurse named Caroline Rasmussen. Nurse Rasmussen was practically an institution at the school, known widely for her inflexible disposition.

Tabitha and her fellow nurses heard the rumor that Nurse Rasmussen's uncle had left a sizable fortune to the medical school—cutting out his niece and nephew in lieu of leaving a lasting legacy to his name. The uncle, however, had not forgotten his duty toward Nurse Rasmussen and her brother.

According to the rumors, the uncle's will had stipulated that the school install Nurse Rasmussen (who was, at the time of his death and the reading of the will, already a nurse in good standing at the hospital) as a tenured instructor in the school. The will had also stipulated that the institution employ her younger brother in a laborer position suited to his abilities.

The school trustees were all too willing to accommodate the stipulations in return for the promised perpetual endowment—an ongoing source of funding for the school.

As Tabitha and her classmates assembled in a line before the stern nurse, Tabitha had a sudden, disconcerting premonition.

Nurse Rasmussen, a solidly built woman in her early fifties, her mouth set in disapproval, examined each student until the young woman quailed. Four of Tabitha's classmates had wilted under Nurse Rasmussen's scrutiny.

When she reached Tabitha, fifth in line, Tabitha met the older woman's look with respectful composure. They stared at each other for several minutes. Each passing moment grew tenser, until Tabitha realized her mistake. She dropped her eyes in deference, but it was too late to escape Nurse Rasmussen's ire.

"Miss Hale, is it?"

"Yes, Nurse Rasmussen."

"You are rather too old to be attempting a career in nursing, aren't you?"

Tabitha flinched and fumbled to find a suitable response.

"I spoke to you, Miss Hale."

"Yes, ma'am. I beg your pardon," Tabitha answered quietly. "It is true that I am older than the other students. I believe my age was discussed and taken into account when I applied to the school and my application was accepted."

"A pretty answer." Nurse Rasmussen growled. "However, given your age, I expect more of you than the other students. See that you are a good example and influence. And I will have you know that I suffer no impertinence. Is that understood?"

"Yes, ma'am," Tabitha replied as meekly as she could muster.

"Then do something about that hair. It is entirely out of keeping for a nurse."

Tabitha's hair was tightly bound at the back of her neck, not a strand out of place. She was amazed by the instructor's order, and the words that popped out of Tabitha's mouth reflected her surprise.

"In what respect, Nurse Rasmussen?"

"Are you questioning me?" the charge nurse sputtered.

"I beg your pardon if it sounds as though I am, ma'am," Tabitha hurried to soothe. "I only ask what it is you wish me to do differently with my hair."

"The color, Miss Hale, *the color*. Dyeing one's hair is an immodest, unsuitable practice for a nurse," the woman rasped.

"Yes, ma'am, I quite agree. However…" Tabitha focused on Nurse Rasmussen's collar and nursing pin as she spoke, making sure that she did not raise her eyes to challenge the nurse.

"However, what?"

Tabitha took a deep breath. "Unfortunately, this is my hair's natural shade."

If the other students had been submissive and cowed prior to this, they were now frozen with trepidation. Nurse Rasmussen's cold, silent consideration lingered on Tabitha.

O Lord! How did I manage to fall utterly afoul of this woman?

Tabitha struggled to keep her composure—and her temper—in check.

After staring at Tabitha for what seemed like an eternity, Nurse Rasmussen muttered, "Indeed, Miss Hale."

"Yes, ma'am." Tabitha nodded her head once. The senior nurse sniffed and moved to the last student in line, but Tabitha had a nagging suspicion that this would not be the last conflict she would endure while under Nurse Rasmussen's supervision.

CHAPTER 10

DECEMBER 1911

Tabitha rubbed her sticky, tired eyes and focused on the patient charts. She was working the night shift and it was late Christmas Eve. In just an hour it would be Christmas Day. Only the sickliest patients, those so unwell that they could not spend Christmas at home, remained on this floor. And only one nurse—and a student nurse at that—was on duty to care for the nine patients in the ward.

Most of the staff had been given the night off to enjoy the holiday eve with family. Tabitha's shift would end at six in the morning. Of course, Tabitha had not been left unsupervised. A single charge nurse (not, thankfully, Nurse Rasmussen), was on duty to supervise this ward and two others. The charge nurse made rounds between wards every hour.

As she studied the latest entries on the charts, Tabitha listened. The ward was still except for the breathing of sleeping patients and an occasional drowsy muttering. Then a patient coughed—a long, protracted cough—and Tabitha glanced up, her eyes now alert.

That would be Mrs. Daniels, she told herself, *the elderly woman with advanced cancer.*

The cough subsided and Tabitha turned back to the charts. During the night shift there was not as much work to do: Administer medications at the prescribed time. Clean bedpans and linens soiled in the night. Offer water to those who were weak or failing. Monitor the patients' condition and ring the charge nurse if a patient took a turn for the worse.

I am merely holding down the fort, she sighed, *while everyone else spends Christmas Eve and Christmas Day at home.*

Tabitha had asked for a four-day pass in November to spend Thanksgiving at Palmer House. *Denied.*

Earlier this month she had asked for three days to spend Christmas in Denver. That request, too, had been rejected.

Christmas and Thanksgiving were not the only holidays or celebrations she would miss or had missed. Mei-Xing and Minister Liáng had married in early November in Denver. Tabitha had requested a three-day pass to attend the wedding. It had been her first furlough request; it had been the first request denied.

Although she had explained her deep friendship with Mei-Xing, the secretary in the Dean's office had not been swayed. "I am afraid your request has been denied, Miss Hale," was all she would say.

It wasn't that Tabitha was still behind on her classwork or that her grades were poor—in fact, she was inching up in her class's academic standings. But no matter how well she was doing, she consistently received the worst assignments, the more difficult or onerous jobs and shifts—what the other girls labeled "punishment duties." Such punishments were usually assigned to students for poor academic performance, egregious clinical mistakes, or other infractions against the school rules.

As assignments were posted weekly and Tabitha continued to be placed on "punishment duties," the other students had pulled farther away, as though close association with Tabitha would cause her "bad luck" to rub off on them.

I work nights so often that I miss every opportunity for a respite. To be accepted by even one of the other students. To share in any fun activities.

Her thoughts turned back a week or so to the wonderful, spicy aroma that had filled the dormitory when she awoke one afternoon. Tabitha often snatched sleep from the only time she could spare: after classes and practicums and before her shift began. She had awoken thinking she was at home with the smells of Marit's ginger cookies wafting up the staircase from the kitchen.

Tabitha had traced the delectable scents to an empty box in the trash bin. Someone had received a gift box from home and had shared it around the dormitory while she slept.

"And they did not save so much as a cookie for me!" she had mourned.

Do not dare start feeling sorry for yourself, Tabitha Hale! She clamped her lips together and returned to the patient charts.

Mrs. Daniels coughed again and then her cough became a spasm. Tabitha heard the woman's whooping efforts to breathe and hurried to help her. She reached an arm behind the elderly woman's pillow and lifted her to a sitting position until the spasm passed.

"Thank you, dearie." The old woman's words rattled in her throat.

"Is there anything else I can do for you? A sip of water?" Tabitha already had the glass in her hand.

"Yes. Please."

The little bit of water set off another coughing fit and, as Tabitha held the woman and wiped away the spittle, Tabitha prayed for her. Without realizing it, she began whispering her prayer aloud.

"Father, you see this precious woman. You have said in your word that you love her. Give her strength and courage, O God, our Father, to face what is ahead. Lord Jesus, please draw near to her, because you love her so very much."

She eased the woman's thin body back onto the bed and straightened her pillow. The woman clutched her hand.

"Why?"

The question was only a faint, watery whisper.

Tabitha bent near. "Why what, Mrs. Daniels?"

"Why ... why would he love me?"

Tabitha pulled a chair close to the bed and sat down, still holding the woman's hand. "He made you, Mrs. Daniels. You are as dear as his child. Do you have children?"

Her patient was silent for a moment. Tabitha wondered if she had drifted off to sleep.

"My ... my son ... haven't seen him in years."

"I am so sorry." Tabitha bowed her head.

O Lord! Give me the right words!

"Do you miss your son?" she asked.

"Yes. Would give ... anything to see him again."

Tabitha nodded. "And do you still love him?"

"Yes." The word was stronger, emphatic. "He is still ... my son."

"Then you have your 'why,' Mrs. Daniels. God, who is the Father of all creation and who made each of us in his image, still loves you, even if you have been far from him for many years. He is still looking for you, seeking you, hoping you will come home."

"Do you ... really think so?"

"It is what the Bible tells us: *But God commendeth his love toward us, in that, while we were yet sinners, Christ died for us.* He is waiting for you to come home, even now."

"How?"

Tabitha squeezed the woman's hand. "Admit that you ran from him, that you disobeyed him. Tell him you are sorry. Ask for mercy and forgiveness because of what Jesus did on the cross."

"Yes ... I-I do. I need mer—"

Her chest was seized by another fit of coughing, and Tabitha held her upright until it passed. When Tabitha laid Mrs. Daniels down, the woman was exhausted.

"May I lead you in prayer, ma'am?" Tabitha asked.

Mrs. Daniels did not reply, but Tabitha felt a light pressure on her hand.

"O Lord," she prayed, her mouth near Mrs. Daniel's ear. "I have gone my own way most of my life. I have willfully ignored you and sinned against you. Please forgive me—not because I deserve your mercy, but because Jesus paid the price for my disobedience in his death on the cross."

The wasted hand in Tabitha's contracted and squeezed hers.

"O Lord, I humbly repent and turn from my own ways. I ask that you forgive me and receive me into your kingdom. Cover me in the precious blood of Jesus and wash me clean!

Tabitha sensed the Holy Spirit moving. "Thank you for being true to your word, true to what you have said, *That if thou shalt confess with thy mouth the Lord Jesus, and shalt believe in thine heart that God hath raised him from the dead, thou shalt be saved.* Thank you for hearing me and saving me. Amen."

Mrs. Daniels stammered a weak, "I-I-I do. A-a-amen."

Tabitha left the woman after she fell asleep. *Thank you, Lord, for the privilege of leading one of your lost sheep back to you, our great Shepherd!* she rejoiced within herself.

A few minutes later the charge nurse appeared at her elbow. "How are things, Miss Hale? Anything to report?"

"All the patients are sleeping, ma'am. Mrs. Daniels had a bad bout of coughing a bit ago, but she is sleeping again."

"Very good." She turned from Tabitha and walked with a practiced silence through the ward, stopping at each bed to listen and occasionally touch a forehead or take a pulse. She returned to the nurses' station and nodded to Tabitha before walking on to the next ward.

At six the following morning, one seasoned nurse and two of Tabitha's fellow students relieved Tabitha of her duties. She wandered on weary feet across the frosty campus to her empty dormitory. Other than herself and her two unfortunate classmates, the dormitory was abandoned. The remaining students were home for the short Christmas break.

Tabitha stripped off her uniform and collapsed into bed. "It is Christmas morning," she muttered.

She fell into a deep sleep thinking about Palmer House and all the fun and gaiety she imagined they were having. *Marit is baking cinnamon rolls and frying sausages. The house is filled with the spicy scents of nutmeg and cloves...*

By the time she opened her eyes again, it was midafternoon, Christmas Day. She washed and dressed and wandered downstairs, her destination the hospital cafeteria. The cook had promised to leave a cold Christmas dinner for the hospital staff.

When Tabitha stepped outside into the dim afternoon light, a drawling voice greeted her.

"There you are. I had almost given up on you, Tabs."

Tabitha jerked at the familiar voice and her mouth fell open. "Mason?" She shook her head. "I mean, *Mr. Carpenter*. But what are you doing here?"

He took her arm and urged her to walk with him. "At the moment, I am freezing to death! Good heavens, I have been waiting for you for two hours. If I do not move my feet, they will shortly be solid blocks of ice."

"But-but, I mean, what are you doing *here*?"

He chuckled. "Well, it is Christmas after all, and Miss Rose invited me to join everyone at Palmer House for Christmas dinner—a delightful prospect, I assure you—but I just could not accept. And do you know why?" He stopped walking and looked to Tabitha, demanding an answer.

"Why, no; I mean, should I know?" Tabitha thought she knew, but she was not going to presume to answer for him.

"You know quite well *why*, Tabs. Being at Palmer House when you are not there is painfully frustrating. And the more I thought about it, the more I thought of *you*, here at school but alone on Christmas—a totally unacceptable situation. I decided that just would not do."

He tugged her forward again. "Besides, how else would I get to see your face when you open my Christmas gift to you?" He stepped up his pace.

"Wh-what? Where are we going?"

"Ah! I am staying at the Palindrome Hotel, and they have promised to lay on a delectable Christmas dinner—but you have slept so long that nothing will be left if we do not hurry."

"But I—" Tabitha pulled back on her arm and managed to bring Carpenter to a stop. "*Mr. Carpenter!* I *cannot* accompany you. I cannot, in fact, even leave campus except to attend Sunday service without a furlough from the dean. I *particularly* cannot accompany a gentleman anywhere."

Carpenter grinned. "Ah, yes. I forgot to tell you. I arrived yesterday and paid the dean a visit. I had an appointment, to be specific. I explained that I was in town to convey Christmas greetings and gifts from your family in Denver. His assistant apprised me of your schedule and when you should be available today. Er, after I made a small contribution to the school's endowment fund."

"After you—" Tabitha huffed. "Oh, I see! And after you had made your 'small contribution,' did Dean Wellan also apprise you of the school's code of conduct? As I said, I cannot leave the school and hospital grounds without a written furlough—and I cannot be seen alone in the company of a gentleman."

Carpenter's grin widened. "Well, it seems that the dean has some discretion in these matters. I have here a two-hour pass for you, specifically to accompany me to Christmas dinner at the Palindrome."

He waved a sheet of paper under Tabitha's nose.

She grabbed it away and, stunned, read the short note. "Why, however did you manage this?"

Carpenter snatched the note back. "I can be very persuasive, Tabs and, er, he could not very well have said *no* when I was waving a check in front of his face, could he? However, this pass says I must have you back no later than five o'clock in the evening, when the doors are locked, regardless of when the two-hour period begins—and it is already 3:10. Really, you've slept away ten minutes of our time, Tabs, so pray forgive my insistence that we hurry!"

He took her arm again and they trod briskly along the walkway until Tabitha spied Carpenter's motorcar idling alongside the curb. Banks jumped from the driver's seat and opened the back door of the car for them.

"Good afternoon, Miss Hale, and a Merry Christmas to you," he smiled.

"Banks! Oh! but it is lovely to see your face. You remind me so much of home, and I fear I have been missing my beloved friends and family!"

As she slid onto the seat, Carpenter followed, grumbling, "What am I? Chopped liver? No 'lovely to see your face' for me?"

Tabitha laughed as they sped away. "Chopped liver? Ugh! I detest liver!"

The lobby of the Palindrome Hotel was festooned with Christmas greenery, bows, and garlands. The dining room, despite Carpenter's worries, was bustling with other Christmas diners. Before the maître d' seated them, Carpenter had a word with Banks, who nodded and hurried away.

Many of the women seated around them wore Christmas finery, jewels, and furs. Tabitha was more than a little self-conscious. "If I had known, I would have dressed more appropriately," she murmured.

"And yet, you are the most beautiful woman in the room," Carpenter replied in a quiet voice. "You are not even aware of the heads that turned as we walked to our table."

Tabitha blushed and touched her napkin to her mouth to hide her discomfiture.

Carpenter grinned and motioned to the waiter. As the waiter approached, Carpenter asked Tabitha, "I believe the chef has but one menu for this holiday dinner. Are you ready to eat?"

Tabitha nodded. "I am famished. I worked the night shift and fell asleep directly. I haven't eaten a thing since dinner yesterday!"

"We are ready to begin," he told the waiter.

Then he smiled at Tabitha. "I am glad you have a good appetite, but I was surprised to hear from the dean's assistant that you appear to work nights on a fairly regular basis. Is this normal for students?"

She made a wry face. "Well, someone has to work nights. Usually, the harder shifts are spread out rather evenly. I do not understand why I seem to be assigned to more than my share of them."

"Oh?" Carpenter's eyes fastened on her. He was just noticing the dark circles under Tabitha's eyes.

"Well, I do not mind working the night shift, except that it leaves me little time to study and sleep—but I *am* catching up on my studies! However, I sometimes tend to doze during lectures—and receive a scolding for it."

"I see." He did not, but wondered if he should investigate a little on his own.

After all, I have a few days at my discretion, he thought.

They enjoyed a fine dinner of sweet tomato bisque, roast goose and cranberry sauce, glazed baked ham, mashed potatoes and gravy, sweet potatoes glacé, and steamed asparagus with hollandaise sauce. During each course, Carpenter related the news from Denver. His descriptions, like his letter, were so insightful and many times humorous, that Tabitha sighed and laughed in turn.

"I can hear dear Mr. Wheatley speaking in my head," she confessed, "saying just what you said in his own unique way. And Charley! How I wish I could see Marit and Billy's baby again while he is still little. And Will and Shan-Rose. I miss them terribly—but I miss everyone. Most of all, I long to see Miss Rose."

"And they miss you, too," Carpenter replied. A contented smile played about his lips as he watched Tabitha's enjoyment of the meal and his news.

When they finished dinner, they were each served a slice of pecan pie. "It's too much!" Tabitha declared, nudging her plate with a half-eaten slice away from her. "I cannot eat another bite!"

"Nor can I—" Carpenter looked down at his last bite of pie. "—No; I just cannot leave that last bit of deliciousness." He forked it into his mouth and sighed. "Wonderful. Not, though, as good as Marit's pie, but quite wonderful."

"But can anyone make pie better than Marit?" Tabitha demanded.

"No one. If I did not know that I would never be forgiven, I would lure Marit and Billy away from Palmer House. I would offer them more money than they could possibly turn down to come work for me."

"You are quite right, Mr. Carpenter. We would never forgive you." Tabitha's eyes flashed, but she was smiling.

She glanced around the dining room once more. *What a wonderful day this has turned out to be,* she admitted.

Her eyes softened. "Thank you, Mr. Carpenter. Thank you for coming to see me and for this lovely Christmas dinner."

He pulled his watch from his vest pocket and checked the time. "Ah. We have but thirty minutes before I must have you home. A cup of coffee? No? Very good, then. May I help you from your chair?"

"Yes, but—"

A cup of coffee *did* sound good to Tabitha just then, but she graciously stood as Carpenter pulled out her chair. He seemed in a rush as he guided her from the dining room into the lobby.

Instead of walking toward the hotel entrance, Carpenter steered her through the lobby and into the hotel's great room. Then she saw Banks, with his hands folded in front of him, standing alongside two chairs tucked into an alcove. On a low table in front of the two chairs she spied a pile of Christmas gifts.

"Would you care to be seated, madam?" Carpenter murmured, indicating one of the chairs.

"But-but, what is all this?" Tabitha gestured toward the gifts.

"I could not come all this way without bringing gifts from Palmer House, now could I? Please bear in mind, that the time is now 4:31, and of our remaining twenty-nine minutes, I require fifteen to convey you to the school and escort you to your dormitory."

Tabitha just stared at the stack of presents before her.

"My dear, please open your bounty," Carpenter urged. "If I cause you a bad mark on your record, I will never forgive myself."

Tabitha began opening her gifts—a bottle of hand lotion from Mei-Xing, new stockings from Joy and Sarah, cookies and fruitcake from Marit and Billy, two handkerchiefs from Breona, a book from Rose, and a new box of stationery from Mr. Wheatley and the rest of the girls. There were notes tucked into every gift and Tabitha sniffed as she read the note from Rose.

My dear Tabitha,

We miss you and pray for you daily. Our God shall uphold you with his strong right hand, and we are confident that by his power you will do great things for him.

All my love,
Rose Thoresen

"I am sorry, but you really must wait until later to enjoy their notes," Carpenter whispered. He flipped open the cover on his watch and frowned at the time.

The last gift on the table was a small square box, glittering in gold foil. Tabitha picked it up and was surprised at its weight. Then she read the tag: *As L. Frank Baum suggests, "There is no place like home." Please receive this remembrance of your home as a small token of my esteem. M. Carpenter.*

Tabitha gnawed on her lip. *He must know that I cannot receive anything of a personal nature—anything that would imply more than a friendship.*

Carpenter snapped his watch shut with finality. "Really, Tabs, you are as slow as molasses, and I shall be forced to demand that Banks break all speed limits in order to return you in proper time!"

Tabitha snorted and tore into the beautiful wrapping paper. She uncovered a white box. She unclasped the box's lid and, from within a wealth of soft tissue paper, extracted a snow globe.

As the snow fell away to reveal the miniature house encapsulated within, Tabitha gasped. "But-but it's Palmer House!" She shook the globe and stared, charmed, at the precise replica within—every tower, gable, and turret exquisitely reproduced.

"Oh, it is *so* lovely!"

"Finally!" Carpenter glared at Banks in mock disdain. "She finds something other than *your* stodgy face to call lovely!"

Banks smirked and tipped back on his heels—in a manner not at all in keeping with chauffer-like decorum.

"Very good, very good," Carpenter added, now all business. "I am delighted that you like it. And now, we must clear all this away and pack up your loot. Time is of the essence."

"But how? Where? Where did you ever find Palmer House in a snow globe?"

Carpenter was helping Banks pack Tabitha's gifts into a large shopping bag. "Find it? No, of course not. I made it."

He offered his arm. "Ready?"

"You *made* this?" Tabitha stared agape at the work of art shimmering inside the globe.

"Don't drop it now. Banks—the door, please." Carpenter had but one goal on his mind at present. He steered Tabitha through the hotel doors onto the walkway. "Yes, I made it."

"Stop." Tabitha slid her arm from his. "Stop a moment."

Sighing, Carpenter halted. "Yes?"

"You made this precious, this perfect replica of Palmer House? You did? With your own hands?"

"As I said," he replied. His eyes, suddenly nervous, shifted away from hers.

"Mr. Carpenter, please look at me."

He did so. With reluctance.

"Thank you. From the bottom of my heart, I thank you. It is the most thoughtful Christmas gift you could have imagined."

He acknowledged her thanks with a brisk nod and they walked together to the waiting motorcar. Banks pulled away from the curb and the motorcar roared down the road toward the school.

With Carpenter urging her to walk as quickly as she could, Tabitha made it to the front door of her dormitory two minutes before the stroke of five o'clock. However, just as she reached for the handle of the imposing door, she heard the distinctive "snick" of the lock. Engaging.

Shocked, Tabitha glanced up to the door's window and saw the silhouette of Nurse Rasmussen, her stony face looking first from Tabitha to Carpenter and back.

"Nurse Rasmussen, please open the door." Tabitha's voice sounded calm enough to her own ears, but the joy of the day was ruined, and she bit her cheek to curb the dismay rising within her.

"I believe the rules are quite clear, Miss Hale. They are quite clear as to when the doors will be locked and clearer still regarding *gentlemen* callers."

An edge had crept into her voice. And something else. Something triumphant.

"Nurse Rasmussen, is it?" Carpenter nudged Tabitha to the side and, from a step below the door, he stood face-to-face with the older woman behind the door's window.

"Nurse Rasmussen, I would like you to look at my watch." He pushed the face of his pocket watch against the window. "The time is, precisely, 4:59 at this moment. It was 4:58 when we arrived and Miss Hale reached for the handle. The doors, I believe, are not to be locked until five o'clock? And," he added dryly, "I assure you that my timepiece *is* precise."

Nurse Rasmussen ignored him and focused on Tabitha. "You are aware of the rules pertaining to men, Miss Hale. I will be making a report to Dean Wellan regarding your behavior first thing in the morning."

She sniffed and turned to go, but Carpenter's palm pounded on the door and he raised his voice. "Nurse Rasmussen! If you would, please be so kind as to read this note." He plastered the dean's pass to the glass of the window. "Now, since we have settled the matter as to what time Miss Hale returned to her dormitory, be so good as to read this pass issued by Dean Wellan himself yesterday afternoon."

Nurse Rasmussen drew a pair of eyeglasses from her pocket and placed them on her nose. She perused the note once and a second time. Her mouth thinned as she read. With a great huff, she removed her glasses and returned them to her pocket.

A moment later, the lock on the door clicked open. Tabitha looked at Carpenter, but he was staring fixedly at the nurse on the other side of the door.

"Excuse me, Mr. Carpenter," Tabitha whispered. "Thank you for the wonderful Christmas dinner—and for everything."

She took the shopping bag with her gifts in it from his hand and, juggling the snow globe, struggled to open the door.

Carpenter snapped out of his reverie and held the door for her. "Merry Christmas, Miss Hale," he replied.

But as Tabitha slipped inside and past the hard-faced matron, she knew that Carpenter was angry—certainly angrier than she had ever seen him.

Not that it matters, Tabitha sighed as she climbed the stairs to the dormitory. *If Nurse Rasmussen did not have it in for me before, she surely does now. And Carpenter can do nothing to prevent me from being the recipient of her ill will.*

CHAPTER 11

JANUARY 1912

Tabitha tore into the letter from home and devoured Rose's flowing script.

My dear Tabitha,

We at Palmer House received your greetings from Mr. Carpenter and were delighted to hear of your lovely Christmas dinner. He described everything in such vivid detail that each of us felt we had, through his eyes, shared a small bit of Christmas with you.

Rose wrote further of their Christmas celebration; she paid particular attention to Will and Shan-Rose's fascination Christmas Eve when the family decorated the tall pine tree—including three strings of enormously expensive tree lights gifted by Mrs. Palmer—and gathered to sing Christmas hymns. Then she described Christmas morning from the eyes of the two children.

What a blessed time! We did not spoil the dear ones—although we could easily have done so. No, we kept our focus upon Jesus and on the manger scene, placing the infant in the manger, reading the Scriptures, and exchanging modest gifts. You have spent Christmas at Palmer House, my dear. You know the holiness of that day. I need not say more.

On another note, dear Tabitha, just prior to Christmas I submitted three handwritten copies of your testimony to a Christian stationer for whom Pastor Carmichael vouched. This stationer, who also restores and binds books, bound the copies of your testimony with lovely blue covers.

I distributed the copies to our newest girls first and they have already read them with a voracious appetite. One by one, they have come in private to speak to me of what they read, and each girl has shared that she sees herself in your story. I see a hope in them now that was lacking before. I am so grateful that your example has sparked that hope.

Oh, thank you, Lord! Tabitha rejoiced. *It was worth it!* Recalling how difficult it had been to tell Rose of her past, Tabitha was glad she and Rose had pressed through to complete her account. She savored each line of the letter and sighed in contentment—until she read Rose's closing remark.

Marit asks how you and your friends enjoyed her Christmas goodies. She sent the package ahead of time and packed it overfull with a wide assortment of cookies, candies, and cake to ensure that you had plenty of treats to share with all your fellow students and friends.

Tabitha frowned. *But I did not receive any packages.* Frowning a little more, she added, *And I have no friends here.* She snorted. *When would I have time for that?*

Still confused about the box she should have received, Tabitha folded the letter away and crossed the campus to the school's mailroom. She greeted the plain-looking but cheerful woman who dispensed the mail.

"Good morning, Mrs. Davis. Would you be able to help me? My friends tell me in their latest letter that they sent a large box of holiday baking to me some time before Christmas. However, I did not receive their package. I was hoping you could tell me if it arrived here?"

The woman, who had met Tabitha with a smile, stilled. Her smile stiffened and then slipped from her mouth. She cast her eyes down and began sorting mail on the counter in a nervous manner.

Clearing her throat, Mrs. Davis managed to reply, "I-I assure you, Miss Hale, that I do not have a package here for you."

Tabitha cocked her head on one side and considered the woman's guarded expression and vague response. "Very well, but—if I may be so bold—I asked if a package for me had *arrived*. Did a package for me arrive? Did someone else pick it up?"

Mrs. Davis looked down, even more uncomfortable. "M-miss Hale, I hope you can understand… h-how very much I n-need this job. I have a daughter… I am raising alone."

Tabitha's mouth started to work but she closed it with a snap. Her thoughts spun in circles. *So the package did arrive? Someone took it? But who in the world?*

And then it hit her.

"Mrs. Davis, did Nurse Rasmussen pick up that package?"

The woman flinched. "P-please, Miss Hale! She happened to be here when it arrived and when she saw it, she insisted on taking it to you—even when I told her it was against the rules. She-she *said* she would deliver it to you!"

Tabitha's face heated. "So you gave it to her. You gave *my* package to Nurse Rasmussen."

Mrs. Davis twisted her hands together. "I-I protested, truly I did, Miss Hale! B-but when I refused to give her your parcel, she insinuated that she would complain to the college administration, tell them that I was not performing my job well—she hinted that she could cause me to lose my position!"

Mrs. Davis licked her lips. "Surely you know how she can be?"

Oh, yes. I know how she can be, Tabitha told herself.

The woman swallowed and sent an imploring plea toward Tabitha. "Miss Hale, if you raise a question to the school administration about the package, it won't matter what happens to Nurse Rasmussen—I will still lose my job for breaking the rules."

Tears of defeat leaked from the woman's eyes and ran down her cheeks, and Tabitha grasped how terrified Mrs. Davis really was. She comprehended the tight corner into which Nurse Rasmussen had painted Mrs. Davis.

And me, too, was her grim verdict. *That old witch bullied this poor woman into giving her my package. Nurse Rasmussen knows that if I were to demand the parcel of her, she would say that, as a courtesy to me, she collected it and left it for me in the dormitory—and has no idea what became of it.*

Tabitha frowned. *I can't do a thing about this. Nurse Rasmussen knows that if I were to report her, no one would dare consider that* she *had done anything amiss—but Mrs. Davis would surely suffer the loss of her job.*

Tabitha left the mail room fuming. She was positively stomping across campus when a memory intruded. Tabitha stopped and remembered, her jaw working.

The afternoon I awoke to the delicious aroma of baked goodies and the empty box in the trash bin ...

"Why, those were *my* treats!"

Tabitha balled her fists in fury. She itched to hit someone—and preferably Nurse Rasmussen.

No doubt she told the other students to help themselves—and I am certain they enjoyed every one of Marit's candies and cookies!

Tabitha clutched her middle, trying hard to master her temper. But the more she envisioned the standoffish young women in her dormitory devouring her treats, the angrier she grew.

"And without so much as a 'by your leave'!" she grumbled. It had been a long time since she had allowed her temper so much loose rein.

Then she sighed. *As frightened as those girls are of Nurse Rasmussen, not one of them would dare defy her or speak out against her.*

Taking a deep breath, she admitted, *Nothing can be done. I must let this go. Lord, please help me to let it go.*

After a long walk to calm herself—while she should have been studying—Tabitha pondered the mounting evidence pointing toward Nurse Rasmussen. It all suggested that the nurse was working against Tabitha: The regular punishment duties—including the never-ending night shift! The avoidance and silent treatment from the other students. And now this intentional theft.

Not to mention her locking me out of the dormitory Christmas Day!

Another thought shook her. *I wonder what my marks look like? No! Surely, Nurse Rasmussen has not given me undeserved poor marks? Surely she has not influenced other staff members against me?*

"I would have heard by now if any complaints had been lodged against me," she reminded herself. "That, at least, I do not need to be concerned about."

Tabitha rubbed at the aching spot between her eyes. "But why? Why does she treat me this way? Why should she 'have it in for me'? What have I done to her?"

Even though she had no answer to those questions, as Tabitha headed back to her dormitory, a settled conclusion slipped from her lips. "Nurse Rasmussen is doing her best to discredit me and have me dismissed."

But why?

That evening, Tabitha wrote a response to Rose's letter. She shared all she could about her progress in school, taking care not to give any indication of the increasingly difficult pressure under which she labored. At the end of the note she added a carefully crafted thank you to Marit.

Please tell Marit how I love her and thank her for her thoughtfulness! When I smelled her goodies, I felt as though I had been transported home for Christmas. I can assure you, all the girls in my dormitory enjoyed them immensely.

"Yes," she groused, angered again. "I am certain sure they did!"

She shook her head at her outburst. "Lord, I do not wish to be held captive by someone else's hateful behavior. Please help me to forgive Nurse Rasmussen and the girls of my class. O Lord, I give this hurtful situation to you. Please send your Spirit of Peace to guard my heart and mind."

As her classes continued, Tabitha still felt as though *something*, something unseen, were working against her—and yet she could not decide what it was. She shrugged.

I can only do my best. I trust you, Lord, to guide me through this ordeal to your perfect will for my life.

The academic year resumed and marched on, and so did the classes, study sessions, exams, practicums, and work shifts. Tabitha caught up on her studies and did well on her exams. She would have been proud and content with her progress—if her energy had allowed her to stop and reflect. But she was now assigned to the night shift six days a week!

Her only sleep was what she could snatch in the evenings between dinner and her shift start and the occasional nap between classes, practicums, and "punishment duties." She often forewent lunch to steal an hour of sleep.

I do not know how long I can keep this up, she worried, rubbing bleary eyes. But when doubt came upon her, when she feared she would crumble, she would recite the words from Rose's Christmas gift, words she knew by heart:

Our God shall uphold you with his strong right hand, and we are confident that by his power you will do great things for him.

"You uphold me with your strong right hand, Lord! Without your strength, I would fail," she prayed, "but because I know you are upholding me, I can persevere."

A slow, beautiful spring rolled onto the hospital and school campus. Tabitha tried to capture and enjoy a moment of it as she raced down the paths between dormitory and classroom, cafeteria and hospital. But it was all she could do to acknowledge the changing of the seasons as she sped across the campus.

Two months in advance, Tabitha applied for a furlough for the spring term break. *I have not been home since fall term began,* she rationalized. *Surely they will approve it!*

And it was important for Tabitha to go home: Breona had at last consented to marry Pastor Carmichael.

Tabitha was hopeful of this request and began to plan her brief visit to Denver. "I must see my friend as a bride!" she laughed, grinning in anticipation.

Then the answer arrived. She stared in disbelief at the short response from the dean's office: "Your request for a furlough has been denied."

Why? Why, Lord? Tabitha could not understand, but she knew that questioning the Dean's decision would be fruitless.

Three more times that spring she felt someone watching her, but each time she stopped and stared around, her heart pounding, she spied no one near her except other students or staff and campus workers.

Twice, after dark as Tabitha walked to her night shift at the hospital, she heard footsteps behind her. She called out, asking who was there, but no one answered. As she walked on, she no longer heard the soft pad of steps following, but she could not shake her sense of unease.

Another instance, in the full light of day, she glared with suspicion at a gardener, a shriveled man of indeterminate age, but he was busy trimming a shrub. Tabitha shrugged and, with an eye on the tall campus clock tower, ran for her next class.

CHAPTER 12

JANUARY 1913

Another year has passed, Tabitha thought. *When I believed I could endure no more, you, Lord, sustained me. You are faithful, O God. So faithful.*

Tabitha had now worked an entire year of night shifts with no respite, no holidays, and no furloughs. She had worked night after night in addition to her classes, practicums, and exams; she maintained her grades in addition to hours spent cleaning the bloody aftermath of surgeries or scrubbing beakers and other medical instruments, wrapping them in brown paper, and sterilizing them in the autoclave.

The same unrelenting duties were not assigned to the other nursing students. Yes, all the students rotated through night shifts, but Tabitha was never taken off the night roster. And only when a classmate made a significant error or broke a rule were they given work in addition to their daily duties.

Tabitha knew that she had Nurse Rasmussen to thank for the "punishment duties" she never escaped. *I just do not know why, Lord*, she fretted.

"Lord," Tabitha whispered, "I give my life to you to do as you wish. Let me be like the Apostle Paul!" and she quoted a passage from 2 Corinthians aloud as she stood long hours in the wards each night.

> *Always bearing about in the body*
> *the dying of the Lord Jesus,*
> *that the life also of Jesus*
> *might be made manifest in our body.*
> *For we which live are always*
> *delivered unto death for Jesus' sake,*
> *that the life also of Jesus*
> *might be made manifest in our mortal flesh.*

She no longer requested furloughs. After having her requests rejected five times, she had given up asking for leave.

While most of the students vacated the campus between terms, Tabitha and a handful of other students remained in residence in the dormitory, working extended hours to maintain staffing levels at the hospital.

Though the hours were long, term breaks also had their bit of silver lining: With no classes in session, Tabitha could sleep all day, sleep until her exhausted body received its full complement of sleep.

Besides, the end of her ordeal was in sight. Within a few weeks the spring term would commence—and at its end, she would graduate!

Then I will go home.

Home! She counted the months that had passed.

I have not been home in fifteen months.

An entire spring had passed. An entire summer had drifted by. Another fall and another Christmas had come and gone.

Carpenter had visited again at Christmas, and Tabitha cradled those precious memories close to her heart. She had even begun to entertain hope that she and Mason could have a future together.

If it is your will, Lord, she prayed, *but I know you have called me to nursing. Help me to follow hard after you, giving you my all, so I might satisfy your purposes in my life.*

Carpenter, too, seemed to have new purpose. "I earned my pilot's license, Tabs, and Cliff is teaching me how to instruct. He has a small pilot's school, and I shall be his partner."

"But what shall you do with this flying, Mr. Carpenter? What is its objective?"

He cocked his head, thinking before he framed an answer. "I am not certain, but I cannot escape the sense that we are preparing for something important, something momentous."

As am I, Tabitha admitted to herself. *Something important, only I do not know what it will be.*

Still, she longed for her schooling to be finished so that she could return to Denver—but she also harbored some anxiety.

When I return to Palmer House, so much will have changed. I will meet girls who live there but who do not even know me. And neither Mei-Xing nor Breona reside at Palmer house any longer.

Tabitha made herself stop thinking along those lines. "Keep your eyes upon your goal, Tabitha. Fix them upon graduation.

"Think of nothing but receiving your nurse's cap and pin—focus on what life will be when June arrives, after which you will leave this place forever."

Tabitha threw her shoulders back and stood straighter. Taller.

I will not disappoint my Lord, and I will not disappoint those who have invested so much in my education, who trust me to do my very best.

January passed into February and then early March. The winter term ended, and Tabitha welcomed the break between classes, and not only because of the welcome extra sleep, but because she also anticipated a visit from Mason Carpenter.

It seemed that Carpenter managed to schedule some business appointment in Boulder every time the school term ended. And somehow he also managed to appear with a two-hour pass from the Dean to take Tabitha to dinner and to deliver notes and gifts to her from her friends at Palmer House.

"How is it that you can wrangle a pass from him when I cannot?" Tabitha inquired as they sped from the campus toward a local restaurant.

"Oh, well. Perhaps the school is grateful for the generous donations I make," he drawled.

She slapped his arm in mock alarm. "No! Is this true? Do you bribe Dean Wellan into these furloughs?"

He chuckled. "My dear, how can the dean refuse to grant me a two-hour pass with you when I am dangling a check under his ample chin?"

"You are incorrigible," Tabitha pronounced.

"Money has its good uses as well as evil, Tabs," was all he replied.

They dined with hearty appetite, and yet Tabitha was hungrier for news than for food. She devoured every word Carpenter shared from home, every description of her friends he could provide.

"And Joy? Is there no word on her little Edmund?"

"None." Carpenter grimaced, suddenly out of humor. "For all the devoted efforts of Mr. O'Dell and having spared no expense to track Morgan, the trail has run cold."

"Having spared no expense? Mr. Carpenter," Tabitha asked, parsing her question with care, "are you providing the funds in the search for Edmund?"

He turned his head and avoided her question. "Mrs. Michaels is a great testimony to me. Her godly character and faith inspire me and those who know her."

He then turned the conversation back to Palmer House and provided many more tidbits of news, to Tabitha's delight.

"You make the separation from all of them bearable," she admitted. "Thank you."

He smiled. "You are most welcome."

Tabitha sighed, happy for the reprieve from her duties, filled with good food, and comfortable in Carpenter's company. She spoke before she realized how forward her questions would be.

"Mr. Carpenter, how is it you have never married? Settled down?" She reddened and slapped a hand to her mouth. "Oh! I do apologize. That was inappropriate. Inexcusable."

But he had only cocked his head again and studied her, as though deciding how to reply. Then he touched his napkin to his mouth.

"I have often wanted to tell you, Miss Hale, about my ... wife."

Tabitha's lips parted. She could not speak.

"Do not worry, Miss Hale, I am not married." Carpenter's smile was crooked. Sad. "I married young and impetuously. I loved Christ, but I did not listen to the Holy Spirit when I fell in love with Maudie. I was not wise and did not concern myself overmuch with her spiritual desires or aspirations—I was too enamored with the blissful life I envisioned that we would share.

"Her picture of our married life, as it turned out, was vastly different than mine. She desired the whirlwind life of a socialite, while I despised the vapid, pointless machinations of high society. We were not happy together, but we were also not long together. She developed acute appendicitis. The doctors performed surgery, of course, but afterward Maudie developed an infection. Following a week of fever and horrible suffering, she slipped away. We were married less than two years."

Carpenter stared at Tabitha, his jaw working. "It was a mistake to marry Maudie with no thought to her spiritual condition. As it is, I fault myself that she passed into eternity with no relationship with Christ."

Tabitha dropped her eyes, afraid of the view Carpenter had opened into his soul, afraid of the raw pain she had glimpsed.

"I promised my Lord that I would not make such a mistake again, Miss Hale," he murmured. "I will remarry only when and if I and the woman I choose are spiritually compatible and God approves of our union. I want God's best. Until then, I am content to wait."

The break ended, and Tabitha's last term began.

She was crossing the lawn from her dormitory to the classrooms, keeping to the cobbled walkway, when she passed one of the school's caretakers. He was pushing an edge trimmer along the walkway. She had not paid much attention to the several caretakers in the past. However, as she drew abreast of the man, he raised his head and they made eye contact.

His stare was appraising.

Tabitha nearly stumbled and her face flamed.

I know this man!

Tabitha forced herself to keep walking and not look back. She ran up the stairs to her classroom as if pursued and slid into her seat. When the lecture began she had trouble concentrating. She was distracted and upset.

With a start, she realized the physician teaching the class had spoken to her. "I asked you a question, Miss Hale."

"I beg your pardon, doctor. I am afraid my attention was elsewhere. I apologize; it will not happen again," Tabitha answered.

"See that is does not," he snapped.

Tabitha nodded and opened her book, but she could not get the image of the caretaker from her mind. He was short, middle-aged, and grizzled.

Not much had changed from when she had seen him last.

Nearly four years ago.

In her room at the *Silver Spurs*.

Lord, does he remember me from there?

She played back the chance encounter, the fleeting exchange. Had she seen a blink of recognition on his part? Had he turned as she passed by? Had his eyes continued to watch her?

Tabitha gnawed on her unanswered questions during the class and remembered nothing of the lecture when the bell rang.

As she gathered her things and exited the building, she peered anxiously about her, looking for the muted green of the caretaker's uniform.

I must avoid another encounter with this man at any cost, she told herself.

April arrived with rain and sleet and departed on a warm breeze. And then it was May. Final exams would begin in two weeks. Graduation was scheduled for mid-June.

Tabitha's days and nights passed by in a haze of study and work, but she knew the end was near and that she was prepared.

I will more than pass my exams, she exulted. *I am in good standing and, because of God's sustaining grace, I will acquit myself well.*

Tabitha returned to her dormitory after classes hoping to snatch an hour of sleep before group practicums. One of her fellow students handed her a note.

"This came for you," she said.

"Thank you." Tabitha slid the note into her pocket. She was bone tired. *What I would give for a whole night of sleep*, she fantasized.

An hour later she scrambled from her bed and made it to her group practicum with only minutes to spare. Halfway through the afternoon, she remembered the note in her pocket.

After she read the note, she stared around, hunting for a clock, and was horrified to see that it read 3:15. She shoved the note back into her pocket, explained her departure to the charge nurse, and raced for her dormitory, the words of the note burning in her head.

Miss Hale,

You will report to the office of the Dean of Medicine at 3:30 to address a deficit in your training. Please do not be tardy.

Emilia Gunderson, Dean of Nursing

A sense of dread descended upon Tabitha, and she took the steps up to the dormitory hall two at a time. Ignoring the startled looks of the housekeeping girls, she stripped her soiled apron from her uniform, tied on a clean one, and felt her hair to ensure that it was tightly bound behind her cap with its blue band marking her as a student nurse. Then she ran down the stairs and across the campus toward the dean's office.

Tabitha managed to arrive at exactly 3:30 and was ushered into a conference room. Dean Wellan and Dean Gunderson were seated at the end of the table; the four members of the board of regents lined the sides of the table.

"Please be seated at the end of the table, Miss Hale," Dean Wellan instructed. He was perusing a stack of papers on the table in front of him.

Tabitha seated herself. She was still out of breath from running straight across campus, and her pulse pounded in her throat. The members of the board, their expressions guarded, looked her over. Dean Gunderson, who had always been gracious to Tabitha, said nothing, but Tabitha thought she appeared stiff. Nervous.

Then Dean Wellan glanced up and, squinting a little, regarded Tabitha with a frown. "May I ask, Miss Hale, if you have been ill?"

Tabitha was surprised. "No, sir. I have not."

His frown deepened. "I ask because you look quite fatigued. Not at all as I remember you last we met."

Tabitha squirmed inside. "Dean Wellan, sir, if I appear fatigued, it is only due to the rigors of classes and work. I can assure you that I am well—and up to the challenge."

He said nothing for a moment, merely studied her. Then he turned his attention to the papers before him and cleared his throat. "Miss Hale, your academic record is acceptable—quite fine, in fact.

"Dean Gunderson and I had our doubts as to whether you could make up the work you missed your first year, but you have done so successfully. You are in high standing in many of your classes."

He frowned again. "You can, perhaps, understand my confusion when we, upon determining your eligibility for final examinations and graduation, discovered a marked deficit in several practicums."

The dean looked at the papers. "Every student nurse is required to log one hundred sixty hours of nursing care in each nursing specialty. Your record, however, indicates incomplete hours in three areas: obstetrics, surgical, and pediatric nursing. You are lacking a combined three hundred sixty hours of nursing experience in these areas."

He removed his spectacles and turned his attention to her. "Dean Gunderson and I are both at a loss as to why you have not served your complete rotations in these areas."

Tabitha was so shocked that she blinked stupidly and could think of nothing immediate to say. After a moment, though, her mind sorted the puzzle pieces and—at last—thought she understood.

This is Nurse Rasmussen's doing! Oh, how could I have been so blind?

"Dean Wellan, Dean Gunderson, we students work the shifts we are assigned—we do not have any say or control over our work assignments. I was assigned to work nights, sir, ma'am, primarily in the general wards."

Dean Wellan studied her with a quizzical frown. "Yes, yes. All students take their share of night shifts. I do not appreciate a student complaining over this necessity. What I do not understand is why your required hours in these specialties are lacking."

Tabitha drew a slow, measured breath before answering. "Sir, I was assigned and have worked nights *exclusively* for the last year and a half. I work six nights each week. I have not been assigned to any shift *other* than nights for more than a year."

She looked away briefly. "Of course, I worked on the floors in question with my cohort for practicums—but only as we covered those specialties in our curriculum. And, occasionally, my night shift assignment placed me on these floors. But only occasionally."

"I beg your pardon, Miss Hale. Perhaps I do not comprehend you perfectly. Do you mean to tell me that you have worked a graveyard shift for an entire year and a half? That you have *regularly* worked eight-hour nights while still attending classes and practicum clinics?"

Tabitha shifted uncomfortably. "Yes, sir. I do not understand why I was assigned thusly, Dean Wellan, but yes. I have worked nights for the past eighteen months, even during term breaks and holidays."

"Six nights a week? Without a day—er, *night*—off? Ever?" He sounded incredulous. "To whose cohort does Miss Hale belong, Dean Gunderson?"

Dean Gunderson's lips tightened. "Third cohort, Dean Wellan. Nurse Rasmussen."

"Excessive night shifts are usually assigned as corrective measures, are they not, Dean Wellan?" one of the board members inquired. "As penalty, say, for poor performance or insubordination?" The board member scrutinized Tabitha. "Does Miss Hale have disciplinary marks against her that would explain this unusual situation?"

Dean Wellan perused Tabitha's record. "Well. I am surprised. Indeed, I see several notations to that effect."

Tabitha jerked and sat forward. "I beg your pardon?"

"I will read from these notations," Dean Wellan said. "Let me see. October 1, 1911. 'Student Hale was insolent and haughty today. She spoke back to a staff member when corrected.' January 17, 1912. 'Student Hale was reprimanded for tardiness.' February 28, 1912. 'Student Hale was reprimanded for five instances of tardiness to class this month.' April 11, 1912. 'Student Hale demonstrated a disregard for sanitary procedures today.' May 5, 1912, 'Student Hale's performance on the surgical floor . . .'"

He went on, listing a total of fifteen complaints.

Forcing down the bile bubbling up from her stomach, Tabitha spoke quietly but firmly. "I have never heard these complaints, Dean Wellan. Except for the first week back after my leave of absence—a year and half ago—I have not been reprimanded or given any sort of disciplinary counseling, and I can think of no instance in which I was late to any class. Your reading of this list is an utter surprise to me."

She cast about in her mind for someone or something to corroborate her response. "Were these complaints lodged by several staff members or only one? Surely my instructors could verify whether or not I was tardy to classes? As I said, I had no knowledge of these complaints. Could they be the product of a single individual? Someone who has a grudge against me?"

Dean Wellan's expression darkened at her suggestion, but he looked carefully at the complaints nonetheless. After several minutes of examining them he pursed his mouth and slid the file over to Dean Gunderson.

The older nurse donned her glasses and peered at the notations in Tabitha's record. After she had read through them, she inclined her head toward Dean Wellan and they spoke in whispers. Dean Wellan huffed and shook his head at something the Dean of Nursing suggested.

Holding up his hand, he broke off their conversation and lifted his eyes to Tabitha. "I shall need some time to look into your situation, Miss Hale."

"Did you find something?" she asked eagerly. Tabitha knew she was overreaching, but she was almost frantic. "Was it Nurse Rasmussen? I am convinced that she has something against me. She—"

"*Miss Hale!* That will be quite enough!" The dean stared her into submission. "You do not disparage our school's excellent staff."

"I apologize, sir, to you, Dean Gunderson, and to the board." Tabitha licked her lips. "May I have permission to speak candidly before you, Dean Gunderson, and the board?"

The dean looked to the board members and back. "Very well. In the spirit of fairness."

"Thank you, sir." Tabitha took a moment to frame clear, concise thoughts.

Lord, please help me!

"Sir, if, as these complaints allege, my behavior has been consistently unsatisfactory over such a long period, would not you, through Dean Gunderson's office, have been notified quite some time ago? If I understand the college's guidelines correctly, a discipline issue that continues for more than a month is to be addressed at your level with the student placed on strict probation.

"In my case, not only have you been unaware of these complaints, but I, also, have been unaware of them—for going on two years. Someone—I do not name or disparage that someone—but it appears that someone on the staff, rather than following school policy, has assigned me to night shifts and various other punishment duties."

She softened her voice. "It occurs to me that my unusual work assignment has been a deliberate attempt to prevent me from logging the required hours in the specialty nursing areas you noted."

Tabitha looked at Dean Wellan and willed him to hear her heart. "I beg you to believe me when I say that I had no knowledge of these complaints. However, I confess that I should have raised the issue of my work assignment with Dean Gunderson long before today. I should have asked why I was being subjected to ongoing punishment duties without due process.

"But I was afraid. I was afraid that my questions would be viewed as immature complaints, as murmuring or rebelling against authority."

She sighed. "I see now that my work assignment has created a deficit in my practical experience. And I am … concerned that both my work assignment and these complaints are the concerted efforts of one individual to discredit me."

The dean and the board exchanged troubled looks, but Dean Gunderson sat rigid in her chair, looking straight ahead.

No one spoke for several minutes while Dean Wellan considered his response. When he did speak, his voice was gentle.

"I must agree that there *is*, ah, something irregular about your record, Miss Hale. I wish you to be assured that we will conduct a thorough investigation and get to the bottom of this.

"If," and here his expression clouded, "as you suggest, wrong has been perpetrated against you by a member of the nursing school's staff, we will rectify the situation to the best of our ability."

Tabitha nodded. "Thank you, sir."

He paused as though he wished to say something else.

"Sir?"

"I only wish to say that I would not have thought it possible for a student to work an ongoing night shift … while still managing the heavy class load and study schedule required of our students. It is a mark of unusual tenacity and dedication that you have done so for such an extended period.

"And," he added in a sober tone, "it explains to me why you appear so very poorly. I assure you that this situation, one way or another, will not continue."

Two of the board members nodded in agreement. Dean Gunderson did not move or shift expression.

"Thank you, sir," Tabitha answered, but her heart was heavy.

I believe you, sir, but can an investigation alter the fact that my required specialty training is incomplete? Surely nothing you can do will permit me to graduate with my class.

"You may go, Miss Hale."

Tabitha raised her chin and, with as much decorum as she could muster, walked from the room.

Dear Miss Rose,

Oh, how I wish you were here, how I wish I could speak to you face to face and, perhaps receive wisdom from your heart! Things have gone all wrong and I do not know what to do.

I was called to the dean's office today—before him and before the dean of nursing and the board of regents. I was told that the practicum portion of my training is incomplete. It is all because I have been assigned to night shifts for the entirety of the last eighteen months and, thus, have missed a large portion of required nursing experience.

In addition, the dean read aloud a long list of complaints lodged in my record! I was mortified, Miss Rose, and dumbfounded. I knew nothing of those complaints, but I could see on his face that he doubted me.

I thank the Lord that he brought the school's disciplinary procedure to my mind. I reminded the dean how, under the school's procedure, any ongoing complaints should have been brought to his attention after which I would have been placed on probation.

Thankfully, he agreed with me that something was not right, and he assured me that he would look into the situation.

I know someone has worked behind the scenes to besmirch my reputation. I do not understand why, but I believe I know who has done so. And it must also be the same person who kept me assigned to nights, knowing I would miss the required hours in several nursing specialties.

But, Miss Rose! The fact remains that my practicums are incomplete. Whether the dean uncovers the truth or not, I am certain that I will not be allowed to graduate next month.

Please pray for me, for I am struggling to understand why God would allow this to happen. I am grieved beyond measure that the work of Palmer House might be affected.

Your devoted daughter,
Tabitha

Tabitha placed the letter in the outgoing mail box and then fell into her bed. She was worn in mind and body.

I do not care what I miss or what goes by the way this evening, she realized. *None of it matters anymore.*

She fell into a deep, exhausted sleep.

CHAPTER 13

Tabitha awoke with a start in the dim light of early morning. Her fellow students were just rising and preparing for the day. She was confused for a moment and then panic struck her.

Oh, no! I slept through the night! I missed my work shift!

"Must be nice for a change, huh, Red?" The girl who addressed her had one hand on her hip and a toothbrush in the other.

"Wha-what do you mean?" Tabitha scrambled to make up her bed and get into a clean uniform. She was so shaken that she forgot to remind the girl *not* to call her "Red."

"Why, not having to work nights for a change, of course. Must be a relief to finally be off night shift." The girl gestured with her toothbrush toward another student who was just dragging herself into a nightgown. "Henderson, there, caught your shift last night, poor thing."

She pointed her toothbrush at herself. "And *I* am the poor sucker tonight!"

Tabitha glanced at the student she knew as Nancy Henderson. "Henderson worked my shift last night? I was not on the roster?"

"Of course you're on it, just not on nights. Looks like you have a stint in pediatrics. Evenings." She wandered toward the communal sinks at the end of the dormitory.

I am not on nights? I did not oversleep?

Tabitha's schedule had, indeed, changed! In fact, the entire schedule had been adjusted. She saw her name on the revised schedule for evening shifts in pediatrics, 3-11 p.m., for the next week. Where she had been on nights, seven girls from her dormitory were scheduled for one night each.

As it should have been all along, Tabitha noted.

She washed, dressed, and fixed her hair with more energy than she had felt in a while, and arrived at breakfast with a healthy appetite. Her day was long and busy, but she smiled every time she remembered that she would be climbing into her bed and spending the entire night there at the end of it.

Over the next few days she continually wondered how Dean Wellan and Dean Gunderson were investigating the complaints against her and what progress they were making. Twice she thought she caught Nurse Rasmussen watching her, but she could not be certain.

If you are behind all of my troubles, Tabitha thought, *God himself will deal with you.*

She pushed down a more worrisome thought: that the Deans might *not* uncover any wrongdoing—and she would be dismissed from school in disgrace.

O Lord, she prayed, *please help me to give this situation to you. I know I have been unjustly accused—but how much more unjustly were you treated? You kept your peace when they accused you! If you help me, I know I can bear whatever comes of this. I so want my life to honor you. For your name's sake, please do not allow me to be disgraced.*

She received a letter from Rose and took heart from the encouragement penned in Rose's familiar handwriting.

My daughter Tabitha, I hope that you will not give in to fear. If God leads and guides your way as he has promised to do, he will make that way plain. Again, I say, do not fear what "man" can do to you, for God himself will walk with you, even through fire. We have Jesus' sure promise: "I will never leave you nor forsake you."

"Yes. I know you will never forsake me, Lord," Tabitha whispered. Still she could not shake an ominous feeling, a strong sense that something else was about to go wrong. And at the end of the week, she received another summons.

Miss Hale,
You will report to the office of the Dean of Medicine at 1:30 to address a complaint. The charge is of a serious nature. Please do not be tardy.
Emilia Gunderson, Dean of Nursing

The dean's secretary again showed Tabitha into the conference room. Dean Wellan, Dean Gunderson, and the board of regents faced her. The scene was much as it had been a week ago—with one exception: The expressions on the faces turned toward her were grave.

Dean Wellan's voice was stiff as he began the meeting. "Miss Hale, we have investigated the situation around your training deficit and the complaints in your records. Sadly, another issue, one much more serious, has been brought to our attention."

Tabitha froze at the icy detachment in his voice.

"Miss Hale, students at this school must possess an unblemished reputation. They are required to behave according to the highest standards of virtue. We have received information from a reliable source that you have a sordid past, one that precludes you from attendance at this institution, one that I hesitate to even speak aloud in these chambers."

He cleared his throat. "Can you answer to these charges?"

Tabitha could not speak. She shook her head a fraction, but she could form no words. All she could think was, *O God! Would you redeem me from my past only to have it disgrace me now?*

"You do not answer, Miss Hale?"

Tabitha looked at him and said nothing.

Dean Gunderson's chin dropped a little. Tabitha imagined the disappointment and humiliation the senior nurse was feeling.

Without conscious forethought, Tabitha whispered, "Dean Wellan?"

"Yes? What do you wish to say?"

"Sir, I am ... overcome at this moment. May I ... may I have a few days to prepare a statement to you and to the board of regents?"

Where did that response come from? Tabitha wondered.

One of the board members expostulated, "Really, I do not see—"

"Enough!" It was the first time Dean Gunderson had spoken, and the single word crackled with stern authority. "The seriousness of this charge should allow Miss Hale some latitude. After all, she has comported herself with honor *for three years*. Is all of that to be disregarded and her reputation ruined without hearing from her? I say, give her the time she requests to respond to this charge."

The men in the room were as startled at Dean Gunderson's vehemence as Tabitha was. Dean Wellan surveyed the board and received several nods and one sheepish shrug in response.

"Very well, Miss Hale." He paged through a small book and added, "Since this is Wednesday, we will reconvene on Monday, five days from today. Will that be satisfactory?"

He again looked for a response from the board. Then he addressed Tabitha.

"We will hear from you on Monday morning at ten o'clock. Until then, you will continue your school and work activities as usual."

Tabitha left the administration building on legs that barely obeyed her commands.

The same question swirled in her head and repeated itself. *What am I going to do?*

She was surprised to feel a hand upon her shoulder. "Miss Hale?"

Tabitha turned and blinked. Dean Gunderson's concerned face stared back at her.

"Miss Hale, whatever your past *might* have been, do not allow those men to denigrate you. What you *were* is not who you are today. I understand that they have a single witness who will testify against you. I suggest that you withstand him to his face."

"Withstand him? Do you mean lie? You are saying I should lie?"

The old nurse's expression softened. "Nursing has come a long way, Miss Hale, but part of its history was neither noble nor honorable. Even fifty or sixty years ago, before the War between the States, most nurses were 'retired,' er, whores."

She straightened. "We need bright, committed women like yourself in nursing today. So, yes. If you have to lie to them, do so. I will support you."

Tabitha could not believe what the dean suggested. "Who is this witness?"

Dean Gunderson snorted. "A low-life reprobate with whom the school is strapped."

Tabitha turned her response over in her mind. "Is he … related to Nurse Rasmussen?"

The dean nodded.

"Is he a caretaker here? A groundskeeper?"

Dean Gunderson gave only one bob of her chin.

Tabitha sighed. Perhaps things did make sense. "Thank you, Dean Gunderson. From the bottom of my heart, I thank you for your encouragement—but I will not lie."

She turned to go, but Dean Gunderson caught her arm.

"Then what will you do?"

Tabitha surprised herself by smiling. "I will pray, Dean Gunderson. I will pray. If the God of all grace wishes to save me from this humiliation, he will. I place myself in his hands."

When Tabitha returned to her dormitory the other students were still in their afternoon practicums. Tabitha knelt by her bed and prayed,

Lord, I am calling upon you. You are my Help, my Fortress, my Defense. The waves are crashing over me, and where can I go but to you? You set my feet high upon the Rock, Christ Jesus, where the waves cannot reach me! Because you hold me, the waves cannot dash me to pieces. Speak to me, Lord! Show me what I am to do and I will obey.

She knelt there until she felt a small, slight nudge, an urge to do something. Standing, she went to the nightstand beside her bed and dug in its drawer until she found the tiny volume she sought. She then found the entry she needed and trod down the stairs to the dormitory's lobby where the telephone resided.

She lifted the receiver and placed it to her ear. "Operator? I would like to place a trunk call to Denver. Yes. My name is Tabitha Hale. Please place the charges on my account. Thank you. I have the number."

She recited the number and waited until the operator told her she was connecting the call. Tabitha heard the line ringing from far away.

"Denver office of the Pinkerton Agency. How may I help you?"

"Hello. Yes, this is Miss Tabitha Hale calling. I am a friend of Mr. Edmund O'Dell. I need to speak with him most urgently. Yes, I will wait."

Monday morning at ten o'clock, Tabitha was seated in the dean's reception area. With her were Edmund O'Dell, Marshal Jake Pounder, Mason Carpenter, and Rose Thoresen. Rose sat beside Tabitha. They held hands and prayed softly. The men with them did not sit. They shuffled on restless legs and feet. O'Dell's fingers twirled his bowler hat, and Tabitha noted the solemn, implacable lines of the men's faces.

"Thank you, Lord, for godly men," she whispered.

According to the message Tabitha had received earlier in the morning, the witness against her was already ensconced with the deans and the board of regents. When he concluded his testimony, Tabitha would be allowed to face her accuser.

Shortly after ten, the door to the dean's conference room opened and Dean Gunderson herself emerged. She surveyed the group that accompanied Tabitha with raised brows and asked, "Are these folks here for you, Miss Hale?"

"Yes, we are," Carpenter answered. He faced the senior nurse and added, "Actually, Miss Hale will not be speaking this morning. I will be speaking for her."

"I see." Dean Gunderson looked at each of them carefully, noting the determined air of the group, and her mouth curved in the ghost of a smile. "Then I wish you well. This way, please."

Carpenter led the way into the conference room. Tabitha and Rose followed behind and Marshal Pounder and O'Dell brought up the rear. Before anyone within the room could express surprise, Dean Gunderson announced, "Miss Hale is here and has brought character witnesses to speak on her behalf."

As the group took the seats pointed out to them, Tabitha noted that the arrangement of the room was the same as last time with one exception: Nurse Rasmussen perched rigidly upon a chair at the side of the room and a grizzled man slouched beside her. Tabitha recognized him immediately: He was the caretaker she had encountered weeks before, the one she feared had known her.

If he is the witness against me, then the deans and the board already know about my past, she realized in dismay. Her heart pounded against her ribs. *Lord, please help me! I pray that no shame falls upon you because of me.*

Dean Wellan responded to Dean Gunderson's announcement. "Miss Hale, will you please introduce your guests?"

Before Tabitha could respond, Carpenter stood and replied, "Good morning, Dean Wellan. You and I are already acquainted; however, Dean Gunderson and the board do not know me. My name is Mason Carpenter. May I also present Mrs. Rose Thoresen, Marshal Jake Pounder, and Mr. Edmund O'Dell, all of Denver, Miss Hale's home town."

The dean nodded. "Very well. Miss Hale, are you prepared to respond to the charges against you?"

Carpenter, still on his feet, answered, "Dean Wellan, Dean Gunderson, and members of the board of regents, Miss Hale will not be speaking today. I and my companions, Mr. O'Dell, Marshal Pounder, and Mrs. Thoresen, will be speaking for her."

"This is quite unusual, Mr. Carpenter," Dean Wellan answered.

"Perhaps. However, we have information as to the reliability of the witness against Miss Hale. As his testimony is the only voice speaking against her, you and the board should be apprised of this information."

Nurse Rasmussen sat up and called out in a shaky but strident tone, "How dare you! You have no right to speak against my brother!"

"Indeed, we do, Nurse Rasmussen. This man," and Carpenter pointed to the slouching figure next to her, "has disparaged the character of a fine young woman and an exemplary student of this school. If his testimony is to be given credence, then *his* character must also be scrutinized."

Dean Wellan studied Carpenter for several moments before saying, "Very good, Mr. Carpenter. You may continue."

Carpenter nodded. "Thank you, Dean. My companion, Mr. Pounder, is a United States marshal. Mr. O'Dell is the head of the Denver office of the Pinkerton Detective Agency. Mr. O'Dell, would you please tell us what you know of the witness?"

Carpenter sat and O'Dell stood. Tabitha thought he cut an impressive figure in his black three-piece suit. As he spoke, his voice was low but authoritative, forcing the room to quiet in order to hear him.

"Ladies and gentlemen," he said, "Arnold Rasmussen lived in Denver for many years and is well known there. Last Friday and Saturday, in my capacity as a Pinkerton agent, I interviewed a total of six individuals acquainted with Mr. Rasmussen."

O'Dell slipped his hand into his breast pocket and removed a sheaf of papers. "I have here the sworn affidavits of those six individuals. The affidavits affirm that the interviews I recorded here are true. As all of the interviews are markedly *similar* in content, I will read from only one of them before submitting the six interviews to you for your examination."

He placed the papers on the table, selected the top one, and began to read from it. "'I have known Arnie Rasmussen for more than ten years. He and I worked on the railroad together. Even though Arnie was married and had young ones at home, he spent every penny of his wages in the saloons and bawdy halls—'"

"Stop! You have *no right* to say such vile things about my brother," Nurse Rasmussen shouted.

"Nurse Rasmussen!" Dean Wellan's voice overpowered hers. "You will be seated and will not speak unless asked. Do I make myself clear?"

Nurse Rasmussen, shaking with anger from head to toe, sputtered into silence.

"Madam, I insist that you answer me," Dean Wellan commanded. "Do you understand?"

She slowly nodded. "Yes. Yes, sir."

"Be seated and do not interrupt again. You are already in jeopardy of losing your position for violating the school's disciplinary policy— regardless of your so-called justifications for doing so."

After staring her into submission, Dean Wellan nodded to O'Dell. "You may continue, sir."

O'Dell scanned the document before him. "Thank you, Dean Wellan. 'Even though Arnie was married and had young ones at home, he spent every penny of his wages in the saloons and bawdy halls. He often returned to work on Mondays hungover or still drunk and was frequently reprimanded. The railroad finally fired him. His wife took the children and moved to Cheyenne to live with her parents. Last I heard, Arnie moved back to Boulder where he came from.'"

O'Dell extended the sheaf of interviews to the closest board member. "Most of the other interviews are similar. They describe a man who drank to excess, who neglected his family, and who could not keep a job."

He nodded to Pounder. "Marshal Pounder will elaborate on my findings."

Marshal Pounder, rougher than O'Dell but no less authoritative, rose from his chair. "I received my information from Denver's chief of police: Arnold Rasmussen, age 47, has two outstanding arrest warrants in Denver for damages caused by drunk and disorderly conduct and one for failure to appear before a magistrate. I have copies of the warrants right here."

He removed some papers from his jacket and jerked his chin at the man. "When this proceeding is finished, I am going to arrest him and take him back to Denver."

Rasmussen snarled at Pounder and cursed. "You ain't takin' me nowhere!" He jumped to his feet and ran for the door, but Pounder and O'Dell were waiting for him. A scuffle ensued and ended with Rasmussen face down on the floor, his hands behind his back. It took Marshal Pounder only seconds to put Arnie Rasmussen in restraints. The crusty old marshal jerked his prisoner to his feet and walked him from the room.

Nurse Rasmussen shouted after them, "Stop! No! No! You cannot do this!" She wheeled toward Tabitha and screamed, "This is all *your* fault, you-you *whore*! You and your whoring *red hair*! He's obsessed with you and that hair of yours! *Obsessed!* Has been for years! He—"

"Nurse Rasmussen!" Dean Wellan was also on his feet.

"This is your fault!" the nurse screamed. "*Your* fault! You should never have been admitted—"

"NURSE RASMUSSEN!"

Muttering and breathing heavily, Nurse Rasmussen subsided into her seat.

Several moments elapsed, during which the board of regents watched the nurse with wary and disgusted eyes. Finally the dean cleared his throat.

"Nurse Rasmussen, your behavior has broken all rules of moral and ethical conduct. Regardless of the terms of your uncle's endowment to this school, you are dismissed from your position. I am certain your uncle's attorneys will not dispute my ruling."

Nurse Rasmussen pulled her lips into a tight, flat line but said nothing. She shot a single baleful look at Tabitha and followed her brother from the room.

Dean Wellan motioned for Tabitha's defense to continue.

Carpenter addressed the Deans and the board of regents again. "I would like to have you hear from Mrs. Thoresen at this time."

Slowly, her legs a little shaky, Rose stood to her feet. Tabitha was grieved to note the stiffness of Rose's muscles and the new lines upon her face. But when Rose opened her mouth, she was anything but shaky or weak. It seemed to Tabitha that she grew taller and a soft glow settled upon her.

"I do not presume to speak for Miss Hale or to her experiences," Rose said, her voice filled with the calm composure known well to those who loved her.

"However, I can relate my own experiences with Miss Hale, and you may draw inferences from them. I live in Denver where I manage a home for women who have been rescued from slavery."

She leveled her steady gray eyes upon those seated at the table, seeing the shock or disbelief on their faces.

"Yes, I do mean slavery."

Her chin dipped to affirm her words. "The women who live in our home were coerced into lives of . . . horrible, unspeakable servitude. Some were lured to Denver or nearby towns by offers of 'legitimate' employment. However, when they arrived, they were met and taken captive by unscrupulous men and, sadly, even those of their own gender. Other girls in our home committed youthful misjudgments or made, perhaps, a single wrong choice—and were, as a consequence of their error, ensnared by similar ungodly individuals.

"At Palmer House, we rescue women. We rescue women as young as *ages thirteen and fourteen* from the clutches of those who beat them, starved them, and debased them until they capitulated to their captor's demands. We rescue women who wish to escape from such a life."

The soft glow about Rose grew, and Tabitha shrank back, in awe.

"We tell these women, these lost girls, of the love, mercy, and grace found in Jesus Christ. We show them from the Bible how the blood of Jesus cleanses us from all sin. *All* sin. We point to the Bible where it reads, 'Therefore if any man be in Christ, he is a *new creature*: old things are passed away; behold, *all* things are become new.'"

She again peered into the eyes of the men and one woman lining the conference room table. Dean Gunderson's eyes were moist and she would not meet Rose's penetrating appraisal. Neither would several of the men.

At last she said, "I wish to ask each of you a question. Are you a Christian?"

Reluctant faces turned her way, and she forced them to acknowledge her. "Are you?" she repeated. She held each look until she received a nod or shrug of response.

"If—*if*—you call yourself a Christian, then you must admit to the Bible passages I have quoted. No one who has been *made new* by the blood of Christ is what they were before. That former person is gone, and God says that he remembers their sins no more."

No individual in the room moved except, perhaps, to blink moist or conscience-stricken eyes.

Rose lifted her chin just a little, but the power around her, touching them, was palpable. Tabitha found that her cheeks were wet, streaked with salty moisture, and her fears had washed away with her tears.

"If *God* has forgiven and forgotten the sins of these women," Rose whispered, "who are we to shame them?"

Having finished her statement, Rose fumbled for the arm of her chair, and Tabitha helped steady her as she sank into her seat. The only sound for several moments was the clearing of throats and a few surreptitious sniffs.

All eyes focused on Dean Wellan. "Thank you, Mrs. Thoresen," he murmured. He turned to Tabitha. "Miss Hale, if you and your friends would leave us for a few minutes, we will discuss our findings. You may wait in the antechamber until we call you back."

One of the board's members, a short rounded man, sputtered an objection. "But-but, Dean Wellan, we still have not heard Miss Hale's response to the charge against her!"

Dean Wellan and the rest of the board glared at him. "Clark Framson, I have always considered you an obtuse man, but I had no idea you were this dull-witted. I may have to recommend a vote of confidence to determine your competence to continue as a regent."

Growls of affirmation issued from the other board members, and the unfortunate Mr. Framson found himself in disfavor, alone in his objection.

"The charge against Miss Hale has been levied by an unreliable witness," Dean Wellan barked. "Has anyone other testimony against her? No? The charge is dismissed."

"Hear, hear," one member muttered.

"Please be excused, Miss Hale, until the board determines how to remedy your scholastic standing."

In a daze, Tabitha found Mason Carpenter escorting her from the room.

An hour later, Tabitha was recalled to the conference room. Her friends took seats behind her and listened to the dean pronounce the board's findings.

"Miss Hale, I regret to inform you that, through no fault of yours, you will not be able to graduate with your class next month."

Tabitha nodded once in silent acceptance.

"We will, however, allow you to take your written exams. I have no doubt that you will pass them with exceptional marks."

Tabitha's countenance lightened a little. "Thank you, sir."

Dean Wellan lightly tapped a pen on his desk. "As a respected institution of nursing, it would be, er, *understandable* if we wished to sweep this unfortunate blemish to our school's reputation under the rug as quickly as possible. We could offer you the option of returning this summer to work your incomplete rotations and, at the end of your rotations, award you your degree.

"If that is your choice, we will make arrangements accordingly—and we will pay your expenses while you do so. Unfortunately, you would miss commencement and leave school with little fanfare."

He eyed Tabitha. "Personally, I feel that would be a shame."

"Sir?" Tabitha had already resigned herself to such a solution.

"I say it would be a shame, particularly given all you have battled and overcome in your life."

There was no missing his allusion to her past life. Tabitha blushed but fought to keep her expression placid.

"When you graduate, Miss Hale, I wish you to celebrate the event with all the pomp and circumstance such an accomplishment warrants. You deserve nothing short of a full graduation ceremony and the receipt of your cap and pin with all of the public honor attached to that ceremony."

Tabitha looked down. "It is kind of you to say so, sir."

He nodded. "Yes, and that is why—and I hope you will agree—I do not wish you to select the option I have just outlined. Instead, I wish you to return to our school for the fall term."

Tabitha opened her mouth, and the dean held up his hand to hold off her protest.

"Miss Hale, the board of regents and I extend our sincerest apologies to you for the ordeal you have undergone in our school. We cannot make up to you for the hardships you have patiently suffered, but we can attempt to make amends."

He cleared his throat. "We would like to extend an offer to you that will, we hope, soften the blow of another year's wait until you graduate. If you accept our offer, we intend to create a new position here at the school, one of Head Proctor, and offer this position to you."

Tabitha blinked. "Sir?"

"The number of students who fail or drop out during their freshman year is disturbing—particularly if, as the Red Cross suggests, many more nurses will be needed to serve worldwide by the time this fall's incoming class graduates.

"As Head Proctor, you would be tasked with mentoring new students with the goal of preventing them from failing or becoming otherwise discouraged. Your job would be to ensure, as far as lies within your scope and abilities, that our next freshman class remains intact."

Tabitha's thoughts were whirling. *But how would I pay for another year? Surely the women's society that provides my scholarship would balk at an extra year?*

Her mind stopped cold when he added, "This would be a salaried position, Miss Hale. You would be a member of the staff. You would pay no tuition or board; rather, you would be paid while completing your rotations and functioning as Head Proctor. When you graduate, you will have a year of valuable work experience to add to your nursing credentials.

"In the spring when the class graduates, you will stand at the head of it. What do you say, Miss Hale?"

Tabitha turned and looked from Rose to Carpenter for help. Rose's tearful smile and Carpenter's grin told her that they approved. She had only one more concern.

"May I ask a clarifying question, Dean Wellan?"

"Of course, Miss Hale."

"You mentioned that the Red Cross may be asking for more nurses. Could you elaborate, please?"

"Ah, yes." He fiddled with his spectacles a moment. "Wars and rumors of wars, Miss Hale. Prognosticators and scaremongers within the government see a buildup toward war in Europe. They may have war *there*, but I sincerely doubt that we, the United States, would involve ourselves in a distant regional squabble. However, should war break out, the Red Cross organization predicts that the world will face a critical shortage of skilled nurses."

He placed his spectacles on his nose. "The government has said nothing officially, of course, but we do not wish to be found wanting, should the call come."

"I see, sir." Tabitha thought for a moment. "One further question, sir?"

He inclined his head.

"If I were to accept your generous offer, would I be permitted to take advanced courses in specialties of my choice?"

"I do not see why not. What specialty areas are you considering?"

Tabitha nodded. "In the areas of contagious sicknesses and traumatic wound care, sir."

His brows arched. "Very ambitious selections, Miss Hale. May I ask if you have a personal reason for studying contagious sicknesses?"

Her throat closed up as she tried to speak. She threw a look for help toward Rose, who nodded her encouragement. After a few swallows, Tabitha whispered, "A dear friend of mine, of ours—" she indicated her friends from Denver, "passed away due to complications from influenza." Her voice stuck and would say nothing further.

"Miss Hale nursed our entire household through that influenza, Dean Wellan," Rose supplied. "With no training except what our family physician provided over the telephone, Tabitha introduced strict protocols that kept others from falling ill. She cared for all who did fall sick. We knew then that she had a call to nursing. However, we lost one dear member of our family during that ordeal."

Dean Wellan sighed. "As hard as we try and work, we always lose some patients." He nodded to Tabitha. "I give my permission to your request. I will speak to the dean of the medical school. The courses you suggest would be taken with graduate nurses and student physicians."

"Then, sir, I accept your offer, with thanks."

They both rose and Tabitha shook Dean Wellan's extended hand.

Almost as an afterthought, he exclaimed, "Dear me. I almost forgot."

He found the paper he had tucked into the sleeve of his ink blotter and handed it to her. "It appears you have not been home in quite some time. A five-day pass, Miss Hale. Please return by the date noted. You will be on the work schedule for the next day and will be allowed to take your final exams at the end of the month. Have a nice visit with your family. You deserve it."

Tabitha, Carpenter, Rose, and O'Dell left the dean's conference room in silence. Tabitha was overcome and stared at the pass.

"Five days!" she murmured.

"Will you pack and come home with us, dear?" Rose inquired.

"What? Oh, yes! How wonderful! I will see everyone again—it has been such a long time."

"We should get on the road as quickly as we can," Carpenter suggested. "Although it is still early afternoon, we will likely be late for dinner."

He took her arm and they walked ahead of Rose and O'Dell. He was anxious to have a private word with Tabitha.

"I must say something to you, Tabitha; I must confess something that lies heavy upon my heart."

"What is it, Mr. Carpenter?"

"You told me on Christmas day as we ate dinner at the Palindrome Hotel—a year and a half ago!—that you were working all nights. I knew it wasn't right! I could see how exhausted you were. I even decided to look into your situation—and I could have easily asked Dean Wellan to explain."

He sighed and squeezed her arm. "And yet I promptly forgot. Even when it crossed my mind later, I did nothing. It is my fault that your circumstances were not rectified in time to ensure that you graduated with your class."

Tabitha was silent for many steps. "I accept your apology, Mr. Carpenter; however, I do not fault you, even a little. No, I believe God has been working his will in my life through this difficult time."

"Can you tell me what you mean, Tabs?"

A smile curved her mouth. "The Book of James tells us to 'count it all joy' when we suffer various temptations. Well, I have been tempted many times. I have been tempted to give up—but God would not allow me to. I have been tempted to lose my temper—but my Lord forbade me. I have been tempted to strike out at Nurse Rasmussen. I have been tempted to hold what she has done against her and even tempted to give in to hatred and unforgiveness. In all these trials, he has shown me that I cannot call myself a Christian and live in such a manner.

"And so, I see that through all these difficulties, God has been working, working to refine *my character*. My unruly temper is my greatest enemy—and now I realize how necessary the refining of my temperament is. I believe, as it says in the Book of James, that these trials have worked God's purposes *in me* so that I will be whole, complete, and lacking nothing.

> *"Knowing this, that the trying of*
> *your faith worketh patience.*
> *But let patience have her perfect work,*
> *that ye may be perfect and entire,*
> *wanting nothing."*

Carpenter squeezed her arm again, signaling that he understood.

As they walked, Tabitha added, "And I perceive, although not clearly yet, that the Lord has a plan for me, a plan that requires a refined heart and character. I cannot wait to discover what that plan might be!"

He grinned down on her. "I so appreciate your absolute confidence in God's guidance, Miss Hale. Yes, I, too, cannot wait to see his plan for you unveiled!"

They arrived at the walkway to Tabitha's dormitory. Rose and O'Dell caught up with them. Tabitha was still thinking of the coming year and her new role in the school.

"It will be a great responsibility," she whispered, more to herself than to any of them.

"It will be a great honor, Tabitha," Rose assured her.

O'Dell and Carpenter agreed.

"I have only one thing to say against Dean Wellan's proposal," Carpenter said.

They looked for him to expound.

"It will keep Miss Hale *here*, in Boulder, for another year. *That*, my friends, I am not fond of. Not at all."

They laughed together with good humor and tripped down the walk to the dormitory's front doors, Rose on O'Dell's arm, and Tabitha on Carpenter's.

CHAPTER 14

FALL 1913

Tabitha sat on the platform with the staff nurses and waited for their audience to settle. She felt stiff and uncomfortable under the speculative glances of the incoming freshman class.

Lord, I do not really belong up here—I am not an instructor; I am scarcely more than a student myself and still wear a blue-banded cap.

Then she remembered. *I told Mr. Carpenter that the Lord had a special purpose to my being here. I must look for that purpose in all I do this year.*

She took a deep breath and sat a little straighter in her chair as Dean Gunderson stood and moved to the lectern. "Ladies, if I may have your attention, please." The shuffling and whispers died. Forty nervous young women looked back at her.

Not all of them are nervous, Tabitha noted. *Some are as excited to begin their training as I was.*

Dean Gunderson, her expression serene, addressed the incoming students. "Good morning to you all and welcome. Before we begin, if any of you have chewing gum in your mouth or on your person, please proceed immediately to the trash bins at the back of the hall to dispose of it."

Amidst a low grumbling across the hall, several girls jumped to their feet and hurried toward the trash bins. Tabitha watched one young woman swallow (with difficulty) the gum in her mouth. A little knot of three girls near the front frowned and murmured complaints among themselves. Their chomping jaws slowed to a stop, but they remained seated. One of the girls made a face; her friends giggled behind their hands.

Dean Gunderson may have taken note of the varied responses, but she gave no sign of it. Instead, she continued, "Ladies, you are here to become nurses, and your goal is an excellent one. Nursing is a vocation of service to humanity, a dedication of one's entire self to the healing care of all peoples and their physical needs.

"However, the work of nursing is hard, demanding, and inglorious. The hours are long, and—*I must assure you*—the discipline is rigorous. If—" now she bent a penetrating look upon the three girls who had grumbled the most, singling out their leader— "*if* you find the discipline of following our rules too discommoding, please do yourselves the kindness of acknowledging that nursing is not for you and withdraw today. We have other candidates standing by should you choose to . . . drop out."

She stared at the offenders and waited. Two of the girls swallowed their gum on the spot. The third slid to the aisle and trotted toward the trash bin.

Dean Gunderson delayed until the chastened student returned to her seat and lowered her head. "Thank you. As I was saying, nursing is a pursuit of great worth. That said, in return for your dedication, you will receive neither riches nor acclaim. Your reward will not be in the recognition of others but within yourselves, in knowing that you have served well.

"By your enrollment in our school, you have stated that you wish to don this mantle, the heavy responsibility of a nursing professional. I commend you for this first step, but it is only the first step of many to come.

"Your training, which commences today, will test your resolve in every manner and at every juncture. Do you have an unshakable calling? Will you endure? Will you stand the test? That remains to be seen.

"I urge you, then, to gird up the loins of your mind. I counsel you to hold this selfless goal in front of your eyes and seek no other end or ambition but the one that is before you today."

Tabitha thrilled to Dean Gunderson's words. *For you, Lord! Let all my efforts and service be for you!*

As the senior nurse continued to challenge the incoming class, Tabitha's attention strayed. She lost herself in the earnest faces turned toward Dean Gunderson, many of them shining with excitement, others troubled or uncertain, some even fearful.

My job will be to counsel and encourage these young women, to help them overcome when they are struggling.

Tabitha swallowed at the immensity of the responsibility before her. *Lord, I will not be able to do this without your help. I thank you that you have given me your Holy Spirit, who is my Counselor and Helper. I can do what you have called me to do, if I lean upon, if I rely on you.*

Tabitha's attention returned to the podium. Dean Gunderson began introducing the staff and eventually made her way to Tabitha, the last in line.

Tabitha flushed as the attention of all present turned upon her. She tried not to shrivel under the scrutiny of so many eyes.

"Miss Hale is the school's freshman proctor. She is, herself, a student near to graduation; however, she is near the top of her class and has earned the respect and esteem of the staff and administration.

"As proctor, Miss Hale's primary responsibility will be to ensure, to the best of her ability, that not one of you falters or fails. She will monitor your progress and will advise and counsel you as needed. Her hours of availability will be posted on her office door. Please take advantage of them; you would do well to heed her guidance and instruction."

Tabitha took her seat again and sat tall and still. The meeting went on for a while longer, with various staff members setting out the school rules and policies.

As she listened with only half of her interest, Tabitha was drawn to a young woman on the far right of the auditorium. She was fair and slender, perhaps even slight. It seemed to Tabitha that the girl had intentionally sat alone, for several unoccupied seats were between her and the next student in the row.

She hadn't realized she was staring so intently until the girl nodded and smiled a shy acknowledgment. Tabitha started and then smiled back. Something about the girl resonated in Tabitha's heart.

When the meeting ended, Tabitha followed Dean Gunderson's instructions to mingle with the students and form some initial attachments. She did not have to try hard: The eager students lined up to introduce themselves and ask her questions. Tabitha tried her best to greet each of them with grace, but their trusting, practically adoring looks almost undid her.

Goodness, she sighed inside. *This will take some getting used to. They act as though I am the answer to all their problems—when I am struggling just to learn their names!*

Tabitha extended her hand to the next girl in line. "Good morning. Welcome to our school."

"Good morning, Miss Hale. I am Claire Silverstine."

There she was, that smiling, wan-looking girl, the one who had sat apart from the rest of the class.

Tabitha studied her. "Good morning, Miss Silverstine. I am pleased to meet you."

"Thank you! The pleasure is mine." She looked aside for a moment and then smiled and turned back to Tabitha. "I am not a freshman, actually. I had to drop out for health reasons at the end of my freshman year, so I am a second-year student. Do you remember me? We had a class together—Dr. Monroe's anatomy."

Tabitha frowned and tried to place her. "No ... that is, perhaps? Have you lost a great deal of weight, Miss Silverstine?"

"Yes! You do remember me, then. Indeed, I was a bit on the chubby side then, but I have lost all my 'baby fat' as my brother calls it. And then some."

"But are you quite well now? Your stamina has returned?" Tabitha examined her more closely, a little concerned.

"I have recovered from my illness, yes, although my strength is not yet what it once was. We shall see. God willing, I shall rise to meet expectations."

"Please come see me if you find yourself struggling—or if you just wish to talk over your progress," Tabitha offered. "Although you are not a freshman, I would be happy to help in any way … even pray with you."

"I knew it," Claire smiled wider. "I just knew you were a Christian when our eyes met earlier. Thank you. I will most certainly take advantage of your kind offer."

She nodded a goodbye, still smiling. As Claire turned away, Tabitha smiled back and reached to greet the next student.

The term was vastly different than any previous term Tabitha had experienced. In some regards it was easier; in other respects, Tabitha felt stretched to the breaking point.

Rather than a narrow bed in the open upper floor of one of the two freshman dormitories, Tabitha now had a small first-floor bedroom. Her room was adjacent to a tiny office, and the office had its own door that opened to the dormitory's common area.

No sooner had she posted her office hours upon the office door—two hours each afternoon—than the signup sheet for each day began filling. Students could request time in increments of fifteen minutes but no more than thirty in a single session. Almost immediately, every minute was filled for the next two weeks.

Tabitha's schedule presented new challenges, too. She worked her assigned hospital shifts in the evenings, with Dean Gunderson herself double-checking that Tabitha's required obstetric, pediatric, and surgical hours were satisfied first.

The two specialty classes Tabitha had requested met in the mornings. That left late mornings and early afternoons for Tabitha to study before she unlocked her office for the scheduled appointments. The appointments themselves opened her eyes to the diverse situations or issues confronting new students, problems that the students often viewed as insurmountable obstacles.

In that first week Tabitha realized that she also needed to allot sufficient time to tutor flagging freshmen. To that end, she established a study hall before breakfast. Then there were occasions where she needed to meet with Dean Gunderson for advice on how to address a particular student's needs.

Fortunately, Tabitha had only the two classes. *And only because I insisted on taking them*, she recalled with wry semi-regret.

The first class Tabitha attended each morning was on public healthcare nursing, including the prevention and containment of contagious diseases. With the exception of herself, all the students were licensed, seasoned nurses.

If that class were not sufficient to illustrate Tabitha's unusual position in the school, her second course, traumatic wound treatment, did the trick: The class was composed entirely of second-year medical students—all males. As the only woman amid the dozen young men, her classmates' pointed stares and whispers made her discomfort worse.

Now I know what a lone grasshopper in a crowded chicken coop must feel like. She snorted to herself and shook her head.

Her discomfort remained until a second woman breezed into the room. Spying Tabitha, she slid into the seat next to her and held out her hand. "Cathy Worth," she murmured. Her dark hair was cropped close to her head; her manner was brusque but pleasant.

"Tabitha Hale," Tabitha whispered back. "Am I glad to meet you! I thought I would be the only nurse in this class."

Cathy, fixing Tabitha with a cool, detached eye, replied, "You still are. I am a medical student."

"Truly? Why, how wonderful," Tabitha enthused—a little in awe.

"Yes, I am glad to be studying to be a doctor, Miss Hale. However, I would not describe the *experience* as wonderful." Cathy graced Tabitha with a mock smile. "You will see as class goes along."

And Tabitha did see, beginning that first morning, the subtle and not-so-subtle jabs aimed at Cathy—and at herself. Even the male physician teaching the class, Doctor Cranston, managed to differentiate between Tabitha as a student nurse specializing in wound care and Cathy as a *medical student*. His emphasis established his point of view: Nursing was for women; doctoring was for men. And, of course, nursing—and women—were both below doctoring.

Cathy's male counterparts, for the most part, ignored Tabitha, but they glared at Cathy with undisguised dislike.

"They see me as a threat," Cathy mentioned to Tabitha, "because I occupy a spot another man was refused."

"But surely you earned your place," Tabitha sputtered.

"Oh, indeed, I did. That only makes them more defensive."

Cathy, however, did not seem fazed by her treatment. She immersed herself in the learning, and Tabitha followed her example.

Claire Silverstine came to Tabitha's office at the end of the first week.

"What can I help you with, Miss Silverstine?" Tabitha did not like how frail the student appeared.

"I am not sleeping well, Miss Hale. If I could sleep properly, I know I would regain my strength eventually..." Her sentence drifted off, unfinished.

Tabitha remembered the deep fatigue of the past two years. "Is anything in particular keeping you from sleep, Miss Silverstine?"

Claire shook her head. "I tend to worry. I know it is wrong to worry, but I worry that I will become ill again and be sent home—and those thoughts keep me from falling asleep. Even when I do fall asleep, I have restless, disturbed dreams. When I wake up, I cannot get back to sleep."

Tabitha thought for a minute. "Is there an aspect of nursing that particularly interests you, Miss Silverstine?"

"Oh, yes. I hope to work with ill children. My family has a little farm in Wyoming, and I always nursed the sick animals; my folks say I have a way with animals, but I love children even more. I might not be strong enough to work in a hospital, but I could care for an ailing child in his or her home. I know that families with sickly children need good nursing care—and I could tell them about Jesus at the same time."

Claire's face came alive as she described her goal.

Tabitha noted the transformation and replied, "I grew up on a small farm, too, Miss Silverstine. May I make a suggestion?"

"Of course! Please do."

"I would like to suggest that before you retire each night, you lay this dream of nursing children before the Lord. Tell him how you desire to serve him in the capacity of a nurse. Then lay your worries before him. Scripture admonishes us as Christians to *cast your care upon him, for he cares for you.* If our great God wishes you to serve him in nursing, then will he not empower you to do what he has called you to?"

Claire's eyes brimmed with tears. "That is it, exactly. I must give my nursing to him—if my call is *his* call, then I cannot fail. Thank you."

"Shall we pray before you go, Miss Silverstine?"

"Oh, yes."

They bent their heads together and lifted their concerns to God. As they finished, Tabitha prayed aloud, "Lord, in all things, we are yours. You have promised peace to us who keep our minds stayed upon you. Thank you for good sleep for Claire this very night. We pray in the name of Jesus, your Son and our Savior. Amen."

The following week, Tabitha nodded as Cathy Worth took the seat beside her in their shared class. "Good morning."

"'Morning." Cathy hid a yawn behind her hand.

Doctor Cranston called for attention. "Gentlemen. *And ladies.* If you would be so good as to follow me, we will make rounds. This morning I will demonstrate the practice of debridement on a particularly interesting case."

He opened the classroom door and the students filed out behind him. They crossed the campus mall in groups of two or three and entered the hospital through the back entrance. Tabitha and Cathy brought up the rear of the line of students.

The patient in question had a severe case of cellulitis (a bacterial skin infection) within the dermis of his calf. Tabitha slanted her eyes at the young, inexperienced medical students and was amused to note their horrified or disgusted expressions—and more than a few swallows of nausea.

"We must remove the necrotized tissue to prevent gangrene, gentlemen. Who will volunteer to assist me?"

"I will, doctor." Cathy Worth and Tabitha had spoken at once.

Doctor Cranston frowned at the two women but nodded. "Very well. Miss Hale, please assist."

By that, Tabitha knew he meant her to assist him as a *nurse*, the proper woman's role. She was astounded when Cathy suggested, "Perhaps Miss Hale could assist me, sir?"

Doctor Cranston, still frowning, sputtered, "Really! I wonder that you have the skill for this delicate of a procedure, Miss Worth."

"My father is a physician. I have done such a procedure under his tutelage several times, doctor." Cathy was respectful and matter-of-fact, and Tabitha admired her even more for her composure.

Under the disapproving glare of some of their classmates, Cathy and Tabitha worked together to debride and clean the patient's infected calf. Tabitha assisted Cathy as she would any other doctor, but she also spoke as they worked, providing a running commentary for the rest of the class, describing the instruments and steps as Cathy performed them.

When she happened to look up, she was gratified to see that the male students were too engrossed in the procedure to be shooting Cathy and Tabitha dirty looks. Even Doctor Cranston nodded in grudging approval as Cathy and Tabitha finished up.

"Well! Hmm. Just so. Very good, Miss Worth, Miss Hale." Clearing his throat he addressed the male students. "It seems that Miss Worth and Miss Hale have established the standard you must come up to, gentlemen. See that you do."

Tabitha was pleased to see the male students studying Cathy, some with respect, a few with guarded speculation. Cathy and Tabitha exchanged careful glances, and neither of them changed expressions, but Tabitha sighed with relief and pleasure.

It was a good day. It would be a good year, too.

ᴄHAPTER 15

JUNE 1914

Tabitha peeked out from behind the heavy velvet curtain and scanned the packed auditorium. The room was too full for her to be able to locate her friends, but she knew they were there.

Today was the day. After all of her hard work, she was, at last, finishing nursing school. For a moment she allowed the accusations, harassment, and intimidation of her second and third year of school to intrude. Then she set them aside and closed the door on that difficult period. For good.

I have no room in my heart for the pain or offenses of the past, she told herself. *Today is for celebrating. Today I am graduating!*

"And not at the bottom of your class, either, Tabs," she whispered. No, the extra year she spent tutoring and coaching and the extra year of increasing responsibilities had honed her own knowledge and nursing skills. She held the second rank in today's graduating class.

O Lord! You always work things around for my good—and for your glory, she rejoiced.

She walked toward her place in the line, passing Claire as she did so. Claire was toward the head of the line, one of the undergrads carrying the school's banner. They grinned at each other before Tabitha slid into her position in line and settled.

All the graduating nurses were dressed in their best uniforms and capes. They had arranged their hair to receive the caps that would be placed upon their heads in this solemn ceremony—caps with the wide black bands signifying their status as nurses.

Strains of "Land of Hope and Glory," a march that was becoming the standard for commencements, filled the hall. The line began to move.

Dean Gunderson smiled into Tabitha's eyes when she fastened the cap on Tabitha's head and placed the nursing pin in her palm. "Well done, Nurse Hale," she whispered.

Tabitha thought her heart would burst. *Oh, thank you, Lord! Thank you for this dream becoming a reality*, she sang within herself. *Truly, you have given me beauty for ashes and turned my mourning into joy.*

When the ceremony ended, the graduates filed from the hall and waited on the lawn for their families to join them. Tabitha did not have to wait long before Rose, Joy, and Breona enveloped her in their arms.

"'Twas easy findin' ye in th' crowd," Breona grinned, "yer hair bein' a beacon fer us, so t' speak!" She and Tabitha hugged with the fierce love and respect they shared.

"Oh, my dear, we are so proud," Rose murmured into her ear. "Everyone from home sends their congratulations—but of course you shall see them all soon and they will be able to tell you themselves."

"We are going to have a *very* large party for you when we get back home," Joy added as she hugged Tabitha. Tabitha was pleased to see Joy looking so well, so rested. And then she spied Edmund O'Dell standing not far away.

"Why, Mr. O'Dell! I must say I am surprised to see you! I am delighted, of course, but I cannot believe you came all this way just for my—" Tabitha's words were cut short as she watched Joy slip her arm into O'Dell's. They looked into each other's faces and smiled, then smiled together at Tabitha, both a little self-conscious.

"Well! What is this?" Tabitha demanded.

She would have put her hands on her hips, but Breona and Rose each took one of Tabitha's arms and began pulling her away, steering her through the crowd.

"That, my dear Tabitha," Rose chuckled, "is an engagement."

Tabitha craned her head around to stare at the moonstruck couple who were following behind. "An engagement! Oh, my!"

"Yis," Breona laughed. "'tis weddin' bells in January we'll b' hearin'!"

"Oh, but I am so happy for them!"

Tabitha wanted to stop and offer them her congratulations. She tried to turn, but Rose and Breona would not release her arms. They seemed intent on pulling her along toward an unseen destination.

"Why, Miss Rose, where are we going at such a fast clip? And Breona, did you come without your husband?"

Rose and Breona only laughed and would not answer. They steered Tabitha with a determined purpose toward the street until Tabitha saw a familiar automobile ahead of them and the happy, smiling faces of Carpenter and Banks standing on the curb.

Carpenter's arms held a wealth of flowers enveloped in tissue paper. He walked the last few steps to greet her. "Congratulations, Tabs," he whispered.

As he placed the flowers in her arms, their sweet and heady fragrance flooded Tabitha's senses. She inhaled deeply and reveled in the splendor of dark rose and blushing pink stargazer lilies, white Easter lilies, and the delicate tendrils of white spider chrysanthemums nestled in a bed of green fronds.

"Thank you, Mr. Carpenter," she whispered back. They stared at each other for a long moment and then he bent toward her and placed a chaste kiss upon her cheek.

"I am so very, very proud of you, Tabs."

Tabitha flushed with pleasure. "I value your esteem more than you know, Mr. Carpenter." She looked past him toward the grinning Banks and waggled her fingers at him. He rocked back on his heels and grinned larger.

"I have a bit of a surprise for you, Tabs," Carpenter added. He looked down. "I hope you will not be too shocked; I pray you will receive my gift in the spirit of true friendship."

Tabitha's brows arched. "Shocked?"

He nodded, first at her and then, turning to Banks, nodded at him. Banks opened the door of the car and handed out a faded middle-aged woman from the back seat. She was followed by a stooped, gray-headed man whom Banks assisted to stand.

The couple was dressed modestly; they seemed overwhelmed, though, out of their depth—until the woman caught sight of Tabitha. Her tired face lit with joy.

"Mama?" Tabitha said the word before her mind could grasp it. Images from her childhood flooded in—she and her mother pumping water and gathering eggs together, her mother's face singing over her at bedtime.

"Mama?" She tore her eyes from the woman and fastened them on the man. "Daddy?"

They started toward her, her father leaning heavily upon Banks. Tabitha shoved the flowers at Carpenter and ran to meet them.

"And once again ... I am only chopped liver," he muttered, but his eyes misted over as he said it. With glad satisfaction he watched Tabitha and her mother embrace and then Tabitha take her father's hand, kiss its palm, and press it to her cheek.

Rose Thoresen placed her hand upon Carpenter's arm. "Well done, Mr. Carpenter. I have prayed for God's timing for this reunion. Thank you."

He tucked her hand into the crook of his elbow and included Breona as she drew near and put her arm about Rose's waist. "Her father is not well, I am afraid. I had not realized it until they arrived. I took him 'round straightaway to my doctor. He prescribed a medication that makes his chest easier, but ..."

He shook his head. "I am glad they are here, that Tabitha will have some time with them."

"Will they stay, do you think?" Rose asked. "Will they stay in Denver to be near her?"

He shook his head. "I think not. Tabitha may be able to persuade them otherwise, but they insisted to me that they will remain a fortnight and then return to their farm."

Joy and O'Dell came close to hear their conversation. "Are those Tabitha's parents, Mama?" Joy asked.

"Yes. Mr. Carpenter brought them here from Texas as a surprise for Tabitha."

"Oh, my!" Joy did not want to stare at the tearful scene taking place a few yards away. She stole another hasty look and turned her back to them.

Rose asked, "Could we make up a room for them at Palmer House, Breona? What do you think, Joy? Tabitha will want them near her during their visit."

"Yis, a'course," Breona agreed. Joy nodded, too.

"Then we would love to have them at Palmer House the remainder of their stay," Rose suggested to Carpenter.

"That would be the best arrangement for Tabitha," he admitted. "Yes. If they are willing, I will have Banks move their belongings tomorrow—not that they brought much with them."

Breona noticed a young girl watching Tabitha and her parents. The girl was slight, pale and fair. A wistful expression played over her face.

"Ah. One moment, if ye please," she said to her friends. She marched over to the girl.

"Hallo. Air ye bein' Miss Tabitha's friend, Claire?"

The girl started and then smiled. "Yes. Tabitha and I are friends from school. And you are?"

"M' name tis bein' Breona Carmichael." Breona flashed a grin at the girl and offered her hand. "Ony friend o' Tabitha ist a friend o' mine."

"Breona! She has told me so much about you! I am Claire Silverstine."

"Aye, an' Claire tis bein' a foine Irish name!" Breona chortled. "Coome, Claire. Coome meet Tabitha's other friends, eh?"

Breona escorted Claire over to Carpenter, Rose, Joy, and O'Dell and made introductions.

"You did not graduate this year?" Joy asked when names and pleasantries had been exchanged.

"No, Tabitha is a year ahead of me," Claire replied. "I should have graduated this year, but I had to interrupt my studies for a year over health reasons.

"When I returned to school I was still a bit weak and sluggish. Tabitha befriended me and helped me to regain my footing and go forward at a steady pace."

She shrugged, that gesture a little sad. "I shall miss her dreadfully now that she has finished. But I shall graduate next year, God willing,"

"In the three and a half years Tabitha has been at this school, you are the only real friend she made," Rose murmured. "When she told us about you in her letters, we loved you from afar." She took Claire's hands and squeezed them. Joy and Breona added their agreement.

"Do all of you live at Palmer House?" the girl asked. "Tabitha has told me so much about it. She considers you her family."

"Mr. O'Dell and Mr. Carpenter do not live at Palmer House, of course," Joy replied. "Breona did live at Palmer House. She is still our housekeeper, but she is a married woman now, and lives with her husband, Isaac Carmichael. Mr. Carmichael is our pastor," Joy added.

Soon Tabitha waved them over and introduced her parents to them.

"And this is my dear friend, Claire," she told her mother.

Tabitha's mother shook Claire's hand, bobbed her head, but said nothing. It was obvious to all that she was more than a little overcome.

"Tabitha, perhaps we should have something to eat and then get on the road," Carpenter suggested.

"Yes. I am all packed."

"If you will lead the way, Banks and I will bring down your things and put them into the trunk. And perhaps Miss Silverstine would accompany us to lunch?"

"Are you able to come, Claire?" Tabitha asked, glowing with the happiness of this day.

"Oh, yes! I would love to. The term is over and I am on furlough now." She made a little face. "Able to leave campus without permission, you know."

"Excellent," Carpenter proclaimed.

They filled a long table at a local tea room and ordered soup, a selection of sandwiches, and cake. Tabitha seated her mother on one side of her and Claire on the other. Carpenter seated Tabitha's father across from his wife and daughter and took the seat next to him.

Tabitha could scarcely believe she was surrounded by so many of her loved ones. She kept glancing at Joy and O'Dell, watching how they tipped their heads toward each other when speaking. She sighed in contentment. *Their new love is so beautiful, Lord.*

"Tabitha," her mother asked, "what will ya do now that ya are a real nurse?"

Tabitha smiled. "There is a position waiting for me at the hospital in Denver, but I have a month's holiday before I start. I hardly know how I shall spend an entire month, though. I have not had any time for my own devices in three years." She laughed and the others joined her.

"What kind of nursing will you be doing when you take up your position?" Rose asked.

"Ah. I will be working in the hospital's emergency services to begin with. However, I have a keen desire to work in public health, in disease prevention. When a suitable position in public health nursing opens, I hope to be accepted."

"And you, Miss Silverstine? What kind of nursing appeals to you?" Rose asked.

Claire ducked her head. "I love working with children, ma'am. I hope to do private pediatric nursing when I graduate."

"What will you do over your furlough?" Joy inquired. "Where do you call home?"

"I am from a little farming community in Wyoming, ma'am," Claire replied. "My brother will be here tomorrow to fetch me home."

After lunch, the group sorted themselves into the two vehicles—Rose, Breona, Joy, and O'Dell in one automobile; Carpenter, Claire, Tabitha, and her parents in the other.

When Banks assisted Claire to disembark at her dormitory, Tabitha got out with her and they embraced.

"I shall miss you so much, Tabitha," Claire whispered.

"Until we meet again, sister of my heart," Tabitha murmured in return. "Remember to write?"

"I shall," Claire promised.

The thirty-mile drive from Boulder to Denver took three hours and involved one changed tire. "Someday the roads will allow us to travel at higher speeds and someone will invent automobile tires that do not blow out over every little rock or hole in the road," Carpenter groused amiably. In a soft voice he added, "In any event, I shall be glad not to make this tedious drive again for a time."

"Not as glad as I shall be," Tabitha laughed in whispered response. "I do not care to *ever* make this journey again!"

She smiled at her father, seated across from her next to Carpenter. Her father dozed, his chin bobbing gently on his chest.

Without Carpenter saying anything, Tabitha's nursing senses had already observed and concluded that he was unwell. She gently squeezed her mother's hand.

"We are s' very proud of you, Tabitha," her mother murmured. The sentiment seemed the only thing that she could say, but Tabitha understood: Her parents were overwhelmed—dazed by their journey from Texas by train, by their luxurious apartment in Carpenter's home, by being whisked to Boulder and back in Carpenter's automobile.

By meeting their daughter, back from the grave.

I doubt they have ridden in a motorcar before now, Tabitha realized. *They must be so discomfited, so out of their element.* She raised her mother's rough hand to her lips and kissed it.

"I am so glad you are here, Mama."

Across the car in the dimming light, Carpenter's eyes watched her.

"Thank you," Tabitha mouthed.

Carpenter walked Tabitha up the porch steps to the door of Palmer House. "I shall bring your parents to you tomorrow afternoon," he assured her. "Your father will be more rested then, and Breona will have prepared a room for them."

As Tabitha reached for the venerable old door to the house, she spied something new: a shiny metal sign nailed to the house, just to the side of the door. Her fingers traced the graven words, *Lost Are Found*.

"What is this?" she asked Carpenter.

"Mr. Wheatley's work, at Joy's request. A reminder to us all that God knows where Edmund is. A reminder to us all that we are to pray and not give up hope."

Tabitha stared at the sign with new understanding. Then she placed her hand on it and prayed aloud. "O Lord, we do not forget: We have asked you to bring Edmund home. Your eyes are upon the whole earth, and you see him, even right now. Father, we trust you to bring him back to us, for in you, the lost are found."

"Amen," came Carpenter's heartfelt response. When Tabitha opened her eyes, his palm was upon the sign, next to hers.

Tabitha's return to Palmer House was all that she had wished for. Her friends greeted her at the front door and gathered around her in the great room to welcome her home. Though she was meeting several girls for the first time, the spirit of the old house had not changed: It was still home to her, and she delighted in the unfamiliar as well as familiar faces.

"Will! What a great big boy you are now." Tabitha knelt next to Marit and Billy's tow-headed child.

"I'm gonna be six, Aunt Tabitha," he announced with pride.

"I can hardly believe it, sweetheart." She hugged him but, as boys that age generally do, he wriggled free from her embrace and raced away giggling.

"And little Charley? Charley, is this you?" The toddler, suddenly shy, buried his face in Marit's neck. Everyone laughed and Marit tried to coax him to say hello, but he was having nothing to do with Tabitha.

"He is going on three, now," Marit apologized to Tabitha, "and is very villfull and full of mischief. Ven he makes up his mind, ve cannot change it."

To underscore Marit's explanation, Charley peeked out at Tabitha. "No!" he hollered.

"Don't worry; he will warm up to you," Billy promised.

"No!" Charley pronounced a second time.

Everyone laughed, which only mortified the little boy. He buried his face in Marit's bosom and burst into tears.

When the bustle of Tabitha's homecoming subsided a little, Sarah and Corrine took hold of her arms and pulled her up the stairs. The two young women who worked for Joy in her fine home furnishings store had shared the room next to Tabitha's since Palmer House opened.

"You lucky thing, you," Corrine grinned.

"Me? What do you mean?" They reached the second floor landing, but the two young women guided Tabitha to the staircase leading up to the third floor.

"You, dear girl, no longer share a room on the second floor with one of us peons! Miss Rose has given you a room on the top floor," Sarah informed her. "She felt that if you are required to work long shifts at the hospital, you needed a 'quieter environment in which to take your rest.' I believe those were her exact words."

Corrine glanced at Sarah and they burst into giggles.

"Why, whatever could Miss Rose mean by that?" Sarah giggled again.

"A 'quieter environment'? Yes, whatever *could* she mean?" Tabitha snorted—and the three of them giggled together.

Sarah stopped before one of the three turret rooms of which Palmer House boasted. Corrine threw open the door. "Welcome home. You have a room all to yourself, Tabitha!"

Tabitha gaped. "Really? I have never had such space before—or such a lovely room!" She entered and turned in a circle, relishing the simple but warm furnishings.

"It was Joy," Sarah said, clapping her hands. "She chose these things from the shop especially for you, and we all pitched in to decorate the room for you."

"We agreed—we wanted your room to be special," Corrine added, "to celebrate your great accomplishment. To welcome you home."

"Do you like the new wallpaper?" Sarah asked.

"What about the curtains?" Corrine added.

Tabitha could not speak. Her heart was too full.

Then the three of them were hugging, and Tabitha's heart overflowed. *Thank you, Lord, for bringing me home again. How I love you!*

The next morning Tabitha helped Breona make up the parlor for her parents. Because of her father's ill health, going up and down a staircase was out of the question. The parlor was the only room on the ground floor, other than Mr. Wheatley's two little chambers (the former butler's pantry and quarters) that could accommodate them. Breona and Tabitha slid the small settee against a wall and set up the two bedsteads Billy had brought down from the attic.

"I am sorry the parlor will be unavailable while my parents are here," Tabitha said to Rose.

"Do not be sorry, Tabitha. Their visit is an answer to our prayers," Rose replied.

Not long after lunch, Carpenter and Banks arrived with their precious cargo. Carpenter helped Tabitha's father navigate the front steps and Banks brought in their single suitcase.

As Carpenter and Banks were leaving, Carpenter stole Tabitha aside for a private word. "I will be away on business for a fortnight, Tabs, and shall return on the second Friday from now. May I call on you and take you for a drive the following day?"

"Yes. I would like that." They smiled, easy with each other. Tabitha added, "I believe my parents will be leaving that Wednesday. They have shown me their return tickets and seem quite set on it."

"I believe it would be difficult for them to adjust here," he answered. His voice was silky soft, and Tabitha's heartbeat quickened a little

She nodded and looked down. "I have not properly thanked you for bringing them all this way to be reunited with me."

Carpenter grew more serious and asked, "Perhaps we can speak of that when I return?"

Tabitha's heart thumped harder. "Of course."

"Until then," he whispered.

After showing her parents their room, Tabitha settled them in the kitchen with Breona, Marit, Billy, and Mr. Wheatley. Her mother was talking the women's legs off, while Mr. Wheatley was talking her father's arm off.

Tabitha sighed and smiled. It made her happy to see her parents looking so content and comfortable with her friends, but she also had a concern: Sooner or later, the origins and purpose of Palmer House would come out—and so would Tabitha's reason for living in the house.

It will not be an easy conversation to have with them, Lord. I ask you to guide my words when I tell them of my past. I pray you will help me to glorify Jesus—I pray that they will see him in me when it is all said and done.

The days flew by, however, and neither of Tabitha's parents asked her to explain why she was living at Palmer House, nor did they even turn an inquiring eye upon her. Each morning Tabitha took her mother on a short walk. Her father, unable to join them, spent the time they were out playing checkers with Mr. Wheatley—to that gentleman's everlasting delight.

Tabitha and her mother would walk arm-in-arm to the little park a few blocks away and wander along the pine trees lining the paths that wound through it. After their third walk to the park, Tabitha came to the realization that her mother would not be bringing up the difficult topic.

They usually sat down on a bench near the middle of the park to just enjoy their surroundings. They spoke of many things, mostly about Tabitha's childhood home and the nearby farms and people she remembered, but each time their exchange veered toward Palmer House, Tabitha noticed how her mother steered the conversation in another direction.

Only once did Tabitha glimpse something, a hint of understanding in her mother.

"When you left with thet Cray Bishoff, I knewed it would lead t' sorrows fer ya, Daughter. I'm ever s' glad thet you have come to this place in yer life, glad thet you are happy now."

"I-I wasn't always happy, Mama," Tabitha said softly. She was ready to admit to the truth—but her mother forestalled her.

"Them days is all in th' past, Tabitha. All in th' past. Thet's where they should stay put." Her mother stood abruptly and glanced at the cloudless sky. "Gonna be a hot one agin t'day. Shall we hev anuther go 'round th' park while it's still cool?"

She offered her hand to Tabitha and they, mother and daughter, arms about each other, walked on.

Tabitha's mother muttered, "A'course a hot one here ain't got nuthin' on Texas, do it?"

Tabitha laughed, her mother chuckled, and Tabitha understood that the topic she had feared was closed, not to be broached again.

Almost two weeks later, Billy drove Tabitha and her parents to Union Station. As much as they had relished every moment spent with Tabitha, relief showed on their faces. Tabitha knew they were anxious to return to their farm.

"Do you have your tickets?" Tabitha asked for the third time.

"Yeah, girl. An' th' wonderful lunch Marit done give us." Her mother, tears starting in her eyes, placed a rough hand on Tabitha's cheek. "Ya have a good life here, Daughter. We be so glad fer ya."

Tabitha hugged her parents close to her. "Daddy . . . Mama, I love you so much. I-I want you to know that Jesus loves you even more than I love you."

Her father, usually quiet and unspoken, cleared his throat. "We are a-seein' the difference in ya, child." He turned away from her, self-conscious of his moist eyes. He sniffed and wiped them with his hand before turning back. "Miss Rose prayed with us last night t' become Christians—real Christians."

Tabitha's mother nodded, affirming her husband's declaration of faith. "Th' day ya left us was th' worst day of our lives, Daughter. We thought th' day we got yer letter was th' best. But now thet we have seen ya ... now thet we know ya hev a good life ... well, now we kin—"

Her mother broke off on a sob and Tabitha's heart filled in the blanks: *Now we can die in peace.*

Tears dripping freely down her face, Tabitha waved at the departing train until it wound down the tracks and out of sight.

CHAPTER 16

In the days following her return to Denver, Tabitha could not pin down her emotions—yes, she was relieved and overjoyed to be finished with her grueling education . . . but she was also sad and bereft because those days were gone forever. She was not accustomed to having so much time for herself and suffered a restless itching because she would not start work at the hospital until the end of June.

As he had intimated he would, Carpenter called on her Saturday, midmorning. "Could we take a drive, Tabs?" Carpenter asked. He tucked her hand into the crook of his arm and they descended the front steps of Palmer House together. Carpenter led her down the walkway and out to the street where Banks had the car waiting.

"Where are we going?"

"It is a surprise," Carpenter grinned.

For a change, Tabitha felt free—as light as a feather. For no particular reason, she laughed aloud.

"You are happy," Mason remarked. He grinned again. "I like seeing you happy, Tabs."

Twenty minutes later they pulled onto the edge of a grassy field and Carpenter's surprise became apparent. Tabitha stared out the window at the short line of aeroplanes ahead of them.

"Wh-what are we doing here?" Tabitha stuttered.

"Do not worry. I am not planning to take you up today. But I wanted you to meet my friend and see the plane I am thinking of buying."

"Very well." Relieved, Tabitha blew out a great breath and then asked, "Will I be able to go close to one of the aeroplanes? Perhaps touch it?"

"Certainly. If you like, we can let you sit in one of them. Is that something you would enjoy?"

She swallowed. "Perhaps. I do not know."

This time he chuckled. "You will never have to do anything that makes you uncomfortable when you are with me, Tabs. I do not believe in forcing others to do what amuses me. Let us just have some fun together, shall we?"

She nodded, further relieved, and felt herself growing a little excited. "All right. Yes!"

A tall, gangly man waved at them from down the field. "That's Cliff. He was my instructor. Now he is quite a good friend. He owns the biplane I hope to purchase."

"Why is he selling his aeroplane?" Tabitha asked. "Is there something wrong with it?"

"No, not a bit of it. We have been using this aeroplane to give lessons. But, the thing is, he is leaving for England shortly and is in a rush to sell it before he goes."

"Oh? Why is he in such a hurry?"

"Ah, well, he is volunteering to train British pilots."

"England does not have flying instructors?"

Carpenter shook his head. "You know the Brits are expecting war to break out in Europe any moment, Tabs. As a Canadian, Cliff feels honor-bound to help the Empire. The British wish to have many trained pilots who can fly reconnaissance for the military. It is a brilliant idea, of course. From an aeroplane a pilot can see for miles in all directions."

"I see," Tabitha answered him, but her heart was troubled at the mention of a coming war.

Banks parked the car a short distance from the line of planes and Carpenter helped Tabitha to step out. "Do watch where you step, my dear. We pilots lease this field from a farmer but his steers also graze here." He snorted. "And they—and what they leave behind—can be quite the impediment when trying to land."

"I grew up on a farm," Tabitha laughed, "so thank you for the warning!"

They drew near Carpenter's pilot friend and Carpenter introduced Tabitha. "Miss Hale, may I present Mr. Clifford St. Alban? Cliff, this is Miss Hale."

Tabitha shook hands with St. Alban while studying his strange attire—warm trousers, a padded, belted coat, and a wool scarf. She was particularly caught by the soft leather hat that completely enclosed his head and the odd eyewear dangling from around his neck.

St. Alban saw her eyes lingering on his getup. "Up in the air the temperatures are much cooler than here on the ground, sometimes quite cold. We bundle up before we fly. Of course, wind is a factor, too. My helmet covers my head and protects my ears—and the strap keeps the helmet from blowing away."

"The goggles keep our eyes from watering," Carpenter interjected. "The goggles fit our faces quite snugly so the wind cannot blow inside them or rip them from our faces when we are far up in the air."

Tabitha's eyes grew larger as she understood that Carpenter had been "far up in the air" many times. She glanced up and shuddered. Both men laughed at her shiver.

"Come see the planes, Tabs," Carpenter urged her. They walked toward the four aeroplanes parked alongside the field and Carpenter strode up to the third in the row.

"This aeroplane was made by Mr. Glenn Curtiss. It is a tractor model. Look—it has two seats, side-by-side. When I was learning, Cliff sat next to me while I operated the controls. This is how we train new pilots."

Tabitha did look, more interested than she had thought she would be. Gingerly, she touched the "skin" of one of the wings.

"Why, it is only a light canvas of some kind," she exclaimed, "and seems entirely too-too flimsy! And what are these sticks and wires between the wings?"

"Those are called 'struts,' Miss Hale." Carpenter's instructor pointed to the two wings, one above the other. "The struts are actually quite effective at maintaining and strengthening the structural integrity of the aeroplane's framework. The struts keep the airflow from bending or twisting the two sets of wings out of shape, thus breaking them."

Tabitha ran her hand over the many parts of the plane to get a sense of their weight and stability. "But it all seems so fragile."

Except the propeller. It seemed solid enough—as did the motor mounted just behind the propeller.

"Yes, the planes are lightweight but they are not necessarily fragile," was Carpenter's reply. He looked at Tabitha. "Would you care to sit in it?"

She stared at the two open-air seats not far behind the engine. Her insides felt a little jiggly. "How would I get up there?"

"A step stool, m'lady," Carpenter answered.

Minutes later, Tabitha was sitting on one of the seats, a steering wheel of sorts in front of her at chin level. She adjusted her skirts, hoping no other woman had been nearby to see how scandalously she'd shown ankle and calf while climbing up the steps and stepping over some of the taut wires to reach the seat. Carpenter surprised her by climbing onto the seat next to her.

"W-what are you doing?" Tabitha's throat dried as she spoke.

"I thought I would start the engine and taxi up and down the field a few times."

"You-you won't try to go into the air?"

"Indeed not! No, I promised you. I would never lure you into sitting in the plane for the purpose of taking you flying against your will. I will not take you up until I have your permission."

And that, Mr. Carpenter, I promise you will never have, Tabitha vowed in silence.

Carpenter handed Tabitha a scarf. "Please tie this about your head so that your hair is not mussed up by the breeze."

Tabitha spread the scarf over her head, crossed it under her chin, and tied it at the back of her neck while Cliff and several other men pushed the plane backward and turned it so it was facing down the field. Two of them grabbed hold of the propeller on the nose of the machine and swung it over.

Carpenter made some adjustments with a hand throttle. The motor coughed, turned over, and caught. As if her insides were not giddy enough already, the roar of the engine—bolted only a short distance from her face—sent her stomach into spasms.

Then they were rolling along the grassy field, bumping over rocks and stuttering over dips and holes. The engine grumbled louder still until Tabitha felt that they were rocketing over the ground. She stared out her side of the machine and watched the pasture fly by ... and she was seized by a wild, inexplicable desire.

All Mason would have to do is lift the nose of this plane for us to go up ... up into the air, she realized.

He glanced at her and grinned—his expression shining with joy.

She grinned back and, acting on her unaccountable impulse, lifted her hand, pointing it upwards.

"Are you sure?" he shouted.

He was mad with glee, and Tabitha, still amazed, was, too.

"Yes!"

She glanced down again, mesmerized as the grass below the nose of the plane fell away. They were only feet from the earth, but she could feel the plane lifting. They glided smoothly into the air—and then they were higher than she had ever been in her life, perhaps one hundred feet from the ground!

In reduced size, the world below her was perfect, and all sounds but the drone of the engine and the air roaring past her disappeared. She stared about her, craning her head to see ... *everything*!

It is magnificent, she marveled. And she was not afraid. She was at peace.

A wisp of cloud wrapped itself about the struts and Carpenter began a slow turn to the right. As he turned the wheel, the plane heeled over slightly and Tabitha's view of the world below them was even clearer. The pasture came closer and the ground rose to meet them. And then they were racing along, level with the grass. The wheels settled and bumped and they were no longer in the air.

Tabitha was almost saddened when the plane slowed and Carpenter turned it back toward his friends.

Tabitha could not stop enthusing as Banks drove them back toward Palmer House. "It was the most beautiful thing I have ever experienced," she admitted.

"And all we did was go up, make a turn and come back down," Carpenter grinned. "I thought that was quite enough for your first time. Of course, as aeroplanes improve, we will be able to stay up much longer and go much higher."

They sighed at the same time—and laughed that they had sighed simultaneously.

"I must admit that you surprised me, Tabs," he said in a softer voice.

"Oh, but I surprised myself more, I assure you. I was so afraid—that is, until we were racing across the field and it felt that we almost *were* flying," she replied. "And then I could not let the moment go. If we did not go up, I felt that something in me would have been so grieved."

His hand found hers. "I understand. I do."

They rode in comfortable silence until they reached Palmer House. As he helped her out, he said softly, "Will you take a turn with me through the yard, Tabitha?"

She placed her arm in his and they wandered among the trees and then along the side of the house where they admired the wealth of roses Mr. Wheatley had trained upon trellises.

Carpenter stopped under a particularly lovely arch where golden-pink climbing roses drooped from the stems and perfumed the air. The rose branches formed a dome above them, surrounding them with a crown of buds and blossoms.

Carpenter faced her with an earnest, determined look in his eyes.

"I love and admire you, Tabitha. I have admired you since that moment in the hospital when I saw you first—when you pointed your finger at me and demanded that I give Shan-Rose to you."

They both laughed, but softly. "I was a bit overwrought, I admit," Tabitha confessed.

"Let me see. I believe your first words to me were, 'That is *not* your baby!'"

"Well, she was not," Tabitha sniffed. "There you sat, a complete stranger, a Chinese babe stuffed inside your overcoat, her little head poking out of it, her eyes big as saucers. Admit it, Mr. Carpenter! It was *not* proper, and she was *not* your child."

"Ah, but you do not give me due credit, my sweet one," Carpenter murmured, pulling her a little closer. "After all, it was snowing and the air was freezing when I found Shan-Rose, and she had no blanket to cover her little body. So I put her inside my coat to save her. I saved her and I saved Mrs. Thoresen."

"Oh, Mason! How foolish of me to bring up such silly social mores when you did—you *did* save Shan-Rose and Miss Rose!"

She turned her face up to him. "You saved us from heartbreak upon heartbreak. I can never thank you enough."

Something flickered across his face and his eyes softened. "Then will you thank me now, Tabitha? Will you make my happiness complete? Will you do me the honor of becoming my wife?"

"Oh, Mason..." Tabitha stared into his eyes, sinking into them, getting lost in the love she saw there, forgetting the arguments she had rehearsed so many times.

"You know I love you, Tabs, do you not?" he insisted.

"Yes." Her reply was less than a breath. Her heart pounded in her throat.

"And do you not love me, my darling? Say you do!"

"Yes," she murmured. "Oh, yes."

"And, oh, Tabs! Do you not dream of making a home with me? A family? What beautiful children we will have, Tabitha! Beautiful, emerald-eyed, flaming-haired daughters and sons. Please say 'yes'! Will you marry me?"

A great whooshing rushed through Tabitha's veins and into her ears; the words "a family" clanged alarms in her head—and sent her heart skidding toward a precipice.

"I—No. Oh, no. Please, let me go." Tabitha pushed on Carpenter's arms, pushed until he released her and she stumbled backward, her emotions crashing around her.

"What is it? Did I say something wrong?" Carpenter reached to support her, to keep her from falling. Alarm of his own tinged his questions. "What is it?"

"Oh, no. I-I should have said something sooner. I should not have let this go on, I should have—" Tabitha held her hand over her eyes. "I ... Mason ... Mr. Carpenter ..."

"What is it, Tabs?" Concern etched his face.

She let her hand drop away from her face. "I must tell you the truth, Mr. Carpenter. Should have told you sooner. I cannot have children." She said the words, but she could not look him in the eye.

He stuttered, stunned by her revelation. "But-but are you certain? How ... how can you be certain?"

Tabitha slowly shook her head. *Because, from the age of fifteen until I was twenty-nine, I laid with hundreds of men—perhaps more—and I never once conceived a child. Because I had an abortion. Because I killed my own unborn child.*

"You deserve so much better than me, Mr. Carpenter," she whispered. "I cannot give you a family. Yes, of this I am certain. Please forgive me. I did not know you desired children so much, and it never occurred to me ... I am nearly thirty-three and you are, what? Five or more years older than I am?"

"Why, we are not too old, Tabitha! We are not!" he pleaded. "I have waited so long for you!"

"It is not our age, Mason." Tabitha's words sounded far away to her own ears. "It is me. I am unable to conceive. It would not be fair to enter into marriage with you when I cannot give you the family you desire."

Tabitha drew on all her old arguments, the many reasons she had painstakingly formulated and memorized to contradict the possibility of their marrying. "Too many obstacles are against us. I have a past that, should it ever come out, would ruin your good standing in Denver society. You deserve a wife who can come to you ... pure and chaste. And I cannot give you a family."

She drew herself up. "Besides, I-I have pledged myself to nursing. Please forgive me. I should not have led you on."

She turned and walked away, stumbled up the front steps into the house. Somehow she navigated the two staircases and found her room.

Joy and Rose, standing together in the great room, noted Tabitha's entrance. They were both surprised when, a few minutes later, a knock sounded on the front door. Rose answered it herself.

"Why, Mr. Carpenter! When we saw Tabitha come in, we supposed you had gone—"

She caught sight of his anguished expression. "Oh! What is it, my dear boy?"

He took her hand. "Mrs. Thoresen. Please, may we talk? Privately?"

She nodded and led him into the parlor.

Thirty minutes later the door to the parlor opened and Carpenter walked out the front door on unsteady legs. A moment later, Rose returned to the great room.

"What is it, Mama?" Joy went to her mother.

Tears trickled down Rose's cheeks, but she shook her head. "I cannot speak of it, Joy. It would violate Tabitha's confidence."

Rose sobbed once and Joy reached for her. "I think I understand, Mama," Joy whispered. "Let us pray for them."

For two weeks Tabitha kept herself so busy that she did not have time to think about Carpenter or dwell on her aching heart. She then began her new position at the hospital and threw herself into her work, taking on longer hours, extra shifts, and difficult patients.

She spent her days immersed in the demanding labor of nursing. When she returned to Palmer House she would seek out mindless work—scrubbing floors or bathrooms, doing laundry for the other women. By night she would fall into bed too exhausted to think, too worn to do anything but sleep.

And then one afternoon she returned home from her shift and found a letter waiting for her. She knew it was from Carpenter. Hadn't she received enough of his letters over her years at school to know his handwriting?

Tabitha climbed to the third floor and closed her bedroom door behind her. The envelope trembled in her hand and, finally, tears began to fall.

What can I do? I love him, I do! But what can I do? We cannot marry.

And there was the rub.

Will this letter say he still wants to marry me? she wondered. *Will he try to change my mind? I must harden my heart against him, against all his arguments.*

Fearful of what she would find inside, Tabitha slid her thumb under the envelope's seal and unfolded the pages she withdrew from within.

Nothing could have prepared her for what she read.

August 1, 1914
My dearest Tabitha,

I have spent the past weeks praying and seeking God's face. He has shown me places in my heart where I have been shortsighted and presumptuous.

For years I have felt that we would be together, that I only needed to allow you to follow your heart and first train to be a nurse. When you finished your training, I (in my shortsightedness) believed we would marry. I believed that you would be willing to oversee a local volunteer nursing program or something along those lines—a place of service and ministry that would still allow us to marry and have a family.

I gave no thought as to whether or not we could have a family and I, in my presumption, never broached the subject with you. I did not wish to pressure you while you were in school—but I presumed so much! It is I who should have spoken of these things much sooner. I am so sorry.

After you left me, I spoke to Mrs. Thoresen. She did not give up your confidences, my darling. No, she steadfastly refused all questions but one: She confirmed what you told me, that you cannot bear children. I do not know why or how you know this, only that what you told me is true.

This fact breaks my heart for both of us, and I cannot help but recall my thoughtless words and how they must have deeply wounded you. Please forgive me for the pain I have caused. I have asked the Lord to show me what I should do now that we have parted. Parted? The word tears at my soul, for I do not wish to be parted from you.

But now I understand, now I see clearly: I understand your call to nursing and why you have bent your entire self toward that calling. Now I acknowledge that I must respect your decision, as grievously as it strikes my very soul.

Tabitha found that she was weeping, and the tears that fell from her cheeks splashed over the penned words on the paper. His next words stunned her.

My dearest, you have surely heard the news. Austria-Hungary has declared war on Serbia, Great Britain's ally. Germany has sided with Austria-Hungary. Now the world expects Great Britain—and all the countries of the British Empire—to declare war against Germany and the Austro-Hungarians within the week. Because nations will honor their alliances and treaties, war will shortly engulf all of Europe. I pray America can avoid the fracas. Consensus assures us that a conflict in Europe will be a short one. I hope and pray it is, but can anyone say with certainty how effortless or contracted this struggle may prove to be—or who will prevail?

Tabitha, I am writing to tell you that I have decided to follow Cliff St. Alban to England. He assures me that the British will welcome my help in training new pilots. Cliff has the sense that aeroplanes will change the way wars are fought. I do not know, but perhaps I can be a help and forget myself and my own concerns as I serve.

My darling, I want you to know that my feelings for you are unchanged. I will return to Denver when the war is over, not so many days or months from now. When I do, I will seek you out. Perhaps, by God's grace, he will make a way for us. Until then,

I am always your servant,
Mason Carpenter

Tabitha read and reread his letter, shaking her head and whispering, "No. No!" Her tears smeared the ink in places, and she could not bear for his words to be marred, so she folded the precious papers away and wept into her pillow.

I must stop him, she realized. *I must change his mind. Going to war cannot be God's will for him!*

In the morning, as soon as breakfast was over, Tabitha telephoned Carpenter's home. She was breaking every rule of etiquette and custom, but she did not care. She was determined to argue against his decision, to dissuade him from entering the war—even if England was an island and lay hundreds of miles from where the fighting would take place.

When a voice on the other end picked up, Tabitha recognized it. "Banks? Is that you?"

"Ah. Yes, Miss Hale. It is good to hear your voice."

But Tabitha could hear the sadness underpinning his greeting. "Has he left? Is he already gone?"

Banks coughed a tiny, polite cough. "Yes, miss. Mr. Carpenter left three nights ago."

"But-but I only received his letter today!"

Frustration shaded his response. "Yes, miss. I was instructed to post the letter after he departed."

I am too late, she realized. *He knew I would try to stop him.*

Still reeling, she managed to whisper her thanks and hang up.

Only days later, on August 4, the newspapers trumpeted the headlines:

GREAT BRITAIN DECLARES WAR

か緯め

$\mathcal{C}$HAPTER 17

T he following months were agony for Tabitha. She spent her days in a fog of work, much of it accomplished automatically, without conscious thought.

In November, two weeks before Thanksgiving, Tabitha received a second letter from Carpenter. It was postmarked from a hamlet in England whose name she did not recognize. She tore into the envelope, hungry for news—eager to know he was safe. The letter began formally and, as Tabitha devoured his words, it grew more so. By the time she finished it, she was terrified.

Sunday, October 11, 1914
Dear Miss Hale,

I received a message from Banks that you had called after I left for England. I am sorry if my abrupt departure caused you concern. I wish you to know that I am in good health.

Cliff and I are posted at Catterick Airfield in Yorkshire, northeastern England, and are training young men to fly reconnaissance over France and Belgium. You should have no anxieties for Cliff or for me. The British Army's Royal Flying Corps recruits pilots only to age thirty and, thus, considers both of us too old to fly actual missions. Most of the men we train are but boys in their early twenties.

At present, the RFC has about eighty-four aircraft, and we lose a few aeroplanes—and precious men—every mission. We do our best to prepare these young men to undertake their dangerous assignments. They fly their aeroplanes across the channel into Belgium and France where the Germans are invading. The pilots seek out the enemy's positions and scout their troop movements for the British Expeditionary Force fighting there. Gathering the desired information is one thing; communicating it to the front where it is needed is quite another, and is proving problematic.

The British have a saying: "Necessity is the mother of invention." I cannot help but believe that this war and its harsh necessities must breed better and more reliable aircraft, more effective means of communications, and other new inventions, for on the ground (I am distressed to report), the conduct of the war has begun badly.

The BEF, under the command of Sir John French, suffered a great rout almost immediately. One arm of the German invasion into France through Belgium, at a place called Mons, defeated the BEF in early August. The Germans advanced and pushed the Brits back to the outskirts of Paris itself.

Then, last month, the BEF joined the French to hold the German horde at the Marne River. While their combined forces kept the Germans from encroaching farther, the price for their success was terrible indeed. We have heard reports that the French suffered a quarter million casualties. We have also heard that German losses were roughly the same. More than half a million lives wounded or lost in mere days? It confounds the mind and ravages the heart.

The BEF suffered "only" eleven thousand wounded and nearly two thousand deaths. British losses were fewer only because their overall troop sizes were so much smaller than those of the French Army's. Still, the deaths of two thousand young Englishmen? Young men who will never return to their parents or sweethearts? Such a loss is devastating. Cliff and I pray daily for the souls of the men we train.

Universally, the military and civilian populations of the Allied Forces expected a quick victory over the Germans. Cliff and I watched English men march off to war with a careless, merry attitude. They, their families, and the commanders of the military believed they would make quick work of the invaders and kick the Huns back to Germany where they belong.

It appears now that they were wrong. Following the Battle of Marne, the Allied Forces dug a line of trenches opposite the trenches of the German army. We hear reports that the Germans occupy higher ground than that of the French and British, making it impossible for the Allied forces to advance. In point of fact, neither side has won any ground in weeks, but the losses in human life continue to mount.

Miss Hale, I must apologize for sharing such horrors with you. I will leave off my observations now.

I hope this letter finds you well, content in your chosen work, and growing in the grace of God. Please extend my greetings to Mrs. Thoresen, Mrs. Michaels, all the souls under the roof of Palmer House, and those whose friendship we share. I send my fondest regard to each of them, and to you. I confess that I think of you often, but I will not presume to reopen that painful chapter.

Miss Hale, I pray that you consider me your most faithful friend. I have given Banks instructions: Should you need for anything, he will assist you. He has my authorization to aid you in any matter should you call upon him. I have already given him instructions regarding your parents—they shall never want, Miss Hale. I assure you of this.

In return, I covet your prayers. We are daily sending these earnest young men to their deaths. Please pray for me that I will fearlessly testify to the hope of Christ wherever I am and whenever I can.

Most sincerely,
Mason Carpenter

Carpenter's ability to describe his surroundings and experiences in vivid language had brought the dreadfulness of war home to her—and it did not escape her notice that he said nothing of his return to the States.

How long will this war last? He said only a few weeks or months! Will he stay with the British until it is finished?

Her thoughts took another wrenching corner. *October 11! His letter took an entire month to reach me? So much will have changed by now... over there.*

And why would he give Banks instructions concerning me? Concerning my parents?

Given that she had refused his offer of marriage, his ongoing care for her and provision for her parents was unwarranted and not entirely proper.

Why would he give such instructions—unless he fears he will not return?

It was at that moment that Tabitha gave way and admitted to the extent of her love for him.

How I love him, Lord! How can I live my life without him?

*O dear God of all grace! Please be near my beloved! Oh, I know I have no right to say he is mine, but he is **yours**, Lord, and I pray you keep him safe in your arms!*

Unsure of what to do, Tabitha sought Rose for advice. She poured out her confusion and shared with her the last lines of Carpenter's letter.

"Miss Rose, I know it would not be proper to reply to his letters. To write him would, perhaps, give him a false hope regarding our future, but..." Her words trickled to an end.

Rose considered Tabitha with compassion. "Do you love Mr. Carpenter, Tabitha?"

Tabitha bowed her head. "Oh, I do! I do, but you know that I cannot give him children, Miss Rose. And he told me how dearly he wanted a family."

Rose's smile was tender. "Tell me, dearest, how would you describe and what would you call our little group here, those of us who live under the sheltering roof of Palmer House?"

"I-I do not understand."

"Would you deem us mere friends? Only fellow Christians? Companions and sojourners upon this earth?"

Tabitha slowly shook her head. "You are also my family—in Christ and so much more in my heart."

"Yes, and you, Tabitha, are my daughter. You see, dear girl, while every child needs a father and mother, not every son or daughter comes from our womb."

Tabitha stared at Rose, opening and closing her mouth as the alternative Rose implied came clear to her. "But-but I do not know… would he consider such a thing? Oh, I just do not know!"

"And yet I know two things with certainty." Rose lifted two fingers, "First, I know that Mason Carpenter loves you and wishes to marry you, Tabitha. He told me so himself. And second, I know that our great God is able to make a way where, in our own small sight, we do not see a way."

Rose patted Tabitha's hand. "Mr. Carpenter has now written you twice. He has taken pains to secure your parents' future and has made provision for you should you need anything… or should something happen to him. Has he not demonstrated his commitment to you? Write him back, Tabitha. Do not withhold the hope he longs for. Allow God to make a way for you."

Tabitha took a deep breath and settled. Galvanized with new courage, she whispered, "Thank you, Miss Rose." She raced up the stairs to reply to Carpenter's correspondence.

November 14, 1914
Dear Mr. Carpenter,

I received your letter only yesterday. The war must be having an effect upon mail services for it to have taken so long to reach me. I have passed on all your greetings to everyone at Palmer House, but the most joyfully received greetings were those you sent to me.

Tabitha rambled on for paragraphs, including every tidbit of news she could imagine would cheer him. In closing she wrote,

I return your fondest regard, Mr. Carpenter. Your thoughtful care for my parents and for me only increases my regard for you. While you are away, I will pray that God grants you a harvest of souls for eternity.

I will also, while you are engaged in such important work, pray daily for your continued safety—waiting with an expectant heart for the day you are restored to us.

With my warmest wishes,
Tabitha

Until she could look him full in the face and they could come to an agreement about their future, Tabitha did not want to pen the many words of love and desire bubbling within her. So she carefully phrased her letter, knowing full well that he would read her change of heart both between the lines and in her signature—simply *Tabitha*, rather than the more formal *Tabitha Hale*.

However, as she addressed the envelope, one unhappy truth was becoming clear to her: The war that both sides of the conflict had believed would end in decisive victory after mere weeks would be neither quick nor decisive.

No, the ugliness of this war would not end simply or soon.

At Palmer House, Rose encouraged everyone to pray about the war more than they talked about it. But at the hospital, nearly all the gossip and news regarded the war. Tabitha tried not to listen, but her heart would not allow her to disregard the conversations.

Before long, she could converse as well as anyone on the foibles of the ruling houses of Europe and the treaty system that had dragged most of the world into what was, essentially, a territorial dispute between the Austro-Hungarians and the Serbs.

The orderlies and doctors watched the progress of Kaiser Wilhelm's campaigns and discussed at length the fearsome weaponry being unleashed upon the battlefields. They commented on the propaganda wars and watched for news of every new battle.

Tabitha soaked it all in.

"I don't understand how the Kaiser can wage war against Britain," one doctor complained. "It is his own mother's home country! His grandmother was queen of England, for heaven's sake."

"Bah! He is a German through and through. He cares only to increase Germany's might and to best the British at sea. Those Germans are obsessed with power."

"Well, if Queen Victoria were still alive and on the throne today, I doubt Germany and Britain would be at odds."

Tabitha absorbed the informally obtained information and read the newspaper accounts for herself until she could follow the progress of the war as well as any man. She joined the rest of Palmer House in praying for Carpenter and Cliff St. Alban, but her own prayers were more heartfelt and specific: *O Lord, whatever happens, I pray that you will allow Mason to hear from my own lips that I am his, that I trust you for our future together.*

Another Christmas season arrived with all the baking, bustle, fun, and blessing the holy days brought with them.

Lord, I am so glad to be home this Christmas, Tabitha rejoiced on Christmas Eve. *If Mason were here, I would not be able to contain all the joy in my heart.*

Snow was falling all around the real Palmer House, blanketing the world in a hush of glory. Alone in her room on the third floor, Tabitha lifted the little snow globe containing the miniature of Palmer House and shook it. The white flakes floated down around the tiny house Carpenter had fashioned with his own hands.

"Wherever Mason is this night, Lord, I pray he is worshipping you and remembering your birth as we are."

She set the globe on her bureau, kissed the tips of her fingers, and touched them to the globe. "Perhaps next Christmas, Father God!"

Then she joined the others downstairs to sing Christmas hymns.

The next letter from Carpenter arrived immediately after the New Year, but Tabitha counted it the best of all Christmas gifts she had received.

My Dearest Tabitha,

I hope you will receive this letter by Christmas Day, but the mail is slower and less reliable than ever before. Whether on time or late, I wish you not a Merry Christmas, but a Happy Christmas, as I hear the English offer their greetings.

In my prayers, I ask our Lord to daily direct my heart to his will. We who call ourselves Christians no longer belong to ourselves: We belong to him. We no longer decide our own fates; rather, we trust in God to lead us in paths of righteousness for his name's sake.

I read your letter with increasing joy and hope. If I were with you right now, I would take your hand, gaze into your eyes and, with my heart in my throat, ask, "Is it true? Has God spoken to your heart regarding our love?"

My desire is to serve him all of my days, long or short. When I next see you, I will ask again that you be my partner in this lifelong service. Please hear me, dearest Tabitha: If it is God's will that we not have a family, so be it. I will be content in his will.

He went on to share news of the war, but Tabitha could scarcely take it in. The words of his letter echoed in her heart: *When I next see you, I will ask again that you be my partner in this lifelong service. Please hear me, dearest Tabitha: If it is God's will that we not have a family, so be it. I will be content in his will.*

"Yes!" she breathed. "Yes, I will be your partner, Mason."

CHAPTER 18

JANUARY 1915

With the Christmas season ending, another joyous event lay before those at Palmer House: The wedding of Joy and Edmund O'Dell would take place on the first Sunday of January.

"We desire only a simple, sacred ceremony before our Lord," Joy told them, "conducted by Pastor Carmichael in the great room of Palmer House and witnessed by those we love best."

While everyone who knew and loved Joy and O'Dell rejoiced for them, their marriage also signaled great changes for Palmer House: Following the wedding, Joy would leave the little cottage she had shared with Grant at the back of Palmer House's grounds. The newly married couple would begin their married life in their own home.

"It will be an adjustment for all of us, but I fear I shall miss her the most," Rose admitted at breakfast the morning before their wedding. "I lean upon Joy to help me manage Palmer House; her strength and wisdom fill up what I am often lacking."

Aside, Rose confided to Tabitha, "I confess that, with Mei-Xing happily married and in her own home and Joy soon to do the same, I feel a great sense of loss. I am so grateful that Breona consented to continue as our housekeeper after her marriage. But that, too, cannot last forever. Someday God will need to raise up others to fill their places."

Tabitha nodded and, again, looked closely at Rose, noting the years creeping up on her. Rose was every bit as vital and vibrant as she had always been, but she tired more easily and had taken to retiring to bed early each evening.

"I am here with you, Miss Rose. You may count on me," she whispered.

Rose squeezed her hand. "That means more than you know, dear Tabitha."

Joy and O'Dell were to be married Sunday afternoon after church services. Early Saturday, the girls of Palmer House, led by Breona and aided by Billy and Mr. Wheatley, cleared away the Christmas greenery and threw themselves into a thorough cleaning of the first floor. The busy workgroup removed drapes, trudged through the January snow, shook the drapes, and hung them on the frigid clotheslines to air. They dusted walls and ceilings and scrubbed mantels and hearths.

Billy and Mr. Wheatley rolled and removed carpets, taking them out-of-doors for a thorough beating. Once the carpets were out of the way, the women swept and cleaned the floors, waxing the hardwood planks and rubbing them until their arms ached and the wood glowed.

They cleaned the gaslight fixtures and wiped their globes; they washed every window until the glass gleamed and met with Breona's approval. They polished furniture and rehung the drapes. Finally, they festooned the windows, walls, and doorways with the costly greens and hothouse flowers Martha Palmer had insisted upon ordering and sending to them.

Tabitha and Sarah stood back with the others, admiring their combined efforts and breathing in the lily-perfumed air. "It will be so beautiful for them," Sarah smiled.

"Aye. That it will." It was all Breona could muster. With the corner of her apron, she dabbed at her eyes.

Later the same day, under a bright winter sun, Joy and O'Dell, accompanied by Rose, Billy and Marit, Tabitha, Sarah, Corrine, and Mr. Wheatley, rode in two motorcars to Riverside Cemetery. Pastor Isaac and Breona Carmichael, with Yaochuan, Mei-Xing, and Shan-Rose Liáng, met them there.

Together, Joy and O'Dell placed a garland of flowers upon the simple grave of Grant Michaels. Joy wept unabashedly. When she placed her hand upon Grant's headstone, O'Dell, with his hand covering Joy's, whispered, "Grant, my dearest friend, you already know that I am doing my best to fulfill my promises to you. Joy and I will stand before God tomorrow and make our solemn vows of marriage, but we do not forget you … and we do not forget Edmund. When we find your sweet boy, I will fulfill my pledge to you to raise him as my own."

Joy and O'Dell bowed their heads to pray silently.

In his own silent prayers, O'Dell added, *And, Lord, please bless our friend Mason Carpenter. Where we have exhausted our own means, he has poured from his wealth into our search for Edmund. Lord, our friend is not far from where the war rages. We ask you to keep him safe and bring him home to us.*

The adjustment was, as Rose had suggested, difficult for those left at Palmer House. Joy and O'Dell departed on their honeymoon trip and were gone for three weeks. When they returned, radiant and rested, Joy again took up the reins at Michaels' Fine Household Furnishings and O'Dell his management of the Denver Pinkerton Office. The newlyweds set up housekeeping in a tiny house O'Dell rented for them.

Joy and O'Dell made a habit of meeting the Palmer House residents for church on Sundays and having dinner at Palmer House afterward, but Rose keenly felt the increased burden of Joy's absence from the day-to-day running of the house. More than that, Rose missed the daily presence of her daughter.

"It is only right and normal," she insisted, but Tabitha did what she could to fill the void Joy's departure had created.

I can never fill Joy's shoes, she admitted, *but I want to do whatever I can to ease Rose's loss.* She surprised herself when she added, *Even if it is only for a short while.*

Weeks after the wedding, Tabitha received an unexpected communication from Mason Carpenter. It was only a note, dated February 7. It arrived February 26.

My Darling,

If you have heard the news, I did not wish you to worry. Yes, the Germans sent their airships across the Channel to bomb eastern England, but we are much farther north than Great Yarmouth where they did the most damage. We do not know if the clouds obscured their pilots' view or if their targets were intentional, for the airships did not bomb any military bases. Instead, they hit innocent civilians. Sadly, several villagers were killed.

In response to this cowardly attack, the Army has directed the Royal Flying Corps to mount guns upon its aeroplanes so that our pilots can shoot down German airships before they can release their bombs. We are working out how to best do so, and hope to prevent another such incursion by the German "blimps" or Zeppelins as some call them.

As I said in an earlier letter, the Army has a limited number of aeroplanes, and we have lost a third of them already. We hear that the French are building newer model aeroplanes, apparently in response to new German models. The British Army has asked to purchase a number of these French planes. I sense a great shift in the war coming upon us. The Allied Forces are now considering the use of aeroplanes to bomb enemy troops and to shoot other planes from the sky.

Tabitha, the wounded are arriving from the front in more numbers daily. Every hospital in England will soon be filled and yet the end of the war is nowhere in sight. We are also hearing disturbing rumors from Eastern Front, rumors of German shells filled with poisonous gasses falling upon Russian positions. If the report is true, this is devilish behavior indeed.

I will write more as I can, but I must get this note onto the mail truck before it leaves. Be at peace, Tabitha. Our times are in his hands.
With all my love,
Mason Carpenter

Tabitha replied to his letter that evening. As she wrote, his words regarding the wounded overflowing England's hospitals occupied her thoughts and she found herself, in her imagination, caring for them and providing solace. She could not shake the images of the wounded before her.

When she had completed her letter to Carpenter, she rested her chin upon her folded hands thinking. The pictures of the wounded in her mind were insistent. Urgent.

Finally, she bowed her head and prayed. *Lord? Am I hearing you? What are you asking of me?*

The following Sunday, those who lived at Palmer House occupied their customary two rows at Calvary Temple. Tabitha closed her eyes and lost herself in the worship of many voices raised in unity to glorify God.

When the singing ended, Pastor Isaac Carmichael stood to bring the message. He took his text from Romans 12.

> *For as we have many members in one body,*
> *and all members have not the same office:*
> *So we, being many, are one body in Christ,*
> *and every one members one of another.*
> *Having then gifts differing according*
> *to the grace that is given to us,*
> *whether prophecy, let us prophesy according*
> *to the proportion of faith;*
> *Or ministry, let us wait on our ministering:*
> *or he that teacheth, on teaching;*
> *Or he that exhorteth, on exhortation:*
> *he that giveth, let him do it with simplicity;*
> *he that ruleth, with diligence;*
> *he that sheweth mercy, with cheerfulness.*

"I wish us to first look at a very profound statement," Pastor Carmichael said. "*So we, being many, are one body in Christ, and every one members one of another*. In plainer language, God's word tells us two important and connected truths:

"First, Christ has but one body. His body is not *this* church. It is not the church down the street. It is not one denomination or another. Christ's body includes *every individual connected to Jesus through his blood*.

"The second truth flows from the first: All parts of Christ's body are *members one of another*. How can we restate this, *members one of another*, with greater clarity?"

He leaned toward his congregation and they inclined their hearing toward him.

"Let me be plain," he said softly. "We belong to each other."

He stood tall. "We belong to Christ. Christ has but one body, and every part belongs to the others. You," he made eye contact with several individuals, "and you, and you, and you, belong to each other."

He let his words sink in then continued. "The rest of the passage, regarding the gifts God has given us, refers back to these two truths. Whether we prophesy, minister, teach, exhort, give, rule, or show mercy, our gift belongs not to ourselves, but to the other members, to the rest of the Christ's body.

"And I cannot put too much emphasis upon this: What gift God has given you is necessary. Important. Vital. For Christ's church to accomplish its mission, every part must work together. For Christ's body to minister to the world, every piece must be present and functioning.

"Do not think you may elect not to serve. No, you and your gift belong to Jesus—and he has said you belong to each other."

He stared around at his congregation. "Every piece. Every part. Every one of us. We are necessary. Important. Vital. We are Christ's hands and feet upon the earth."

A few nights later, Tabitha and several of the girls decided to assemble a jigsaw puzzle. The Christian women's society that often aided Palmer House had donated several boxes of used puzzles, all with intriguing images on their box lids.

"Ohhh! Do look at this one," Gracie suggested. Her selection was of a large passenger ship plowing through a turbulent ocean.

"Shall we make it first, then?" Flora asked. "It is very dramatic, I think."

Tabitha regarded the image and experienced a peculiar pull toward it. "Yes, that one will do. Shall we turn all the pieces right side up and separate them into edges and non-edges first?"

"To build the outside you mean?" Gracie had already dumped the many pieces upon the table and was sorting a handful.

"Um-hm."

The girls were content and quiet as they turned, sorted, and separated the small pieces. Soon they had identified three of the four corners and were connecting edge pieces onto the corners to form the puzzle's frame.

As Tabitha uncovered another edge piece her attention lurched to a standstill.

A voice, one she immediately recognized, spoke to her heart. *Every individual I call is necessary for the success of my work. The work cannot be complete without all the parts and pieces.*

The words were so clear that the hair upon Tabitha's arms lifted. Gracie and Flora did not notice that Tabitha seemed frozen.

The edge piece between her fingers grew warm.

I call some to be the frame for the work, to make the vision plain. Those whom I call to frame the work are vital to my plans, the voice spoke. *They lead so that others may follow.*

Tabitha scarcely breathed. *Lord, I am listening.*

She opened her hand and stared at the edge piece resting in the hollow of her palm. Except it was not an edge. The fourth corner of the puzzle stared back at her.

You are vital to my work. The whisper of His voice faded.

You are vital to my work.

"There it is!" Flora pounced on the corner piece and placed it on the table. "See! These all fit together now. Goodness. I had begun to think the last corner was lost—and then where would we be?"

"Excuse me. I-I have something pressing I need to do." Tabitha pushed away from the table and stumbled upstairs to her room.

"Well! We wish you would have thought of that before we began!" Flora grumbled to her back. "Olive! Jane! Do come and help us. Gracie and I can't do this all on our own."

Tabitha sank to the floor next to her bed. "Lord, I feel your call upon me. Please show me what I should do."

She prayed for some time. Then, with a nod of decision, she picked up pen and paper.

Dear Dean Gunderson,

Greetings from Denver. I hope this letter finds you well and flourishing in the grace of God. My work in the hospital here is quite satisfying, and I am often grateful for the excellent training I received from our school in Boulder.

However, with the war in Europe increasing, I find that I have a strong desire, a calling from God, to serve the wounded of this conflict. I am seeking God's will in this direction.

You once told me you had connections with the American Red Cross. If so, and if you are inclined to recommend me to their ranks, would you kindly forward my letter and nursing credentials to them? I would be most appreciative.

Cordially,
Tabitha Hale

She reread what she had penned and nodded. *If this is your leading, Lord, I trust that you will confirm it with an open door.*

CHAPTER 19

APRIL 1915

The unexpected spring snow lay more than a foot deep—and more threatened to fall from dark, low-hanging clouds. Tabitha could feel the icy moisture in the air, dampening her clothes, even penetrating her thick wool coat as she struggled to break a path from the trolley stop to Palmer House.

Earlier, as she had climbed aboard the trolley, the driver had warned her that he had been ordered back to the terminal. "Th' snow downtown is s' deep th' trolleys are a-gettin' stuck," he explained. Huffing, he added, "Spring in th' Rockies, eh? Never know what yer gonna get."

I am so grateful to have caught the last car going my direction! Tabitha thought as she trudged through the drifted banks. *I am not so very far from Palmer House. I can make it.*

Tabitha had three blocks to traverse on foot, but many of the walkways along her route were impassable. Biting her lip, she slogged through the wet, frigid slush in the gutters.

Her boots were soaked through. Her feet could have been bricks of ice. Worst of all, a coating of ice clung to the hem of her coat and skirts, weighing down every step.

"But I am nearly home," she mumbled. "Almost there."

Home!

Tabitha envisioned what awaited her there: The two fireplaces at either end of the old mansion's great room would be blazing merrily. Her friends—her dear family—would rise from their cozy chairs to welcome her home from her long shift in the hospital. They would strip away her cold, sodden outer wear and knock the ice from her dress. They would urge her toward the warming fires. And the rich scents penetrating the air would foretell the dinner they would sit down to enjoy together.

"I know Mr. Wheatley and Billy will have cleared Palmer House's walkways," she said aloud to encourage herself.

But she wasn't quite home, and she shivered, chilled all the way through. Although the early spring days were growing longer, the looming, snow-laden clouds had turned the late afternoon light to near darkness. Gaslights along the street did little to diffuse the foggy gloom—or penetrate the thick columns of snow now falling all around her.

"Just what we needed," she grumbled. "More snow."

Beneath the heavy scarf muffling her throat and face, Tabitha prayed, *Lord, you always comfort me in my afflictions. You are with me even through the dark valley. I will fear no evil; you lead and guide me. You lead me in paths of righteousness for your name's sake.*

She sighed with relief when she stepped from the gutter onto the walkway bordering Palmer House's iron fence. Here the slushy snow was passable, mere inches deep.

"Bless you, Billy! Bless you, Mr. Wheatley!" she murmured. Surely they had shoveled the walk fronting Palmer House no more than an hour or two before.

She stumbled down the walk toward the tall wrought-iron gate and yanked it open. The cold hinges protested their opening and closing, but Tabitha thought of nothing but the cobblestone path ahead of her and the warm house where the path ended.

She dragged her ice-filled skirts up the steps toward the door and noted, as she always did, the little sign to the side of the door.

Lost Are Found, it read.

Tabitha touched the sign tenderly and murmured, "Lord, in you the lost are found. We trust you."

She had to shove on the heavy entry door with all her strength before it gave way: The freezing dampness had swelled the wood and bonded the door to its posts. When the door released, Tabitha almost tumbled into the foyer beyond. She caught herself and collapsed, instead, against the open door, her strength gone.

Almost immediately her friends surrounded her. "Lord be praised, 'twas that worried we were growin' o'er ye," Breona fussed. Then she snapped over her shoulder, "Dinna be standin' there gawking, Gracie. Be shuttin' thet door."

Gracie and Jane rushed to push the solid door closed and latch it. Other hands guided Tabitha from the foyer into the great room and voices clucked over the chunks of snow and ice clinging to her clothing.

"A bucket an' towels, if ye please," Breona growled. "Mind th' ice on th' floors."

Someone fetched a straightback chair and urged Tabitha into it. Capable hands worked the boots from her feet and mittens from her hands, while others pulled at the ice on her skirts.

Tabitha sighed as the weight came off. "I caught the last trolley, but the snow … it is so deep and wet."

"Aye. Billy was jest bundlin' up t' go out an' seek ye," Breona muttered. "Are you all right, Tabitha?"

Tabitha found Rose's gray eyes studying her, and she smiled. "I will be, but I do not care to do that again anytime soon!"

"Indeed, no," Rose agreed. "Most of Denver's businesses closed at noon. No one has ventured out for hours. Breona cannot even go home to her husband."

"The hospital never closes." Tabitha could feel the heat of the fire beginning to penetrate her bones, and her eyelids grew heavy. "I have thought of nothing but your dear faces and this warm fire for most of the past half hour."

"I can believe it took you that long to walk from the trolley stop," Sarah chimed in while chafing Tabitha's hand. "It was difficult enough earlier in the day! You, my dear Tabitha, are a trouper."

Rose nodded. "Yes, you are. And just as soon as we peel most of this ice off your skirts, we will get you upstairs and into dry things. Marit has been waiting dinner until you arrived."

Tabitha smiled again. *Dinner ...*

Clad in dry, warm clothing, Tabitha descended the stairs and hurried to join the others already at the table. She was just passing Rose's desk when she noticed the letter propped against her pencil jar. Tabitha plucked it up and stared at the return address.

Her heart quickened. She tucked the envelope into her pocket. *Is this the answer I have been waiting for, Lord? Will this letter confirm what I feel you have spoken to me?*

Much later, as she was preparing for bed, she remembered the letter, tore the sealed envelope open, and scanned the contents with eager eyes.

Dear Miss Hale,

We have received your letter of interest forwarded by Dean Gunderson. The American Red Cross welcomes your application. We have inspected your credentials and Dean Gunderson's letter of reference. We find your qualifications and character most suitable, particularly your training in the care and treatment of traumatic injuries.

You are correct in saying that the situation for the war wounded in Europe grows daily more alarming. Reports from the front are distressing.

Unfortunately, our organization's focus must remain, for the time being, primarily upon our mercy ship, the SS Red Cross. Our present task is to keep the ship adequately fitted with medical supplies and personnel and to position the ship to accomplish the greatest good, providing relief wherever we can, while strictly observing neutrality and impartiality.

That said, our leadership anticipates that the United States will, eventually, join the fight. When that occurs, the need for doctors and nurses will be far greater than our present numbers could possibly supply.

In response to this future need, we are screening and approving the applications of nurses such as yourself but are constrained from doing more. If you will, please hold yourself ready for our call. It may be a few months; it could be much longer.

However, Miss Hale, if you are quite prepared to serve in a more immediate capacity, may we suggest an alternate course of action? England is begging for skilled nurses.

At the onset of the war, Queen Alexandra's Imperial Military Nursing Service created the Reserve and the Territorial Force Nursing Service. The QAIMNS mobilized these nursing branches to serve the British Expeditionary Force. Presently, the Territorial Force Nursing Service has a presence on every front of the war.

This has left England herself short of nurses, and the war wounded are returning to England for extended care by the thousands. The QAIMNS draws qualified volunteer nurses from the British Red Cross to work with them in English hospitals overflowing with wounded from the European front. Your credentials make you an excellent candidate for their need.

You may write to the address below to submit your application and may include the letter of reference I have enclosed. If you are accepted and travel to England, please keep us apprised of your whereabouts. When the President grants us authorization, we will be organizing base hospitals overseas and will be pleased to enlist your services at that time.
Sincerely,
Marjorie Oxman-Steel, RN, advisor to the American Red Cross

Tabitha stared at the address below the nurse's signature. "England! I will write. And Mason is in England. This cannot be a coincidence," she whispered. Not wanting to lose any time, she composed her letter that same evening.

It was two more days before the spring storm subsided and she was able to post it.

On May 8, only weeks later, newspapers reported the sinking of the American passenger ship, *Lusitania*, torpedoed by a German U-boat. Tabitha swallowed hard when she read the account herself.

"If those Germans think the United States will take this lying down, they had better think again," Tabitha heard one doctor at her hospital declare in anger.

If I am called over to England to serve, could my ship suffer the same fate? Tabitha wondered.

No. God will not call me but that he will not also make a way. Tabitha put her chin up and tended to her duties.

The United States, in response to Germany's sinking of the *Lusitania*, protested heartily, but the president did not declare war as some had hoped he would.

Late in the month, Tabitha received a letter from Claire.

Dear Tabitha,

I have passed all my examinations and will graduate June 12. I so look forward to entering nursing. I know I am not strong enough to work in a hospital ward as you are doing, but I hope to find a family with an ill child whom I can nurse back to health. Perhaps in this way I will render service to God by being a blessing to them.

Is there any possibility you could come to my graduation? My entire family is coming, and they have planned a light lunch after the ceremony. I would count it an honor to have you here and to introduce you to them.

Tabitha shared the letter with Rose. "I would dearly love to go," Tabitha confessed, "but going by train would mean staying overnight, maybe even two nights. The hospital would not grant me that much time off."

Rose thought for a moment. "Could Mr. Carpenter's man perhaps drive you? It would make for a very long day but we did so for your graduation. Two or three hours to Boulder and the same back, returning late?"

Tabitha's answer was dubious. "I am not certain. Mason did say to call upon Banks, but—"

"If Mr. Carpenter were here, he would, no doubt, take you himself," Rose answered.

Tabitha nodded. "Yes, he would."

"Then, I should think Claire's graduation is an occasion to contact Mr. Carpenter's man."

Banks called for Tabitha early the morning of Claire's graduation. Tabitha sat alone in the spacious interior of Carpenter's motorcar, cradling a bouquet of flowers that filled the car with their fragrance. She was still marveling at Banks' response to her telephone call. He had not paused or hesitated a moment over her request.

"But of course, Miss Hale! It would be my pleasure to drive you to your friend's graduation. I know Mr. Carpenter would send his congratulations to Miss Claire as well. I shall order flowers for Miss Claire in Mr. Carpenter's name."

When they arrived at the school, Banks opened the door for her near the entrance to the school's great hall. "I shall be parked just there, miss." He pointed with his chin to a patch of grass already filling with other motorcars. "If you would care to stand here on the curb, I will watch for you and bring the car around directly."

"Thank you, Banks," Tabitha whispered, struck by his kind attention. He smiled, nodded, walked around the vehicle, and drove away to make way for others pulling up to the entrance.

When Tabitha disembarked on the familiar campus, she viewed it with fresh eyes. *It is so hard to believe an entire year has flown by,* she reflected.

The crowd was pressing her, so Tabitha moved with the flow to enter the hall and find a seat. Soon after, the graduation ceremony began. Tabitha stood with the crowd to honor the new nurses as they paraded into the hall. Dean Wellan and Dean Gunderson addressed the graduates, commending them for their achievements—and their dedication to a profession that would entail even more commitment and hard work.

Afterward, the graduates filed onto the platform and, one by one, received their caps and nursing pins. Tabitha smiled with pride as she watched Claire receive the marks of her accomplishments.

When the ceremony ended, the graduates filed out. The crowd took many minutes to exit the hall. When Tabitha emerged from the building, she looked for Claire and found her friend surrounded by her happy, proud family.

Just as I was only a year ago, Tabitha recalled. As she drew near, it was obvious that Claire had been watching for her.

"Tabitha! Oh, I am so glad you came!" She reached for Tabitha and the two of them embraced.

"I am so proud of you, Claire," Tabitha murmured into Claire's ear. "These are from Mr. Carpenter."

"Oh!" Claire's eyes glistened. "He is so generous." She hugged Tabitha again.

When they broke apart, Claire introduced Tabitha to her family. "Tabitha, these are my parents, Mr. and Mrs. Silverstine, and my brother, Robert."

"We have heard many good things about you, Miss Hale," Claire's mother said as she squeezed Tabitha's hand. "You were a strength and encouragement to Claire when she returned to school. Thank you. Thank you for helping her."

Tabitha's smile was glowing. "I saw Claire as the answer to *my* prayers, Mrs. Silverstine. She was the friend I never had at school. I am grateful to God for her."

"Will you join us for lunch, Miss Hale?" Claire's father asked.

"I would be honored. I am here with a friend's car and driver. May I meet you at the restaurant?"

Tabitha thoroughly enjoyed her time with the Silverstines. She could see that they were a simple, close-knit family. Their pride in their daughter was evident, and Claire basked in their approval and love.

As the little celebration began to break up, Tabitha said her goodbyes. "I shall watch for your letters," she told Claire, "and I expect to hear soon that you have found a good situation."

They embraced again, and Tabitha walked outside to find Banks and the waiting car.

As the next days passed by, Tabitha began to believe that she would not receive an answer from the British nursing service.

I prayed and asked you to lead me, Lord. I am sorry if I jumped ahead of your plans for me. I trust you, Father. I will continue to serve you here until you lead me otherwise.

But an answer did arrive, and its impact was immediate.

Dear Miss Hale,

We have reviewed your credentials and accept at once your kind offer to volunteer with Queen Alexandra's Imperial Military Nursing Service. Your services are needed most urgently. You will be enrolled in a Voluntary Aid Detachment through the British Red Cross and seconded to the QAIMNS.

We have arranged for you to come to us aboard the U.S. passenger ship Arabic, departing New York harbor July 1, scheduled to arrive in Liverpool, England, July 8.

Please make your way to New York City in a timely manner and present your U.S. passport at Pier 114 no later than June 30 where you will be issued travel papers and itinerary. Keep expense receipts from Denver to New York for reimbursement purposes.

We will receive you at the enclosed address, our headquarters in Surrey, where we will process and assign you to an appropriate hospital accordingly.
Cordially,
Lady Marie Perth–Lyon, Assistant to Dame Flora Becher,
Matron-in-Chief QAIMNS/QARANC

Tabitha gulped. "Lord, you did answer! And I leave soon. So soon!" The two words caught in her throat. "My ship leaves in only two weeks. I shall have to tender my notice at the hospital immediately. I must factor in how long it will take me to reach New York by train so that I arrive in time. I—" The nearness of her departure stunned her.

Tabitha reread the letter and had another realization. She found a map of England and scanned it anxiously. Her breath hitched when she located it: Surrey was in the south of England. Yorkshire, the location of Catterick airfield, was north and east.

"Not close, but not too far! Close enough that, when I am able to obtain a pass, I could go to Mason," she whispered, "although they may certainly post me to a hospital elsewhere."

She grasped at another insight. "Oh! I must tell Rose I am leaving! O Father, I know she has grown to depend upon me. Please! I ask that you bring someone to fill my place, to ease the many burdens on her shoulders."

When she finished praying, Tabitha went downstairs and found the puzzle box with the ship on its lid. She took the box upstairs, dumped the pieces on her bed, and sorted through them. When she located the corner piece she sought, she set it aside and scooped the remaining pieces into the box.

I hope they are not terribly put out when they cannot find the last corner piece next time they assemble this puzzle, but I must take this with me as a reminder of what God spoke to me.

"Miss Rose? May I have a word with you?" Tabitha waited until morning after the girls had left for work before approaching Rose. They sat down in the great room, as they often had while Tabitha was dictating her testimony, and faced each other across the low table.

"What is it, Tabitha?" Rose asked. She appeared calm, but Tabitha noticed the hanky she clenched in one hand.

She knows. She knows something of what I am about to tell her, Tabitha perceived, and her heart ached. *I am one more support Miss Rose so depends upon who will be leaving her. O Lord!*

Tabitha licked her lips. "Miss Rose, the letters from Mr. Carpenter have spoken of the great need for nurses in Europe," she began. "The numbers of war wounded are filling British hospitals to overflowing."

Rose nodded. Her grip on the hanky tightened.

"I-I felt the Lord lead me to volunteer with the Red Cross, so I wrote to them. As it turns out, they cannot do much more than they are doing at present unless the United States enters the war." Tabitha stared at her hands folded in her lap. "They suggested that I might serve in the British Nursing Service as a volunteer. I wrote to them weeks ago."

Rose sighed and nodded again.

"Yesterday I received their reply. They have accepted me." Tabitha swallowed. "They have already booked passage to England in my name. I must leave in less than two weeks," Tabitha whispered.

Rose nodded a third time but still said nothing.

"Miss Rose? Please do not be disappointed in me. I need your blessing—I could not go without it."

Rose lifted her tired eyes to Tabitha's. "My darling girl. I am not disappointed in you! How could I be? You must do what the Lord leads you to do."

They studied each other, many unspoken words flowing between them, before Tabitha choked out, "And will I go with your blessing?"

"Of course you shall have my blessing," Rose murmured. "And you know I will keep you in my prayers." She smiled as she spoke, but Tabitha had never seen such sadness in a smile. She could not bear it.

"I am sorry, Miss Rose," Tabitha sobbed.

Rose went to her and gathered her into her arms. "We must never be sorry for following where Jesus leads us."

"But I am hurting you," Tabitha sniffled, "and I said I would be here for you! This house and all its cares are too much, too much for you to bear alone!"

Rose did not say anything for a long time. She just kept her arms about Tabitha and kept stroking her back in a soothing manner. When she did speak, her voice had a dreamy quality.

"Once, long ago, God spoke to me to leave what remained of my family. I recall how hurt my mother was, how she protested my leaving her, my brother, and my childhood home."

"What did you do?" Tabitha lifted her wet eyes to Rose's.

"I did what God called me to do," Rose answered, still far away in her memories. "I never saw my mother again. She passed away a year or so later."

Rose took a cleansing breath and returned in her thoughts to the present day. "If I had not followed the prompting of the Holy Spirit? If I had listened to the voices of 'reason' and 'convention' rather than to God?"

She smiled and Tabitha was comforted to see the well of strength Rose still possessed. "If I had not obeyed God, I would not be here with you today. Look at all the things that would have gone undone had I not obeyed God when he spoke to me."

Rose gently took Tabitha by the shoulders and turned her so she could look in her eyes. "God called Abraham out of his own country and into a land he did not know. God called, but before he could show Abraham all he had in store for him, Abraham had to leave all he knew. In the same way, at some point in our lives, God calls each of us to 'go,' often without knowing what he has in store for us.

"Tabitha, my daughter, as much as it pains me to see you leave us, it would pain me more to see you disobey the call of God on your life. You have my blessing and my love. Whatever lack we suffer here when you depart, the God of all grace will fill out of his abundant provision."

Tabitha laid her head on Rose's shoulder. "Thank you, Miss Rose. Thank you for obeying God. I cannot imagine where I would be had you not followed his leading."

They were both thinking of the old Tabitha, the selfish, angry, bitter woman Marshal Pounder had delivered to Rose years before.

Rose placed her hand on Tabitha's fiery hair and stroked it. "God has redeemed and restored you, Tabitha. Now it is your turn to follow as he directs. Go and bear much fruit, my daughter."

Tabitha's preparations were complete: She would leave Denver in two days. Her train would take her to New York; there she would find the berth reserved for her on the White Star Line liner, *SS Arabic*.

As it was a Sunday afternoon, some of the Palmer House family were gathered in the great room; others were clustered in the gazebo where Corrine was reading aloud to a small knot of the young women while they did light mending or knitting.

Rose was nodding in her chair; Tabitha was in deep conversation with Sarah.

"I am praying," Sarah whispered to Tabitha. "I am asking the Lord if I should leave my position in Joy's shop to come help Miss Rose here."

"If it is God's will, I will be quite glad of it," Tabitha replied as a knock sounded on Palmer House's front door.

Mr. Wheatley answered the door and showed a young woman into the room. Rose awakened from her dozing when Tabitha leapt to her feet.

"Claire!" Tabitha rushed to embrace her friend. "Oh, Claire, my dear friend! I am so happy to see you! Everyone, this is my friend Claire from nursing school." She walked Claire from one to another until they had all shaken her hand. Of course, Rose had met her at Tabitha's graduation. She greeted Claire fondly.

"But what are you doing here?" Tabitha demanded.

"Oh, isn't it wonderful, Tabitha," Claire exulted. "I have just taken a position here in Denver! I arrived last week and am nursing a little boy who survived scarlet fever. His family is very kind to me. I have the whole of Sunday off each week, so we can see each other often and—"

Claire stared at Tabitha's shocked expression. "But aren't you happy I am here?"

"Oh, goodness, I most certainly am." Tabitha wiped away the dismay that her friend had to have seen. "It is only ..."

"What is it, Tabitha?"

Tabitha sighed. "Claire, I am leaving on Tuesday."

"Leaving? But where are you going?"

Tabitha led Claire into the parlor where they could speak in private. After she explained she added, "So you see, I must leave on the train early Tuesday morning if I am to reach New York in time to meet my ship."

"Oh, my." Claire's disappointment was evident. "I had so looked forward to us ..."

"I am so sorry," Tabitha whispered.

"No. You must not be sorry." Claire lifted her chin. "I know you will do great things for God ... over there." She shrugged. "I had high hopes we would have lovely times together. I even hoped I would come to know your friends here at Palmer House, perhaps partake of the amazing fellowship of which you told me so much."

Tabitha smiled. "That hope," she answered, "is entirely possible. Even though you live with your patient's family, I know Miss Rose will welcome you to sit with the Palmer House 'troop' at our church!"

They both laughed. At school Tabitha had described the long line of Palmer House girls marching two-by-two to church each Sunday.

"I know, too, that Miss Rose will enfold you in her little flock, Claire. I am only sorry I will not be here with you."

"You will write to me?" Claire asked.

"Of course! As often as I can."

Quite early Tuesday morning, Tabitha finished dressing and closed the only suitcase she would be taking. The house, for the most part, was still shrouded in darkness and sleep.

I said my goodbyes last night, she recalled. *No one need see me off this morning.*

Tabitha felt in the pocket of her dress. Her fingers traced the edges of the corner puzzle piece. She had pinned a clean handkerchief—with the piece folded within it—to the pocket's inside. Neither the handkerchief nor the puzzle piece would fall out of her pocket.

She slipped on a light sweater, slung her handbag over her shoulder, and carried her case down the two flights of stairs. A cab would be waiting for her at the curb to take her to Union Station.

Resolute, Tabitha stepped toward the front door—but was stopped by the soft glow of a light coming from the great room. She set her case by the door and peeked into the room. She was alarmed to see Rose slumped over her desk, her head resting upon her folded arms.

Tabitha tiptoed to the desk and heard the breathy sounds of deep sleep. Under one of Rose's hands lay her open Bible.

Has she been here all night? Did she stay up late praying for me? Tabitha wondered.

From outside Tabitha heard a horn honk once. *My cab.*

She leaned over and placed a gentle kiss on Rose's hair, careful not to disturb her. Then she let herself out of Palmer House.

Perhaps for the last time?

O Lord! I pray you will not let this be my last sight of this dear house and its dearer people!

PART 3:
A GOOD AMEN

And we have a priceless inheritance
—an inheritance that is kept in heaven…
pure and undefiled,
beyond the reach of change and decay.
(1 Peter 1:4, NLT)

CHAPTER 20

After two days on the train and one night suffered in a strange hotel, Tabitha was relieved to arrive in New York late afternoon of the second day. Yet, when she stepped down from her train, she was stunned by the enormity of Grand Central Terminal, with its forty below-ground lines and platforms and the dust and rubble of ongoing construction.

She allowed herself to be herded along by the stream of disembarking passengers until she reached the main concourse. The immense, open room was overwhelming, but it offered her an escape.

Tabitha set her face and feet toward the nearest exit. She emerged from the station amid many strange buildings and bustling crowds. When she managed to secure a cab to take her directly from the train station to the docks, she slumped with relief in her seat.

"Pier 114, please," she told the driver.

"Sure thing, lady."

The cab wove in and out of late-day city traffic—a jarring cacophony of sight, sound, and chaotic struggle between motorized and nonmotorized vehicles. Trucks, cabs, carts, vendors, farmers, and merchantmen vied for passage through the streets.

Finally, Tabitha saw the glint of water ahead of them.

"Here ya go, miss," the cabby announced.

"Could you wait for me?" Tabitha asked. "I am only picking up my ticket."

The cabby shrugged. "Sure thing, but th' meter keeps runnin'."

Tabitha presented herself at the pier's office window and tendered her newly obtained passport. As the tiny book contained only Tabitha's name, address, and description, the official studied it and then scrutinized her. With a nod, the agent handed back her passport and, after a short search, passed her a sealed envelope.

Tabitha stepped aside and perused the contents of the envelope: A letter of authorization that identified Tabitha as a nurse of the British Red Cross assigned to the QAIMNS. Her boarding papers for the *Arabic*. Instructions for travel from Liverpool to QAIMNS headquarters in Surrey. A voucher for bus and rail travel in England. A small amount of British coin and currency.

They have thought of everything, Tabitha thought with approval. She returned to her cab.

"Could you recommend a clean hotel close by?" she asked the driver.

"Yup." He wheeled the cab in a tight circle. Minutes later, he pulled alongside a modest building. "That'll be dollar fifty," he announced.

Tabitha fumbled for the change. "Could you pick me up tomorrow morning? At eight?"

"Yup."

When she arrived at the same pier the following morning, the scene was very different from the afternoon prior. Vehicles clogged the harbor streets, each trying to edge closer to the pier before disgorging their fares and luggage. Streams of passengers flowed toward the gate leading to the gangway.

"Ya might as well hoof it from here," the cabby observed with laconic logic. "Ya aint' got much t' carry anyways."

"Thank you," Tabitha replied. She handed him his money and joined the throng converging on the ship.

The *Arabic* towered above the pier and yet, at six hundred feet in length, she was not the largest of the White Star Line's ocean-going ships. Tabitha stared up at the single huge stack protruding from the center of the ship and the four masts, two aft and two fore. As she climbed the gangplank, she noted the three decks rising above the ship's main deck and the lines of portholes below the main deck.

Once aboard, Tabitha found a place at the rail among the crush of passengers waving to friends and family down on the docks. She did not want to be in her cabin when the ship slipped its moorings and steamed out of the harbor, so she set her suitcase on the deck in front of her feet, placed her hands on the rail, and surveyed the bustling activity on the pier below.

Tabitha shivered when the ship's engine rumbled and the deck beneath her feet shuddered. Two tug boats nudged the much larger ship and, amid great shouts from the crew and the cries of the passengers, the *Arabic* slid from the pier.

As the distance between shore and ship increased, so did Tabitha's view. Soon she could make out the whole of the island's lower outline, the two rivers bounding the island, and the cities on opposite shores. As the *Arabic* made its heading toward the open sea, Tabitha gazed in awe at the green-gold lady, torch uplifted, guarding the entrance to the harbor.

The crowds of passengers laughed and chattered as they broke away from the rails. Tabitha, too, went in search of her berth. A steward pointed her to a tiny cabin one flight down from the main deck. The room had two beds, one built above the other, taking up the entire width of the narrow room. A grandmotherly woman reclined upon the bottom bed. She raised her head when Tabitha entered.

"Good morning, dearie. I am Mrs. Patch. You do not mind taking the upper bed, do you?" the sweet older woman asked.

"Not at all, Mrs. Patch." Tabitha introduced herself and hoisted her suitcase onto the upper bed. She stared at her berth, at the bars along its edge that would, presumably, prevent her from rolling out onto the cabin's floor in her sleep—or in rough seas.

Hmmm. And just how shall I manage to get myself up there?

"Bit of a ladder there," her cabinmate pointed out.

Tabitha nodded and climbed, a little awkwardly, onto her mattress to try it out.

"I've been in the States for two months, visiting my children and their families in New Jersey. Headed home to England now," Mrs. Patch offered. "What are your travel plans, dearie?"

"I am a volunteer nurse with the Imperial Nursing Service," Tabitha answered. It was the first time she'd called herself part of the service.

"Bless you, dear! Bless you! Leaving your home to help us? Oh, the Lord bless you. And what part of this country do you call home?"

"Denver. In Colorado."

"Oh, my. America is so big. Where would this Denver be, dearie?"

"In the west," Tabitha replied. "In the Rocky Mountains."

"Merciful heavens! America has such tall mountains!"

A knock sounded on the door. "All passengers report to the main deck. All passengers please report to the main deck." The voice repeated the command as it faded down the passageway.

"It is the safety drill, dearie," her English shipmate informed her.

When the majority of passengers had assembled on the open deck, the captain, standing upon a box, raised his voice and bellowed, "I am Captain William Finch, master of the *Arabic*. In the event of an emergency, every passenger must know his or her lifeboat number and assembly point. First Mate Kirby will explain the process. You will give him your full attention."

The first mate took the captain's place on the box and described the manner in which cabin numbers and lifeboats corresponded. "Your cabin and lifeboat are on the same side of the ship," he shouted.

"Port side cabins, port side boats. Starb'rd cabins, starb'rd boats. D'ye see? Your lifeboat number is painted on the backside of your cabin door. Memorize it! Your life vests are stowed in cabinets directly across from your lifeboat. D' I make myself clear?"

A general murmur wafted back to him.

"I said, DO I MAKE MYSELF CLEAR?" he roared.

This time the response was quicker and louder. "Yes!"

"If the ship's claxon sounds, you will gather your party and proceed immediately to your assigned lifeboat. You will retrieve a life vest from the cabinet opposite your assigned lifeboat, and don it. You will take nothing with you other than the clothes you wear. You will *not* go back to your cabin to fetch anything. You will queue up with your backs against the ship's wall opposite your assigned lifeboat.

"You *will not* approach the rail until a crewmember sways the boat over the deck and bids you to enter it. You *will not* attempt to enter your lifeboat before you are ordered to. You *will not* attempt to board any lifeboat other than *your* assigned boat. ARE MY INSTRUCTIONS CLEAR?"

"Yes!" The passengers responded as one.

The mate stepped down and Captain Finch again climbed upon the box. He cleared his throat.

"People, we are all nervous about German U-boats patrolling the seas and sinking innocent passenger vessels. Our concern is understandable. God willing, we shall make this crossing without encountering the German Navy.

"To that end, this ship runs dark and silent at night. Come dusk, all cabin windows must be closed and covered. No exceptions. The crew will black out all windows in the dining room and salon and will douse all external ship lights save the minimum running lights needed for safe navigation."

He frowned mightily and glared around at the cowed passengers. "After dark there shall be no loud noises: No loud talking. No shouting. No singing. No music. No slamming of hatches or doors. No dropping of heavy objects. Immediately following dinner, passengers will retire to their cabins and remain there, engaging only in low conversation. In any and every event, passengers will follow crew instructions promptly and without argument."

He drew himself up. "America is not in this war. However, we are living in a time of war, and we are entering a war zone. The safety of this ship and its passengers is my responsibility. Have no doubt: *I am master here*. I will brook no deviation from these rules or any questioning of them or of a crew member's directives. Am I understood?"

"Yes, Captain!" The passengers were well and truly terrified by now, Tabitha included.

"Don't worry, dearie," Mrs. Patch soothed as the passengers dispersed. "I've crossed over many times on the *Arabic*. The captain gave the same talk on the way over. He is really quite a charming man—when there isn't a war on."

Tabitha just nodded. This was her first time aboard a ship and, as the ship left land far behind and she could no longer glimpse the shore, the expanse of open ocean turned her legs to boneless rubber.

Six days and five nights glided peacefully by. Even on the third day, when the weather had strengthened a bit, Tabitha had counted the rough sea a blessing—if the weather kept the German threat at bay.

So long as this ship stays afloat, Lord, I am content, she had prayed.

"The captain wishes me to announce that we expect to make port tomorrow by 10 a.m.," the first mate informed the passengers at dinner the evening of the sixth day.

With the news that they had made good time on their crossing and would reach Liverpool early the following day, Tabitha and her fellow passengers were elated. What the mate had omitted to mention was that the last eight hours of their journey would be the most dangerous portion of their crossing.

Tabitha rose not long after dawn to the general stirring of the ship and its passengers embarking upon a new day. She dressed, washed her face, and combed out her hair before pinning it in the severe lines she was now accustomed to as a nurse.

"You have such lovely hair, dearie," her little roommate commented. "Such as shame to keep it all bound up like that."

Tabitha smiled. "I am in the habit of it, I suppose, Mrs. Patch."

"I want to thank you, Miss Hale, for coming over to nurse our bonny boys."

The older woman's gratitude touched Tabitha's heart. She ducked her head a little, acknowledging her cabinmate's appreciation.

A shuffling and low commotion in the passageway interrupted them. Tabitha put her head out of the door and saw crew members urging passengers into the passageway and up the stairs. It was being done with as little noise as possible.

One of them noticed her. "Miss! To the dining room, right quick! Everyone!" he whispered.

"We have to go, Mrs. Patch. Right now!" Tabitha grabbed her sweater and handbag and bolted for the door.

"What is it?" Mrs. Patch followed suit and clutched her sweater and handbag to her chest.

"Shhh. Just come. Hurry, now. And quiet like," Tabitha insisted.

They joined the line of silent passengers—some in a confused state of attire—that streamed up the stairs to the main deck and into the common areas. The entire ship's complement soon crowded into the dining room and salon, and yet the room was hushed. No one dared to ask questions, but those nearest the windows scanned the sea with anxious eyes.

The ship's doctor and second mate stood upon chairs, head and shoulders above the passengers. Their threatening scowls and gestures forbade any questions.

The second mate motioned for attention. When even the faint shuffling of feet settled, he whispered, loud enough for most to hear. "Ship's lookout sighted a periscope off our starboard bow. We have radioed for assistance. If a ship of the Royal Navy is nearby, she will come."

Tabitha's throat threatened to close up on her. She heard more than saw other women nearby gasping for air.

"Silence!" the second mate growled, *sotto voce.*

The passengers stilled again, all but for a small disturbance off to Tabitha's left. She heard a man whispering as loudly as he could, "Help! My wife needs help!"

Tabitha did not hesitate. She pushed her way through the close-packed bodies, hissing, "Make way! Make way!" as she did. When she arrived at the prostrate woman, the ship's doctor was close behind her.

"Seizure," Tabitha whispered to him, taking in the woman's stiffened, jerking body at a glance.

He dropped to his knees to examine the woman. He looked up at Tabitha. "You are a nurse?" he asked softly.

She nodded and dropped to her knees opposite him. She folded her sweater and, while the doctor lifted the woman's head, she placed it underneath. The violent thumping of the woman's head against the deck was not as worrisome once Tabitha's sweater cushioned the blows.

The seizure lasted all of two minutes. As the woman began to come around, she moaned and thrashed in her confusion.

Tabitha leaned her mouth near the woman's ear. "Please lie still and quiet. You have had a seizure, but you will be all right. Please lie still and be quiet."

The attention of the assembled passengers, which had been riveted on the small drama playing out before them, suddenly shifted. They all heard the engines of their ship throttle up. The regular, dull rumbling of the engines driving the *Arabic's* twin screws, the low growl to which they were so accustomed, swelled and rose to a higher pitch.

"We're speeding up," someone whispered.

"We can't outrun a U-boat!" a man cried.

"Silence!" The second mate's glare skewered the offending passengers.

Without warning, the ship heeled over. "The captain's tryin' t' ram the U-boat," someone hissed.

"The Germans'll sink us now, f'sure!" another man groaned.

"Shut yer pie hole!" whispered several voices at once.

The *Arabic*, as unwieldy as she was, was now running hard through the dangerous waters off Ireland, scrambling for her port. Still kneeling near the woman who had suffered a seizure, Tabitha began to pray aloud in a soft voice. "O God, I do not believe you have called me to serve the war wounded only to be sunk at sea. Lord, in the name of Jesus, I beg you to save the lives on this ship! We are calling upon you, Lord! Please help us, Father God!"

"Amen," the doctor breathed.

"Yes, amen," the woman's husband added.

The *Arabic* shuddered again as the captain ordered the helm hard over. The floor of the salon tilted, and the passengers slid and struggled to keep their footing. Moments later, they both heard and felt the jarring grind of the ship's port side raking across metal. Some passengers lost their balance and fell down only to be accidentally stepped on as the deck lurched again and their fellow shipmates stumbled and tripped. Excited and terrified murmurs erupted across the salon.

"Rammed her, by God! Rammed that U-boat!" someone called.

The murmurs grew into shouts and shrieks that were drowned out by the ship's sudden, sharp claxon.

"To your lifeboat stations!" the second mate bellowed. "To your lifeboat stations!"

Tabitha's heart thumped and raced, but she made herself assist the doctor as he lifted their patient to her feet and into her husband's arms. "Get moving, man!" the doctor urged her husband. Tabitha looked about in the melee for Mrs. Patch, but could not see the tiny woman in the panicked crowd.

"Look!" a man screamed. He pointed out the port side windows of the salon. Many necks craned to see what was happening.

"It's a battleship!" another shouted. "British! Thank God!"

Tabitha caught the barest glimpse of iron gray sliding past them—and then the BOOM of guns.

"Get to your lifeboats!" the second mate bellowed again. He jumped from his box and ran to assume his own station.

"Mrs. Patch! Mrs. Patch!" The salon emptied as Tabitha sought her roommate.

"Go!" one of the crew commanded.

Tabitha raced for her cabin's side of the ship and fought her way down the deck toward her assigned lifeboat. When she reached the cabinets where the life vests were stored, she was relieved to find her roommate already lined up against the wall of the ship opposite the rails.

"Hurry, dearie!" Mrs. Patch called to her.

Tabitha reached for one of the remaining vests and struggled to put it on. A crew member grabbed it and jerked the vest over her head.

"Tie it off here and here," he instructed before turning away.

But Tabitha was staring at the scene in the sea before her. The British battleship, perhaps a quarter mile off the *Arabic's* port side, was sending lifeboats of her own into the water.

"Captain Finch scraped that U-boat's side, he did, and the crew took shots at it as we came close," Mrs. Patch said from Tabitha's elbow. "Some was saying the German boat could not go under the water after that. The battleship arrived before the U-boat could get away."

"What are they doing?" Tabitha screened her eyes with her hands but could only make out dots bobbing in the water.

"Our boys sank that U-boat, thank the good Lord! Now they are trying to save the Germans who jumped as their boat was going under."

Tabitha stared—and finally understood that the "dots" bouncing in the frothy sea were *men*.

The claxon overhead ceased. Tabitha's ears still rang from its harsh blare, but she sighed in relief as the order went round, "Secure lifeboats! Secure lifeboats!"

The danger was over.

From the rails of the *Arabic*, Tabitha watched the docks of Liverpool drawing closer. She and her fellow shipmates exchanged sighs and shy glances, mutual expressions of relief, of freely drawn breaths and slowing heart rates.

Tabitha sucked in the tangy salt air and blew it out. *I do not care to repeat such a scare, Lord.*

Thirty minutes later, they docked and passengers began to line up to disembark.

"Goodbye, dearie." Mrs. Patch patted Tabitha's arm and padded off toward the gangplank, her suitcase in hand. Tabitha soon lost sight of her.

Down on the docks, Tabitha clutched her own suitcase and handbag and looked about for the bus service her instructions promised. She knew those instructions by heart: She was to take a bus from her port of entry to the rail yards. There she would board the next train to London's Victoria station. From Victoria station she was to catch the Brighton line to Surrey.

Tabitha felt in her pocket for the folded paper that identified her as a VAD for the nursing service. She need only to show the letter on the bus or train to be given a ticket.

From the docks to the rail yards, Tabitha looked about her with wide eyes. The bustle was much like what she had seen in New York, but something about the people was different: They carried themselves with grim determination and rushed at their duties or raced to their destinations with dogged haste.

War, Tabitha comprehended with a shiver. *They are at war. How many here have already lost son or husband, brother or cousin?*

Despite her instructions, Tabitha lost her way in Victoria station and had to ask for directions to the Brighton line. After she reached the right platform and boarded the train, she settled herself in the compartment and watched the green of the countryside chug by.

The trip was not long; the clock in the station where she disembarked read 2 p.m. She passed vendors in the street, many selling foods.

I am starving, Tabitha realized when her stomach lurched. *I have not eaten today!*

Fumbling for the British money in her purse she approached a vendor selling pastries. "What are those, please?"

"Meat pasty," the vendor answered. He cocked his head at her. "You a Yank?"

"I beg your pardon?"

"Yank. American."

"Oh. Yes." She pointed at a steaming pie the size of her palm. "I'll take one, please."

He wrapped the pie in a piece of brown paper. "That'll be twelve pence."

Tabitha opened her palm and studied the coins there. "I apologize. I am new here. Could you help me?"

He stirred the coins in her palm and picked out one. "Shilling. Same as twelve pence." he slapped the coin on the counter, pointed to it, and then studied her a moment, puzzled. "Not many tourists knockin' down th' door t' Merry Old England these days."

She shrugged. "I am not a tourist, actually. I am a nurse. I'll be reporting to the QAIMNS today as a volunteer."

"Cor! A VAD? From America?" He seemed astounded.

Tabitha shrugged again. "Yes."

He looked away and then pushed the shilling toward her. "Pie's on me t'day, miss. And thank ye fer yer service."

Tabitha hesitated before she picked up the coin. "You are most kind."

"Bloody war. Lost m' baby brother in France last fall," he muttered. He looked away again, but not before Tabitha saw the glimmer of tears in his eyes.

"I shall do my best here," she whispered. "God bless you."

CHAPTER 21

That evening Tabitha was given a bed in a VAD dormitory. She was exhausted and did not pay much attention to her surroundings. In the morning, however, she awoke with fresh eyes and ears.

Around her three nurses of a Volunteer Aid Detachment (she had heard the man at the lunch counter yesterday call her a "VAD," pronouncing each letter) readied themselves for their shift at the nearby hospital. They eyed Tabitha, and she listened to their chatter, but they did not speak to her. Tabitha, for her part, had difficulty understanding them, so broad and strange were their accents and many of their words or phrases.

The three VADs were clad in simple blue-gray dresses, immaculate aprons, and typical white nursing hats, each sporting a small red cross. The girls tugged on white oversleeves designed to protect their dress sleeves, and each girl wore a single white armband with a red cross upon it.

The three VADs were nearly ready to depart as a group when Tabitha asked, "Pardon me. I am new here. Before you go, could you please tell me where I am to report?"

They had watched her, curious but silent—until she opened her mouth.

"Blimey! She's a Yank!" one expostulated.

"You daft? You never seen a Yank?" another jeered.

That girl, sandy haired and bright-eyed, pointed her chin toward the window behind Tabitha. "Report t' matron 'cross th' yard, Yank. She'll put you right. And chivvy along. She runs peevish midmorning."

"Um, thank you kindly," Tabitha replied, not following half of what the girl said.

"Ooo! So posh, is she," the first girl commented with a little sneer.

"Oh, budge up, Nancy, and let me at th' sink. We're late as is."

The three VADs at last clattered down the stairs leaving Tabitha alone. She peered out the window and noted her destination, the official-looking row of buildings on the far side of the grass.

Tabitha took extra care with her toilet that morning and made certain not one strand of her flaming hair escaped the severe knot she pinned at her neck. She gathered her handbag and made sure she had the envelope she had picked up at the pier in New York. It contained the letter identifying her as an incoming VAD. She patted her pocket: Her handkerchief and its precious corner piece were secure.

She marched up the steps to the building and introduced herself to the receptionist typing away inside. "Good morning. My name is Tabitha Hale. I am here to report for intake."

She handed the letter to the woman, who examined it and nodded. "One moment, please." She was back in another moment. "Please go right in."

Tabitha slipped through the door the receptionist indicated. There she found two other women, one behind a sizable desk, the other standing close to it.

"Good morning, Miss Hale. I am Lady Perth–Lyon, assistant to the Matron-in-Chief. This is Sister Alistair. I take it your crossing was uneventful?" Lady Perth-Lyon was a mature woman with pleasant features. Her head bore a crown of graying braids.

Tabitha thought of the *Arabic's* near disaster with the U-boat but did not mention it. Instead she nodded. "Thank you, yes."

Lady Perth-Lyon set her head to one side and studied Tabitha. Tabitha realized both women were examining her. She remained placid under their scrutiny.

Finally Lady Perth-Lyon broke the silence. "We are in a bit of a quandary about you, Miss Hale."

Tabitha raised her brows. "I beg your pardon?"

"Yes. Quite ..." The gray-haired woman tapped her pen on her desk pad and bent a questioning eye on Sister Alistair.

Sister Alistair wore a pale blue-gray dress similar to the VADs Tabitha had met in her dormitory but, at present, no apron. Tabitha noted two inch-wide bands of scarlet set upon her sleeves just above the white cuffs. Around her shoulders and under a stiff white collar she wore a short cape—its color a darker blue than her dress—trimmed with a wide band of scarlet.

An oblong medal at the end of a short ribbon hung from the nurse's cape just over her breast. Tabitha recognized the medal as the symbol of the QAIMNS. And rather than a nurse's cap, Sister Alistair's head was bound in a simple white wimple with a veil that hung down in the back just past her shoulders.

Lady Perth-Lyon smiled a little. "You see, Miss Hale, Queen Alexandra's Imperial Military Nursing Service belongs to the army and has very strict standards of admission. QAIMNS nurses must, first of all, be British—and you are not British, of course."

Tabitha nodded her understanding. "Yes, ma'am."

"Our nurses must also be ladies of good social standing and have completed a rigorous course of training—three years at an approved hospital, in the main."

Tabitha nodded again. "Yes, ma'am. I am aware."

"Our VADs, on the other hand, come to us primarily from the ranks of the less educated. They are not trained nurses, nor are they necessarily of good social or, er, moral standing. Many of our volunteers are simple, rough, frequently coarse, and without proper qualifications—except that they are willing. They often serve, not in any nurse's aide capacity, but as cooks, kitchen maids, laundresses, and clerks."

Lady Perth-Lyon sighed and studied the papers on the desk before her. "However, you, Miss Hale, have been very well trained and have nursing specialties we covet. We normally do not interview our VADs. They are recruited elsewhere and sent on to us through the British Red Cross. But you ..."

She turned that discerning eye upon Tabitha again. "Until we could meet with you personally, we could not form an opinion regarding your character or professionalism. What we observe at present seems to confirm the glowing recommendation of—" she looked down again, "One Emilia Gunderson, Dean of Nursing at the school you attended in Boulder, Colorado, and from which you graduated ... with honors."

Sister Alistair stirred. "You see, Miss Hale, we cannot place you in the QAIMNS where by training and character you belong. We cannot even enroll you in the QAIMNS Reserves. Times are changing and the need is great, but the standards have not yet shifted to meet the need. And yet, you are far *too* qualified to be wasted in the ranks of the VADs. This is the quandary of which we spoke."

"I see," Tabitha murmured.

Well, Lord? she inquired. She waited for the two women to decide her fate.

Lady Perth-Lyon looked again at the papers on her desk. "It says here that you were proctor to the incoming freshman class in your school? What can you tell me about your responsibilities in that role?"

Tabitha raised her brows in surprise. *I do not wish to discuss my problems at school and how Nurse Rasmussen sabotaged my graduation— that would only lead to more questions.*

Instead she answered simply, "Mine was a new and somewhat unique position, ma'am. I had to leave school in my freshman year to address a family emergency, thus delaying my graduation."

She swallowed hard and pushed ahead into safer topics. "In my last year at school, I needed only to complete my required core nursing hours. However, it was then that Deans Wellan and Gunderson offered me the position of Head Proctor. I held office hours, mentored struggling students, and helped them to address particular needs when they arose. During my last year I also took two specialty courses, one in infectious diseases and one in traumatic wound care."

"Yes, both courses are of interest to us," Sister Alistair murmured, "as is your experience as Head Proctor."

Lady Perth-Lyon folded her hands and stared at Tabitha. "Tell me, Miss Hale. Why are you here?"

Tabitha thought for a moment. "I am here to serve, ma'am."

"But in what capacity?" Sister Alistair insisted.

Tabitha turned toward her. "Ma'am, I hope to be of service where I can best be used, but I am not afraid of hard work. Wherever the need is, I am willing."

Lord, wherever you need me, she pledged silently.

The two women opposite her exchanged glances, and Sister Alistair nodded.

Lady Perth-Lyon pursed her lips and replied. "Very well, Miss Hale. We thank you in advance for your service. We are sending you to Colchester Military Hospital as a VAD. Colchester is an army hospital in Essex, not far from here. Sister Alistair is also posted there and you may see her occasionally.

"Understand that wounded soldiers are treated first at casualty clearing stations and then field hospitals. Those who require ongoing surgeries, hospitalization, and convalescence are sent home to military hospitals such as Colchester. You will see every kind of injury possible at this posting, and they are quite in need of skilled nurses. We may, later on, have something more suitable for you."

She signed some paperwork, folded and sealed it into an envelope, and extended the envelope to Tabitha. "Please report to Matron Edwynna Stiles, chief nurse of the hospital. Give her this letter. The receptionist outside my office will provide you with directions."

"Thank you, ma'am," Tabitha answered.

A young volunteer put Tabitha aboard a bus later that morning, and Tabitha arrived at Colchester Military Hospital late in the afternoon. The hospital lay within an army troop and cavalry station.

Army administration buildings and a myriad of tents, stables, and parade grounds formed a labyrinth. The hospital itself was an imposing collection of three-story brick buildings, a few topped by crenelated battlements and towers.

Tabitha, after asking directions several times, presented herself to the matron's office. Her interview with Matron Stiles went much as her meeting with Lady Perth-Lyon and Sister Alistair had gone.

After perusing the letter from Lady Perth-Lyon, the matron asked, "Are you willing to undertake the same duties as any other VAD?" Matron Stiles was a stern woman, but something about the set of her mouth gave Tabitha hope that she was also a fair one.

"Yes, ma'am, I am."

"You will call me Matron, Hale. QAIMNS nursing sisters in charge of hospitals are addressed as Matron. Other nursing sisters are addressed as Sister. VADs are addressed by their surnames, although patients often call them 'nurse.' I dare say many things are different here than where you trained. Please make an effort to adapt yourself."

"I will, Matron," Tabitha answered.

"Draw your uniforms from the supply window. My clerk will assign you to a dormitory and a ward. Good day, Hale," Matron Stiles dismissed her.

That evening Tabitha again slept in a dormitory of VADs. Ten young women in total occupied the top floor of a brick building poorly illuminated by dormer windows. As Tabitha introduced herself, the girls, all of whom were younger than her, had the same reactions as the VADs in Surrey.

"You American, then?" one asked.

"Yes, I am," Tabitha answered.

They silently took Tabitha's measure, and several of the girls whispered together. In the end, they offered to show her where to pick up her uniforms and where to take her meals.

Tabitha received a cap, two uniform dresses (with admonitions to wash one each day), four aprons, and four sets of oversleeves that afternoon. She was told to report to her ward promptly at seven the following morning.

After dinner she ironed and hung her uniforms. As she undressed for bed, her fingers touched the hanky and puzzle piece pinned inside her pocket. Tabitha unpinned them and held them in her hand a long moment.

Then she tucked them into the corner of her suitcase.

"VAD Hale reporting, Sister," Tabitha said in a quiet voice, but she was staring down the long ward at the rows of beds all filled with men. Wounded men. Every patient an amputee.

The collective groaning, murmuring, and sighing of the patients was, in itself, indicative of the level of pain they were suffering.

The harried nursing sister who oversaw the ward looked up from her charts and sighed. "Another new one, eh? And likely you canna even make a proper bed." She waved for one of the VADs Tabitha roomed with to come over. "Darby, be showin' Hale here about and have her follow you today."

"This way," Darby motioned. Away from the sister, Darby frowned. "Look lively, Yank. I will tell and show you something but one time."

"Got it." Tabitha ground her teeth to bite back a smart retort.

I am here to serve as you wish, Lord. Please help me to do so humbly and to have and keep a meek heart.

Then she had a disconcerting realization: *My trials at school taught me how to exercise control over my temper and acid tongue.* She chuckled inwardly. *That self-control should serve me well here.*

Darby pulled a stack of linens from a deep closet. "We keep clean linens here. Dirty ones go in that bin. Night shift feeds the patients breakfast at six; we come on and clear away the remains, after which we change all the linens in the ward."

Tabitha noticed the other two VADs stacking dishes and collecting trays.

"Pay attention." Darby thumped the stack of linens into Tabitha's arms and retrieved another stack from the closet. "Our patients are not amb'latory—that means they cannot get out of bed on their own—so changin' linens is a trick. We work two nurses to a bed to shift the boys while we remove the soiled sheets and replace them with clean."

She leaned toward Tabitha, her brows pulled down. "They's already in pain enow. Have a care you don't hurt them more, eh?"

Darby motioned Tabitha to the other side of a bed. "Stand over yon." She gripped her side of the bottom sheet.

To the legless patient she said in a bright voice, "Good morning, love," and rolled the man toward Tabitha.

Of course, Tabitha knew what to do. She and Darby changed the patient's linens, rearranged his pillow, and disposed of the soiled sheets in less than two minutes.

"Ye've done this b'fore, I wager." Darby waved an accusing finger under Tabitha's nose.

"I wager." Tabitha's response was dry.

"S' you're not a green VAD?" She considered Tabitha with a glimmer of respect.

Tabitha lifted one shoulder. "Never said I was."

"Ha!" Darby grinned and they moved to the next bed. The ward had twelve patients down each side of the room. Tabitha and Darby, working more and more as a well-oiled team, changed the linens of the entire ward in less than an hour.

As they finished, Tabitha noticed the Sister checking their work. The nurse nodded in approval. "Well done, Darby, Hale."

"That's high praise, I'd say," Darby whispered.

"What is her name?" Tabitha asked.

"Sister McDonald. C'mon, then. Let's get the bin to the laundry. I'll show you the way."

Tabitha worked hard that day and took pains to catalog the differences between the manner in which her hospital in Denver did things and how Sister McDonald ran her ward. Tabitha observed a process closely before attempting a duty. The other VADs on the ward, two of them, said nothing to her, but they watched Tabitha with growing approval, as she mastered one duty after another.

Shortly after the VADs had served lunch to the patients, a grizzled older doctor whisked into the ward. "Where is Sister McDonald?" he demanded. "I have post-surgery wounds to examine."

Tabitha could see how frazzled the doctor was. *I can't imagine how overworked this poor man must be*, she thought.

"She is at her lunch, Dr. Furler," Darby answered. "I am certain she did not expect you. You are usually here an hour from now."

He cursed under his breath and growled, "I have an amputation in an hour and cannot be late. One of you will have to assist me in my examinations here."

The other two VADs skittered to the end of the ward and busied themselves there. That left Darby and Tabitha staring at each other—and Darby shot Tabitha a plea for help.

Tabitha shrugged. "I would be happy to assist, doctor," she offered.

The doctor grunted and moved to his first patient. "Hurry up, then."

"Darby, where are the wound care trays?" Tabitha hissed.

Darby jumped to show Tabitha where the supplies were kept. Tabitha, armed with the appropriate dressings and instruments, moved alongside the doctor and wordlessly anticipated and supplied what he needed as he removed dressings and examined or treated wounds.

In America, the status of a doctor was far above that of a nurse and, Tabitha saw, it was no different here. She was silent as she worked with the doctor, but she was trained to foresee a physician's needs. If Dr. Furler scowled at what she presented to him, she had a second option already in hand.

They reached the last of the five patients he had come to examine. Private Pierce, perhaps age eighteen, had lost his leg below the knee. Tabitha smiled at the boy, hoping to reassure him.

The doctor began to gently work the sticky bandage free from the boy's stump. Just as he pulled it away, blood spurted from the wound. Great pulsing jets of it shot across the end of the bed and onto the floor.

The doctor swore and clamped the soiled bandage onto the wound. "Hemorrhage!" he snarled.

"Here, doctor." Tabitha slapped a sterile cloth on the bed and dropped a scalpel and a clamp followed by a thick pad of bandages onto the clean surface. She wrapped her hands about the soiled bandage and took over the task of keeping pressure on it. As soon as the doctor released the pressure for her to maintain, he grabbed the clamp and pad. Moments later, he had sliced open the stitches on one side of the stump's flap, located the bleeding vessel and clamped it.

Blood was everywhere—staining the floor, spattered on the bed, covering Tabitha's gloved hands. Tabitha called to Darby, "We need sutures and needles. Several sizes. And clean gloves. Right away!"

Darby jumped to gather what was needed and delivered them to her. Tabitha stripped off her soiled gloves. Darby awkwardly helped her don fresh ones. While Darby regloved the doctor, Tabitha sorted through the needles and sutures and presented her estimate of the best size to him.

"Very good, nurse," he muttered. Within moments he had tied off the ruptured blood vessel and removed the clamp.

"I do not like the looks of this stump," he muttered aloud.

Tabitha leaned closer, sniffing and noting the puffiness. "Something in the wound is suppurating."

"Yes," Dr. Furler agreed. "I need to open the flap all the way and look for the source of infection. Can you prepare for that?"

"Yes, doctor," Tabitha answered. She rattled off a short list of instruments to Darby who now stood by to fetch anything they needed. The other VADs hovered nearby, watching with interest.

Tabitha spoke to their patient. "Private Pierce, the doctor must open your stump to clean it. It may pain you, but you must keep entirely still. We do not want to cause more bleeding. Can you do that?"

She gestured with her chin at one of the VADs. "Bollard, please stand by Private Pierce's head to calm him. The girl moved to obey Tabitha.

The doctor clipped the remaining stitches around the stump's flap and laid it open. Before Tabitha could stop herself, she pointed. "There."

"Indeed," Dr. Furler muttered. "The tissue here has necrotized. Scalpel."

Tabitha had the sharp instrument at the ready. As the doctor cut through and removed the dead tissue, Tabitha offered sterile water for him to rinse the wound.

He frowned. "How does this look, nurse? I am afraid my sight is not all it used to be."

Tabitha leaned in again. "Is that a tiny bone fragment, doctor?"

He looked where she pointed and took a pair of tweezers from her hand to probe it. "Yes, it is. You have good eyes," he mumbled.

Fifteen minutes later, the doctor had finished redressing the stump and Tabitha was gathering the bloodied instruments and soiled bandages.

"Darby," she said, "Let's change Private Pierce's bed again, shall we?"

That was when she noticed Sister McDonald. The nursing sister, hands clasped behind her back, was observing and nodding. "You did well, Hale."

"Yes, she did. What is she doing in a VAD uniform?" the doctor complained with a scowl. "Obviously she is a skilled nurse."

"Yes, doctor. We are aware. However, this is only Nurse Hale's first day with us."

He rounded on Tabitha and she stepped back, a bit startled.

"Do you have surgical experience?"

"I-I am trained in all aspects of nursing, doctor, but have not worked surgery since school. However, I took a specialty course in traumatic wound care, and I worked in the emergency services ward at my last hospital."

"And where, pray tell, was that?" he demanded.

"Denver, Colorado, doctor."

The other VADs were ogling Tabitha with wide eyes now. Darby stared at her with something close to awe.

"American. Right! I heard we had an American volunteer. A unique situation." He turned to Sister McDonald. "Well, she is wasted as a VAD, do you not think?"

"We have plans for her, Doctor. We hope to utilize her better as soon as she has settled in."

Tabitha, startled again, wondered, *What does that mean?*

The doctor harrumphed and checked his watch. "Late. I'll be back this evening to see this patient."

Sister McDonald looked at Tabitha, a ghost of a smile playing on her lips. "A fine first day, Nurse Hale. Carry on."

"Wot? She called you *Nurse Hale*," Darby whispered.

Tabitha laughed. "I guess she did."

When their twelve-hour shift ended, Tabitha was exhausted but elated. *Thank you, Lord! Thank you for helping me, for strengthening me today.*

She fell into bed after dinner and slept until six the following morning, when Darby shook her awake.

"I say, *Nurse Hale*, you sleep like th' dead. Get up now or we'll be late."

Tabitha groaned but rolled out of her cot. Her first sight of the day was Darby's grinning face and the curious eyes of her fellow dorm mates.

"Don't think we've been prop'ly introduced," Darby smiled, holding out her hand. "Ellen Darby, VAD."

"Tabitha Hale, quite out of my league, I fear," Tabitha returned with a yawn.

"Cor, and I doubt that." Darby grabbed Tabitha's arm. "Come on, now. You mustn't be late, *Nurse Hale*."

The other girls in the dorm giggled, but they were good-natured giggles.

Thank you, Lord! Tabitha prayed. *It is going to be all right.*

CHAPTER 22

All but two of the VADs in Tabitha's dormitory had Sunday off, and Tabitha finally had the time and energy to write letters—one home to Palmer House, one to Claire, and one to Mason Carpenter. She took her time on the letter to Carpenter, knowing that its contents would astonish him, but she could not stop smiling as she wrote it.

My dear Mr. Carpenter,

I pray that, by God's grace, you are well and fruitful in your walk with him!

I have something to tell you, dear friend. Your letters speaking of the overflow of wounded in British hospitals spoke deeply to my heart.

After much prayer, the Lord led me to volunteer with the American Red Cross to nurse the wounded. Unfortunately, at this time, they have a presence in the war zone only on their hospital ship, the SS Red Cross. They did, however, suggest that I volunteer with Queen Alexandra's Imperial Military Nursing Service, via the British Red Cross, to serve in a Voluntary Aid Detachment.

This I did and was accepted. I arrived in England a week back and was posted to Colchester Military Hospital in Essex. The administration does not yet know quite what to do with me as I have been trained as a nurse and most VADs have not; however, I am content to serve where the Lord places me.

For the past week I have worked in a ward of amputees. I cannot tell you how these young men touch my heart. I often sit by their bedsides to talk with them or write letters for them. Only two days past, I was honored to pray with a young soldier to receive Jesus as his Savior and Lord. Although he is racked with what is called "phantom pain," I see the peace of Christ now resting on his brow, and he smiles with a joy that makes every difficulty bearable.

My dear Mr. Carpenter, please do write to me at the address below? I hope and pray that Colchester is not too far from Catterick and that, someday soon, I will have earned a two- or three-day pass and can come to visit you.

Yours always,
Tabitha

The Monday after Tabitha had worked on the ward for two weeks, Sister McDonald called her into the little closet the ward used as an office.

"Nurse Hale, you will please report to Matron."

"Yes, Sister." But Tabitha felt frozen and could not move.

"Nurse Hale, you are adapting to our ways. Obviously you are a fine nurse." Sister McDonald's eyes crinkled in a friendly fashion. "Go on, now. Matron Stiles wishes to speak to you."

When Tabitha appeared before Matron Stiles, Tabitha was amazed to see Sister Alistair with her. The nurse nodded at Tabitha. "Good morning, Nurse Hale."

"Good morning, Sister."

Matron Stiles did not beat about the bush.

"Nurse Hale, we have a proposition for you, one that will utilize your skills and experience even though we cannot muster you into the QAIMNS. Would you be interested?"

"Yes, I believe so, Matron. Um, what do you have in mind?"

"We would like to appoint you head of Colchester's nursing VADs."

"I beg your pardon?"

"Nurse Hale, we wish you to manage our VADs. Oh, not all of them; I am speaking of those who are medical aides. We wish you to manage their training, discipline, keep them in order, that sort of thing."

"Me?" But Tabitha felt herself growing a little excited.

"Yes. We nursing sisters quite flinch when new VADs arrive. Some are minimally prepared; most are not. A few are entirely unsuitable." The matron leaned toward Tabitha, her smile growing. "I think you would agree that the VAD ranks are quite a mashup. However, we are so short on nursing sisters, that we must find ways to improvise, to stretch and better manage our resources.

"Mind you, what we are proposing is novel. Some would—and I dare say, *will*—call our idea unorthodox or revolutionary. Nevertheless, Matron-in-Chief wishes us to proceed. My nurses cannot leave their posts to train these volunteers, but you can."

Sister Alistair spoke for the first time. "Sister McDonald has reported on your performance and your willingness to work hard to her exacting standards. We have also received a good report from Dr. Furler who, it seems, is outraged that we are underutilizing you."

"Quite so, Sister." Matron Stiles bent her gaze on Tabitha. "We would like you to take charge of the hospital's VADs and bring them up to our standards. In a limited capacity, of course. What do you say?"

Suddenly Tabitha grinned. "I say *yes*, Matron. It would be my pleasure to serve in this way."

"Excellent. We shall reassign you to different lodging and—"

"Um, no, thank you, Matron. I should like to remain where I am, if that is acceptable."

The two older nurses studied her. "Very well," the matron conceded. "If you think it wise."

"Do I understand correctly that I will remain a VAD?" Tabitha asked.

"Yes," Matron Stiles admitted. "That is true."

"Then I should prefer to lead by example, wherever possible," Tabitha explained. "My presence in the dormitory will help."

Sister Alistair queried the matron. "American egalitarianism?"

Matron Stiles said nothing, but she finally nodded. "Very well. We shall see how you get on."

Word of Tabitha's appointment spread through the hospital ranks. Her fellow VADs did not know how to react. They stepped back from Tabitha and waited to see what would happen.

Tabitha, relieved of her nursing duties, began visiting every ward in the hospital to evaluate the working VADs. She studied the expectations of the nursing sisters, made notes of areas of incomplete (or utterly lacking) VAD training and, with Matron Stiles' permission, instituted mandatory hour-long classes each evening directly after the day shift ended and each morning as the VADs came off night shift.

The timing of the classes was hugely unpopular with the VADs, but they had no choice in the matter. Each shift had nearly one hundred VADs: The sullen volunteers gathered in the basement classroom Tabitha had appropriated, and the enormity of the task before Tabitha became clearer.

Tabitha studied her students and saw the widest array of backgrounds and aptitude she could imagine. She discovered that not all the VADs assigned to the hospital were young girls either. Some were middle-aged spinsters or widows, some older than she.

Tabitha huffed. *Lord, this will be like chasing chickens around my father's barnyard!*

"Our goals," Tabitha began, "are to become exemplary volunteers and to disprove the notion that VADs cannot assume and adequately perform many daily nursing duties. If you have a desire to make nursing your permanent vocation, I can help you. I can help you *if* you work hard."

She noted the women whose interest she had aroused. "If you set your mind to learn and you acquit yourself satisfactorily, I will note your progress in your record. When opportunities for advancement arise, your training will be your friend."

Tabitha focused an entire week's classes on a single, specific set of nursing duties or skills. "Each week, once you perform well on the week's tasks, you may be excused from the remainder of the classes for that week," she informed the surly volunteers. "However, if you are sloppy, slow, or incorrigible, you will train extra hours until you are proficient. And you will become proficient. Those who do not become proficient will receive a poor report. Two such reports and you will be removed as a nursing aide."

The VADs looked at each other. A few straightened.

At the end of the first week's classes, Tabitha took each shift and broke it into two cohorts. She appointed the two most competent VADs from the shift to be cohort proctors. One of the appointed proctors was Ellen Darby.

"I will address you," Tabitha announced, pointing to the group on her left, "as Colchester Green. You," she pointed to the cohort on her right, "Will be Colchester Blue. Night shift cohorts are Colchester Red and Gold."

Curious and excited rumblings ran through her class.

Then Tabitha called the proctors to her side and gave the two women narrow armbands the color of their cohort's name to wear above their Red Cross armbands. Tabitha herself wore a wide red armband designating her as Head VAD.

Tabitha addressed the two proctors. "Please wear your armbands whenever you are in uniform. Wear the symbols of your leadership proudly and acquit your cohort well, but understand that only the best VADs may wear these armbands—they are not permanent appointments."

Tabitha observed as the other VADs began to comprehend the armbands' honor and significance.

"You can see how large our cohorts are," Tabitha added, keeping her voice casual. "If others of you demonstrate your competence to my satisfaction and show an eager willingness to improve the performance of your entire group, I may be inclined to break the two cohorts into four and appoint additional proctors."

The two proctors considered each other, and speculative eyes followed Tabitha.

The following Monday, as the classes focused on a new set of skills, Tabitha noted a shift in morale. The VADs began to willingly assist their fellows, and a sliver of competition grew between the cohorts—a competition that spurred overall class progress.

Very good, Tabitha breathed.

Tabitha's days were long. She arose early to instruct the outgoing night shift and stayed late to teach the day shift. From the start of the first class she established high standards, and she allowed no VAD to fall below her expectations.

Tabitha coached the VADs in proper etiquette when interacting with doctors and nursing sisters: She drilled the women on the correct manner in which to answer a physician's or nurse's questions, how to respond to their instructions, how to ask clarifying questions, and how to properly report on a patient's condition.

She evaluated every VAD's posture and deportment. She demanded that each woman stand tall with hands at her sides or clasped in front of her.

"No nurse or aide stands, sits, walks, or works in a sloppy, lackadaisical manner. Every movement is to have purpose; every task is to be done well. Our very presence, wherever we go, should inspire confidence in our abilities and professionalism."

Tabitha reprimanded any VAD who slouched or slumped. She corrected posture so often in the first weeks that merely her entrance into classroom or ward produced a general "snapping to attention."

She instructed the VADs in basic sanitation rules and expectations. The volunteers learned the importance of personal and nursing hygiene. They practiced cleaning and sterilizing instruments using boiling water, chemicals, and the autoclave. She emphasized sanitary processes to prevent necrotic and bacterial gangrene, other bacterial infections, or infectious disease.

"A hospital is the perfect breeding ground for contagion," Tabitha insisted to her students. "Our cleanliness—the care we take in washing our hands, wearing clean garments, and using only sterile fields and instruments—can prevent infection or disease. Think of our patients! They are vulnerable and we are their guardians. We must not be sloppy or inattentive to our duty."

Then Tabitha moved on to the differing care for their patients' many and varied injuries: shell-shock, amputations, gas inhalation, brain trauma, burns, bullet wounds, and internal injuries.

The gas inhalation cases that came to them from the field hospitals of the Western Front were beyond horrible to treat. The patients often developed pneumonia or emphysema and, despite the hospital's best efforts, died horrible, suffocating deaths. The pitifully few men who survived suffered scarred lungs and a lifetime of illness and disability.

Tabitha reminded her students that the majority of gas cases died immediately when the heavy chlorine gasses sank to the bottom of the soldiers' trenches. Worse, those soldiers who survived but had inhaled lethal doses died only days later.

Tabitha taught the VADs how to write letters for the soldiers. She taught them to suggest salutations and letter closures, how to identify themselves as the letter writer, how to best describe the soldier's wounds and treatment to his family, and how to include cheerful tidbits. She also taught them how to write to a deceased patient's family. She demonstrated how kind, well-chosen words could provide comfort.

Tabitha stressed proper conversation while treating patients; she instructed the VADs in appropriate responses to inappropriate comments or behaviors and, above all, how to maintain a professional attitude at all times.

The most difficult task to train was how to bathe patients who were bedbound.

"Nursing sisters and orderlies will not always be available to perform this task. Given the shortage of nurses and the overflow of the wounded returning from the war zone, this situation is likely to worsen. We must, therefore, be prepared to take up this routine duty.

"If you have never seen a man's unclothed body before, this task will, initially, seem difficult," Tabitha told them in a matter-of-fact manner. "We will practice in groups of two until you can perform this task well and without qualms."

She began scheduling the groups of two when she could be present to instruct, and made sure that the first students scheduled were not squeamish on the idea. She began in Sister McDonald's amputee ward with Darby and the other proctor, Hensley.

"When you have become proficient at this task," Tabitha informed the two women, "you will assist me in training the others of your cohorts."

Sister McDonald looked on as Tabitha demonstrated how to position the screens around a patient's bed and perform the bath.

"May I assist you, Nurse Hale?" the sister asked.

"I would be honored, Sister," Tabitha replied.

It took four weeks for every VAD to complete the training. Afterward, with the permission of Sister McDonald, she assigned her proctors to oversee the regular bathing of patients in her ward until the VADs were deemed able to perform the task without supervision.

Then Tabitha moved her proctors to another ward and repeated the process. Slowly, the VADs began to assume the responsibility for bathing patients.

Between class times, Tabitha visited wards and monitored her students, lending her hands, modeling correct habits and, when needed, applying discipline.

Discipline, she discovered, was an ongoing problem. A few of the patients were incorrigible flirts—and some of the VADs flirted back. When Tabitha first witnessed one of her VADs flirting, she called the girl into the hall and did not mince words.

"VADs and nurses do not fraternize with patients, Edwards, nor do they, at any time, behave unprofessionally in the wards—regardless of a patient's manner. Do you understand me?"

Edwards, a sulky young woman, pursed her mouth and did not answer.

"I asked you a question, Edwards."

"Yes, I understand," the girl ground out.

"You will address me correctly and with a proper attitude or I shall assign corrective measures." Tabitha's tone was icy.

"Yes, I understand, Nurse Hale," Edwards whispered, but underneath she was still defiant.

Tabitha stared with cold disdain until the young woman's eyes dropped to her shoes.

"You have a good touch, Edwards," Tabitha murmured, "and can make something of yourself without flirting. Do not make the mistake of thinking a *worthy* young man will respect a girl with loose manners."

She softened her tone further. "If you wish to have respect for yourself at the end of the day, do not sell yourself cheap. Rather, give yourself and our profession the honor and attention they deserve. Do I make myself clear?"

"Yes, Nurse Hale. Thank you."

The chastened girl returned to her work and Tabitha was gratified to see her attitude improve. As for the young man who was the other half of the problem...

Tabitha inquired of the nursing sister on that ward who pointed out the soldier at the heart of the issue.

"Sister, may I have your permission to speak to your patient regarding his behavior toward the VADs?" Tabitha asked.

"You have my permission, Nurse Hale. Corporal Perkins needs a good set-down." Sister Ingram chewed her lip a moment. "I believe I shall enjoy watching you administer it."

"Thank you, Sister."

Tabitha strode into the ward and, without hurry, walked from bed to bed until she had made her way toward the loud offender.

His leg was splinted and held in traction; other than that, he seemed in good health. Certainly he was in good spirits: He told loud, animated, off-color jokes and generally enjoyed being the center of the other patients' attention.

For their part, his fellows had tired of the corporal's boisterous manner, but Corporal Perkins seemed to have taken no notice of their cooling regard.

Tabitha walked to his bed and stood by his side, her hands clasped in front of her apron. "Good morning. It is Corporal Perkins, is it?"

"Blimey! Aren't you the Very Adorable Darling! Hair like a fiery sunset, wot? Hey, Red! Come give us a closer look."

Some patients had redefined the VAD acronym to stand for "Very Adorable Darlings." It was the first time a patient had called Tabitha so. She thought it a sweet toast to the volunteers who worked so hard to care for the war wounded—but only when kept in proper bounds.

As for Corporal Perkins calling her 'Red'? Tabitha's fingers hurt as she clasped them tighter and commanded herself to remain cool and calm.

Tabitha was also well aware that Sister Ingram was observing the scene and that the four VADs on the ward—including VAD Edwards— had stilled, waiting to see what the Head VAD was doing.

Tabitha stared, unblinking, at the young man until the noise in the ward died down—until the other patients recognized the drama about to unfold. Until Corporal Perkins himself appreciated that he was the center of attention.

The wrong kind of attention.

"Wot?"

Tabitha continued to look at him until he started to fidget. His head swiveled side-to-side. and he saw that the entire ward was focused on him—and on the beautiful but stern VAD standing before him.

He flushed and licked his lips. "Ah, beg your pardon, miss."

"You will address me as Nurse Hale, Corporal," Tabitha said with quiet firmness.

His mouth opened a little.

"Nurse Hale," Tabitha repeated.

"I, uh, I beg your pardon, Nurse Hale," he muttered.

"I cannot hear you, Corporal."

He flushed again, irritated, but he growled, "I beg your pardon, *Nurse Hale.*"

"Edwards, come here," Tabitha commanded.

Her chastened and embarrassed VAD scrambled to Tabitha's side. "Yes, Nurse Hale?"

"Corporal, do you see this volunteer?"

"Yeah."

"You will address me correctly, soldier," Tabitha snapped.

"Yessir! I mean, yes, Nurse Hale!"

A titter went around the other patients' beds, and the unlucky Corporal Perkins blushed a darker red.

"Corporal Perkins, I am Head of the Volunteer Aid Detachment for this hospital. As such, I am responsible for VAD training and behavior. My VADs are not your 'darlings,' Corporal. They are honorable servants of the Crown and of England. You will not flirt with them. You will not disrespect them. You will treat them with the deference their profession demands. Do I make myself clear?"

He swallowed, glanced around at the nodding, approving glares of his fellow soldiers. He huffed and capitulated. "Yes, Nurse Hale." He swallowed again and, while staring at his coverlet, mumbled to Edwards, "I beg your pardon, miss."

Tabitha waited a long—a very long—moment more, then swiveled on her heel and addressed the patient in the bed next to Perkins. "And how are you today, Private?"

A collective sigh rippled through the ward as the tension eased.

Corporal Perkins, Sister Ingram reported to Tabitha later, was subdued and docile the remainder of the day. "VAD Edwards, also," she added with an approving slant of her eyes toward Tabitha.

As rushed off her feet as Tabitha had been since she arrived at Colchester, she hardly realized that five weeks had passed. In one respect, she felt she had been in England for months. In another, the weeks had flown by.

In all regards, Tabitha was busier in her new position than she had ever been in the Emergency Services ward in Denver. Even so, the mantle of responsibility for the VADs was something she loved from the outset. And Matron Stiles and Sister Alistair, with few words but many favorable nods, told her she was making satisfactory progress with her trainees.

I love these women, Lord, Tabitha admitted. *I love this work… and I am good at it.*

But as she crawled into bed that night, it dawned on her that Carpenter had not replied to her letter. *O Lord, surely he has received my message. Could it be that he is upset with me? That he is angry that I left the safety of Denver and am here near the war zone?*

No, she assured herself as she drifted to sleep. *But it is also not like him not to respond. I am certain a letter is coming. It will be here soon.*

She thought of the three-day pass she had hoped to earn so she could visit his air base. With reluctance, she admitted how unlikely it was that Matron would grant her one in the foreseeable future.

When, with my new duties, will I ever be free to take time off?

Her responsibilities seemed to have no end. As geographically near as Mason's posting was to hers (comparatively speaking), would either of them ever have time to visit the other?

She was writing a letter in the ward for convalescing officers when the Sister in charge whispered in her ear, "Nurse Hale, a message from Matron's office has arrived. Please report to Matron as soon as possible."

Tabitha nodded. "Thank you, Sister. Please excuse me, Captain, but I have been called away. Perhaps Norwich will finish composing your letter?" She beckoned for the VAD to come and take her place.

It was mid-August. The sea breeze that reached the town by way of the Colne River was fresh and did much to alleviate the heat and smoke of the city's factories and wool mills. Tabitha stretched her legs as she walked from the hospital to the administration buildings and closed her eyes momentarily to rest them.

I am tired, Lord, but such a good tired. Thank you for bringing me here, for letting me serve in a meaningful manner.

She tripped up the steps to the matron's offices, a light bounce in her step. "Good morning, Miss Thompson. Matron asked for me?"

Miss Thompson smiled and Tabitha wondered at the glow on her cheeks. "Um, yes. Good morning! Nurse Hale, Matron has granted you a half-day pass. Please be back for dinner."

"Sorry. I do not understand." Tabitha shook her head in confusion, but Miss Thompson giggled a little, lifted a languid hand, and pointed behind Tabitha, to her left. Tabitha followed the direction of Miss Thompson's finger.

"Hello, Nurse Hale."

The air left Tabitha's lungs and her heart tripped. "Mason?"

He crossed the room to her, and their hands met, twined, and clung together. Tabitha could not tear her eyes from his face. "Oh, Mason!"

Miss Thompson coughed a tiny cough behind them. "Do have a lovely afternoon," she murmured. She smothered another giggle before it left her mouth.

Mason drew her toward the door and they walked outside together. He said nothing, but kept leading her away until they reached a shady grove of trees. He led her within the sheltering branches of a willow— then he pulled her into his arms and stared into her face as though trying to commit every part of it to memory.

"Tabitha. My darling girl."

Tabitha did not realize she was crying until he swiped a tear from her cheek. "Mason! How did you get here?"

"Never mind that now. I want to kiss you, Tabitha. May I kiss you?"

She nodded and he drew her closer until their lips met. Tabitha tasted mint and a freshness she could not characterize. She wanted to melt into his strength and remain there, but all too soon their lips drew apart. She rested her head on his shoulder and sighed.

"Mason."

"Yes, darling?"

"Mmm." She nuzzled her face into his neck.

"Oh, I completely agree."

After Tabitha changed out of her uniform, Carpenter took her to a pub for lunch. When they saw how dark and smoky the pub was, Carpenter asked the barman to pack them a lunch.

"Can we get to the Colne River from here?"

The barman looked them over. "For a nice bite on th' grassy, eh? Rec'mmend Castle Park, I do. Nice bit o' th' river flowin' through. A mill with a weir 'crossin' th' river. Perfect for sweethearts, eh?"

Tabitha blushed, but Mason grinned like a mad man. "Thanks, mate."

With a bound paper package in one hand and Tabitha on his opposite arm, Mason followed the barman's directions. They caught a bus to the park and wandered toward a grassy knoll that sloped down to the river's edge.

"This is lovely," Tabitha murmured.

He squeezed her hand and they found a spot not far from the slow-moving water. There they spread their ploughman's lunch on the brown paper they carried it in—crusty bread, cheeses, chutney, pickles and pickled onions, a fruit tart, and two bottles of lemonade.

"What a beautiful old town," Carpenter commented.

"Would you believe it? I have not been off hospital grounds since I arrived," Tabitha admitted.

"Speaking of hospital grounds, Miss Hale, I have neglected to tell you how very angry I am with you."

Tabitha ducked her head. It was softly spoken and partly in jest, but enough of the truth bled through. "Are you so *very* angry, Mason?" She looked at him with adoring eyes and he shook his head.

"You, my darling, are incorrigible. When I opened your letter, my heart fell through my shoes to the ground. Do you know how many ships the German U-boats have sunk?"

Tabitha thought it imprudent to mention the *Arabic's* close call. "I arrived safely, as did you when you crossed over. And the work I am doing is so important, Mason!"

He listened as she described her position in the hospital and her role to better train the VADs.

"Already I can see such changes in these women. They are beginning to take pride in their service and are eager to learn and to grow their skills."

Mason shook his head. "You are a natural leader, Tabitha. I am so proud of you."

She smiled in shy delight. "Thank you. And what of your pursuits? How is your friend, Mr. St. Alban?"

"Cliff? He is well, thank you. I shall tell him you asked after him. He and I work long hours every day with our pilots, primarily in the two-seater *B.E.2* model aeroplane. It is a stable craft, quite suitable for reconnaissance runs. Our pilots fly over the enemy positions while their passengers take photographs and radio back German troop movements.

"The problem we face is that German aeroplanes can outmaneuver the *B.E.* The Huns now have the *Fokker*, a new model aeroplane that employs a machine gun. With this plane, the Germans dominate the sky. We lose planes and pilots daily because of the *Fokker*."

He was quiet a moment and Tabitha realized how painful those losses were to him. He sighed and added, "Thankfully, the RFC is rethinking the role of aeroplanes in this war. The French have paved the way with newer, better models of aeroplanes that are as good as the Germans'. So now the British are scrambling to manufacture new models, too—or order them from America—and I am glad."

He said, as much to himself as to Tabitha, "This war will be fought and won in the air, not merely on the ground. When the British understand this and provide us with better planes, then Cliff and I will need to learn to fly them in order to train our pilots on them."

"How long will you stay and help the British, Mason?" Tabitha asked. She thought she knew his answer, but needed to hear his response in his own words.

"I will answer you, dearest, but you must answer the same question for me. How long will you stay to nurse the war wounded?"

They faced each other and saw the truth in each other's eyes.

"Until they do not need me," Tabitha replied with a shrug to her shoulders. "Surely this war cannot go on much longer. A year, perhaps?"

He looked away. "I wonder. Initially, we thought weeks. And then months. Now?" He shook his head. "I, too, will stay and see it through, but we may both be surprised and dismayed at how long this war lasts."

After lunch, they wandered along the winding bank of the river until they reached a picturesque bridge. Tabitha kept watch on the sun, knowing as it moved farther across the sky, that their time was running out.

Carpenter, too, glanced up. "This," he murmured, "is as good a place as any."

Still holding Tabitha's fingertips in his hand, he sank down on one knee. "I did not ask you properly the last time, my dearest, but I would have this moment, this memory, be special for both of us—this perfect day, this beautiful place, and this one, this very special question: Tabitha, will you marry me?"

Tabitha trembled. "Even if I cannot give you children, Mason?"

He nodded. "Yes. I have been thinking and praying about it. Perhaps we should seek God's will for us concerning adoption? But, my love, you should know: Without you, I would not want a family. You are my only love. Will you marry me?"

"Yes," she whispered. "It would be my honor."

He rose to his feet and there, in front of any watching eye, they sealed their engagement with a soft, chaste kiss. Tabitha was still trembling when he opened her hand and pressed something into her palm, closing her hand around it.

She grasped the warm object and opened her fingers to look at it. A gold circlet set in blazing green stones winked at her.

"Oh, Mason!"

"It was my mother's," he told her. His voice was rough as he added, "I realize that as a war nurse you cannot marry me at present, and I know that as a nurse you cannot wear this token of our pledge, so I give you *this* to keep my ring near your heart until this war is over and I place it upon your hand."

He took the ring, threaded it through a gold chain, and clasped it about her neck.

Tabitha fingered the ring and sighed. "I shall wear it always, dear Mason." She kissed it and tucked the chain and ring into the neckline of her dress.

The ring settled just where Mason had intended.

Next to her heart.

"Nurse Hale, did ye hear th' news?" Litton, one of the VADs in her dormitory, demanded.

"No, I do not think so," Tabitha answered. "What is it?"

"Them bloody Germans sank another of yourn Yank ships, wot," she tossed over her shoulder. "Left th' rag for ye on th' table."

Tabitha frowned but, seeing the "rag," the British newspaper, lying on the table, she unfolded it. The August 19 headline blared:

U-BOAT SINKS SS ARABIC
44 DEAD

"Oh!" The headlines swam before her eyes and she sat down abruptly. When the haze passed, Tabitha skimmed the article, then began at the top and read it again, slowly. When she finished, she folded the paper and let her thoughts wander.

*A German U-boat sank the **Arabic** off the coast of Ireland, just south of the city of Kinsale, on a return voyage to the United States. Despite heaving to and launching lifeboats immediately, forty-four died, because the ship sank in just ten minutes. Captain Finch survived, but of the forty-four who died, twenty-five were **Arabic** crew members.*

Tabitha, eyes wide, heard the shriek of the claxon and struggled against the crush of harried passengers as they ran to their lifeboat stations. She fumbled with the unfamiliar life vest. A crewman helped her to don it.

"Tie it here and here," he had said before rushing away.

Did he die, Lord? Did that young man perish? Did the ship's doctor go down with the ship?

Tabitha was late to teach her class that morning and was distracted the remainder of the day.

Tabitha wrote the news of their engagement home to Palmer House, to Claire, and to her parents. The letters she received in return were filled with joyful congratulations. Rose wrote,

Along with your wonderful news, we can share some of our own. Pastor and Breona anticipate a blessed event in the late spring. Our darling Breona! She is shy to talk about her coming baby, but I know she will be a wonderful mother. Now I covet your prayers! The Lord must provide us with a new housekeeper.

Carpenter visited Tabitha again before the year ended. They spent part of Saturday, Christmas Day, together and met for church the following morning.

"This is Boxing Day," Carpenter told Tabitha. "Traditionally, everyone visits friends and family on Boxing Day. What shall we do?"

"If we were home together, we would be sharing this Sunday with our friends at Palmer House."

"And what would our Sunday look like were we in Denver, sweetness?"

"Oh!" Tabitha waxed bold. "Why, we would attend church with them at Calvary Temple. We would sing from our hearts to God and Pastor Carmichael would feed us a hearty meal from the Scriptures. Afterward, I would hug Breona and feel how her tummy has grown."

Tabitha's eyes shone. "Then we would all meet at Palmer House where Marit and the girls would lay out a wonderful dinner. We and our dear friends would gather around the table to eat, and we would share our stories of what God has been doing in us and for us, and Mr. Wheatley would *try* to commit you to a game of checkers after dinner, and—"

She stopped when he burst into laughter. "What? You asked!"

"Yes, and you describe it to a 'T,' darling. So, please! Continue. What would we do *after* dinner at Palmer House?"

"Well, I would grab little Charley and cuddle him until he squawked, while *you*, my dear fiancé, would allow Shan-Rose and Will to climb aboard your back for pony rides."

"What a wonderful picture you paint," he whispered, "and I pray God we shall do all of that someday soon. However, since we cannot cuddle Charley or play horsey with Will and Shan-Rose on this special day, may I suggest that we do *this* instead?"

"Do what?" Tabitha asked, intrigued.

"Aha! Well, it seems I have arrived in Colchester with two rather overfull suitcases. Imagine it, my dear! These suitcases are packed to their limits with the most delectable and imaginative things children could hope for at Christmas: tins of lollipops, gumdrops, and peppermints; boxes of chocolates and cookies; little dollies, teddy bears, puzzles, wooden trains, and tops. New socks, mittens, hats, and mufflers. Cliff and I collected these goodies and treasures over the past month."

She stared at him. "Why, whatever will we do with all that?"

He grinned. "I have it on good authority that St. Martin's Orphanage, just outside town, is having a party for their children today. That is, *we* are hosting a party for their children today."

Tabitha's eyes widened. "Ohhhh, Mason! You are a beautiful man—how I love your heart! But how shall we get there?"

"Sister Alistair, who, by the way, happened to tell me of this orphanage, has lent me her motorcar. She took the train home to visit her brother's family and left her automobile for me to use—with the stipulation that I not drive it on the wrong side of the road, of course. So tell me, Tabs. Would you care to accompany me to share all these treats with the orphans of St. Martin's?"

When they arrived at the orphanage, they found that the war had swelled the ranks of the motherless and fatherless. Sister Mary Angela showed them into the room where others in the parish were already serving around punch and cookies to the children. Nearly one hundred children sat quietly at tables munching their treats. They stared with curious eyes at Mason and Tabitha—particularly as Carpenter lugged his overpacked suitcases into the hall.

He and Sister Mary Angela and the parish rector discussed how to distribute the candy and other gifts. In the end though, despite their best attempts, it was a happy riot. The children were so eager that Tabitha and Mason grabbed from the open suitcases the first thing that seemed a good fit and handed it to the next child clamoring excitedly at their feet.

All the children received at least one article of clothing, one small toy, and cookies and candy galore. Their shrieks of laughter and pleasure left Tabitha and Mason flushed with joy.

Tabitha sighed in contentment on the road back to Colchester. "What a marvelous thing Boxing Day is, Mason."

"See anything you liked there?"

"What do you mean?"

He grinned. "I am thinking of when this blasted war is over and we can be married. I am thinking of filling that empty old house of mine—of ours—with just the kind of mayhem we witnessed today."

He sighed in contentment equal to hers. "With every child I looked at today, I had the thought, 'Why, this boy could be ours!' or 'What I would not give to hold this little girl on my lap and read her bedtime stories!'"

Tabitha's eyes filled. "Oh, Mason. How I love your heart."

CHAPTER 23

JANUARY 1916

After the New Year, the course of the war worsened, and Colchester Hospital overflowed with patients. Tabitha's responsibilities increased as the British Red Cross sent scores of new VAD recruits to them.

"Obviously, we cannot use this many unseasoned VADs, Nurse Hale, but it seems that word of your program has gotten out," Matron informed Tabitha.

"The Red Cross is, understandably, overwhelmed and is unable to provide the initial—and quite limited—training it usually gives to all new volunteers. They are now sending raw VADs to us to train."

Matron tapped her pencil on her desk, thinking. "If we can manage it without disrupting the hospital, I should like to send *our* seasoned VADs on to new posts. We would keep the raw ones until they, too, are trained and ready to move on."

Tabitha squared her shoulders and rose to the task. She promoted eight of her best VADs to proctor new, smaller cohorts and set them to teach classes she knew they could handle on their own. Colchester, as Matron desired, sent twenty trained VADs on to posts where they were most needed. In a month, twenty more would follow.

As for the nursing sisters, their numbers were increasing also, but not at Colchester. Yes, newer nursing sisters were posted to Colchester, but the more experienced nurses were dispatched to form casualty clearing stations or to staff field hospitals near the front.

Seven of Colchester's nursing sisters left in February, including Sisters McDonald and Ingram. Tabitha found herself owning the responsibility of orienting new sisters to their duties as no nursing sister could be spared for the task.

"Much like a sergeant will acclimate and educate his superior officer on the field of battle, we are leaning upon you, Nurse Hale, to help us acclimate our new sisters," Matron Stiles informed her.

She hmmed a little and then looked up at Tabitha. "We cannot say how grateful we are for your service, Nurse Hale. Your professionalism and your character… You are filling a great need for us, and you are deserving of recognition."

Tabitha was flustered. "Um, I ... I do not know what to say."

"You do not need to answer. Please just know that, with appreciative hearts, we thank you."

Tabitha left Matron Stiles' office with unshed tears in her eyes. She sniffed, self-consciously, as she passed Miss Thompson, but her heart was full.

Mason came next at Easter. It had been months since they had seen each other, and Tabitha was struck with how worn he appeared.

"The war is going badly, Tabs," he whispered. "I would snatch you up and take the first ship home—if I did not fear the journey or what my conscience would do to me if I abandoned our brave young pilots now."

Tabitha clutched his hands. "Tell me what is happening."

He shook his head, slowly. "Our young men do not last even two weeks. We train them for a month, send them up, and often on their first flight across to Belgium or France, they do not return to us. Our most seasoned pilot at present has exactly five weeks of experience."

"Mason!" Tabitha could not comprehend it.

"The RFC is sending newer aeroplanes now. Cliff and I and the other trainers should see them soon. We must learn to fly them and operate the guns on them. We must learn to fight in these planes, Tabs, what they call 'dog fights'—shooting at the German planes while diving down upon them or rolling over and over to escape their guns. The French know how to fight like this, but they cannot spare us trainers!"

"Please tell me you will be careful, Mason," Tabitha begged. "I cannot lose you!"

"Sometimes in life we do not have the choice to be careful, Tabitha. When sudden events demand our response, we must act and pray we make the right call." He sighed. "On that day, I pray I will make the right decision."

They visited St. Martin's again together, bringing cake for the children. The children who remembered them from Christmas greeted them with shouts of "Hallo!" and "Did you bring presents?" When Carpenter revealed the three boxes of cake, the children were as pleased as they had been to receive Christmas gifts.

"You are quite good to us, Mr. Carpenter," Sister Mary Angela thanked him softly. "The blankets and pillows were a godsend during the cold winter months, but not nearly as much as the abundance of heating coal you provided."

Tabitha stared at Mason, stunned by Sister Mary Angela's revelation, overcome again by the fresh revelation of Mason's giving heart.

"Thank you, Lord, for this good man," she whispered.

When Mason arrived in Colchester midsummer for his next visit, he begged her, "Please say we can marry now, Tabs. I know you cannot leave your duties and responsibilities and I will not ask you to. But is there no way we could marry anyway? Then I could dream of you at night knowing that you are mine and that we have a future together. Do say you will ask Matron, Tabitha?"

Tabitha, too, was thinking along the same lines.

For a long time after coming to Jesus, the idea of being with a man— *any man*—had angered her. Repulsed her. But her love for Carpenter was something she had never known. It was holy, good, and safe. She longed to be held in his arms, to belong fully to him, and he to her.

"Yes. I will speak to Matron. I do not know what she will say or what rules could be turned, but I will ask."

"So you will marry me? Now? As soon as we can?"

She swallowed, her happiness overflowing. "Yes, Mason. I would have us married at Palmer House, with our friends as witnesses, but I know they will understand."

Tabitha requested an interview with Matron Stiles the following day. "Matron, you are acquainted with Mr. Carpenter?"

"Yes, Nurse Hale. Sister Alistair tells me good things about him regarding St. Martin's."

Tabitha's voice sank to a whisper. "Mr. Carpenter and I became engaged last year. In the fall."

"I see. I congratulate you," Matron Stiles replied, but Tabitha thought her response measured, reluctant. "Does this mean we shall be losing you soon?"

Tabitha understood. *Ah! Lord, she thinks I will be leaving.*

"No, Matron; that is, not if I can help it. You see, we wish to marry soon, but we are both deeply committed to our work—his in Yorkshire and mine here."

The older woman relaxed. "I see. So ... you are asking to marry, but you hope to continue on here? It would be something of a long-distance marriage?"

"Yes, Matron. I know the rules state that nursing sisters cannot be married, and the VADs are also to be unmarried, but perhaps an exception could be made?"

"Yours is an interesting case, Nurse Hale." Matron steepled her fingers and thought for a moment. "Would you allow me to consult Sister Alistair and, perhaps, Lady Perth-Lyon?"

"Of course, Matron."

Two days later, Tabitha stood again in Matron's office. Sister Alistair was also present. "Nurse Hale, may I reconfirm your intentions? You wish to marry Mr. Carpenter but retain your position with us?"

"Yes, that is correct, Matron."

Matron cleared her throat. "Lady Perth-Lyon, Sister Alistair, and I agree that for you to marry and remain at Colchester would, perhaps, send a damaging message to the VADs. High morale and complete dedication are, during these hard times, difficult to maintain."

"Yes, Matron. I understand." Tabitha felt her heart sinking.

"However..."

Tabitha glanced up. "Yes?"

"Sister Alistair has proposed something of a solution."

Tabitha looked to Sister Alistair.

Sister Alistair's expression was enigmatic. "My brother is the rector of Farring Cross, a small seaside village about fifty kilometers up the coast from here. Would you be willing to take the train to Farring Cross?"

"Are you saying what I think you are saying?"

"Yes. My brother would be willing to marry you and Mr. Carpenter. Quietly."

Tabitha glanced with hope toward Matron Stiles. "We could marry if we kept it a secret?"

Matron inclined her head. "Lady Perth-Lyon agrees it would be the best solution. We would grant you a three-day pass to travel there by train... and to spend two nights before returning."

She looked away. "You are a great asset to us, Nurse Hale, but even darker days are ahead, I am afraid. More of our sisters will be posted to the front soon. I am convinced that sending well-trained VADs with them will be vital to our meeting the challenge."

Turning in her seat as though her muscles ached from sitting many long hours, Matron added, "We need your services to prepare the VADs for service at the front and to train their replacements. Are you willing to marry privately but keep your marriage undisclosed until such a time as wisdom allows us to acknowledge it?"

Tabitha hesitated. "I will have to ask Mr. Carpenter if he is amenable to your suggestion."

"Certainly."

Tabitha, with Matron's permission, used her telephone and asked the operator to place a call to Mason. She then waited impatiently in Matron's antechamber for the call to go through and the operator to call her back.

What if Mason cannot be reached? What if he cannot leave his work to take the call? I cannot wait here all day, either. I have work to do. And what if he disagrees with my superiors' suggestion? Will he ask me to give notice? Oh, but I cannot! I am needed here, more now than ever.

For perhaps a half hour, Tabitha fretted and worried over the situation, becoming first anxious and then fearful. As the minutes ticked by, though, she realized that the Holy Spirit was trying to speak to her.

Peace, that sweet voice whispered. *Stand in the peace that Jesus promised you. Do not be moved...*

> *Peace I leave with you,*
> *my peace I give unto you:*
> *not as the world giveth,*
> *give I unto you.*
> *Let not your heart be troubled,*
> *neither let it be afraid.*

"Oh!" Tabitha sighed. *How can I expect to live and act in God's will if I disregard his admonitions? Lord, I am sorry. I do trust you. In all things, I trust you—even in this. Please help me to wait in your peace for Mason's call. And I commit this situation to you, for you know what is best for Mason and for me.*

Miss Thompson must have heard Tabitha's sigh. She lifted sympathetic eyes. "Is everything all right, Nurse Hale?"

Tabitha shook her head and laughed low in her throat. "Yes, Miss Thompson. Everything is fine."

Minutes later, the phone on Miss Thompson's desk rang. "Colchester Hospital. Matron's office." She paused. "Miss Hale? Yes. One moment."

She looked to Tabitha with some surprise. "It is for you."

"I am to take it in Matron's office," Tabitha answered. She knocked on the door and, when Matron bid her come, slipped inside.

"I will step out for a cup of tea whilst you speak with your young man," Matron murmured. She patted Tabitha's shoulder as she passed by.

"Hello?" Tabitha breathed into the telephone's mouthpiece.

"Call for Miss Tabitha Hale. To whom am I speaking?"

"This is Miss Hale."

"Please go ahead."

Tabitha waited until she heard the sharp click indicating that the operator had disconnected from the call. "Mason? Are you there?"

"Yes! What is wrong? Tabitha, are you all right?"

"Yes, yes. I am sorry I worried you. I just…I needed to speak with you right away about…our wedding."

"Wedding? Did they say 'yes'?" He was as excited as she was.

"They did, only…only they wish us to marry and not make it public just now. Sister Alistair has a brother who is a rector in the little village of Farring Cross not too far from here. He would marry us quietly."

Mason said nothing for a moment, so Tabitha hurried on. "Lady Perth-Lyon and Matron Stiles are in favor of us marrying, but they are concerned that discipline and morale among the VADs might suffer if it were known. The VADs are not allowed to marry while in service, you see, but, well, I am not a British volunteer, and they need me terribly. I could tell that Matron and Sister Alistair were worried I would give my notice."

He was still quiet, so Tabitha asked, "You won't ask me to give notice, will you, Mason? You know how important what I do is?"

He sighed. "Yes, I do, indeed. So they are asking that we marry but keep it secret. Hmm. Well, you and I had already agreed we would not give up our work until the war ended. I suppose—"

"They will give me a three-day pass, Mason. Farring Cross is about fifty kilometers from Colchester by train. We can meet there and spend two nights. Together."

"I like the sound of that, Tabs. When?"

"So you will agree to keep our marriage to ourselves for a time? I am certain that we can tell our friends at home and explain that I will be keeping my maiden name for the time being."

He growled. "Yes, I agree, but the instant we can tell the world that you are Tabitha *Carpenter*, I will shout it from the housetops!"

Carpenter wrote with two proposed sets of dates, dates when his superiors agreed to grant him three days of leave. Tabitha, with Matron's approval, chose the second range of dates: September 20-22.

"Sister Alistair will write her brother, and ask that he marry us on the evening of September 20," Tabitha reported.

"I shall make all the arrangements for dinner and hotel," Mason promised, "and meet you on the Farring Cross train platform the afternoon of September 20."

That evening Tabitha wrote a letter to Rose.

Dear Miss Rose,

I have such wonderful news. Would you please read my letter aloud at dinner when you receive this? I would ask you to read the following first.

Miss Tabitha Kathrine Hale
and
Mr. Mason Albert Carpenter
request your prayers and blessings
as we enter into sacred matrimony
the evening of September 20, 1916.

Mason and I dearly wish you all could be here to share this moment with us. Although it is technically against the rules for VADs to marry, my superiors at Colchester have granted us permission. In return, Mason and I have agreed to keep our marriage a secret at this time and I have agreed to remain as Colchester's Head VAD.

We can consent to their terms only because we had already determined that neither of us can bear to leave the work we are engaged upon: Mason cannot leave off training new pilots, and I cannot leave off training new volunteer aides. What we do is too terribly important to the war effort. We had decided to marry but live apart so that we could continue in our present endeavors.

At least our infrequent times together in the future will be as husband and wife! Therefore, I request that you do not write to me as Tabitha Carpenter, but continue to address me as Tabitha Hale, as I will continue to be known to the hospital and its staff.

As happy as Mason and I are, one circumstance mars that happiness—that all of you will not able to witness our vows. When this war has ended and we return home, we hope to renew our vows before Pastor Carmichael and all of our family in Denver.

Oh, Miss Rose! We are filled with joy.

Midweek, the morning of September 20, after her roommates had left the dormitory, Tabitha packed a small bag. Then she bathed and washed her hair. As far as anyone other than Matron and Sister Alistair knew, Tabitha was taking a well-deserved three-day leave to rest by the seashore.

When she had dried her hair and carefully combed it out, Tabitha donned a new outfit—a flattering sheath of deep green with an overdress of gauzy cream shot with green, gold, and beige flowers.

The waist and bodice of the dress fit Tabitha's figure flawlessly; the diaphanous overskirt flowed around the sheath that hugged her hips to perfection. For once, Tabitha curled her red hair and arranged it around the brim of the darker green cloche she pinned in place.

No unflattering knot or bun at the back of my head today, she thought with a smile. *Today I am a bride!* The radiant woman staring back from the mirror bore testament to the joy swelling in her heart.

Today I am marrying Mason Carpenter, her heart chimed again and again.

Tabitha walked off the hospital campus and met the cab she had arranged for. The cabby drove her to the train station where she caught the noon train. Three hours later, the train steamed to a halt at the small platform that served the village of Farring Cross.

She saw Mason at the same moment he caught sight of her, and she knew he had never looked more handsome, more distinguished.

"My darling," he murmured against her hair.

Sister Alistair's brother, the Reverend Markus Alistair, met them at the tiny village church. His wife and a church elder stood with Tabitha and Mason through the ceremony. The elder's wife handed Tabitha a bouquet of late roses and watched, smiling and sniffing into her hanky, from the front pew.

Reverend Alistair looked from Mason to Tabitha, and said solemnly, "The vows you are about to take are to be made in the presence of God, who is judge of all and knows all the secrets of our hearts; therefore if either of you knows a reason why you may not lawfully marry, you must declare it now."

"I know of no reason," Mason asserted.

"Nor I," Tabitha replied.

The minister smiled. "Well, then. Mason Albert Carpenter, will you take Tabitha Kathrine Hale to be your wife? Will you love her, comfort her, honor and protect her, and, forsaking all others, be faithful to her as long as you both shall live?"

"I will," Mason's voice rang with confident fervor.

"And will you, Tabitha Kathrine Hale take Mason Albert Carpenter to be your husband? Will you love him, comfort him, honor and protect him, and, forsaking all others, be faithful to him as long as you both shall live?"

"I will," Tabitha pledged.

"God our Father, from the beginning you have blessed creation with abundant life. Pour out your blessings upon Mason and Tabitha that they may be joined in mutual love and companionship, in holiness and commitment to each other. We ask this through our Lord Jesus Christ your Son, who is alive and reigns with you, in the unity of the Holy Spirit, one God, now and forever."

"Amen," Tabitha and Mason said together. They both had tears in their eyes when they kissed. The moment his lips met hers, Tabitha felt their healing power—the power of sacred trust and sacred bond.

You make everything beautiful in its time, Lord, her heart sang.

After the ceremony, Mason asked the two couples to join them for a wedding supper at a nearby hotel. The Reverend Alistair, his wife, and their friends were more than happy to accept.

Mason had arranged for everything, from the food to the flowers to the cake. The hotel sat upon a bluff overlooking the ocean, and their wedding table for six, adorned down its length with fragrant stems and blossoms, faced the sea so that the crash of breakers upon the seawall was their accompanying serenade.

The hotelier was delighted to supervise their celebration himself. Under his direction, his servers brought course after course to the table. With each course, the four guests saluted the bride and groom and wished them well.

For the finale of the dinner, the waiters served tiny cups of sherbet and the hotelier's wife bore a small two-tiered cake, artfully iced and bejeweled with sugar roses. All the hotel staff gathered around and applauded as Tabitha and Mason cut the top layer and fed each other a bite.

Then Mason and Tabitha served around the rich slices chock-full of chopped raisins, almonds, and cherries until everyone present had a slice of the cake. Tabitha had the hotelier box up the last large, uncut bit of the cake.

I will save this for Matron and Sister Alistair, Tabitha decided.

The long, happy afternoon wound toward late evening before the celebrations ended. Then Mason led Tabitha toward their hotel room.

The following morning, they slept late and drank their tea on the balcony facing the crashing surf. Tabitha leaned her head upon Mason's shoulder as they watched, mesmerized by the everchanging sea.

"Everything was so perfect, Mason. Thank you."

His fingers pressed hers in acknowledgement. "Could anything make our honeymoon more perfect? Is there anything your heart desires?"

"No, nothing," Tabitha sighed.

"Are you certain?"

She snuggled in closer to him. "I am. I cannot imagine anything more delightful than this."

He chuckled. "Well, my love," he teased, "How would you like to fly over the sea?"

Tabitha was baffled and sat up to look up at him. "Why, whatever do you mean?"

Kissing her forehead he replied, "I mean that I did not take the train here as you did, for I wanted to give you a gift no other bride would likely receive from her new husband. To finagle this gift, I requested a *five-day* pass for our wedding. I knew Catterick's RFC commandant would balk at the length of my request. In actuality, though, I have taken so little leave in the last two years that I believed he would feel obligated to honor my request."

Mason chuckled. "Then, in typical American fashion, I offered him 'a deal,' an alternative: I would reduce my request from five days to three, if—*if*—he would allow me to borrow a plane, one of our older, less-used trainers, thus reducing my travel time. I agreed to pay for the petrol, of course."

"You flew here!"

"I did, indeed. My *B.E.2* is anchored just there." He pointed, and Tabitha followed his finger up the beach until she saw the nose of an aeroplane peeking out from behind a sheltering shed.

"Oh!"

"So I ask you again: Could I, your husband, give you the wedding gift of flying over the sea?"

Tabitha's heart quickened and she breathed, "Oh, yes!"

He bundled her against the cool air they would find above the sea water and made sure the scarf covering her head and ears would not work loose. The seat he buckled her into this time was behind his seat instead of beside it, and the entire body of the plane was enclosed rather than open.

"You cannot fall out, darling," he told her, "no matter what." He pulled the straps snug about her waist and over her shoulders and grinned, "I would not have dared to touch you so familiarly before today, would I?" He leaned closer to brush a kiss across her mouth. "Or dared to do this."

Tabitha sighed in contentment and excitement as Mason undid the anchors on the wheels and grasped and spun the propeller. When the engine caught, he climbed into his own seat, regulated the flow of fuel until the engine purred, and donned leather helmet, goggles, and his own seat restraints.

Then, with a small crowd ogling them from the balcony of the hotel and along the shore, he pointed the aeroplane down the beach and they raced ahead. Tabitha stared, enthralled, as the sand fell away and Carpenter banked toward the sea. For the benefit of those watching from the hotel's balcony, he turned in a wide circle and flew directly over them.

Tabitha shrieked with glee and waved her hands at them. They waved and shouted in return. And then Carpenter, pulling the plane into a long, tilting turn, circled back and flew westward along the shore. He did not fly into the swirling clouds, but kept the plane low so that Tabitha could consider the rows of breakers pounding the bluffs and cliffs and study the villages they passed over.

Perhaps ten minutes later, he turned, following a river inland from its mouth. Tabitha was amazed when the familiar town of Colchester came into view. She was able to see so clearly the layout of the army barracks, stables, parade grounds and buildings. She pointed to her dormitory and the familiar hospital wards as they circled above Colchester twice. Then Carpenter, again following the Colne River, took them back to the sea.

He flew straight out above the sea and took them higher. "Would you like to have some fun?" he shouted.

"Yes!" Tabitha shouted back. She could not believe how much she loved the wind in her face and the earth in miniature below her—the incredibly freeing sense of flight.

"Hang on!" Carpenter yelled.

Tabitha was not prepared for what happened next. Carpenter pulled the nose of the plane back so that they were climbing higher and higher into the sky—and then just as they leveled out, he dove the plane downward, only to put them into a loop-the-loop. When he again leveled out, he banked over into barrel rolls. They rolled over and over until Tabitha was dizzy.

But she was not scared—no! She was thrilled.

"Again!" she screamed. "Again!"

For the next fifteen minutes, Carpenter did everything he knew to do with the plane: He dived, he rolled, he dipped and looped. Tabitha's laughter and screams of delight were his delight, too.

When he turned them back toward Farring Cross they were quiet in their joy, but Tabitha felt that her first day of married life had been perfect.

He knows my heart, Tabitha sighed. *My husband knows my heart.*

Tabitha returned to Colchester Friday evening. Getting on the train and leaving Mason while he stared after her was the hardest thing she had ever done.

The following morning she picked up a small box wrapped in brown paper and took it to Matron's office.

"Good morning, Nurse… *Hale*," Miss Thompson greeted her, her blue eyes dancing.

"Ah, good morning, Miss Thompson. Could Matron spare me a moment?"

After checking, the young woman said, "Please go right in."

Tabitha closed the door behind her and then placed the box on Matron's desk. "For you and Sister Alistair," she smiled. "We thought of you when we were sharing our cake."

Matron undid the paper and eased open the box. "Oh, how lovely! Cake is so dear these days. We shall certainly enjoy this." Then she leaned toward Tabitha. "This is a very generous serving. Perhaps you might offer Miss Thompson a slice?"

Tabitha's brows shot up. "She knows?"

Matron chuckled. "Little happens in this office to which Miss Thompson is not privy. However, she is most trustworthy, I assure you."

Tabitha cut the cake into three portions and laid one slice on a napkin Matron offered her. As she was leaving, she placed the napkin in front of the receptionist.

"Lord love you, Nurse Hale!" she exclaimed, eyeing the cake with avarice. Glancing at Tabitha, she added in a low voice, "And *mazel tov*. We are quite happy for you."

Tabitha went back to her work that day with a spring in her step.

"Quite the rest you had," Ellen Darby remarked. "Us slavin' away whiles you drink in the sea air!"

"It was perfect," Tabitha answered. "The beaches were beautiful and, as you said, I *drank* in the sea air."

In her mind she was flying, dipping down toward the whitecaps, and racing over the surf…. Mason looking back at her and grinning like a lovesick fool.

She sighed. "Most refreshing!"

As Matron had suggested, the struggle on the continent only intensified that fall. No one spoke anymore of the war ending. It stretched out before them, an endless conveyor of the dead and wounded, bad news followed by worse news, defeat upon defeat.

The talk now centered on America.

"If them Yanks don't toss their hats into this war soon, we can start bidding the entire Continent g' morn' in German," one soldier in the wards snarled.

Tabitha heard similar sentiments expressed wherever she went, and she wondered why her own country delayed. Would Congress and President Wilson's deliberations end in a declaration of war against Germany or would America sit back and allow all Europe to be crushed under the Kaiser's boot?

What will become of England if the Germans win? she wondered. She had grown to love her coworkers and their country and feared for them.

Mason's frequent letters were brief and gave her little clue as to how his pilots were faring, but Tabitha knew from the "rags" left in the dining hall how badly things were going.

They met at a hotel in Colchester for Christmas. Tabitha fell into Mason's arms, drinking in his strength. "Oh, Mason! How I have missed you." When she pulled away to search his face, she saw the same shadows lurking in his eyes that she saw everywhere: The shadows of fear and uncertainty. His arms around her were as needy as hers about him.

CHAPTER 24

JANUARY 1917

The year 1916 ended, and no sooner had 1917 arrived than the Germans resumed unrestricted U-boat attacks on American ships. "Iffin that don't light a fire under th' bloody Yanks, noffing will," Tabitha heard an orderly predict.

Finally spring arrived, a bloodstained, horrifying spring. When at last President Wilson called for war and the Congress agreed, Tabitha heard not one voice in the hospital celebrate or applaud. She observed only measured sighs of relief and glimmers of hope in otherwise war-ravaged faces.

Rose wrote her of the American military draft and the many young men from Denver called up to fight.

We were worried that they would call Billy up, but he is safe for the moment, she wrote. And we do not take our joys for granted in these perilous times. We delight in Pastor and Breona's little one and in the hope that Joy and Mr. O'Dell will soon give me another grandchild to fill these aching arms.

Tabitha's tears were happy ones. *I long to see Breona as a mother*, she admitted. *And Joy! Another child for Joy! O God, thank you! And thank you for little Edmund ... wherever he is, we know you have not lost sight of him.*

April arrived, and the British, in a coordinated offensive with the French, launched an attack against the Germans at Arras, France. Tabitha read the reports with a sinking heart: Even though the offensive was considered successful, more than 300 RFC aircrew perished and 245 aircraft were lost providing support to the troops.

Mason wrote, *Twenty of our pilots, young lads we had scarcely trained, died at Arras. They lasted less than two days after leaving us. We led twelve of them to Christ before they departed, God be praised.*

Tabitha's heart was breaking—for her husband, for the young men and their families, for the British nation, whose very heart was bleeding and broken.

O Lord! Use me, Tabitha prayed. *Use me! Do not let me send our VADs to the front without you!*

As uncomfortable and unprepared as she felt, Tabitha began organizing afternoon and evening Bible studies for the VADs and led the studies herself. Matron placed the weight of her office firmly behind Tabitha's efforts.

As word of the meetings got around, the study groups and prayer times grew. VADs who worked nights flocked to the afternoon sessions before they ate dinner and commenced their shifts; VADs who worked days ended them with God's word and prayer.

Not one VAD who attended was unmarked by the war: All had either brother, cousin, or friend who had perished in the fighting. Two widowed VADs had lost their sons.

Tabitha was wearing thin, but she was no more worn than anyone else, so she pulled on her early memories of Palmer House and the studies Rose had conducted each morning. Tabitha would open to a familiar passage, read it aloud, and ask the Holy Spirit to fill her mouth—and he did.

The numbers attending the study groups grew. Tabitha, by stepping out in faith, began to ask the women if they were ready to surrender to the Lordship of Jesus Christ. "Not to a church, and not to a religion," she explained, "but to Jesus himself. Today you can choose to make him your Lord, Master, and Savior. You can be free of your sins and guilt."

Prayer sometimes lasted hours, and Tabitha was in over her head, but she fell into her bed each night with the satisfied peace that only living fully for God yields.

At the same time, Tabitha intensified her efforts to prepare VADs to work in the field hospitals that operated scant miles from the front. She now had a team of experienced VADs whom she utilized to accelerate the training.

"Please," she begged Matron, "please do not post the members of my training team to the front. All our efforts will slow if you do."

Matron nodded, and Sister Alistair sighed. The need was great and they could not disregard the army's demands for more nurses and aides.

As fast as they could prepare them, newly trained VADs were sent to support nursing sisters in the field hospitals and casualty clearing stations. The clearing stations were often so close to the front that they could hear and smell the battles raging—sometimes only on the other side of a hill or just across a farmer's blood-soaked fields.

Then news arrived of the deaths of some of their own: Sister Ingram and three of her VADs, gone in a brutal instant, their clearing station obliterated by errant mortar fire.

The young women scheduled to ship out next looked at each other with fresh insight—and showed up to Bible study ready to give their hearts to Christ.

Tabitha slipped away one sunny Saturday in May to meet Mason. They would have only the one precious night together, but they first took the bus to St. Martin's where they would, for a few hours, forget the agony they dealt with day upon day.

Mason sat on the floor and crowded children onto his lap. Others leaned against his back and clung to his arms. Tabitha, her own lap and arms full, read aloud from *Peter and Wendy*.

As she read about the boy, Peter Pan, who could fly, she stole glances at Mason. He was laughing and surrounded by happy children. Tabitha tried to capture the scene in her mind's eye.

We can fly, Mason, my love, she found herself thinking. *You are my Peter, and I shall be your Wendy, and you shall teach me to fly. Oh, if only we could fly to Neverland today!*

"Nurse Hale, you are wanted in Matron's office, please." The VAD delivered her message and scurried away.

Tabitha tidied her hair, checked her apron, and walked down the two flights of stairs to the ground level. The June air kissed her face, and she hummed as she walked the cobbled paths to Matron's offices.

"Good morning, Miss Thompson," she said cheerfully.

Miss Thompson's eyes skittered away from her. "Good morning, Nurse Hale. Please go right in."

Tabitha blinked at the young woman as she went toward Matron Stiles' doors and let herself in. She closed the door behind her and turned. "Good morning, Matron—Cliff! I mean, Mr. St. Alban, what are you—"

"I will leave you here, Nurse Hale," Matron murmured. She bit her lip, but her chin was quivering as she passed Tabitha.

Then she was alone with Cliff St Alban, her husband's best friend. He would not meet her inquiring eyes.

"Cliff?"

He reached for her arm as her legs buckled. "Sit here, Miss Hale. Please. Sit."

"Cliff? Is Mason all right? Please?"

He knelt on the floor beside her chair. "No, Miss Hale. I am so sorry. He is gone."

Later, Tabitha played Cliff's words over and over in her head. Even when she did not wish to hear them, his voice haunted her and his words echoed in her mind.

"We always start our trainees in the two-seater trainer planes. Three of us trainers and our trainees were in the air when German planes dropped out of the clouds. They had never attacked our base before! There were two of them, their ugly red crosses clearly marking them. I shouted for my trainee to run for it, but I knew a *B.E.* could not outrun a *Fokker*—and we had no guns.

"Mason was on the ground. He climbed into a fighter, one of our newest models, and took off. The Germans had by then shot down one of our trainers. The plane made it to the ground, but it cracked up on landing. The trainer and his trainee ran from the wreckage, ran from the machine gun rounds chasing them.

"One *Fokker* was on our tail, shooting at us. Mason swung around behind the German and came up from underneath. He shot the tail off that plane and then swung wide to find the second.

"We put down on the ground as soon as we could. The third trainer got down all right, too. By then several of our pilots had taken off in fighters."

Cliff lifted his eyes to Tabitha's. "These pilots are just kids, Miss Hale, most of them as green as grass. Mason knew that. He drew the German plane away and headed out to sea, following the coast. Our pilots followed behind.

"They told me he flew like an Ace, diving, rolling, giving back what that German dished out. He would have won, too—except two more German planes dropped down on him. Then Mason, he hightailed it—far away from the base, away from our pilots. I know it was to save them!

"Our boys followed, though, down the length of England, over Norwich, and out over the sea, toward the coast of Belgium. They-they saw when the Germans shot him down."

The Germans shot him down.

The same five words played over and over in Tabitha's mind.

"Did they ... did your men find Mason?"

Cliff's sorrowing eyes filled with tears. "No, Miss Hale. He was still far out over the sea when his plane went down. Our boys saw it go into the water."

He looked away. "The Germans did not know our boys were following. They brought their fighters up behind and below the Huns and blasted them. Two of the three German planes went down in flames. The other crashed into the water. They made the Germans pay for Mason, Miss Hale."

Do I care? Tabitha asked herself. She fingered the gold band hanging about her neck. *No. It does not bring him back.*

Cliff shook his head. "After, when our flyers circled back … they found no trace of Mason or his plane."

He swallowed hard. "Mason saved those young trainees and their trainers, Miss Hale. He-he saved *me*. He made a tough call … but he did what he felt he had to do."

Sometimes in life we do not have the choice to be careful, Tabitha. When sudden events demand our response, we must act and pray we make the right call.

Tabitha shuddered. *I will never hear him speak again. Never hear his voice.*

Cliff extended an envelope. "I found … this in his things. I-I did not know you and he, that you had gotten married."

Tabitha glanced up. The envelope Cliff held out to her read, *Tabitha Carpenter*. In Mason's handwriting.

"We kept our marriage a secret because of the rules of nursing. So I could keep training the VADs here."

Cliff nodded. "I-I wondered. I am glad you married him. He loved you very much."

With those words, Cliff ran out of steam. He looked away, unsure of what to do or say next.

Tabitha had attended the deaths of many patients, had delivered bad news many times. Without weeping.

She touched his arm. "Thank you, Cliff. Thank you for coming in person to … tell me," she whispered. Her experience and training were all that kept her together.

When he at last excused himself, Tabitha fingered the envelope. *Do I want to read it here? Do I want to read Mason's last words to me here?*

She immediately answered herself.

No.

Tabitha left Matron's office with eyes straight forward and shoulders squared. She walked on stiff, wooden legs to the grove of willow trees where Mason had taken her … a very long time ago it seemed.

Within the shelter of the same willow where he had kissed her, Tabitha collapsed onto the grass. She sobbed for a while, still numb and unbelieving, before opening his letter.

Dearest Tabitha,

If you are reading this, then something very bad has happened, something neither of us anticipated, but that God has known of since before time began. Do not be afraid, Tabitha. If I am no longer with you, I am with the Lord. I will wait for you here, in his Kingdom, until he also calls you to himself.

I want you to know that I have provided for you, my darling. The moment I returned to Catterick after our wedding and honeymoon, I sent word to Banks and enclosed our marriage certificate. I also enclosed written instructions to my attorney to rewrite my will.

You already know that I made provision for your parents before I left for England. With the exception of a bequest to St. Martin's and for Banks' and the other servants' pensions, you are my sole heir, Tabitha. Everything I own—my house, all that is in it, my car, my accounts—they are all yours. You shall never want for anything.

I make only one request, or perhaps a suggestion if, some day, you can bear it: Fill our home with children who need a mother's heart. I cannot be there with you, but that old mansion could be home to many a brokenhearted child—and this war has left so many alone. If you think you can do this, please know that I would approve.

My darling wife, you are the bravest woman I have ever known. To survive what you survived and grow into the woman of God you have, has made me the proudest of husbands.

I waited many long years for the woman of my dreams before I met you, Tabitha. You were worth waiting for.

With all my love,
Mason

Although she felt as though she were clawing her way through a dense fog, Tabitha kept moving. One hazy, confused step after another, she got up each morning. She taught, monitored, counseled, worked, and slept again.

It was clear to those who knew her that she had suffered a great blow, but she refused to speak of it and refused to pause ... or even slow down to feel her own pain.

I am not the only one suffering in this war, she told herself. *I am but one of the far too many brokenhearted. I must do my duty just as they are doing theirs.*

Mid-July a letter from the American Red Cross reached her.

Now that the United States has entered the war, we have a mandate from the president to work in Europe. We invite you to join our ranks in France.

"No," Tabitha spoke aloud.

Then she pondered her decision. *No, I cannot abandon my VADs or the nursing sisters. I must stay here at Colchester. It is where God himself placed me.*

Her heart added, *These were the last places I saw Mason. No, I cannot leave. I cannot leave ... him.*

"I should like to send you on a small assignment," Matron Stiles announced to Tabitha in early October. "The children of St. Martin's Orphanage need inoculations and screenings. You will leave tomorrow and return in two days."

Tabitha's eyes narrowed and her old anger threatened to surface. "Why would you send *me*, Matron? Any trained VAD can perform this task."

"Because you need to go, Nurse Hale." Matron Stiles' tone brooked no further argument.

And then Tabitha saw it, a tender, caring tightness about Matron's mouth.

Tabitha stared at the floor. "Very well, Matron."

That evening she packed a small bag with a nightgown and a clean uniform. In the morning she drew the supplies she needed and trudged to the bus stop. As the bus trundled along, the changing scenery, the grass and trees, the little cottages as the bus left Colchester proper, began to speak to Tabitha's frozen heart.

She remembered Boxing Day, the first time she had taken this same route—with Mason in Sister Alistair's motorcar.

It was cold that day, she recalled, *when Mason and I brought Christmas presents and candy to the children. But the last time we came, the sun was fighting through the mist and warming ditch banks covered in cockle shells. Tulips nodded in pots by front doors and roses climbed upon trellises.*

Something peaceful and right wrapped itself around her as the bus chugged ahead.

When she knocked on the weathered old orphanage door, Sister Mary Angela gave her a warm welcome. "Please! Come in. Matron told us to expect you."

In the morning, the children queued up for their exams, and Tabitha recognized many of them from past visits.

"Where's that man?" one boy asked. He was eager, expectant.

The sister shushed him, and Tabitha, while grateful that she did not have to explain, could not miss the hurt on the boy's face.

He knows, she sighed. *He knows how dads and mums go away and never come home.*

Tabitha released the child she had just examined, and a tiny girl with fiery red hair stepped forward. The child edged up to Tabitha, placed her hands on Tabitha's knees, and stared at her with wide, expressive eyes.

"You m' mum?" she demanded.

"I beg your pardon?" And then Tabitha saw her, truly saw her. The tot was, perhaps, age four. Her wild, curling locks were nearly the same shade as Tabitha's hair.

"Said, you m' mum?" the girl insisted. She pointed at Tabitha's hair and reached to touch it. The hand she stretched out had been badly burned. Two of the fingers were bent; the scarred skin stretched taut over them was marbled red and white.

O dear Lord, Tabitha mourned. *So much hurt and pain in this world.*

She pulled the child up onto her lap and the girl instantly sank against her breast.

"Smells good, it do," she announced.

"This is Sally, Nurse Hale," a nun whispered.

"Hello, Sally. May I look at your face?" Tabitha helped her to sit farther out on her knees so that Tabitha could examine her. Tabitha looked in Sally's ears, eyes, nose, and mouth.

Sally's blue eyes studied Tabitha in return. "You m' mum?" she asked the third time.

Tabitha shook her head. "No, darling. I am not. But your hair is a lovely color. Very like mine, do you not think?"

"Nay," Sally disagreed, shaking her head. "M' hair's nasty."

Tabitha flinched. "What? Who says so?"

"They all says so," Sally sighed.

"The other children?"

"Yah. Ev'ryone. They calls me Red."

A font of ire burbled up inside Tabitha and, against her will, her heart went out to the child. "Tell me, Sally. Do you think *my* hair is nasty?"

Sally considered Tabitha's question and then shook her head no. "Nay. Youse pretty."

"Well, so are you, Sally. Your hair is like mine, so you are pretty, too."

Sally watched Tabitha as if judging her words. Then she leaned into Tabitha and wrapped her arms about Tabitha's neck. "I likes you."

As Tabitha hugged her back, her heart shucked off a sheet of ice.

This is good, Lord. Matron was right. I needed to come back here. Thank you for making her send me here.

After that, Tabitha spent every Sunday afternoon at St. Martin's Orphanage. Since the buses did not run on Sundays, she begged the use of Sister Alistair's motorcar.

Sister Alistair did not object: Petrol was dear and costly, so she rarely drove. Tabitha was happy to pay for the fuel out of the ample funds Banks had forwarded to her.

Another Christmas neared, and with it the end of 1917. Tabitha wrote home to Palmer House.

Dear Miss Rose,

Perhaps my heart is beginning to mend. I know, at least, that it is still alive and not a dead, insensible stone as it had felt before.

I have returned to the orphanage Mason and I visited regularly. We had hoped to adopt two or more of the children when the war ended. The children! I care so deeply for these children. How I live and breathe and go on each day is still a mystery to me, but when I visit St. Martin's, I know I am alive. And I know that I live to serve my Jesus through two important causes, nursing and these children.

These little ones have suffered more than I have. Still, each Sunday they come running to greet me, their faces alight and merry. They think I come bearing treats and fun, and I do, of course. However, each week I also bear a heavy heart when I come to them. And yet, after each visit, I return home lighter. The children have no idea of the gift they give to me.

I am determined that the money Mason left to me will be well used for Jesus' sake when this war is done. I may not have a solid plan as yet, but I have, at least, sent my own will and testament to Banks. Should anything befall me, Mason's wealth will be distributed as I have directed. I know he would be pleased.

❧ ❀ ❧

$\mathcal{C}$HAPTER 25

MARCH 1918

Tabitha waited for Matron or Sister Alistair to speak, wondering why she had been sent for. Matron consulted the report on her desk before she answered Tabitha's question.

"A contagion has reared its head on the Continent, Nurse Hale," she began. "It appears to be quite serious."

Tabitha noted the solemn set of the two nurses' expressions. "You are concerned, then?"

"We are, yes. The newspapers are calling it the Spanish Influenza, as though it began in Spain or is contained there." Matron frowned. "That story is likely not true. Last week Dame Becher, QAIMNS Matron-in-Chief, received a letter from the matron of the army hospital near Étaples, France. It was a letter that the matron was able to send by hand, thus, ah, bypassing army censors. What her letter describes is ... quite disturbing."

Matron stared at Tabitha. "I may as well tell you that the matron of whom we speak is Sister McDonald. You know her well. You know her nursing skills and professionalism. Sister McDonald's letter insists that the infection began at the troop staging center near Étaples. This center adjoins the army hospital of which she is nursing matron.

"As soon as affected solders were admitted to the hospital, the entire facility fell to it, overwhelming their capacity to handle the outbreak. The subsequent mortality rate was high. *Very* high. From Étaples, it spread to troops in the field and other outposts. To other Allied Forces."

Matron sighed. "We are now hearing of similar cases here in England. Should this influenza get out into the general population? The effects could be devastating."

"What is to be done?" Tabitha asked.

Matron nodded at Sister Alistair, who shifted on her feet and spoke.

"I shall be leaving for France within the week, Nurse Hale. If we are to prevent an all-out epidemic among our soldiers, we must put in place the severe measures needed to curtail the disease's spread. We need nurses who understand such things, who have appropriate training."

"Y-you are referring to my training in infectious diseases," Tabitha whispered.

"Yes, Nurse Hale. Although I cannot compel you, I am asking you to come with me. If you agree, we will take a small band of your best VADs with us. You will have three days to impress upon them the preventive sanctions we must practice, teach, and put into place. The powers-that-be have given us the authority, the extreme latitude required to contain the contagion."

"Three days! But-but what of the VAD classes? The ongoing training of new volunteers?"

Matron fixed Tabitha with a serious eye. "Who is your most outstanding proctor, Nurse Hale?"

Tabitha sighed and wiped a hand across her brow in distraction. "VAD Darby, Matron."

"She will assume your teaching and monitoring duties." Catching Tabitha before she could object, the older woman added, "We cannot emphasize enough the importance of this mission. Darby must rise to the occasion like the rest of us. Because you have trained her, I am confident that she will."

"Yes, Matron." Tabitha blinked, sorting through the many details she would need set in order.

Matron and Sister Alistair exchanged glances. "Do you accept our assignment, Nurse Hale?"

Tabitha straightened and squared her shoulders. "Yes, of course, Matron. I will go."

"Very good." Matron stood and came around her desk to face Tabitha.

"I have been authorized by Dame Becher herself to offer you this symbol of our fellowship, Nurse Hale. You cannot wear the uniform of the QAIMNS nor can the British Army command you as it can command us. You will still, outside this office, be known as Nurse Hale. However, this badge will mark you as the outstanding nursing sister you are and will garner you the respect you have earned."

Sister Alistair moved to Matron's side and snapped opened a small velvet box. Matron removed from the box a medal suspended by a striped ribbon.

Tabitha knew the distinctive medal—how could she not? It was a cross set within an oval, a stylized "A" set upon the cross. Inscribed on the oval band surrounding the cross were the words, *Queen Alexandra's Imperial Military Nursing Service.*

The medal was worn proudly by every nursing sister of the QAIMNS.

Tabitha trembled as Matron pinned the medal to the right strap of her VAD uniform apron.

"In recognition of the selfless service you have rendered to England, I, Matron Edwynna Stiles, by the authority of Dame Flora Becher, Matron-in-Chief QAIMNS/QARANC, bestow upon you the medal of Queen Alexandra's Imperial Military Nursing Service."

Tears streamed from Tabitha's eyes. "You honor me," she sniffled.

"You honor your vocation, Sister Hale. You honor us."

"Yer want me—*wot*? Yer jokin', Nurse Hale, yeah? I know nuffing of nursing loike you do!" Darby's eyes were wide. She had reverted to the broad accents of her home, and she clutched at her apron as though it were on fire.

"Do you not know every skill I have taught the VADs?" Tabitha demanded. "Have you not proctored and overseen every class I have taught? Is there anything we expect of a well-trained VAD that you do not know and practice yourself?"

"No, but … *cor*! I-I-I'm not *you*!"

Tabitha mouth curved into a smile, a bit of sadness tinging that curve. "No, dear Ellen, you are your own self: You are a well-trained and disciplined VAD. When you are in the wards, you are a consummate professional. Now, in your new role as Head VAD, you must be a professional at all times, not only when you are in the wards. And I assure you, if you will lead and not give in to fear, the VADs will follow."

Tabitha fumbled for her armband and tugged it off. "You must put this on. For the next three days, you will be my shadow, and this band will announce your new status. Where I go, you will go. Everything I do, you will emulate."

She twitched the band into place above Darby's oversleeve. "And when I leave, you will carry on. I have confidence that you will do a smashing job … *Nurse Darby*."

Darby's complexion had taken on a green tinge, but she pointed with her chin. "You-you're wearin' the QAIMNS medal."

"Stranger things have happened in war, I hear," Tabitha shrugged. "It is, however, the greatest and most singular honor of my life."

The next days were a whirlwind of activity. Tabitha taught the VADs everything she knew for containing the influenza.

Matron had Miss Thompson dog her footsteps, taking notes and staying up late into the night to type the procedures.

Darby attended Tabitha the way a drill sergeant attends a commander, correcting in a low, authoritative growl any VAD who failed to learn and do so quickly enough.

Tabitha spent her last evenings writing letters home to her parents, Palmer House, Claire, and Banks explaining her new assignment. She packed and repacked her bag, not entirely certain what she would require in the field.

The VAD in the supply office added to what Tabitha had packed: a sewing packet, candles and matches, heavy stockings and rubber boots, a rain slicker, and extra uniforms.

"Got t' have th' right kit, Nurse Hale, wot?" she assured Tabitha. "'Tis bloody spring, an' th' Frenchys' roads an' fields will run wi' mud."

At the end of the week, Sister Alistair, Tabitha, and five VADs—all strong, healthy, well-trained, and disciplined women—lined up beside the bus taking them to their departure port. Much of the hospital staff and many ambulatory patients turned out to send them off.

"We hope to hear from you soon, Sister," Matron spoke to Sister Alistair. She nodded to Tabitha and the other VADs. "Colchester is proud of you, ladies. We send you on now, in the grace of God."

Their ship sat in port, a great hulking mass of iron painted the color of an angry gray sea. The ship looked all the more ominous for the rain streaming from a gunmetal sky.

German U-boats still plagued the shipping lanes, sinking with impunity any vessel they could. Thankfully, this journey across the Channel would be one of hours rather than days, and other vessels, including armed naval ships, would travel with them through the thick of the German threat.

Still, Tabitha was not the only woman in their party to swallow anxious nerves. As she climbed the gangplank, she recited lines from Isaiah 43.

Fear not: for I have redeemed thee,
I have called thee by thy name; thou art mine.
When thou passest through the waters,
I will be with thee;
and through the rivers, they shall not overflow thee:
when thou walkest through the fire,
thou shalt not be burned;
neither shall the flame kindle upon thee.

Tabitha and Sister Alistair, clad in their rain slickers, stood together at the rails but alone in their own thoughts. Their VADs clustered together in a tense knot not far from them.

Tabitha forced her face into calm, stoic lines. *I will not be afraid, Lord, for I know you are with me,* she prayed. *You are my Refuge, O God. Therefore I will not fear.*

Then the ship's engines growled and the ship eased away from the docks. It steamed from port down river and into the open sea where it took up station among a convoy of ships crossing over to the coast of France. The waves of the Channel ran high that day; they pitched the ship—and its passengers' stomachs—in a fitful, unpredictable cadence.

Hours later, under a clearing sky, their ship broke off from under the watchful guns of several destroyers and made for the calm of a French port. Tabitha and Sister Alistair exchanged relieved glances when the ship's hands ran the gangplank onto the docks.

A booming voice hailed them when their feet touched the dock's steady planks. "Sister Alistair? I am Sergeant Franklin." He saluted. "I have orders to escort you and your aides during your posting in France. If you will come with me, please?"

The stocky army sergeant's roughened face and short, salt-and-pepper hair showed him to be middle-aged, likely in his mid-forties. He gestured toward a dull green canvas-covered truck. "This will be your conveyance and here is your driver," he said by way of introduction. "I and another soldier will lead you in the vehicle just ahead."

He pointed to an open passenger car painted the same dull green as their truck.

Handing a sealed packet to Sister Alistair, the sergeant added, "These are your orders, Sister, and our itinerary. We shall leave as soon as you are ready and spend the night at an outpost a few miles east of here."

Sister Alistair stepped aside to peruse her orders. When she had read them once, she motioned Tabitha to her side. "Please read these through, Nurse Hale."

Tabitha did so. "We shall be busy, Sister."

"Indeed. Well, let us be off."

Armed with the authority they needed to execute their orders, Sister Alistair, Tabitha, and their VADs climbed into the back of the truck and sat upon the hard benches on either side of it. Their driver handed in their bags, tied the canvas closed, and followed the passenger vehicle ahead of them down the road and into the murky spring dusk.

They stopped well after dark at a supply outpost. That night they slept in two tents set aside for them. Sister Alistair insisted that Tabitha share her tent while the VADs shared the other.

"I wish you to grow accustomed to this arrangement, Nurse Hale," Sister Alistair informed Tabitha. "Yours is a leadership role in our mission, and I want it understood as such at each hospital or clearing station we reach. You will act on our orders with authority—subject only to me."

"Yes, Sister," Tabitha answered, but her eyes were open wide as she tossed and turned upon the unfamiliar cot. Though she stared into the tent's darkness, she saw her open hand and a puzzle piece resting in its palm. An edge piece. A corner.

Oh, Mason, she thought. *Who could have foreseen my life taking this curious turn? Only our great God.*

Early the following morning, their two-vehicle caravan began its journey. Sister Alistair's orders were for their nursing troop to visit as many British and Allied Forces camps and outposts as they could reach. They were ordered to train the resident medical and volunteer staff in proper quarantine and preventive methods so as to curtail the spread of the influenza that was beginning to ravage the armies on both sides of the war.

When their convoy arrived at the first outpost, Sister Alistair presented her orders and requested that the commandant or senior officer call the remaining officers and medical staff together. Sister Alistair described the course of influenza, how it was often most fatal to the very young, the elderly, and the infirm—such as those who were already wounded.

Tabitha outlined quarantine procedures. "If the infection takes hold in the wounded wards, those patients will likely die, despite our best efforts," Tabitha informed the medical staff. "Therefore, separate wards for the infected and wounded must be established now. These wards must be erected safe distances from each other. At the first sign of infection, the symptomatic patient must be removed to the quarantine zone.

"And you must enforce strict boundaries between those who are nursing the infected and those who are nursing the wounded. Doctors, nurses, VADs, and orderlies nursing in the influenza wards are not to approach the non-infected zones or any non-infected part of camp," Tabitha decreed. "They must even eat and sleep in separate quarters."

Tabitha gestured to her cohort of VADs. "These VADs are trained in the particulars of handling influenza patients. For the next three days they will hold clinics for your VADs and orderlies to demonstrate the care of infected patients and the prescribed protocols to protect aides and orderlies. Sister Alistair and I will do the same for physicians and nursing sisters. We will oversee the establishment of the separate wards and protocols until they are working as required."

The medical staff eyed Tabitha, garbed in her common VAD uniform yet working side-by-side as a peer with Sister Alistair, and issuing orders with calm authority. They noted, too, Tabitha's American accent and the distinctive medal pinned to her apron strap. Whispers and conjecture about her circulated among them, but no one questioned her role.

Not all camps Sister Alistair and her VADs visited were unprepared for the influenza: A few had alert doctors or nurses with knowledge of the newest epidemic procedures. Those camps needed less assistance from Sister Alistair's little band.

In other camps, however, the medical staff did not possess the authority to demand—and receive—complete cooperation of the camp's commandant and staff. In effect, the medical staff were unable to enforce the protocols necessary to stop the spread of influenza. In those instances, the overarching authority of Sister Alistair's orders required the camp's officers to accede to her every demand.

Sister Alistair's and Tabitha's best hopes were for the hospitals and posts where the contagion had not yet shown itself. But often their convoy arrived too late, and the disease was already running rampant through every part of the camp. The dead were buried in mass graves by the few who were not ill themselves.

In those situations, Sister Alistair declared a complete quarantine around the camp itself.

"You cannot mean it!" one exhausted commandant protested. "We cannot leave or receive reinforcements? No supplies? No mail?"

"No one enters the camp except properly trained nursing help and no one—*no one*—leaves," Sister Alistair repeated. "This rule must be strictly enforced. Supplies and incoming mail must be left at the camp entrance. No outgoing mail may be picked up lest it spread the contagion. We must have your complete cooperation in this procedure, sir. The quarantine is not to be lifted until the camp has been free of infection for two weeks."

"But what of the wounded? Where will they be taken?"

"They must be rerouted to a field hospital that has successfully separated the wounded from the infected," Sister Alistair insisted. "Even once your quarantine is lifted, incoming wounded—and *anyone* wishing to enter the camp—must first be screened for fever and cough."

"Yes," Tabitha added. "Even right now, while your camp is quarantined, we must still attempt the separation of the infected from those not yet symptomatic. You will protect some of your patients and staff in this manner and will be prepared to receive the wounded when the quarantine is lifted."

Their group spent one to three weeks at each camp or hospital, depending upon its size and needs, before moving on. Their convoy visited so many troop staging areas and medical outposts that Tabitha lost track of where they were or had been.

She and Sister Alistair, of course, even instructed and enforced proper protections upon Sergeant Franklin and their drivers. She had the VADs employ the men to demonstrate chemical-treated handwashing and the use of face masks to camp orderlies. The three soldiers, having been pressed into burying the dead several times, obeyed without complaint.

Their vehicles traveled the dangerous and war-torn roads from troop staging point to field hospital to casualty clearing station. They crisscrossed the midsection of France from northwest to southeast, but always west of the fighting.

Their truck bore the Red Cross, the universally recognized symbol of medical personnel, on its canvas sides and even on its top. According to the first and second Geneva Conventions, the markings would protect them from intentional attack.

Still, many of their destinations were near the battlefields. They often heard the thunder of artillery guns and felt the ground shake from the impact of shells. One day an artillery missile landed so close to their speeding caravan that its concussion rocked their truck, tossed the lead car into a ditch, and covered both vehicles with dirt and debris.

Sister Alistair and Tabitha scrambled down from their truck and found Sergeant Franklin's driver pinned beneath their automobile. He suffered a few cuts, but seemed fine otherwise.

Sister Alistair bandaged the driver's wounds while the driver of the truck, Sergeant Franklin, and the combined efforts of the remainder of the nursing team set the automobile back on its wheels. The truck driver then attached a chain to the car and pulled it from the ditch.

More than once on their journeys they heard the scream of German aeroplanes diving toward them, only to hear the planes pull up and roar away from their tiny convoy as the enemy spied the truck's Red Cross.

The howl of the fighter's engines terrified the other women in the back of the truck, Sister Alistair included. Several of the VADs sobbed or shrieked with hysteria, but the familiar whine and grumble of engine always turned Tabitha's thoughts toward Mason.

You and I crested the waves of the sea, Mason, my love. It was our honeymoon, and you flew me toward the moon itself. You scribed somersaults in the sky to thrill me, and we shouted with the joy of it.

How I loved your heart then. How I will always love your kind, generous heart.

In the last days of July, their entourage pulled back to a British base and hospital just outside Paris. There they received mail for the first time since leaving Colchester in March. Tabitha found a letter from Rose waiting for her.

My dearest Tabitha,

Joy and Mr. O'Dell's son, Matthew, will soon have a brother or sister. Matthew is a lovely boy. He is now walking and chattering in the most darling manner.

We have quite an active nursery when everyone is here, and I am blessed to be grandmother to them all: Billy and Marit's Will and Charley, Minister Liáng and Mei-Xing's Shan-Rose, Pastor Isaac and Breona's Sean, and Joy and Mr. O'Dell's Matthew—with more to come!

Your friend Claire has become a great favorite with the children— and with us. She meets us at church every Sunday and spends the afternoon and evening with us. We love her dearly.

We cannot help but hear and read alarming reports of the influenza, so we are praying daily for you. Do not be afraid, dear daughter. The Lord holds you in his mighty hands.

Everyone here sends their warmest love and greetings. Now that our soldiers have joined the war, it must end soon, mustn't it? And then you will come home to us. Please come home to us soon.

Love,

Rose

CHAPTER 26

AUGUST 1918

S ister Alistair's little band was exhausted beyond measure. They had traveled and labored steadily for months, yet their orders allowed them mere days to rest and prepare for their next assignment.

The new orders, when Sister Alistair received them, were a shock to all of them: Sister Alistair was appointed matron of a casualty clearing station outside the Argonne Forest, replacing the camp's previous matron whose health had broken under the strain. Only a single VAD of Sister Alistair's selection was to accompany her.

She chose Tabitha. "You are a strength to me that I cannot do without, Nurse Hale," Sister Alistair whispered.

Sergeant Franklin was ordered to escort Sister Alistair and Tabitha to their station and then return. The remainder of Sister Alistair's VADs were assigned to other locations. Their two drivers had already been dispatched elsewhere—they did not even have the opportunity to say goodbye.

"I do hate for our merry band to be broken up," Sister Alistair sighed, "but I am very glad you shall accompany me to our next posting, Nurse Hale. And I am hoping we have seen the worst of the influenza."

But the contagion was not played out.

Not by half.

Before Sister Alistair and Tabitha left for their new post, a doctor returned from Brest, a town near the westernmost point of France. He reported on a second wave of the infection striking troops there. He addressed the assembled medical staff with news of the infection's rekindled threat: a new and deadlier strain.

Sister Alistair and Tabitha attended his debriefing. His report was terse.

"As you are aware, influenza deaths normally occur among the very young, the elderly, the wounded, and the chronically infirm. However, it appears that the Spanish Influenza has changed. Mutated. With this alteration, we are seeing fit, *healthy* soldiers contract the disease—and pass away within days, despite our best efforts to save them. Doctors and nurses in their prime are suffering the same fate.

"We have received word of this same mutated virulence from Allied Force doctors in Africa and from the United States. This new strain of the influenza seems to invoke a very strong reaction in the young and able-bodied man or woman. The patient's immune response to the contagion is so severe that the infection overwhelms his or her system."

Sister Alistair and Tabitha glanced at each other. Sister Alistair bowed her head; Tabitha followed suit.

Lord, Tabitha prayed. *Where can we go but to you? Keep us close to your heart.*

A grueling three days later, Sister Alistair and Tabitha arrived at their new post northwest of the Argonne forest. This casualty clearing station was not one their influenza prevention convoy had visited. The station was well supplied, but the personnel were exhausted.

Sister Alistair—now Matron Alistair—pressed her lips together and took up the reins of nursing leadership. She placed Tabitha in charge of the station's VADs, but not before she made clear to her staff of nursing sisters that Tabitha was a trained nurse, every bit as much a nursing professional as any of them.

"It seems our reputation has preceded us," she confided to Tabitha. "The nursing staff is thus also aware of your work with VADs. Sadly, the previous matron refused to relax the stringent class distinction between professional nurses and volunteers. She would not allow the sisters to train the VADs or delegate any but the most mundane nursing work to them."

Matron Alistair sighed. "What a waste. The sisters are overwhelmed to the point of breakdown—not unlike their previous matron! I believe the sisters are willing now to relinquish their bias against VADs and allow them to share the load more equitably. Therefore, I wish you to train these aides with all possible speed to assume more nursing duties."

"Yes, Sister. I beg your pardon—yes, Matron," Tabitha answered.

Matron frowned. "This station's influenza containment procedures must also be revamped. The nursing sisters are so run-down that I am quite concerned. Should the new strain arrive here, our staff will be quite vulnerable."

The task of a casualty clearing station was to save and stabilize as many wounded as possible before sending them on to surgery in field hospitals or, if the soldiers could be patched up, to return them to their units to rejoin the fight.

As the battlefront shifted location, so did their station. The soldiers and their commandant, a major who had lost an arm in the second Boer War, stood by only to guard the medical staff and move the station to best serve the closest battles. The station's personnel, equipment, supplies, belongings, and tents often changed location three times in as many months.

The flow in and out of the station was dizzying. As soon as their patients could be sent elsewhere, they were. Sadly, their station also became the burial ground for many souls who did not survive their wounds.

"'Tis our lot," a VAD named Moira MacTavish informed Tabitha as she walked through the wards the first time. "Been like this since I got here. Canna remember what a full night's sleep is. Th' doctors and sisters patch up the soldiers best they can and send them on t' hospital—or back t' th' front, poor devils. We VADs do th' laundry, change th' linens, scrub th' bedpans, feed th' patients, listen t' them talk and grieve, and write letters home for them."

Whether MacTavish understood Tabitha's role and authority over the VADs or not, Tabitha appreciated her candor. The young woman glanced up, and Tabitha glimpsed the pain in her shadowed eyes. "I dinna think I can bear t' write one more bonny boy's g'bye letter—but what choice d' I have when they're a-dyin'?"

Tabitha gripped the VAD's shoulder. "We cannot do this under our own strength or courage. We must draw our courage from the One whose strength never fails."

MacTavish stared at Tabitha and then nodded. "Aye. You are right. Thank ye."

Before dinner that evening, the camp commander and Matron Alistair called for a meeting of the entire camp. Doctors, sisters, aides, orderlies, and soldiers assembled on the sunburned grass outside the mess tent. The August sun beat down on them, sapping the little strength they had left.

"We have just received word," the commandant told the assembly, "that a large convoy of wounded is on its way to us. We believe it will arrive a few hours from now, after dark. Please eat well—I do not know when or if we shall get to bed this night, and you will need your strength."

"Do we know how many patients to expect, Major?" Sister Alistair asked.

"I cannot say, Sister," the commandant answered, shaking his head. "'Large convoy' was the only information I received. Oh, and our patients may be from all the Allied Forces: British, French, Australian. Even American. We shall sort them out to their own hospital units after they are stabilized."

"Yes, Major. And I should like to press your men into service as orderlies," Matron Alistair said in front of the assembly.

The major stuttered and frowned, not appreciating having been put on the spot in public.

"It has not been done, Matron," he finally managed.

"And yet they should not stand about idly while the medical staff are taxed beyond their ability, to the detriment of the wounded. Do you not agree, Major?"

Staring daggers at Matron, the commandant gave her a curt nod. "As you say, Matron."

"Thank you, sir." Matron Alistair turned to her nursing staff. "Please pair the new orderlies with experienced ones who can show them the ropes. And be watching for patients showing influenza symptoms: fever, cough, respiratory distress. Take all proper precautions and send symptomatic patients to quarantine immediately. Now, as the major said, eat well. We have a busy night ahead of us."

The trucks began to arrive sometime after eight in the evening. The nurses and orderlies lined up to unload the stretchers. The station's personnel were masked and gloved.

Tabitha and two nursing sisters worked to assess the condition of the incoming wounded. They directed orderlies to carry those needing immediate care to the surgery. They instructed that the patients who could wait for care be laid under a tent near the surgeries.

For another group of patients, the nurses simply instructed, "Keep them comfortable." It was heartrending to decide when a soldier's wounds were so grievous that precious resources could not be wasted trying to save him. Those patients were carried to yet another tent where, under the care of a nursing sister, they were administered morphine to ease their pain and their passing.

The night slipped by in a blur of sweat and labor. Tabitha identified two of the most likely VADs and summoned them to work alongside her.

"You will be assuming more duties," she explained, "nursing duties you were not previously allowed to perform. I expect you to look lively and follow my instructions immediately."

The VADs stuttered a "Yes, Nurse Hale," but jumped to follow Tabitha's orders. By the time the last casualties had been unloaded and cleared, the two women were proficient at several new tasks.

At dawn Tabitha sent them to breakfast.

"Thank you, Nurse Hale," one of the nursing sisters murmured. "These women are not stupid and they are willing to learn. I have been trying for months to pass more nursing responsibilities onto their strong shoulders, but..."

Tabitha nodded her understanding and they stumbled off to the mess tent in companionable silence.

"Nurse," the voice was weak, one of the many voices that called as the figures of the VADs bustled through the ward. "Nurse. Water. Please."

With no other VAD in sight, Tabitha poured a glass of water herself and lifted the patient's bandaged head to drink from the glass in her hand. He swallowed with difficulty and sputtered and coughed, dribbling water down his face onto the sheet.

"Take your time," she encouraged him. "Drink slowly. I am not in a hurry."

Finally, he managed to swallow the glass's contents. "Thank you," was his whispered reply.

Tabitha looked him over with a practiced eye, wiped the droplets from his chin, straightened his bedding and pillow, and checked the dressing around his head that covered the side of his face.

"Everything here looks fine," she said automatically, although she knew that the horrible wound would require significant care in a hospital. The man, an American soldier, she noted, would heal, but he would never look the same.

She unbent, set down the glass, and turned to leave.

"Wait. Please!"

Tabitha paused and the skin along her arms turned to gooseflesh before she understood why: She knew his voice.

"Tabitha? Is it you? Could it be?"

Slowly she turned back around. With that recognition in mind and acknowledging the more than twenty years that had passed, she studied the man in the bed before her.

"Hello, Cray."

"It *is* you! Impossible ... but how—"

Neither of them could speak—and yet far too much lay between them. They simply looked at each other.

Tabitha saw a caricature of the Cray Bishoff she had known, the young man she had followed blindly into Arizona: He was older, of course, malnourished and worn from months at the front, and grievously wounded.

"You are a nurse?" he whispered. She heard the wonder in his voice ... and the charged questions behind his wonder.

"Yes." She shrugged, not wanting to say more.

"I ..." Tears stood in his eyes. "I ..."

From far away, Tabitha heard Rose Thoresen's quiet voice.

Tabitha, you spoke of hate earlier, the hate you had for the man who left you alone in the desert and who sold you to Opal.

Cray. Cray Bishoff, Tabitha had whispered.

Have you consciously, deliberately forgiven him?

I do not know, Miss Rose. I try not to think about him or any part of my past.

May I suggest, dear Tabitha, that you think about forgiving him? I suggest this not because he deserves your forgiveness or has asked for it, but because forgiving those who have wounded us sets us free. And I would have you perfectly, completely free, my daughter.

Tabitha knew by heart the prayer she had spoken to God that day: *Lord, I forgive Cray Bishoff. I forgive him for leaving me alone and . . . for selling me to Opal. I forgive him, Lord, as you have forgiven me in Christ. I let go of the hate I held toward him. Father, please set me free in every part of my life so that I can glorify you with every part of my being.*

Amen, Rose had murmured.

"I forgave you, Cray," Tabitha murmured. "I forgave you years ago. Because Jesus forgave me."

"You-you forgave me?" he stammered. "But-but I-I, but what I . . ." Even now, he could not speak of the horrible truth resonating between them.

"Yes, Cray. I forgave you. And I forgive you now, afresh. I want you to know that Jesus died so that we can be absolved of even the unspeakable things we have done. Jesus died for *you*, too, Cray. If you will confess your sins to him, he will forgive you."

They said no more. Tabitha nodded and, as she walked away, tears trickled and then streamed down her cheeks.

Thank you, Lord, she rejoiced. *Thank you for using Rose to show me how to forgive. I am free, Father. Truly free. You have made me free in every way.*

The new strain of influenza arrived mid-September. At the same time, to the east and southeast of their station, they heard that the combined Allied and American armies were staging their troops for what would, some said, prove to be the bloodiest, most difficult offensive of the war.

Matron Alistair insisted that Tabitha head the team receiving new casualties so that preventive and quarantine procedures were strictly enforced. Tabitha had never worked so hard in her life. There was no respite. Convoys carrying the wounded arrived day and night without advance notice.

The saving grace of a clearing station was that it often had no patients in camp when the next batch arrived, meaning that if new patients brought influenza with them, they could not infect patients already in the wards.

Still, the contagion found them.

"This man!" Tabitha shouted through her mask. "He is feverish and coughing." She pointed to a sister, an aide, and two orderlies. "The four of you will take him to quarantine. You are now assigned to the quarantine ward. You know the quarantine rules.

"The rest of you—" Tabitha turned aside and dipped her rubber gloves in a bucket of water liberally dosed with carbolic acid.

The staff receiving the casualties knew what Tabitha's orders signaled. They followed suit, rinsing their hands in the same bucket, and awaited her directions.

"Every patient who came off these trucks must be more carefully evaluated," Tabitha ordered. "If they show any symptoms at all, have them moved to quarantine immediately."

The remainder of the casualties and those already unloaded were reexamined. Three patients were sent to quarantine. Tabitha assigned another VAD to the ward.

"We have influenza," she informed Matron later, "and we have done what we can. Now we must be vigilant."

She was trembling as she made her report. By all accounts, the virulence of the second wave of influenza would exceed anything they had seen or dealt with. Its arrival in camp evoked the first real fear she had tasted since arriving in France.

"Thank you, Nurse Hale," Matron replied.

But Tabitha saw a shadow cross her face as she spoke.

That evening before she fell into an exhausted sleep, Tabitha searched her small bag. She exhaled in relief when she found what she was looking for: The corner puzzle piece folded in her handkerchief.

She made herself open the hanky and stare at the piece. As before, the sight of the corner piece called up that same still, small voice.

I call some to be the frame for the work, to make the vision plain. Those whom I call to frame the work are vital to my plans, the voice spoke. *They lead so that others may follow.*

"Things never come out quite how we expect them to, do they, Lord? I confess to harboring a bit of grandeur in my heart, of thinking *I* would accomplish great things for you."

Her laugh was rough. Wry. "I know a little better now, though. Your purposes are far higher than ours—and all the glory belongs to you."

Turning the piece over in her hand, she prayed, "Lord, you have called me here to lead through the very great danger of this plague. So be it. I-I consecrate my life to you anew. Though war surrounds us and disease stalks us, I choose to trust you. Help me to lead unafraid, to offer my service as worship to you alone. Even unto death, Lord, I give you my life."

She folded the piece back into her hanky and tucked the hanky into the deep pocket of the apron she would wear on the morrow.

"You will remind me why I am here," she whispered.

"We must close this station entirely until the contagion is under control," Matron Alistair insisted, "or we run the risk of every wounded man sent here contracting and dying from this disease!"

The major sighed and rubbed the bridge of his nose. "I quite agree, especially as our armies are engaged in the new offensive. I will apprise our command of the situation."

Every able-bodied man or woman in camp was pressed into nursing the ill. Tabitha policed their preventive procedures and corrected sloppy practices with stern rebukes.

"Who will nurse you if you fall ill, Dunstead?" she chastised one careless VAD. "You cannot, *even one time*, put your contaminated hands to your face!"

Dunstead did fall ill. Soon after, two of her roommates came down with fever. Then one of the nursing sisters collapsed and was put to bed. Four more joined her. Followed by the cook and several orderlies.

Faced with fewer nurses and more patients, Matron Alistair joined her staff in the wards. "We are in this alone and must all persevere!" she exhorted those about her.

"We may be the only ones left on our feet soon," Tabitha murmured. Her mind and heart were numb from the suffering around her. She no longer retired to her cot to sleep; she snatched minutes or an hour sitting in a chair in the wards when she could be spared.

She frequently touched her apron, feeling for the outline of the small, precious object tucked within a deep pocket.

Even unto death, Lord, I give you my life.

The new strain was as lethal as the reports had indicated it was. Their patients' fevers rose. They coughed, sneezed, and complained of unbearable headaches, sore throats, and aching limbs. Some vomited; others suffered nosebleeds.

A week passed by. Two weeks.

And then, as the infected appeared to be recovering, many of them relapsed. Fevers soared and could not be brought down. Lungs filled with fluids and hemorrhaged.

And the deaths began.

Dunstead, the VAD Tabitha had chastised for her carelessness, died the following day. She was followed by one out of every three who contracted the influenza. The progression of the influenza and its march toward death was brutal. Merciless.

To the station's east and south, British, French, Belgian, and American soldiers were engaged in what was now termed the Battle of Argonne Forest, the tipping point of the war. For miles around the station the fighting thundered, but the quarantine held, and no wounded arrived at their camp.

The calendar read October 23. More than a month had passed before the medical staff declared that the influenza had run its course. Four recovering patients remained in the wards. When those patients were judged to no longer be contagious, the camp's quarantine would be lifted.

When that decision was made, the flow of wounded from the raging Grand Offensive would resume.

The news the major reported to the staff that day was of victory after victory for the Allied Forces and American troops. The death toll was terrible, but it was victory, hard-won victory—not defeat, not stalemate.

"My counterparts at Headquarters tell me the Germans are pulling back and considering terms of surrender."

"Can it be true?" one of the sisters asked in wonder. "All these years . . ."

"They believe it is so," the major replied. "They tell me it will soon be over."

Days later, the major announced new orders: "Our station is to be upgraded to a field hospital and will receive those leaving the battlefield for good. We will process the healthy and send them on, but we will also have surgical staff to care for the wounded more adequately before they are moved."

Tabitha heard the news but could scarcely care. Yes, only four recovering influenza patients remained in the wards, but the cost of saving them had been far too high.

She turned from the major's briefing and stumbled from the tent. Whipping her apron from her thin, exhausted body, she threw it aside and ran from the camp.

When she reached the woods, she kept running. She kept moving, tripping and stumbling, until she fell upon a dim, solitary place to weep alone.

O Lord! My heart is broken to pieces. Broken! I cannot bear any more. I would rather you had taken me, Lord, than to leave me alone to bear these losses.

Forty-seven wounded soldiers in their care had perished from the Spanish influenza.

Five VADs had died nursing them.

Three nursing sisters.

Two orderlies.

The camp's cook.

And Matron Alistair.

Army trucks loaded with more tents and equipment arrived. They brought fresh personnel: More doctors. More nurses. More support staff. A new matron. Reinforcement troops began to overhaul the clearing station to bring it up to a working hospital in the field.

Tabitha plodded on weary feet toward the dispensary when a familiar voice called to her.

"Nurse Hale! Nurse Hale!"

Tabitha stopped and held her hand over her eyes against the bright morning light.

The woman who had shouted raced across the grounds and came to a stop in front of Tabitha.

"*Cor!* You are a blessed sight t' m' eyes, Nurse Hale."

"Darby? Darby! You are here?"

"Aye. Bin sent t' help out, me an' some of our best." Ellen Darby was rosy-cheeked and resplendent in clean uniform, cloak, and hat. She pointed with her chin toward the five VADs behind her.

All of them, Darby included, appeared healthy and rested.

Darby and her volunteers studied Tabitha; she, in turn, wondered how she must look to them: Her hair, while neatly pinned, had not been washed in a week; her relatively clean uniform was stained and worn beyond repair. And she had missed far too many meals and hours of sleep.

"We shall be glad of your help, Darby," Tabitha whispered. "It has been... hard going, particularly this last month. We lost many to the influenza. So many. Sister Alistair..."

Darby's brows drew down in stark denial. "Wot? No!"

Tabitha shook her head and stared into the distance, blinking against tears. "She is gone, Darby, and I am too grieved to speak of it yet."

She looked back and took a deep breath. "Let me . . . let me be happy just to see you. To welcome you and your VADs. To feel that hope is alive here again."

She raised her chin and inspected Darby's volunteers more carefully: The women were still, orderly, full of quiet strength.

"Your aides are nicely turned out, Darby." Tabitha smiled a little. "You have done well. I knew you would."

"'Cause o' you, Nurse Hale," Darby insisted. "'Cause ye gave me th' courage t' be somethin' more'n I were."

Darby's broad, homegrown Northumberland accent grew broader still and unshed tears stood in her eyes. She leaned toward Tabitha.

"Yer near a legend back o' Colchester, Nurse Hale. Yer an' yer band o' VADs and Sister Alistair and all yer done t' quash th' influenzer. Legend! And we're that proud o' ye. We are."

Tabitha lifted her hand and cupped Darby's cheek, surprising them both. "Oh, my dear, dear Ellen. Our lives belong to the Savior who redeemed us. To him be all the glory," she whispered.

Darby covered Tabitha's hand with her own and pressed it; tears rolled off her cheek to drip on their joined fingers.

She sniffed and whispered, "Aye. T' God be all th' glory."

$\mathscr{C}$HAPTER 27

NOVEMBER 11, 1918

The armistice was signed. The war was over. Newcomers in camp celebrated. Tabitha and her fellow nurses looked at each other and smiled, but their smiles were heavyhearted. The war was over, but the damage was not.

All around them lay the broken bodies of soldiers, many whom would return to their families minus arms or legs. So many more would not return home at all.

The flu had taken its heavy toll, too. Of the station's surgical and nursing staff when Tabitha and Sister Alistair arrived, little more than half had survived and were still serving in the hospital.

Tabitha could not join in the relief and celebration. She was too numb and too drained to rejoice.

We still have so much work to do, Lord, she prayed. *Please help me to remain strong for those who rely so heavily upon my care.*

Then she shrugged. *But I am grateful, Lord, that no more young boys will be thrown to the cannons and then brought here, wounded and bleeding. Or dead.*

She gazed down the long lines of occupied cots and tried to imagine the numbers of them lessening, the flow of the wounded decreasing until no more came.

Her thoughts returned, as they often did, to Mason. *I am grateful, O God, that he will never be counted among those who are suffering as these men are suffering. I thank you that I am assured of where he is— that he is free from the heavy cords of this life.*

Tabitha touched her apron pocket, but it was empty. At some point while the plague ravaged the camp, her hanky had fallen out. She must not have pinned it well, and now the corner puzzle piece—that visible reminder of the word God had spoken to her—was gone. Its loss stung her heart, but she surrendered even this small grief to God.

It is all right, Lord, she prayed. *Your purposes are burned into my heart.*

"Nurse Hale!" A doctor called for her.

Tabitha pointed her weighted feet toward his voice and willed them to trudge forward. As she stumbled toward the doctor's voice, Tabitha recalled the letter she had just received from Claire.

Dearest Tabitha,

The influenza arrived in Boulder in late September. It descended with such virulence upon the military academy at the university that newspapers posted a plea to graduates of the medical and nursing schools: Come back to Boulder and help nurse the sick! Of course, I had to answer the call—how could I not?

I hope you will not be too severe on me. I know my constitution is weak, but I promise I am taking every precaution. They call this influenza a pandemic, a worldwide epidemic, but I would wager you already knew that.

I understand now, at least a little, the horrors you have been through. No one could know how it is without seeing it. Hundreds of young men from the Student Army Training Corps sickened from the influenza. We have lost a few of that number but hold out hope for most of them to recover. We do, however, have a long journey ahead before they are safe.

Who do you think I met while I was nursing in the wards? You must remember your classmate, Cathy Worth, from school. She is a doctor now. I did not recognize her at first, as we all wear masks. When I realized who she was, I spoke to her.

She asked me to pass her regards to you. Of course I told her you had volunteered with the British Nursing Service four years ago now, and that you were nursing the wounded in France.

Well! She expressed such pride in you. "I always knew Nurse Hale would be a credit and an honor to us all," she said. Wasn't that wonderful of her?

I, too, am so proud of you, Tabitha. When you come home, perhaps we can do something great for God together. I am praying on it.

It was Claire's closing line that occupied Tabitha's thoughts: *Something great for God together.*

Within a week of the armistice, soldiers released from German prisons began making their way into France. A steady stream of men came, directed to the hospital by the troops tasked with repatriating them. The soldiers arrived by truck. By wagon. On foot.

The French prisoners of war arrived first. Another week went by before British and American prisoners of war trickled into the hospital.

The soldiers were malnourished. They suffered from all the ailments that run rampant where starving, mistreated bodies are packed together in crowded, unsanitary conditions: rickets, lice, fleas, worms, skin eruptions, intestinal disorders, respiratory infections, and festering sores.

The doctors and the new head nurse, Matron Merriman, ordered strict protocols be instituted to prevent the spread of disease-carrying pests—or another outbreak of the influenza.

Once more the hospital was separated into two sections separated by a large parade ground. One side was for patients who showed symptoms or were suspected of carrying influenza or other infectious diseases, the other side for returning prisoners needing surgical or other nursing care.

Returning prisoners of war who were not in need of urgent care were routed directly to the showers. Orderlies relieved the men of their vermin-ridden clothes and piled the rags into wheelbarrows. The men were then herded into the showers where other orderlies helped the weak arrivals to scrub thoroughly with strong disinfectant soap. Two orderlies at the end of the shower administered delousing powders to rid the men of lice and fleas. After delousing, the men received clean clothes.

Gloved and masked women volunteers from surrounding villages collected the soiled garments and wheeled the filled barrows to open-air laundry vats. So filthy was the never-ending flow of laundry, that the many vats of boiling water and lye soap were emptied, scrubbed clean with harsh chemicals, and refilled several times daily.

Once the arrivals were showered and dressed in clean clothing, they lined up for medical exams. The physically depleted men sank down upon the ground where other volunteers fed them small, soft meals as their stomachs were not ready for heavy foods.

Tabitha and her VAD assistant, MacTavish, were assigned to Dr. Clemente as he examined new arrivals and made determinations for treatment. A new British volunteer, a young girl named Margot, took patients' names and set up their charts as the doctor made his examinations.

Tabitha assisted the doctor in his examinations. Afterward, she and MacTavish administered medications, cleaned and bandaged wounds, and listened. As long as they could, they listened to the men talk.

Most of their patients had not seen a woman since before they had been captured. Some rambled on about lost comrades or sweethearts waiting at home. All expressed wonder that the war was really and truly over, that they would, in short order, be shipped back to their families.

Once the returning soldiers were fit enough to answer questions, the military staff debriefed them. The officers in charge of the debriefings made a record of each man's account, his sworn testimony of the care he received while in enemy hands.

Lieutenant Smythe blew out a frustrated breath as he talked with Tabitha during a moment of rest. They stood between graying buildings, sheltering from a chilling wind.

"They are reluctant to complain about their treatment," the Lieutenant grumbled, "even those who were horribly abused."

"Why ever for?" Tabitha leaned her back against the building, hoping to soak up any warmth the pale, distant sun may have infused into the weathered slats.

"They think it will delay their being shipped home."

Tabitha thought for a moment. "Well, will it, Lieutenant?"

Lieutenant Smythe shrugged. "Possibly. If the major wishes to delve into their claims and seek corroborating testimony."

"Then I do not blame the men for their reluctance," Tabitha murmured. "I do not blame them at all."

CHAPTER 28

DECEMBER 1918

The flow of prisoners returning from captivity in Germany and Switzerland had been steady for weeks. Then the nurses working the hospital wards noticed that beds were emptying and not refilling. The examination lines were shortening; tent wards were clearing.

"We are comin' t' the end of it, Nurse Hale," MacTavish sighed. Her voice held a hint of awe.

"Yes. It has to end sometime, does it not?" Tabitha murmured.

The third week of December, Matron Merriman and the hospital commandant ordered that the two sides of the hospital be consolidated and unused cots and tents be broken down. It was the first step toward dismantling the hospital.

The head nurse called her staff, Tabitha included, together after dinner to give them news. "Ladies, our work here in Europe is nearly done. Some of us will have the opportunity to go home soon, perhaps by Christmas."

The worn face of the head nurse smiled for the first time in many days. "We shall require a number of volunteers to accompany and see to the needs of the remaining wounded soldiers on their way back to England."

The gathered nurses dissolved into excited babble.

"Quiet, ladies, if you please," Matron Merriman remonstrated. "I have more and important information to give you."

When the nurses quieted, she continued. "Many of you will be discharged from service to the Army soon. However, while we may not need you here, we do need you, at home and elsewhere. The pandemic is still raging across the world, in England and across Europe, in America and Canada, in Australia. Red Cross Headquarters has asked for nurses to meet this need. Please consider volunteering for an assignment back home."

"In any event," she said, smiling larger, "We anticipate dismantling this field hospital within thirty days."

She looked over her weary but work-hardened staff. "You have comported yourselves in the most honorable and professional manner I could have asked for," she whispered.

"I know we have miles yet to go, but I could not speak to you this night without telling you how very, very proud I am of all of you. Years from now, no one will believe all we have done, the lives we have saved … the sacrifices we have made."

Suddenly Tabitha felt too warm and the room felt too close. Other nurses around her must have felt the same. Throats tightened, eyes misted, and feet shuffled as they received such high praise from their superior.

"Thank you. That is all." Matron Merriman nodded, turned, and left the tent.

"I have seen nothin' of Europe other than these stations and hospitals," MacTavish grumbled after Tabitha had conveyed the news to the VADs. "I should like t' see somethin' other than blood an' death afore going back to m' da's farm. P'raps the Red Cross would take me on in a convalescin' center for a wee bit. I should like t' see some of th' grand cities of the Continent, I would."

Tabitha shrugged. "Somehow I doubt many of the 'grand cities' will much resemble what they were before the war."

"Well, I will stay, if I am 'cepted," MacTavish said stubbornly. Then she asked, "What will you do when it comes time t' leave, Nurse Hale?"

"I had thought to help the American Red Cross manage the pandemic in the States," Tabitha answered, "but I believe I shall return to England instead."

"Why, whatever for?"

"I hope to rent a cottage or a house in Colchester, near St. Martin's."

MacTavish was surprised again. "St Martin's Orphanage, is it?"

Tabitha nodded. "I wish to spend time with a little girl named Sally. See if we suit each other."

"You want t' adopt? But … aren't you bein' a single woman?"

Tabitha's smile was wan. "Actually, I am a widow, but my husband left me with the means to raise a child on my own."

MacTavish's eyes widened. "I-I'm that sorry. I dinna know."

"Look lively, ladies," one of the new orderlies called. "Stragglers come in t' camp. We're a-cleanin' them up now."

Tabitha and MacTavish straightened their shoulders and raised their chins, their response automatic after the many crises through which they had served.

"Shall I fetch Dr. Clemente?" MacTavish offered.

"Yes. And I will set up the exam trays."

It was after dark, but the hospital—and all its staff—were accustomed to functioning whenever the need arose. Tabitha lit lanterns in the exam tent and set about preparing the implements, bandages, salves, and medicines they might need. She also set out the medical charts Margot would fill as the soldiers were treated.

Thirty minutes later they had received five new patients and Margot reported that they only had three to go.

"Thank you, miss," Dr. Clemente murmured. "Go ahead and start their charts."

"Yes, doctor," Margot answered.

Tabitha was carrying a tray of clean bandages to the table when she heard Margot ask from just beyond the tent flap, "Your surname, please?"

"Carpenter," was the low, sluggish reply.

"First name?"

The response was slow in coming, as though the man had to think upon his answer.

"Mason. Middle initial A."

The tray Tabitha held tipped; the rolled bandages toppled and slid onto the dirt floor.

"Nurse Hale!" MacTavish hissed. "Have a care!"

But Tabitha did *not* care. She dropped the empty tray on the table and stumbled toward the tent entrance.

"Mason? Mason?" She stood panting, staring up at the soldier. In the faint lantern light from within the tent, he was a ghost of the man he'd been.

But she knew him.

She clutched his arm and tugged on it. "Mason, my love. It is Tabitha. Please look at me!"

Glazed eyes rotated toward her. "Tabs?" He stared and blinked, uncertain.

"Yes! Oh, yes! But-but, Mason! They told me you were dead!"

Carpenter raised one hand to Tabitha's cheek and touched it, as though he could not believe his senses. "I have prayed ... for this day."

Those around them stilled as they grasped the momentous event unfolding before them.

"I-I thought I would never see you again—not until heaven!" Tabitha sobbed.

"Oh, Tabs, my darling. I am happy to disappoint you."

And Carpenter folded her into his weak arms.

❦

$\mathscr{P}$OSTSCRIPT

Nurse Hale, you have requested to accompany Mr. Carpenter back to England. Is that correct?" Matron Merriman looked over her spectacles at Tabitha.

"Yes, Matron. Mr. Carpenter is my husband. We live in the States, but we shall return first to England. The British Army has said it will care for him until he is stronger, and Matron Stiles has agreed to receive him at Colchester Hospital. When he is discharged, we shall stay on a bit longer."

"Do you have family in England?"

"No, Matron. But ... there is a little girl, an orphan. We have hopes to take her home with us."

"Oh? Very commendable. And may I ask where your home is?"

"Denver, Colorado, Matron."

The senior nurse nodded and glanced down at Tabitha's request. "Mr. Carpenter was a volunteer instructor for the RFC, was he not? Up in York? And yet this report says his plane was shot down over the sea not far off the shore of Belgium?"

Her tone was serious, perhaps severe, but her eyes were not. In fact, Tabitha thought they glistened a little.

"Two German *Fokkers* attacked their flight school. They went after inexperienced pilots in their trainer aeroplanes. The trainers had no guns. The young men were defenseless. Mr. Carpenter went up in an RFC fighter and shot down one of the German aeroplanes. Two more German fighters dropped down on him, so he led them out to sea—away from the base."

Tabitha knew the account by heart; she had memorized Cliff's words over many tear-filled nights. "He flew down the length of England, over Norwich and out over the sea. Toward the coast of Belgium.

"Other RFC pilots, his students, went up in fighters and followed him and the Germans. They managed to shoot down the enemy aeroplanes ... but not before the Germans had shot him down."

The Germans shot him down.
The Germans shot him down.

"He was reported killed in action," Matron stated.

"Yes, Matron. The students saw his plane go into the water."

Tabitha looked up, mouthing the new, unfamiliar ending. "H-he tells me that when our planes shot down the German fighters, a German ship saw them go into the water. The ship raced to rescue them—quite near the spot Mr. Carpenter went into the sea."

Tabitha drew a cleansing breath. "They did not find their downed pilots, but they found Mr. Carpenter floating on a bit of wreckage."

Tabitha saw that she was right about the older woman. A moist sheen glimmered on Matron Merriman's eyes, and Tabitha's eyes watered in response.

"How long ago was he reported KIA?"

Tabitha swallowed the lump that kept creeping into her throat. "A year and a half, Matron. He has been in a prison camp all that time."

"You must feel that he has risen from the grave." Matron Merriman was now staring at a framed photograph on her desk.

"Only Jesus has ever done that, Matron," Tabitha whispered, "but yes, it feels as though Mr. Carpenter has come back from the dead. He was dead to me for so long! Even though I knew I would see him in heaven . . . later, I am grateful beyond words to the God of grace who has seen fit to return my husband to me."

Matron Merriman studied Tabitha for a minute. She cleared her own throat. "Thank you for reminding me that Jesus *did* overcome the grave, Nurse Hale."

She lifted the frame on her desk and, with one finger, touched the face in the photograph. "I, too, belong to the God of grace, as does my beloved husband. He was shot down over Germany. I will have to wait a little longer, but I will see him again."

The matron again cleared her throat and returned the frame to its place on her desk. She studied Tabitha a moment longer and tipped her head toward the medal and ribbon hanging from the apron strap of Tabitha's VAD uniform.

"I heard about you, you know, when you, Matron Alistair, and your VADs came over. We all heard about the fiery, red-haired American who wore the QAIMNS medal on a VAD uniform and commanded a squad of expertly trained volunteers. I will remember to tell my grandchildren about you."

Matron opened a desk drawer and, with two fingers, lifted a wad of dirty cloth from it. "One of the VADs found this. It's a bit worse for the wear, but I wonder . . . could it be yours?"

She held it out to Tabitha.

Tabitha frowned as she received the filthy scrap from Matron. It was a very dirty hanky. She fumbled with a pin and unfolded it. A corner puzzle piece, warped and split from moisture, fell into her hand.

"Oh!" Awe swept over Tabitha's heart.

I call some to be the frame for the work, to make the vision plain. Those whom I call to frame the work are vital to my plans, the voice spoke. *They lead so that others may follow.*

"Th-thank you, Matron. It *is* mine." She forced back the tears that came so easily lately.

Amen, Lord. I will always say 'amen' to your call upon my life.

When Tabitha continued to stare at the object in her hand, Matron Merriman smiled to herself.

"Well, then." She stamped Tabitha's request and handed it back to her. "I wish you God speed. You have served my country—and our Savior—with distinction. Well done, Nurse *Carpenter.*"

Tabitha struggled for composure as she stood.

"Thank you, Matron."

THE END

Read more about Tabitha,
Rose and Joy Thoresen,
and the girls of Palmer House
in the series, **A Prairie Heritage**.

ABOUT THE AUTHOR

Vikki Kestell's passion for people and their stories is evident in her readers' affection for her characters and unusual plotlines. Two often-repeated sentiments are, "I feel like I know these people" and "I'm right there, in the book, experiencing what the characters experience."

Vikki holds a Ph.D. in Organizational Learning and Instructional Technologies. She left a career of twenty-plus years in government, academia, and corporate life to pursue writing full time. "Writing is the best job ever," she admits, "and the most demanding."

Also an accomplished speaker and teacher, Vikki and her husband Conrad Smith make their home in Albuquerque, New Mexico.

To keep abreast of new book releases, visit her website at **http://www.vikkikestell.com/** or connect with her on Facebook at **http://www.facebook.com/TheWritingOfVikkiKestell**.

Faith-Filled
Fiction™